Portals:

Book FOUR

Sigils & Satyrs

Travis I. Sivart

Sigils & Satyrs
Portals: Book 4
Copyright © 2022 Travis I. Sivart
All rights reserved.

ISBN:

Talk of the Tavern Publishing Group

Dedication

To Maria, for more support on a daily basis than she'll ever realize. And to Andrea, the woman who became my wife while I was writing this, and how she helps me in a million little ways every day.

Table of Contents

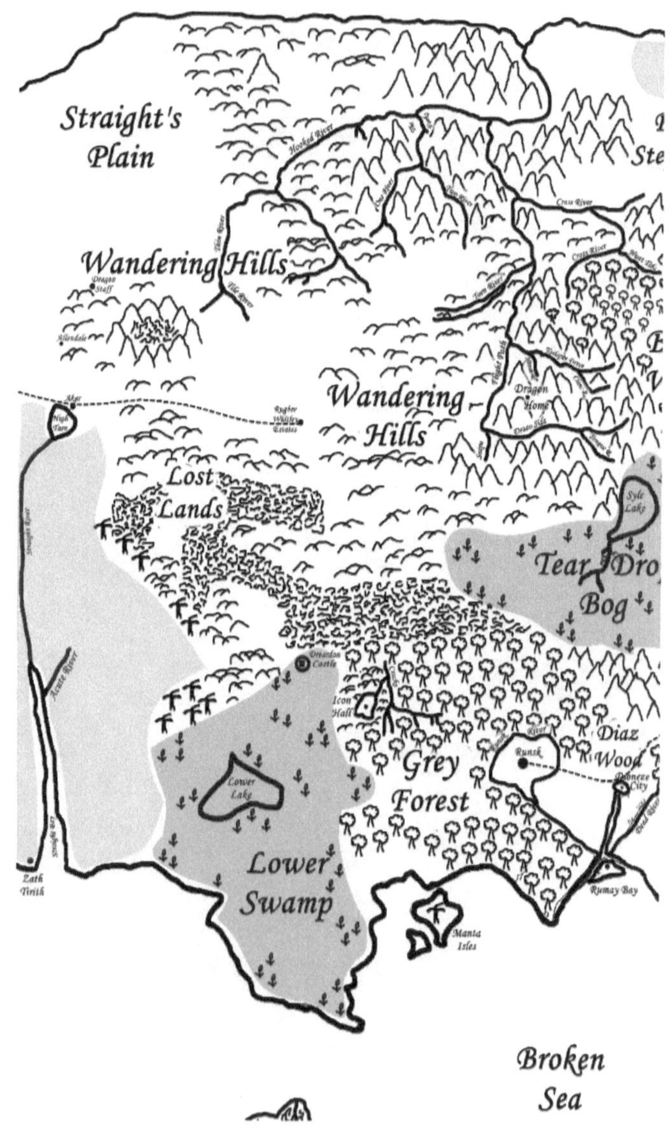

Straight's Plain
Wandering Hills
Wandering Hills
Lost Lands
Tear Dro Bog
Syle Lake
Grey Forest
Lower Lake
Lower Swamp
Diaz Wood
Runsk
Manta Isles
Rumay Bay
Zath Tirith
Broken Sea
Dragon Staff
Aftendale
Akar
High Tarn
Rughr Whitley Estates
Drandon Castle
Icon Hall
Dragon Home
Hooked River
Straight River
Acute River
Tum River
Cross River

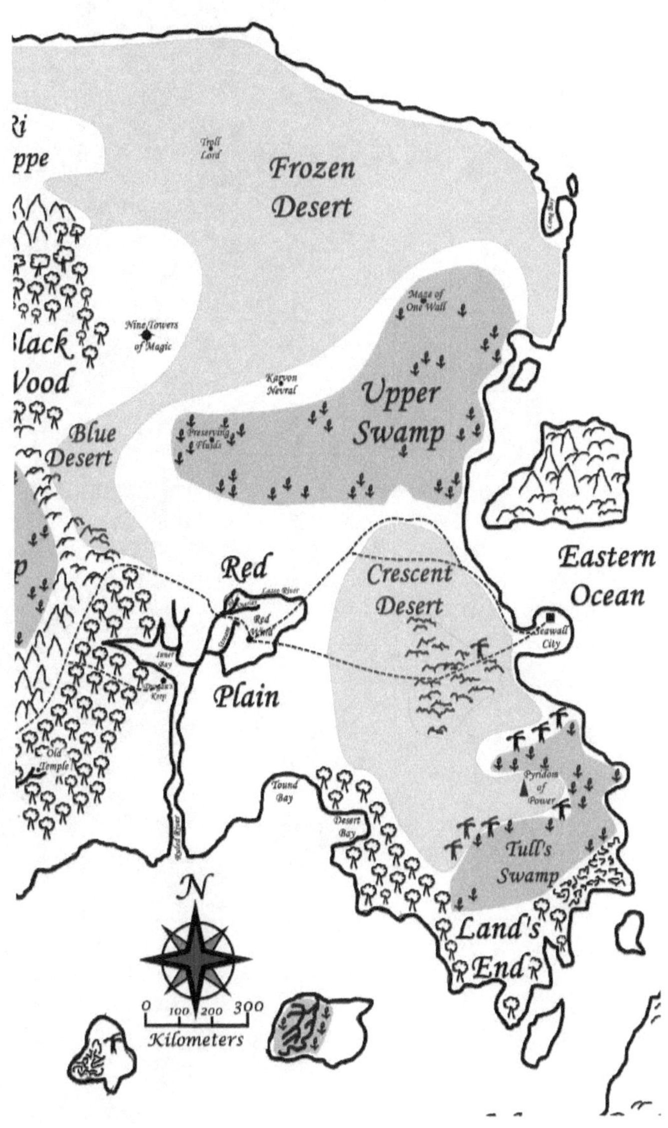

Ri
ppe
Frozen
Desert
Troll
Lord
Mage of
One Wall
Black
Wood
Nine Towers
of Magic
Karyon
Nevral
Upper
Swamp
Blue
Desert
Preserving
Fluids
Red
Lasto River
Red
Wind
Crescent
Desert
Eastern
Ocean
Seawall
City
Inner
Bay
Pyridom
of
Power
Old
Temple
Plain
Tound
Bay
Desert
Bay
Tull's
Swamp
Land's
End
N
0   100   200   300
Kilometers

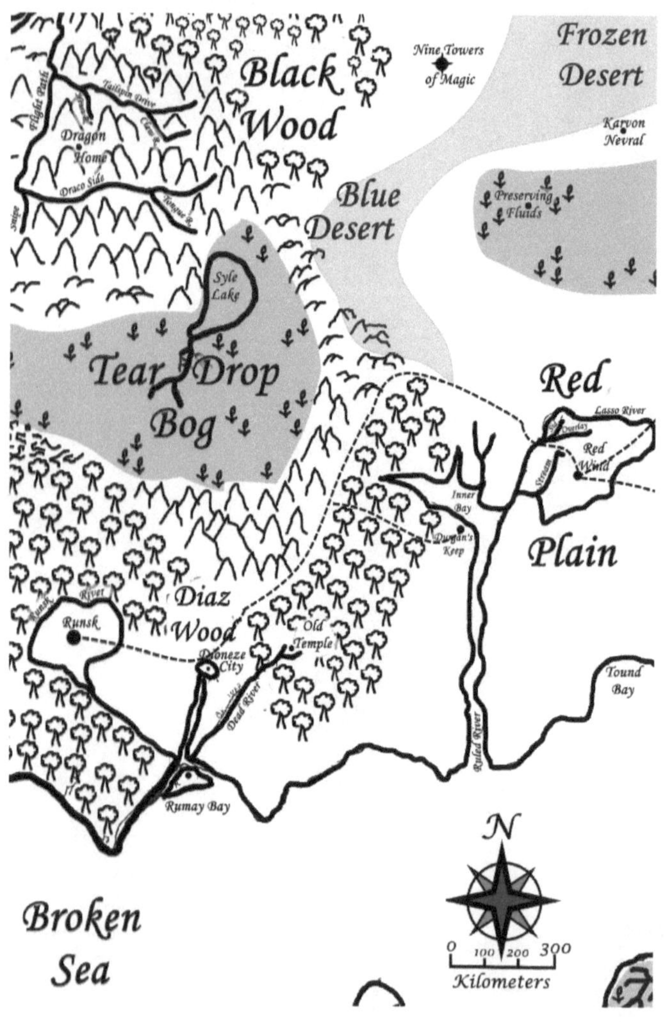
Black
Wood
Nine Towers
of Magic
Frozen
Desert
Flight Path
Tailspin Drive
Dragon
Home
Draco Side
Tongue R.
Snipe
Karvon
Nevral
Blue
Desert
Preserving
Fluids
Syle
Lake
Red
Lasso River
Overlay
Red
Wind
Tear Drop
Bog
Stream
Inner
Bay
Plain
Runsk River
Diaz
Wood
Duncan's
Keep
Runsk
Old
Temple
Dioneze
City
Tound
Bay
Dead River
Ruled River
Rumay Bay
N
Broken
Sea
0   100   200   300
Kilometers

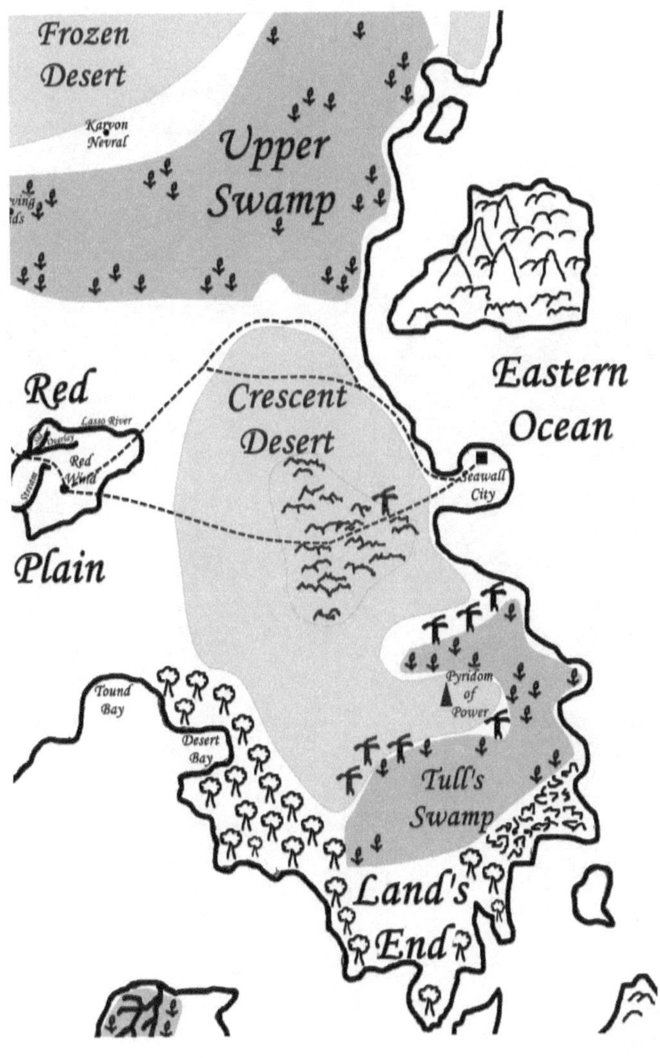
Frozen
Desert
Karvon
Nevral
Upper
Swamp
Eastern
Ocean
Red
Lasso River
Red
Wind
Plain
Crescent
Desert
Seawall
City
Pyridom
of
Power
Tound
Bay
Desert
Bay
Tull's
Swamp
Land's
End

Chapter 1

Aiyana stood on a thin rock column above the murky water of the courtyard. She glanced at Nathan, who was watching the swirling movement causing bubbles to rise to the top while swatting at the swarm of gnats clustered around him.

"Think it's something alive?" he asked.

"Dreardon Castle is rumored to be home to many things," she sighed, "all of them horrible and dangerous. I think we should assume everything wants to kill us here. That's why I asked you to make this pedestal for me."

Nathan stood on the steps leading from the gatehouse into the long-deserted ruins, the rotted doors bracketing him. He grunted, his hands gripping Marcid, his magical battle axe.

The courtyard was large enough to fit a small village, and sculptures of people going about everyday tasks stood in waist deep water. The statues were weatherworn, but the detail and care of the craftsmanship was apparent even in their deteriorated state.

Movement drew their attention. An elongated, algae-green form broke the surface, then disappeared a moment later.

"What was that?" Nathan asked. "A branch? A snake?"

"Not sure." Aiyana shrugged.

"Who builds a castle in a swamp, anyway? And then makes a sunken courtyard?" Nathan shook his head. "It was bound to get flooded, they had to know that."

"It wasn't always a swamp," Aiyana said. "When this place was the seat of power in this area, it was grasslands. But over time, the lowlands flooded and became what it is today."

"You're sure the book you need is in this place?" he asked.

"According to my research, it is." Aiyana nodded.

"And you really need this particular book? It's absolutely necessary?"

"Yes," Aiyana sighed again, "it should help me find where the Aeifain once lived. When we opened the portal network—"

The water erupted, a dozen tentacles shooting from the depths and towering above the two friends. They slammed down on the steps, writhing towards the axe-wielding rokairn.

"Okay," he grumbled, lifting his weapon, "here we go!"

Nathan swung the axe, striking one of the rubbery appendages, and the blade turned sideways, sliding along the length of the tentacle.

More of the alien arms burst from the fetid water at the base of the column Aiyana stood on, ringing her. They fell inward, collapsing around the wizardess.

Flame erupted from her crystal topped staff, and a circle of fire rose in an upward spiral.

The attacking arms twisted away and fell back into the dark waters with a splash.

Nathan backpedaled to the broken doors, stepping over fallen timbers and ducking behind the rusted portcullis that leaned against the wall.

The tentacles followed, snaking along the damp flagstones, seeking its prey.

"A swamp squid?" Nathan shouted, batting away the limbs with the flat of his axe. "Swamp octopus? A swamptopus?"

"It just wants a snack," Aiyana laughed, "and you're snack sized!"

"Fun sized, dammit!" Nathan retorted. "And I don't want anything this disgusting touching me!"

"I'll take care of it," the wizardess said, raising her staff again.

Calling out to the elements, Aiyana drew upon the ley lines of air and water, pulling in the power of nature from around her.

A chill wind cut through the cloying humidity and swept across the flooded area inside the castle walls. A thin layer of frost formed on top of the water, crackling outward from the woman.

The tentacles flailed against the ice forming around them, breaking it, and pulling back under the dark surface.

Nathan stomped from his hiding place, glaring at the retreating limbs.

"Is that going to kill it?" he asked.

"I don't think so," Aiyana shrugged. "I bet this place freezes over in the winter, and whatever that was probably hibernates or something."

"Swamptopus," Nathan said firmly. "It was a swamptopus. I've decided that's what it should be called."

"Whatever it is," Aiyana dropped from the pedestal Nathan had made for her, "it'll come back out when this ice thaws. So, we better be gone before then. On the bright side, now we can walk to the front doors of the castle without having to wade through the water."

They moved across the slick surface, Nathan using slow, solid steps to keep his balance, and Aiyana using her staff.

Nathan, always an admirer of craftsmanship, paused at a statue of a woman carrying a small child. He leaned in, inspecting the detail.

"These are amazing," he called to Aiyana, "so much fine work, right down to individual hairs in the eyebrows. They're so lifelike that it wouldn't surprise me if they started walking around."

"That's unlikely," she called over her shoulder. "As much as they look like living people, they're just statues now."

"Now?" Nathan turned and shuffled along the ice to catch up. "What does that mean?"

"It means they're not going anywhere," Aiyana climbed the steps of the castle, "and we're here. We can discuss them later."

The castle stood open to the elements, the interior foyer littered with leaves, debris, and animal droppings. Moldy tapestries hung in tatters on the high walls, and the few pieces of remaining furniture were in similar condition.

The crystal atop Aiyana's staff flared into a blue light, casting a flickering, otherworldly glow in all directions.

More sculptures stood in the hall and the adjoining rooms, each appearing to be in the middle of some mundane task.

"We see just fine in dim light," Nathan grumbled. "That will only attract attention."

"Or keep the curious away," Aiyana shrugged. "Rats and other vermin will avoid the light. And we can handle anything that shows up."

"But we can't handle roaches and rats?"

"Nathan," Aiyana stopped and looked at the man, "we can't read in this light, and I am looking for something specific, and will need to be able to make out details to find it. Okay?"

"Yeah, fine," Nathan mumbled. "But now I can see the faces on the statues in here. They're creepy. And why does that one look terrified?"

Nathan pointed at a statue posed with one hand held in front of his face, and a sword in the other.

"It's nothing we need to worry about," Aiyana reassured him. "Let's just find this book and get back to The Citadel."

The two searched rooms until they found the library, a vast two-story room with shelves of books that filled the walls from the floor to the ceiling. Padded chairs with the stuffing torn out sat next to gnawed tables.

A podium stood in the center of the room, a dusty glass dome covering whatever was on it.

"There," Aiyana whispered reverently, "that's got to be it."

She hurried to the pedestal and wiped at the caked on grime on the glass with her sleeve. Peeking through the clean spot, she gasped.

"It's here!" she said. "The Tome of Lost Souls."

"Did you ever doubt it?" Nathan asked, watching the door, his back to her.

"Well, there was the chance that someone could have taken it."

Aiyana leaned her staff against a wood column. Moving to the podium, she held her hands above it, closing her eyes.

"Wards," she mumbled, "but nothing too bad. I should be able to disarm them."

"Great," Nathan shifted his grip on his axe, "I'm getting creeped out, and really want to get out of here."

"A powerful priest of Jonath, like you, getting scared of things that go bump in the dark? Aw, that's cute." She teased.

Mumbled arcane words cut off any reply from Nathan.

Aiyana drew upon the mind magics of her people, very different from the elemental magic she used earlier, and traced the unseen lines of protection of the enchantment surrounding the dome.

"And…" she said quietly, "here we go."

Blue sparks showered around her, and she pressed her hands through the glass. Drawing back, she pulled the thick leather and brass bound book from the encasement.

She gazed at the volume, turning it over in her hands.

"It was written by the Lost One," she said, "and they were documenting all the missing races. Not just ones that died out in wars, but the peoples who disappeared without a trace."

Hello, child, a voice in Aiyana's head said, *I feel your desires to find the lost aeifain city, Icon Hall. You want to open their city for the knowledge and expand the portals further.*

Unsure if she'd imagined the voice, or if it was real, Aiyana shook her head to clear it.

"Yeah, yeah," Nathan was grumbling, "I know. You've told me. And this will lead you to your people, the wondrous aeifain, because you can't remember where they lived. Can we go now?"

Aiyana turned, smiling, and pushed the massive tome into her robe. The book slid into the pocket, disappearing into a cloth cavity smaller than it.

"What was that?" Nathan whispered, going stiff. "Did you hear it?"

"I'm sure it was nothing," Aiyana whispered, moving up next to her friend, "but we can go now, anyway."

"If it was nothing," he cocked his head to look up at her, "then why are you whispering?"

"Let's just get to the standing stones so we can portal back to The Citadel," Aiyana said in a conversational volume, moving towards the door they'd come in.

A hissing, slithering noise came from the hall.

"There!" Nathan whispered. "There it is again! You had to hear it."

Aiyana stopped in her tracks.

"Did I mention the cursed queen?" Aiyana whispered.

"Cursed queen?" Nathan sputtered. "No, and don't you think you should've said something *before* we came here?"

"It's just a legend," Aiyana said defensively. "Dreardon Castle was ruled by a queen. No one remembers her name. But she wanted to be a wizardess and control the elements. In her greed for power, she slew all the priests of Jonath, sacrificing them to gain their power over stone. Same for Latress's chosen, for wind, Tarra's for water, and Torr's for fire."

"All the priests of Jonath?" Nathan gaped at her. "I'm a priest of Jonath!"

"Anyway," Aiyana continued, "she collected tomes of magic, and slew whole sects of priesthoods. The gods cursed her, sinking her lands into water and making it so anyone she looked upon turned to stone."

"The sculptures," Nathan mumbled, "that's why you said they were just statues now. They were her people before. And that's why you thought someone may have taken the book!"

"We really should go now," Aiyana stood straight and took a step forward, "if it is her, legend says she can't leave the castle. We'll be safe once we cross the threshold. As long as we don't look back."

"Looking back is what I do!" Nathan hurried to catch up to her. "Fine, but we're going to talk about this habit of yours of forgetting to tell me things later!"

The priest moved in front of the wizardess, Marcid held across his body. He leaned forward to peek into the hall outside the library.

Aiyana put a hand on his shoulder, stopping him.

"Um," she hesitated, "if it is her, maybe looking to see if it is her isn't the best idea?"

She felt him tense under her grip, his muscles hardening, becoming as hard as stone.

"She can't turn something to stone if it's already stone." Nathan said firmly.

Aiyana saw his ruddy skin shift to a pale, pebbled shade of rock.

The gifts of Jonath, she thought, *he can make his skin like stone.*

Let him handle this, the voice in her head said, *keep heading for the portal stones. That is what is important. The priest is not important compared to what you must do.*

Nathan squared his shoulders, set his feet at shoulder width, and took a step forward into the hall.

A dark shape shot from the shadows, bowling him over, and the rokairn tumbled out of sight. A snake tail as thick as a man's body, and the length of three, slithered past.

I can't leave him, she mentally shouted. *He's my friend!*

Then help him, and the world, by doing what needs done, the voice sneered. *Haven't you failed, and let enough people die? Can't you see how important your mission is? Isn't the fate of an entire race more important than one rokairn? Don't let his sacrifice be for nothing.*

Aiyana rushed into the hall, looking to the right towards where Nathan had disappeared, then left towards the exit. The dull glow of daylight seemed further than they'd traveled to get to the library.

Looking into the darkness to the right, she raised her staff, and the blue light filled the hallway.

Nathan was rolling to his feet, pushing a scaley feminine figure from atop him. The woman's lower half was reptilian, and its sinewy length was wrapping around the warrior.

Looking past his foe, Nathan saw Aiyana.

"Run!" he shouted. "Get out! I've got this. I'll be right behind you!"

Aiyana hesitated, going through what she could do to help without hurting her friend.

Nothing, the voice said, *you will only hasten his demise by launching fireballs, or slow his attacks if you use ice. Run, as he told you to.*

She turned and ran for the front door, calling upon the winds to move her faster.

Reaching the threshold, she turned and looked behind her.

"Kaleb triot, denal venitier!" came Nathan's rokairn battle cry from the gloomy depth of the castle.

Aiyana turned and looked at the gate in the outer wall. The summer heat had already turned the ice to slush, and tentacles were tentatively exploring the broken surface.

With a rush of anger, the wizardess pushed the power of wind and water she held and thrust it across the courtyard. The water rippled in knee-height waves, solidifying as the wind ripped across its surface. Tentacles severed, flopping and writhing on the muddy ice.

She ran, her footing supported by the textured surface of the frozen swamp.

Reaching the gatehouse, she turned back to look for Nathan.

The rokairn burst through the open doors of the castle, his beard flapping and Marcid bobbing as his pumping arms matched his feet.

Aiyana thrust her arms forward, and wind rushed past her towards her friend. She spread her arms just before the gust hit him, parting the gale, and brought them back together.

Nathan ran past the wall of weather, but the creature behind him took the full brunt of the hurricane force wind, tossing the cursed queen back into the building. The wind rebounded, catching the rokairn and lifting him into the air.

Lifting the elemental power, Aiyana pulled the air current back to her, carrying Nathan with it.

The rokairn hit the steps, still running, and bolted past Aiyana and out of the gatehouse. He slid to a stop twenty paces outside of the castle wall and bent to put his hands on his knees.

Panting, he looked up at her as she sauntered towards him.

"I," he breathed, "thought I told you to run."

"I'm not very good at being bossed around," she said with a sniff, walking past him. "We should get to the standing stones."

"Why'd you stick around?" he asked, trotting to catch up.

"Thought you needed help." She smiled. "I'll always be there to lend you a hand when yours aren't enough."

"You know I can make hands of stone if I need an extra, right?" he teased.

"Doesn't matter," she shrugged, "I'll be right beside you, helping scoop up clay for you to make them with. Just deal with it."

Ten minutes later, they arrived at the standing stones, and Aiyana used her staff to open the magical doorway.

They stepped through and appeared on the grassy plain of another ring of stones.

"Another hour of walking and we'll be back at The Citadel," Aiyana said, stretching with her face held up to the sun.

"Yay," Nathan pushed a fist into his lower back, grinning as it popped, "more walking."

An arrow shaft clacked off his stony skin, followed by a dozen more that struck the surrounding ground.

"What the hell?" Nathan looked around, bewildered.

"Does this day never end?" Aiyana sighed, waving her staff in front of her and calling the wind to knock another dozen arrows from the air. "Looks like we've got an army attacking us?"

She pointed, and Nathan followed her gesture.

Dozens of humans stood in a loose cluster in a clump of trees a football field length away. They had swords and bows and were charging towards them.

Two men stood apart beside a piece of small siege equipment.

"That's a ballista, right?" Aiyana asked.

"I guess," Nathan shrugged, "but I think it looks more like a trebuchet. Hold on, they're using it. Let's see if it shoots something, or slings something."

The device jerked, and a flaming ball flew in their direction. It jerked again, the top beam sliding back, then forward again, launching a second fiery projectile.

"You got the last thing," Aiyana smiled. "I'll get this one."

She raised her staff, and the wind picked up, gusting past them. Dirt flew into the oncoming men, and the flaming missiles fell downward.

The pitch and flames exploded on the ground in the midst of the soldiers, scattering them and the fire across the field.

She called upon the element of fire and water, spreading the flames, and making smoke to roil across the attacking force, providing a smoke screen.

Gesturing again, she used her mind magics to blanket herself and her companion.

"And now we're invisible to them," she said. "Should we finish them?"

"I think we've done enough for today," Nathan grunted. "Besides, between you and me, I am pretty sure we're unbeatable. We can let this one go."

Chapter 2

The sunlight tickled Reggie's closed eyes as his head bounced against a large, flat stone underneath him. It went up and down to the beat of some sort of nearby rhythmic pounding. In fact, as his surroundings swam back into his awareness, he realized it was getting further away. Another realization was that a crunch, a squelching noise, and/or some sort of terrified scream accompanied each thump.

He groaned and forced one eyelid open, then the other. The left, swollen, was reluctant to go wider than a mere slit. What was in front of him made him blink, and his hand struggled to reach up and rub his eyes.

He got a face full of dirt and leaves. A shooting pain lanced through his fingers—which were bent in many directions, like a gnarled hangman's tree.

Muffling a cry of pain, he opened his eyes wider. Between the twisted digits of his fingers, he saw a large form lumbering away.

At first, he thought it was a trick of perspective. The man (at least, he thought it was a man) would've been huge. Like humongous, bigger than the tallest man Reggie had ever seen. He'd be two and a half meters if he were a centimeter.

Reggie's mind darted to one side, chasing the realization that he'd just done a measurement in metric. Now, that didn't seem odd to him, but an hour ago, it would've seemed extremely off form. He was British and used both standard and metric in his line of work, but always defaulted to standard. Then again, an hour ago he was snug in his bed in his villa in the south of France, with a hot water bottle and a thick down duvet up to his nose.

Now, he was in a…forest?

Yes, pemtie, he realized, and the native word meaning stupid or idiot—foreign to his Earth body—surprised him. *Definitely a forest. And it looks old but was once more than just a forest. The trees are in vague, straight lines. Now, this isn't uncommon in Europe or in Great Britain, but these trees weren't the normal types for that area. These are marsh trees, with dozens of roots, and perched atop small isles with a spiderweb of canals all around.*

His mind cataloged the scene, noting the enormous tower in the distance, and the ogre lurching towards it while idly crushing any of Reggie's men as he wandered past, using a club roughly the size of a horse's haunch.

And where are the horses?

Reggie pushed to a sitting position, his eyes flying wide. The back of his mind registered the pain was considerably less than it had been a minute before, but the front of his mind was too busy having a panic attack to listen to the back half.

Ogre? My men? My horses? Reggie's mind whirled.

With a crunch, the creature stopped and stomped on the ground. The stomping. The cries of the dying and injured. Reggie noted that the whacks of the club was a horse's rear leg torn free.

Reggie realized that between his loud yelp earlier, ragged panting, and accompanying movements, he'd attracted the ogre's attention.

He flopped to the ground like a rag doll, his arms and legs akimbo, playing dead. His body was healing at an incredible rate, much faster than anything considered normal. The dull ache in his ribs—which had been a sharp, jagged pain a few minutes ago—now barely hurt. Surprising after a club had crushed most of his left side.

Or had the pain in his ribs been from a hacking cough, struggling for breath in his bed?

He lay still, silently debating the two perspectives. He was a man of science, observation, and perception and allowed reason, facts, and proof to rise to the surface before he drew any conclusions. Sometimes like curdled cream in his tea, other times like an ancient artifact being washed clean with a brush, or a gentle flow of water.

Reginald Betancourt was an archaeologist. He'd been a part of digs in Egypt, and across Africa. He discovered how the ancient Viking villages depicted their lives through broken crockery and waste from trash pits. He even explored the jungles of Thailand when he was younger, discovering vine and moss-covered temples with stone heads the size of a Studebaker.

But he'd been on his deathbed, or so he was told. Maybe it was consumption, maybe it was pneumonia, but the doctors had whispered (when they thought he'd been asleep) how there was no coming back from this one.

Now, here he was, laying in a heap of mouldering leaves, wondering if an ogre was about to kill him again.

Again? The thought leapt at him like a frightened mouse, scaring him much more than itself.

Yes, he and his men had come into the Grey Forest seeking ruins that may hint at what happened to the Dasism—an elusive race of humanoids that bonded with nature—or traces of the hidden kingdom of the Aeifain, a delicate race of magic-wielding beings. The ogre held two important people of the former, while occupying a ruin built by the latter. Or perhaps to observe the mating rituals of the storm swallows and rock crows, two native species of birds intricately connected to the ecosystem of these woods, and often came before the winds and rains that assaulted the area.

They'd found the tower, and when they went inside to see what they could find, they'd awoken the beast within: An ogre.

That creature approached him again. It had already killed the score of men and women who'd come on the expedition with him. It had even killed the healer. She'd been a beautiful woman, a priestess of Promethene, the goddess of sound and light. In spite of that, she had a fair hand in healing. Of course, ol' Reggie never stood a chance with her since the order was chaste.

The rumbling of the ground as the ogre came closer drew his attention.

Where was his rapier? He'd lost it in the battle, if you wanted to call the massacre a battle. He had his main gauche—wait, that was the French term, not the local term. Main gauche was the translation in his head, it had a different term here that basically meant slap weapon, or parrying blade.

The two worlds in his head collided, and his gorge rose, threatening to heave free and alert the enemy that he was, in fact, still alive.

Was he an old man of science who did tedious study with patience, or was he a young man in his late twenties who relied on impulse and his sword?

But two goals, so different, aligned…to find the lost mystery, discover the reason for a lost civilization that disappeared, and reveal the existence of past knowledge and culture to an ignorant world.

It was a matter of playing the cards life dealt him and hoping he came up with an ace.

In a stroke of genius, or so Reggie liked to think afterwards, he fainted.

Reggie woke.

Rolling his shoulders, he stretched. Wetness crept across his back and hips where he'd been laying on the mat of leaves on the forest floor. But this was partially a marsh, and the tide was coming in, slowly filling the low areas with fetid swamp-like rivulets.

Night was falling, and dusk was the hour of predators, including the worst of the bunch, mosquitos.

He sat bolt upright and slapped at his neck, feeling a tight pinching sensation.

They were here, the bloodsucking beasts that had drained a horse in less than a half of an hour. There were ways to handle them. Mosquito netting used to work, but that wouldn't do here. These were not the tiny insects the size of your fingernail, these were the size of a juvenile's finger, and the adults were larger than a lumberjack's hand.

Few things could deter the pests. He considered the options. So, there was rain. A good torrential downpour drove them to cover. Or the spider trees.

Reggie searched the sky for a flock of storm swallows, the harbingers of the monsoon-like storms that frequented the Grey Forest. Or the rock crows that would point him to solid ground, and maybe help him find the natural shelter of the caves that riddled the land. The interior was a natural repellant to the sturine, the local slang for the insects, since they resembled the long, sleek, and toothy sturgeon fish in the rivers.

Pushing to his feet, Reggie looked around. The interior of the stout stone tower glowed with the orange light of a blaze, thin wisps of smoke trailing out of the windows. The building wasn't on fire, but the wet wood would create enough smoke to keep the miniature predators at bay.

The man stumbled forward, getting his legs to cooperate, and snatched his rapier from the saturated ground. Lurching towards a horse he stopped beside the corpse. It was missing a leg.

"Ew," he mumbled.

Bending, he slipped open the saddlebags to look inside. Nodding in silent agreement that it would have enough of what he needed, he freed them and slung them over his shoulder.

"No crows, no swallows," he muttered. "Looks like I'll have to find the spider trees. Now, let's take a moment…"

He stood, closed his eyes, turned in a slow circle, and breathed in deeply through his nose, searching for the sickly sweet scent that would be a signpost to their location.

"That way seems likely," he said, then snorted. "Talking to yourself, old man, first sign of senility. Well, better madness than dead. Let's get on with it then!"

Orienting on the smell, he loped into the trees, splashing through the rising streams that would soon be sluggish currents between hillocks.

He pulled his sleeves down, preferring the stifling heat over being bitten enough by the sturine to pass out from loss of blood.

It felt good to run. It had been years since he could do this without his knees wobbling, threatening to buckle from torn ligaments, or his breath coming out in rattling coughs from his struggling lungs.

He was young again, though he couldn't guess at his exact age, and it was exhilarating. Not to mention, he was on an adventure again!

In his other life—thinking about it, his mind and body swooned until he stopped trying to figure out which world was the real one—he'd faced mummies, but they'd been wrapped in gauze and long dead. He'd faced tigers, but they ran at the sound of a gun. Usually. He lived through yellow fever, and seen crocodiles, lions, rampant elephants, and more.

This place, though, the threats were different. They were more aggressive, like the others in his previous life were merely a scouting expedition to get him ready for real danger and excitement.

"Magic!" he giggled. "Real damned magic, I mean, I've seen witch doctors and seances, but not wielders of true arcane ability. May Parsay watch over me, and the Traveller guide my steps!"

The two people he called upon were gods, he realized. The former was the god of luck, the latter the god of traveling.

His hand went to his neck, and he felt the chain with a dozen holy symbols—each the size of a coin—jangling on it.

This world had gods!

Unlike the Christian god, or the Norse, Greek, Roman, Egyptian, or other gods of his past, these gods took a much more active role, bestowing blessings upon their followers and priests. The gods here were like the stories of the gods from that other world, where all his memories lingered.

He shook off the thought, immersing himself in this world, this body, this experience. Remembering the fencing sword on his hip, he knew the blocks and parries, the attacks and feints making the weapon a deadly tool. He knew of magic; healing from gods, calling on the elements, mixing of potions, and so much more!

He wanted the adventure this world offered. The opportunity to explore somewhere new and exciting. To uncover places where no one else had been for hundreds of years and to share that discovery with others.

The thick buzz of the sturine brought his awareness back to the moment.

The trees he sought stood about the length of a football field ahead of him, lining a sandy peninsula. The trunks were tall and straight, the leaves forming a thick ball atop them. They could be many types of trees, he knew, but with one difference. Thick, milky-white layers—that made him think of cotton candy, if someone made it with cheese cloth—covered the branches and leaves.

Drawing closer, ducking under the swarm of thin, elongated, flying insects slightly smaller than his head, he saw the fat, black bodies dotting the webbing coating the trees.

He tumbled into the weeds at the base of the trees, rolling to a stop under one. The swarm diverted, heading into the sweet-smelling sheeting of the webs, and sticking there. Black forms moved, dozens of them becoming hundreds, as the spider trees came to life.

Dropping to his back, Reggie laughed. Relief rolled out of him, and he cackled long and hard, clutching his sides until tears streaked his face, creating clean lines down his cheeks.

Preparing to bed down for the night, he tucked the saddlebags under his head, and curled around the scabbard holding his blade, still giggling in fits and starts, the tears of joy changing into something deeper. Excitement crept into him. He was on another adventure.

He fell asleep.

Chapter 3

"They're here," Aiyana's head snapped up, her hair the color of corn silk in moonlight whipping across her face.

"Huh?" Nathan looked at her from his workbench, small wire-framed glasses perched on his enormous nose that protruded over a bushy beard.

Aiyana tilted her head as if listening to a voice only she could hear. Nodding, she looked around.

Wind rippled the thick canvas of the tent, no easy feat considering the heavy material, and that it was magical and built to resist the elements.

Captain Farrell, Aiyana's raven, cawed and flapped across the worktable, before launching across the room to settle atop the blue crystal capping the wizardess's staff.

The rokairn peeled the glasses from his face with one hand, twisting his head to free the curled metal from his ear. It snagged in his thick hair, and he grunted as it tore a few strands free.

Rokairns were hirsute by nature, short of stature, and broad of shoulder. They were a solid folk, who usually dwelled deep inside mountains. Compared to aeifain, like Aiyana, they were a rock to a willow. Aeifain were slight and slender, pale, and delicate, and moved with a grace like dancing. Humans often called the former dwarves, and the latter elves, but most people considered both terms insulting.

Turning in a circle, Nathan watched the walls of the tent ripple, one panel at a time, like a great serpent was slithering along the outside—if that serpent was as tall as a horse, and twice as long.

"Hrmph," Nathan grunted, "either the goddess of wind is teasing a priest of her husband, or something very weird just happened."

"Don't be pemtie. That was not because of Latress or your patron god, Jonath. It was as if something had woken and come into the world. If I had to guess, I'd say it was your friend, Jack Tucker," the aeifain said, snatching herbs and implements from the workbench in front of her.

The priest watched the wizardess pick and choose from supplies, setting them next to a burner and a wok-like bowl. It made him think about how he missed Chinese takeout. Sure, he could pray to Jonath and make the fields grow, or a stone wall burst from the ground, but getting a nice order of General Tso's chicken with crispy egg rolls was impossible. He'd found rice, chicken, garlic, and ginger (or at least their equivalent), but just couldn't get the sauces right. Not to mention trying to deep fry something.

"Oh," Nathan moaned, "fried chicken…"

Aiyana stopped and looked up at her bearded companion.

"My granny made wonderful fried chicken," she said, "and some incredible mashed potatoes with chewy lumps in them. Oh, and the peppered gravy poured over them and the hot biscuits. Oh my, it was a beautiful thing."

Nathan watched the woman, lost in the memory, before returning to her task with a shake of her head to send the fond thoughts away. It was rare for her to acknowledge their old world, the world they'd both lived in before coming here, though a few decades apart.

In the past three years, since Torrents left to find The Kid, and Aiyana constructed a magic staff that could open the portal network throughout the continent, she'd become very focused on her magics.

She was a natural elementalist, but had spent a lot of time learning about alchemy and mind magic. With the combination of the three types of magic, she'd created the robe she wore and the tent they were in, in addition to many smaller items.

The woman knew the value of not having to use her own energy every time she wanted to do something. Instead, she'd imbue an item with the arcane currents. That allowed the object to channel a specific magic many times over, before the magic needed renewed or the item burned out.

The robe she'd created had pockets that held more than most chests, and the items in those pockets could be called upon, so they were there when needed. It also had many mundane items transformed into small patches lining the inside of the robe. She could peel one off, popping the whipstitching that held it to the inner liner, and call the item back into existence. He knew the robe couldn't have patches containing food, water, or any other perishable item.

As far as Nathan knew, she had a shovel, a ladder, rope, and various other useful things. He'd teased her about that, asking when she would ever need a ladder. She just smiled and said, "You never know when I'll want to reach new heights."

Aiyana had even used her mind magics combined with alchemy to create tattoos of items on her flesh.

She could pull a dagger at any time, even after being searched.

The tent was a wonder beyond anything the robe could do, though. When they'd first started searching for the lost Aeifain, they'd needed a place to sleep, research, and hide.

The warlords of Runsk and Dioneze—cities in the plains to the south—hunted the two after they overthrew one city without meaning to. Now, they sought revenge, and the magical wonders Aiyana carried and Nathan protected.

The tent, which the wizardess dubbed 'The Citadel', was huge on the inside but smaller on the outside. Aiyana had explained to Nathan that she'd tapped an interdimensional pocket, using the same magics as the portals, but in a different way. It was a static magic, staying in between places rather than moving to a new one.

Ten paces across, it held their small kitchen and sleeping area in one part, between which sat a table flanked by two rather comfortable chairs. The two would spend their evenings reading next to the glow of the woodstove beside them on the edge of the cooking area.

They dedicated the rest to the workshop and laboratory. Three stout tables, each longer than a tall man, stood in an orderly fashion and took up half of the tent. They lined the walls behind the tables with shelves. One unit held various books; tomes of knowledge, religious texts, histories, and a few of arcane formulas and methods. Another held jars of herbs, ointments, unguents, components, and ingredients for various rituals, spells, or recipes. A third held odd trinkets, many of which Aiyana crafted herself.

Nathan had a small shelf where he kept a few story books, cookbooks, his jewel crafting and carpentry tools, and various bric-à-brac he'd picked up as mementos of his travels. The footlockers, more of a medium-sized chest at the foot of each of their beds, held clothing and toiletries.

Aiyana had created a small, curtained alcove for the chamber pot. It had a keg of water with a hot and cold tap—which refilled itself—in the privy, and a similar one in the kitchen. She'd soundproofed the bathroom wall for the sake of privacy and propriety.

The whole place was lit with a dozen small stones magicked to give off a clean, white light that turned off with a stroke of a finger.

She decided to call it the Citadel because of the equally impressive exterior. The walls of the tent were as hard as thick stone and blended with the local landscape. It could look like a grassy knoll, an outcropping of rock, or whatever else fit into the surroundings. Sound didn't travel out of it—except with the magical command word—but they could roll up flaps in the walls so they could see and hear the outside.

The most amazing thing was when they had to travel and move the tent. Under normal circumstances, it would take a small army of people to tear this all down, load it into a dozen wagons, and haul it to the next stop.

But the Citadel would collapse with a single command word from Aiyana or Nathan and become a single large sheet, with everything still inside it. They'd fold it in half, and again, and again. Each time they folded it; the canvas never got thicker. They'd continue to do that until it was no larger than a common bedroll and looked about the same as well. Strapped to the bottom of a backpack, or slung across a duffel, it weighed about the same as a sleeping bag.

She based the idea of the magic of the tent on what she'd seen on their visit to The Traveller's Inn. Though they hadn't spent long there, Aiyana had delved into the secrets of the place, partially by asking questions, and partially through magical means. The Key of Aiyana—the magical staff she'd created from five ancient, arcane artifacts—was also a key, pun intended, and Nathan assumed some of that portal magic was also part of the tent.

She'd wanted to put chicken legs on it, like the legendary hut of Baba Yaga of their previous world, and allow it to walk the lands, transporting them as they did their work. Nathan felt that was a better option than luring children in and gnawing on their bones.

Local folklore considered Aiyana a hero. The ruling warlords, though, considered her a threat to their rule.

Nathan didn't care about any of that. He just wanted to protect Aiyana and help her in her driving need to find the lost city of her people, Icon Hall. Sure, he'd like to find somewhere to settle down, and a nice woman who would join him in a humdrum normal existence. It probably wasn't his fate, but he could dream.

Captain Farrell cawed again and ruffled his feathers, hunching his head into his chest and tilting it to watch Aiyana work.

The aeifain pulled her wide-cuffed sleeves up on her blouse and tied them above her elbows. She took her gathered materials and added them in precise amounts, measuring each as she went, and in an exact order. She worked efficiently, every movement taking only as much effort as needed.

Aiyana muttered to herself, stopping to tie her long hair back with a leather thong, and looked around the room.

"Wine, water, or spirits?" she asked.

"Sorry, what?" Nathan asked. "I prefer beer, ale, or lager usually."

Aiyana snorted.

"No, silly billy, I need a liquid medium for the scrying. Water is clean, but weak. Spirits are strong, but often clouds things. Wine tints things, but it's a nice balance between the two. Beer and such would never work. I swear, sometimes I think you haven't heard a thing I've said in the past three years."

She moved to the kitchen and ran a finger along the bottles in the wine rack attached to the bottom of a cabinet.

"I've spent countless hours discussing what I am doing as I do it. Granted, it's not all for your benefit. It helps me to study out loud," she continued.

She let out a little huff and pulled out a bottle.

"This'll have to do, I guess," she said, picking up the corkscrew on the counter.

"I'm sorry." Nathan sighed.

The woman paused in her effort to twist the device into the wax and cork plug, tilting her head at him. She studied his face and realized her friend thought he'd failed her in some way.

"No, Nathan, I'm sorry. You've been a superb listener, and a great help these past few years. You made this corkscrew, built the furniture and cabinets, fetched things from towns for me, and countless other tasks. You've been invaluable. I just forget to say that out loud, very often," she said, turning her attention back to the bottle.

"Well, it's not much." Nathan shoved his hands in his pockets—an addition to their clothing he'd made, since pockets weren't a thing in this land, everyone just used pouches—and shrugged his shoulders. "I mean, you're trying to find and save an entire race of people who went missing, open magical doors that could help people travel thousands of kilometers in a blink of an eye, and help save a world recovering from its destruction. Least I could do is cobble together a few things to sit on. And remember, the first things I made were rickety and horrible. It took several tries for me to get it right."

"Don't sell yourself short," Aiyana said, idly patting him on the head as she passed him on the way back to her work area.

She pulled up short, a hand going to her mouth in an 'oh' of embarrassment, her face turning red.

"I'm so sorry, Nathan. That was cruel, insensitive, and offensive of me! I should've never used the word short for a rokairn!"

"Aw," Nathan chortled, "that didn't bother me. But the pat on the head like I was a child is another story."

"Oh! I did that too, didn't I?" Her blush deepened.

"I'm teasing! Now, stop worrying about it, and go do the magic thing. And by the way, who exactly are these 'they' you mentioned? You know, 'they' are here?"

Aiyana nodded, all business again, and continued to the table. She gently poured the wine down the side of the thin, wide, metal bowl, muttering something.

Nathan wasn't sure if she was talking to herself or uttering words of magic.

"They…" she said, pausing to scatter some herbs across the top of the mix, "are someone from our world. And once I get this heated to the correct temperature, then it should clarify, and I should be able to locate the person or persons, and if we're lucky, even see what they look like."

"Ah," Nathan nodded, still unsure, "and how long should that take?"

"I found them!" Aiyana squeaked. "Or should I say, I found him! And we're going to need to hurry. There's something else on its way too. And if we don't beat whatever this other thing is to this man…well, let's just say this won't end well."

Chapter 4

The cloudburst turned from a twilight sprinkle into a night deluge. What had been a light pattering overhead—like the feet of a couple of mice on a waxed paper windowpane—had become a downpour that sounded like a waterfall rushing down a cliff face, interspersed with white hot cracks of lightning turning dark spaces into spectral photo negative snapshots. Under the cover of the branches and leaves of the Grey Forest, the noise of the rain was more of a light shower scattered among the foliage than an actual storm.

Other things made noises in the night, as well. The shuffle of wet leaves, tossed by the wind or quick movement, sounded from the shadows. A low tick-click-click-click echoed from a deadfall around the exposed roots of a fallen tree.

Reggie crouched at the edge of the tree line, ground mists slowly creeping around the black trunks of the forest. He ran a hand along a silvery, twinkling sigil on the moist tree bark, wondering at its purpose. Lights wavered in the clearing ahead, a cluster of buildings barely visible through the rain.

The storm sparrows had been harbingers to the downpour, flocks of hundreds of the small birds moving in chaotic, but precise patterns, overhead. The wonder of nature still captivated the man's attention and adoration as it did things that humans stood in awe of, scratching their collective heads, wondering how nature knew what it knew, and how it did what it did.

Magic, Reggie thought, *the birds, not this village. Though, there may be some of that here, as well. It seems those things do exist in this world.*

He had spent hours traveling northeast, towards where he thought a community was located. The prior inhabitant of his body, and the men under his charge, had left to find the tower. They'd heard the rumor of the ogre, but it had been a handful of years since anyone in Wiley's Station, the village in front of him, had seen the monster.

When the town was new, the ogre often raided it. As the attacks stopped, locals let them fade into stories and legend. People were funny that way, quickly forgetting, always willing to accept that things were dangerous, but also willing to believe they were just tales. Unless you went 'that way' and stirred the hornet's nest. Or ogre's lair, as the case might be.

The village lay on the border of the Grey Forest and the Tear Drop Bog to the northeast, which is why the terrain was as it was, boggy. The swamp seemed to have tides, of a sort, and flooded the corner of the forest for part of the day.

Reggie moved his foot, tossing something slithering across his knee-high boots into the dense shrubbery. It was coming up on dusk, the hour of the predator, and he'd been traveling most of the day.

He watched the lights of the buildings now, debating if the townsfolk had sent him and his men into the forest as a sacrifice or not. They'd warned him of the risk. The barkeep of the only inn and tavern in town refused to talk about what lurked in the woods, but his wife had been full of tales, fraught with drama and danger.

Another man played second fiddle to her stories, raising his hands above his head and his voice in a wailing moan at all the right parts of the tales the woman had woven. It had all been quite entertaining.

Reginald stood, deciding to enter the town and seek a warm fire and bed. He still had gold and silver in his pouches, so he could pay for his food and lodging, as well as repairs to his torn clothing.

He straightened his sleeveless, quilted, red doublet—which took the brunt of the damage—and pulled frilled cuffs over his wrists from under the maroon leather bracers.

Brushing at the mud and stains on his beige breeches tucked into his knee-high black leather boots, he tried to get the worst of the muck off before making an appearance.

Standing, he adjusted the saddlebags on his shoulder, as well as the rapier and main gauche on his hips, then strode forward.

His shoulder-length blonde hair matted to his head within seconds from the heavy rain, and he grimaced, licking the rivulets of water that drizzled past his lips.

He meant to walk with dignity, but found he was doing a hunched, speed-walk by the time he reached the porch of the unnamed inn. The door stood open, the rope handle of the doorknob looped around an iron hook on the wall to stop the wind from catching it and slamming it closed.

The outdoor kitchen had a waist-high wall around it, and a roof above it. They could drop canvas walls into place in cooler weather, but with a cook fire being lit most of the day, it was pretty hot in there, even in the winter. When the snows hit, though, they'd set the walls into place, the canvas creating an insulating layer. It might be raining, but it was summer, and together with the heat from the kitchen, closing the windows and door would make it unbearably hot inside.

All this flashed through Reggie's mind as, coincidentally, a flash of lightning lit up his silhouette in the tavern's doorway. Faces around the long, rough, wooden tables were blotches of pale against the dark timbers of the walls.

Everyone turned towards him.

He stepped into the room, raising a dripping hand, and smiling as thunder rolled in the background, sounding like the low, throaty growl of warning from a celestial guard dog.

"It's me, good ol' Reggie, returning from my excursion." He looked around the room, his hand falling to his side. "Horrible night to be outside, wouldn't you say?"

He laughed, trying to make it light and friendly, but was met with eyes, most wide, but a few slitted in suspicion.

"Of course, it is, dearie," the plump, middle-aged matron of the house shuffled forward, wiping her hands on her stained apron, "you just come right in, and sit yourself by the fire until you're dry enough that you don't be dripping all over everything. Not that we have fine rugs, or posh cushions for you to ruin, but a puddle's a puddle, as my mum used to say."

The usual hushed murmur and scrape of this sort of place faded back into existence as the patrons picked up mugs and conversations, continuing as if they hadn't been interrupted, though most still watched the newcomer from the dark through side glances.

The woman took Reggie's arm and led him to a chair beside the hearth, shooing away three children playing some sort of game with stones on the seat.

"Reggie is it now?" The woman looked up at him through greasy strings of brown hair streaked with gray. "I thought you said your name was something else. Even threw a title around, didn't you now?"

"Ah, yes, that…" Reggie knew that there was a different name associated with this body, which had to be almost fifty years younger than his, "well, allow me to apologize for any airs I put on before, it was for my men. You see, hired men and loyal retainers expect a certain amount of pomp and circumstances, but I'm more than happy to drop them now and just go by my more personal nickname of Reggie. If that's alright with you, mum."

"Oh, I do say," the woman giggled, an odd sound of someone who was quickly heading out of childbearing years, "of course, good sir. Reggie it is, and Reggie it will be."

She patted the chair, letting go of his arm.

"And I'm called Elda. It's Teorge behind the bar tonight, and you'll meet the others soon enough. Now, you sit down right there, and I'll go get you a steaming cuppa cider. Or do you prefer tea? I seem to remember you liked your tea, didn't you?"

"Either would be warming and delightful, but not as much as your company and comfort as my hostess. I shall thank you—and pay you—for whichever you decide to bring." Reggie said, sitting in the chair.

A snort came from the bar at the front corner as the barkeep and owner, who was also the woman's husband, wiped a glass and set it on the planks of the bar in front of him.

"Of course, of course," the woman wandered off to get the drink, "and take off some of your wet clothes. There's a hook beside the fire you can hang them on. And get those soggy boots and stockings off. They'll dry in no time in front of…"

The woman's voice trailed off as she went into the kitchen.

"You better do as she says," said the man from behind the bar, presumably Teorge, "or you'll get a swat with a wet towel along with your mug of whatever she brings."

Reggie looked up at the man and smiled his thanks, surprised to see the man smiling back.

The room wasn't large, but it was full. The bar wasn't any longer than a man was tall, and only as wide as a burley man's shoulders. Teorge had a similar build, a solid rectangle of a body with a square head, and a haircut to match. Age and the weight that comes with it softened his square jaw. His natural look was a scowl that relaxed when he smiled. Which he did a lot, judging by the laugh lines that creased his face.

Behind the keeper were a half dozen tapped kegs, chalk words scribbled on the front showing if they were wine, beer, stout, lager, or ale. The beer had two kegs: 'House Brew' and 'Special Brew'. Three smaller casks sat on the bar, marked as whiskey, brandy, and gin. A well-used broadsword hung horizontally above the barrels, with a belt and scabbard hanging perpendicular from one of the rod-iron hooks.

"You flirt with her," the keep said. "She was the prettiest girl around when we met, and all the boys would come and try to get her fancy. She may be older now, but she's still my flower, and deserves the attention any flower gets from an admirer. Just no touching, now, you hear? That can hurt a flower and make a bee sting if you disturb its source of honey."

"Teorge," the woman came out of the kitchen, carrying a tray with a steaming ceramic mug, and a matching bowl, "don't go harassing the custom, this lad said nothing untoward, so you mind your tongue, and don't go letting that jealous streak of yours cause problems with people who pay."

Teorge scowled at his wife, but once she turned her back to him and set the stew and tea on the table beside Reggie, he smiled and winked at the younger man. His face was a brick again by the time she turned back around.

"Thank you, mum," Reggie said over the rim of the mug, lifting to sip at it. "Mm, this warms me from the inside, while the sight of you warms me from the outside."

Elda giggled again and turned back to curtsey, blushing a little.

Teorge glared at Reggie but nodded, and the corners of his mouth twitched upward.

"You just eat up while I find a warm, dry place for you to sleep, and once that's all taken care of, you can tell us your tale and what happened to all those strapping young men that were with you."

Elda turned away again, her step light, and humming a gay little tune under her breath.

Reggie looked around the rest of the room, using the wooden spoon on the stew—thick with potatoes, leaks, and stringy meat—to get some food into him.

The room was odd, triggering his memory, like remembering a dream. He had no recollection of it until he tried to recall it. Then it sprang to his mind in disjointed bits and pieces, evoked through a fog of memory rolling away.

The whole town—or village, or whatever it was—was like that. A vague idea, coated with the thick disorientation of something seen through a haze of a story.

A dozen and a half locals sat at tables, eating, drinking, and talking. The stout wooden timbers supporting the second story were ringed with oil lamps on two sides, leaving black smudge circles on the ceiling, and hooks with cloaks and drapes on the other two sides.

He recalled the upstairs, a handful of small rooms with even smaller beds, from his previous stay. That night, though, had been full of songs and boasts of his men telling how'd they'd find the beast and slay it.

Reggie had stayed quiet, smiling in the corner, letting his troops burn off their anticipation. He knew some of them would be injured, and probably some would be killed. But he never imagined he'd return alone, as the sole survivor, all others having perished.

The beast had killed him also, but now he walked again, in the same body, but with a different…spirit within.

He mulled the situation over as he ate, drank, and warmed himself by the fire. People needed to know. To understand the danger was still real and present, but they weren't at risk if they stayed away from it. Unless his actions drew the attention of the ogre to this small settlement.

The rest of the town was three streets wide and seven blocks long. It had all the usual shops, a general store of dry goods and household items, a stable, a blacksmith, and so on.

It probably started as a trading outpost for lumberjacks, furriers, and other wilderness sorts. It would've grown into this sort of place, dangerous from the wilds, but safe from the human sort of dangers like warlords and power-mad mages. Or maybe it was the opposite?

Magic. That was something else this world had. He knew the tales from the memories of the body he now wore, stories of necromancers and summoned demons. The civilization side of things was shaky now, rebuilding from the burning ruins of a war that shattered the world. His grandparents lived before it happened, his parents lived through it, and he was born after it.

"Are you done, then?" Elda asked, drawing him from his thoughts. "Ready to tell your tale, or do you need some more time?"

"I think, with a delightful glass of brandy, I'm ready to tell my story."

Reggie stood, waved his hand for quiet, and all eyes turned to him, eager for a story.

He'd tell of his adventures tonight, and tomorrow he'd set out to discover lost things: truths, knowledge, and mysteries. That was his passion, and one best fed with doing.

"What I'm about to say may shock, even frighten some of you…" he began, gesturing across the crowd with his drink, "and I caution and counsel you against seeking any of these things you hear about tonight, for the danger is grave and, in truth, more worrisome than I'd care to admit."

"Get on with it, old man!" Came a shout from the back wall. "We crave adventure, and don't need your warnings!"

"Hush up, Collin," scolded a woman, not unkindly. "He's getting to it."

Scanning the room, Reggie picked out the man who'd heckled him. He raised his drink to the man, winked, and took a deep draught from his brandy.

"Collin, I'll tell you a secret. No, two secrets. At least to start, by the end of the night, there may be many more than that." Reggie said.

Setting down his drink, he began patting his pouches. He stopped at a long one tied around his thigh and drew out a pipe and a leather tobacco pouch.

"First," he put a foot on the chair he'd been sitting on, and propped his forearms across his knee as he pulled a thick pinch of tobacco from the pouch, pausing frequently in his story to load, light, tamp, and puff on the pipe, "let me say that your lack of fear is admirable…"

"That's right!" the young man in the back shouted, and chuckles and a few yells of support erupted from around the room.

"…but foolhardy," Reggie continued, "the things I've seen, no, I don't think this is the way to get my point across. Let me say, I've seen more years than my body shows, thanks to powerful magics that I cannot begin to comprehend. So, yes, I am old. Much older than you may think or expect."

He paused, bent, and pulled three straws from the broom by the hearth. He lit them on the tallow candle on the mantle and pulled the flame into his pipe with quick puffs. The dancing flame ducked into the wooden bowl, then flared in an upward burst, lighting the storyteller's face in eerie shadows.

One of the many skills Reggie had gained from decades of hunting missing treasures and uncovering lost civilizations—forgotten to man and history—was to tell of his ideas and exploits in a way that pulled the attention of others. This was a useful talent for drawing support from the common folk who could influence the opinion of an entire city or country, or the wealthy who could influence funding.

It was also handy for family gatherings when the grandkids sat around him in a semi-circle. He never tired of their honest reactions, their open faces staring up at him with slack-jawed stares of wonder and fright.

Looking up through the flame shooting a handsbreadth above his pipe, he scanned the room to make sure he had their attention.

"I've seen temples laid to waste and swallowed by jungles, only to be discovered by my hand a thousand years later. I've uncovered tombs in deserts, hidden and cursed by man, gods, and time. And now, I share with you a secret, a truth that comes with age, something those of lesser years will deny, scoff at, and not recognize until the shroud of years lays heavy across their shoulders."

He pulled on his pipe, and released a cloud of haze around him, then sent gentle rings of smoke through the center. The mist of tobacco parted with his breath.

"The young claim to want adventure, and they do—there's no denying that. But they are so full of confidence bred with a lack of years, and certainty that what little they know is the piercing truth, that when they're confronted with events that confirm or deny what they think, they react strongly. Fear and hope wash over them, causing them to freeze, run, or fight. It is only with the decades of experience, bitterness, and having what you knew to be true…crushed, that you truly understand what I am about to tell you. The old handle change differently. I won't say better because you would never believe me."

He looked across the crowd and saw the people with grey in their hair and beards, lines around their mouths, and wrinkles around their eyes, nodding. The younger people scoffed, rolled their eyes, or looked dubious.

"Years temper you, granting wisdom, and that allows you to accept more easily something that differs from your thoughts, because you've seen it happen so many times before. We may be more reluctant to change with day-to-day things. But with the big things in life, we know that what we expect and have seen before will eventually come to be proven wrong. Something will cause a great upheaval, and we've seen it before. With each great war, each government overthrown, and each new way of thinking. We've seen it before and know it will change everything and nothing."

Reggie smiled, raised his brandy, and moved it across the faces of his rapt audience.

"Here's to the new, the unknown, which is often just the old raising its head once again."

He drank deeply as others raised their drinks to return the toast, and drank.

"Now," he said, "there was an ogre that was exiled to rumor and tales…"

Chapter 5

Legend told that the Tear Drop Bog was haunted. A place whose marsh had become brackish from the weeping of banshees torn from life by war and misfortune. Their loved ones—and their victims—had added their tears to the waters, filling a once lush valley until it was a swamp bogged down with horrible things, most of which were intangible.

Nathan stood on a crest of a hillock, the symbol of Jonath gripped in his thick, gnarled fingers. Wind wailed around him, though it sounded more like human voices than a breeze.

Aiyana bent double, panting from the exertion of force-creating a portal to these forsaken, forgotten, and fragmented lands. She propped her staff against her hip and tucked it under an arm, tilting her head as if listening to a distant voice.

Captain Farrell took to the air to scout the area. Even the raven seemed disconcerted by the broken landscape, calling to his brethren to find the dangers and pitfalls around the small hilltop.

"Take your time," Nathan said to the wizardess. "I'll stand watch while you recover. I liked the colors of this portal. It had hints of emerald on top of the sapphire and aquamarine. Was that because of the area we were going to, or something else? Doesn't matter, you did good, and that was no easy task, what you did."

He rambled, giving her time to recover.

"The ley lines here," she panted. "They're muddled. Like a knitting pattern that tangled. The earth lines are soft, mushy. The air ones are thick, but wide. The water ones feel tainted. And any fire lines are missing, like they're blocked from entering this place at the border. Something has messed with the entire network."

"Jonath, bring us awareness, gather our strength, and grant us the wisdom to know which path to take to find the new disruption to the land."

The priest's voice was somber and flat in prayer but had an undertone of power and passion.

The air shimmered around the two, which may have been from the magic of Nathan's supplication, or from the thick morning air.

"We go south, as you expected." The rokairn oriented himself in that direction. "You've done well in your spell, bringing us north of the settlement. Wiley's Station should be a few hours walk in that direction.

"You know," he continued, looking at the wizardess who'd sat on the wet grass to catch her breath, "I always liked the cities back home, but here…I've come to love the wilderness. The buildings always felt safe to me. I knew the dangers of civilization, and how to avoid them. Here, though, the cities are full of things that want to kill you, but the countryside is full of things just trying to survive."

The rokairn fingered the shaft of his double-headed axe, Marcid, the thick vines flourishing under his grip. It was an odd dichotomy, the powers of earth and protection that enchanted his weapon. His god, Jonath, and PepperGarten's god, Senaria, had blessed it. The weapon was almost a living thing, though it had no sentience that he knew of.

"Why do we need this man we hunt?" Nathan asked.

"He is of our world," Aiyana answered, rising to her feet, "and you know Jack likes doing things in threes. So, three companions for a quest. But he also carries knowledge that lends itself to my personal quest…to find the missing Aeifain. I need to know what happened to my people. They had so much promise but withdrew from the world. Why? Where did they go? Did they do this for their own reasons, or were they forced to do it? And this man, he's on a similar quest, though I do not know if our goals precisely align."

"Yeah," Nathan drew out the word, "well, I guess we'll find out. Do you think he's an enemy?"

"All people can be an enemy if they stand in the way of freeing a people. They may think they're helpful, but so often rely on the tired defense of…that's the way it's always been."

"That's a bit much, Aiyana, don't you think?" Nathan asked. "Because someone thinks differently than you, relying on their past and experience, they might be an enemy? Wouldn't that make me your enemy, also then?"

The wizardess turned to look at the priest, her gaze calculating as she considered his words.

Nathan tilted his head, wrinkling his brow as he realized she was thinking about it.

"No," she said, laughing, then going serious, "if that were the case, we'd have a serious problem."

Nathan let out a breath he hadn't realized he was holding.

"Oh, the young can be more stuck in their ways than the old, sometimes," he muttered.

"And aeifain have ears that hear more than is meant to be heard," Aiyana replied.

"You're welcome to hear it, if it means you'll think about what I said."

Nathan didn't wait for an answer. He shouldered his pack, lifted his axe, and walked down the slope to splash in the rivulet of a stream between hills.

Standing on a small rise, having followed something that was between a dirt road and a wide animal track, Aiyana stood beside Nathan, looking over the remains of Wiley's Station.

The settlement was a burned husk. Flames still danced among the blackened timbers and charred corpses scattered throughout the town. The bodies showed signs of violence, but no weapons or defenses were in place.

"They used magic in this attack." Aiyana pointed at arcane sigils carved into a freestanding post that once held a porch roof above the now-scorched boards of an abandoned building. A line of red traced through the symbols, traveling from one to the other.

She pointed at burn marks in the road, which started as a small round black circle in the center of the street and widened in a cone-shape until it met a building. Similar marks were visible on the far side of town, running perpendicular to the line of buildings, where three or four would've been set ablaze with a single magical flame.

"You think our man did this?" Nathan asked.

She turned to him and studied him.

Nathan supported himself, using the haft of Marcid as a crutch to lean on. He didn't look directly at the carnage. His eyes avoided the clumps of smoldering bodies in the streets where families had huddled together as a horrible fate befell them.

This was not the work of the one you seek, a voice said in her head. *It was something much more powerful. Working with it would lead to paths you never expected to open before you.*

"No…" she shook her head.

"Good," Nathan cut off her next words, "then we agree. Let's look for…"

The rokairn stopped talking, turning around, and breathing in short, sharp breaths.

"Are you okay?" Aiyana asked, her voice gentle, laying a hand on his shoulder.

"No." Nathan's rough voice broke. "I'm sorry, but how can you be okay? People were killed, and for no good reason. And whatever the reason was, even if they were horrible people doing horrible things, we both know most weren't. Horrible, that is. People follow others, doing bad things, not because they're bad, but because they don't know how to get out of it. There can't be a good reason to kill a whole town!"

"I know, Nathan," Aiyana soothed, "and I remember you telling me the stories of your grandparents and family fleeing Europe during the Nazi invasion, and how you were raised during the civil rights movement. You've seen so much, and I understand. But remember, I've lived a few centuries, and I've seen horrors beyond description…"

Nathan wheeled on the woman, his face red as his distress turned to anger. The man caught himself as his mouth opened to give a sharp retort, drawing in a deep breath to steady himself.

"No," he said, his voice firm, "you haven't. I know the body you have has, and I know you've seen people beaten in the streets as you marched in defense of the rights of black people, but this isn't the same. You, Aiyana, college student and hopeful young woman, have not seen this sort of massacre. And neither have I."

Aiyana's hand dropped, and she turned away so he could only see the side of her face as her hair fell to cover it.

"Yes, that's all true," she sighed, "but I have to draw on what I can, so I don't break down and lose it right now. Does that make sense to you?"

Nathan watched the younger woman shudder. She inhabited a body older than his but was still very young.

He sighed, and his shoulders slumped.

"Yes, of course, I'm sorry," he said.

"Don't be sorry," Aiyana turned and looked at him, her eyes glistening, "just pull it together. I'll give you a moment. Meet me in town when you're ready."

She walked away, her shoulders, back, and spine stiff.

The rokairn watched her go. He'd seen riots in the streets, hidden from them, not wanting to be swept up in the events throughout his life. But she'd always rushed for the front lines, ready to stand up for what's right, to defend those that weren't allowed to have a voice of their own.

He trailed after her.

The two entered Wiley's Station, the smell of burned bodies, buildings, livestock, and goods washing over them.

They left less than an hour later. They hadn't spoken much as they investigated the charred remains of the structures, trying to make sense of what had happened there.

"Hoofprints," Aiyana said.

"What?" Nathan asked.

"The ground was wet, and even all the fire couldn't hide hoofprints. There were lots of them, but only the boot prints of the villagers, or so it seemed. And the hooves weren't shod, no horseshoes."

"Yeah, okay, I saw that, too, now that you mention it. What's it mean?" the priest asked.

"I don't know, but it's odd." The wizardess answered. "I think someone else is hunting our man."

"It could be a coincidence," Nathan pointed out.

"Could be, but unlikely." Aiyana said. "And if it is not, then this man is more important than I thought."

"We're all important when we come to this world. You were, I was, and the others before us were. We're here to make, or help make, some large change that is looming."

"How deep does Jack Tucker go?" Aiyana breathed. "What kind of puppet master is he that the people he brings from our world to this one are the catalysts of significant changes?"

"I've only met him twice, but he didn't come off as a puppet master type, more of the helpful sort."

"Yes, I've met him also, and took time to study his tavern, his *travelling* inn. I saw the threads of magic linked to more than just the ley lines, or even this world. He has some larger thing in mind, but I can't put my finger on what motivates him."

The two moved away from the town at a slow pace, considering the carnage, discussing viable theories about who was doing what and to whom.

"If it isn't your friend Jack, then it could be that mageocrat from Seawall City," Aiyana suggested.

"First," Nathan ticked off items on his fingers, "Jack isn't my friend, more of an acquaintance. Second, that alchemist is dead. It's more likely the petty warlord of Dioneze City still pursuing us. Manalo Maqsher isn't known for his tact and burning an entire village wouldn't be unlike him."

"The mageocrat could've become an undead wizard, a lich. He dipped far enough into weird magical formulae; it wouldn't be unthought of for him to have prepared for the eventuality of his death. As for Maqsher, how would he even have known we were coming up here? How could he have followed us without the ability to use the portal network? And even if he could, how would he have gotten here before us?"

The aeifain turned to look at Nathan, who was staring at her from the corner of his eye, one side of his mouth pulled tight.

"That's *a-mage-ing*," Nathan grunted.

"No," Aiyana shook her head, "don't start that."

"Come on!" Nathan urged. "You used to be a real *wizard* at puns! You'd sling two or three in one sentence, *conjuring* a *hat trick* every time!"

"Look," Aiyana jerked her head back, tossing her long hair over her shoulder, "let me *spell* it out for you, since you're the one *casting* aspersions here, and I'll *ley-line down* the law—puns are not *enchanting*!"

"Khizhane was an alchemist, and a *vial* man, but I don't think he'd have *turned* to his *mummy* the moment he died."

"*Holy* mixed potions and *portents*! Are you mixing priest magic puns in now?" Aiyana raised an eyebrow while wrinkling her nose. "I should've *seen that coming*, or heard it through the *grape di-vine-nation*."

"Oh!" Nathan winced. "I don't know if that one was a stroke of genius, or just a stroke, because it had a lot of heart, but it damaged my brain."

"Were those puns, or just being witty?" Aiyana asked.

"No idea," Nathan shrugged, "you're the judge, jury, and executioner of all things related to *pun-ishment*."

"Aww, lame!" the wizardess lamented. "Should we just *o-pun* the door to the textbook *pun-dits* so they can rob us blind with their blunt *pun-dings* to the head?"

The two continued back and forth, trading verbal spars and barbs, traveling into the Grey Forest, unaware they were being observed.

Chapter 6

Kajuun watched the two people move along the dirt track of the road, the pair winding their way into the shade of the tree canopy.

More intruders, she thought, *coming into the ancient forest and taking what they want with no regard to the life that was always there, trying to survive.*

Wiley's Station had been new…well, for the forest it was. For the humans who'd lived there, it was a well-established town of over two decades. The second generation was already taking over the community. But humans bred so fast and within fifteen or twenty years, the next generation would pull their weight, ousting the oldest.

Kajuun thought the elders usually quit because it wasn't worth the fight anymore, especially among their own kind, when they were just trying to help the younger folks with their years of wisdom and experience. The elders that stuck around seemed to be sick in their brains, greedily snatching at threads of control and power, trying to make their continued existence mean something to everyone but themselves.

The people of the hoof and horn respected, even revered, their elders, asking for their knowledge and advice. When the body faltered, less work was expected, but the mind was still a fine tool to help the tribes. After the mind faded, it was time to share the stories of life with the youngest of the tribe. When the spirit failed, and the body broke down, and the mind became disconnected from the moment, then it was time to give a last celebration before releasing the soul for the next part of its journey.

But one of her people hadn't aged, though he'd been around for much longer than others expected, considering he wasn't of the long-lived species of the Torck. His name was Rauhen, and he told stories from the days when the aeifain still walked the lands. He'd advised her people for decades, using mind magics from a distance, guiding the three tribes to unite, where to migrate to, and how to build their city.

Rauhen had become a leader among her people within a few months of his arrival, his ideas fresh and bold. He'd led them from a ragged experience, scrambling to survive off the land, to a wondrous city with food, education, shelter, and magic available to all.

Returning her attention to the two, she winced at the latest barrage of puns, stroking one hand along the curve of her horns. It was a nervous habit she'd picked up soon after she got her first full twist. Others fiddled with rings, pulled their beards, or any other number of things, but Kajuun stroked her horns, and usually it was the right one on the rear set.

She was one of the rare Shirai, revered as leaders among her people, who had a double set of horns. The foremost set swept back from her brow, set in her skull just above her dark bangs. The rear set began on the top of her head and curled behind her, almost touching the back of her head.

She shifted her cloven hooves, thinking about her people. Once, a peace-loving folk, they'd welcomed humans, dasism, and aeifain into the Grey Wood (as they called it, though the other races now called it a forest), and shared their songs, dances, and wine.

The longevity of the people of hoof and horn, the Torck—better known as the Rammen to the other races, which others pronounced like 'ram' and 'men' but jammed together—varied greatly.

The great-bodied bull men—known as minotaurs—were the shortest lived, and almost never saw a fourth decade, their bodies and minds failing shortly after they entered their third decade.

The satyrs lived longer, until almost seventy most of the time, and sometimes as long as ninety. The fauns, though, they were said to have some dryad or forest spirit in their blood, and they seemed ageless to most of the Torck. They could live a half-dozen centuries or more, though rumors said a few lived more than a millennium.

Kajuun was a satyr, and well into her fourth decade. She'd proven herself a capable warrior, scout, and could commune with the wind and forest spirits.

As she grew older, she shied away from civic duties of planning cities, teaching the youth, or guiding her people in other ways that were usually expected of elders. Instead, Kajuun insisted on continuing the path she'd hewn for her life. They wouldn't put her out to pasture; she'd continue to be a soldier.

The older people scoffed and sneered at the idea, and the younger people mocked and teased her about not wanting to move into her expected role. The elders lectured her about knowing when it was time to step aside for the youth, telling her that her body no longer needed to be put through the rigors of frosty nights spent outside.

But Kajuun stuck to her path, enjoying the time with nature away from all the politics and game playing that comes with a society. The fauns were the only ones who didn't speak against her decision. The fourteen of their race within the community watched and nodded knowingly. Kajuun didn't know what that could mean, but she'd shrugged it off as one of the things the holy elders did.

The young pointed out that since they had created the Torck Horses, scouts and warriors were no longer needed. Kajuun shivered with the thought of the things. She considered them abominations, even though they were made with natural means and forms. Crafted with stone, the constructs had the torso of a man, and the head and two hind legs of a horse, all infused with the magic of the gargoyles.

Kajuun didn't trust the magic.

Minotaurs had bull heads and lower halves, with the torso of the other intelligent races. They were massive and muscular, as befit their root stock. They weren't stupid, but they were rarely creative or attracted to the arts that relied on thought. But, because they preferred a good, hard day of physical labor, didn't mean they weren't good to have as friends or to raise a glass of mead or cider with.

Satyrs had the lower half of goats, wide flat noses, and various versions of horns that generally grew from their temples, between their eyes and their ears. Their ears were often pronounced, and always covered with a soft downy fur. Sometimes they were not much more than pointed, exaggerated versions of human ears, similar to the dasism or aeifain, but with fur. Other times, they stuck out a hand span from the head, and would tilt and pivot to capture sounds.

Kajuun's ears were almost human, and usually hidden underneath her dark hair.

Satyrs also came in a distinct caste separation. One breed was covered in thick, coarse hair across their body, and the other had less body hair on the torso and arms, though they always had some. The first type, known as Natera, was coarse in humor and personality, and thrived on the baser drives and instinct, driven to drink and sex when not on a specific task. The other type, the Shirai—the type that Kajuun was—was thought to be a mix of faun and satyr, lending some of the innocence and introspection of the former, and the passion and impetuousness of the latter.

Some thought that the different horns dictated social standing. The minotaurs thought that the wider horns dictated strength, and satyrs thought that more loops showed savvy.

Kajuun was outside of her own caste, separated by her double set of horns, which often heralded heroes of her people.

Fauns, though, were different. They had the wisdom of children, but with centuries of living behind them. They saw the world in a unique, but simple, way. The complexity of politics, that blocked the way to enjoying life, confused and saddened them.

Physically, though, they were as diverse as the weather. Some looked almost identical to satyrs, whereas others were almost completely human looking except for their shorter, slighter build, pointed ears, and proclivity to wear fewer clothes even in snowy weather.

But these humans…they were just disruptive and destructive. They didn't care if they wiped out entire ecosystems to build their towns and make money.

Money, that was another issue. Placing value on raw materials like gold and silver over their value as beauty and art…it was confusing. To destroy one thing, to horde something that had no day-to-day value and improvement in life made little sense. Those types of views needed removed, even if it meant destroying them.

Her eyes fell on the ground at her hooves. What had been a line of ants carrying bits of leaves had curled into a shape. The insects were moving in a wiggling pattern, drawing out a sigil Kajuun had seen on the post in Wiley's Station.

Something larger was at play here, and she needed to find out what it was before it grew out of control.

"What were you thinking?" Tymere glared at Manalo. "Children are not to be used, not when we have fully grown men that can do the job!"

"Fully grown men cost money, but children can be caught and taught. They do it to please, or to get a crust of bread and a bed. Bed and bread are cheaper than gold." Manalo scratched at his scruff of a beard absently, looking at the maps on the table in front of them.

"I think you're just upset because you don't know where our old friends disappeared to." Manalo shifted to scan the sheafs of papers scattered on the table detailing supplies.

"We didn't really know where they were before." Tymere crossed his arms and scowled. "Those two bastards have been confounding us for years and dodging any magic or foot soldiers we've sent their way. Nathan uses the power of Jonath to protect them from detection, and somehow Aiyana has stolen knowledge from under our noses to increase her power in each of the arcane arts. You've been sending squads of horsemen and warriors to catch them, and I've been scrambling to get enough mystical power to maintain the little lead we have. We're failing. That's the bottom line."

"What do you want from me?" The warlord turned to look at the alchemist. "You expect miracles, when it's a war of attrition and small advances. This is a long game, not a take it all in the next couple of days!"

"I want her staff, and her research!" Tymere uncrossed his arms and thrust them towards the heavens. "She's not sharing! The things she's learned can help all of humankind, not just one person. She's selfish and bent on the destruction of our people."

"And I want to unite the city-states of the plains so we can rebuild what we had a half-century ago, bring people together so we can rise and make our people great again. We both want the same thing, but we've joined so our divergent styles can come together to make this happen."

"Yes," Tymere ran both hands through his hair, "and what do we do to make that happen when we see a surge of magical power and they disappear?"

"You calm down," the warlord's voice was strained, but even, "and use whatever resources you have to find something within range to tell us where they are. If we're going to save humans, we must be fierce, but methodical. Diligent, but decisive."

Thunder cracked and rolled farther to the north. The distant tree line of the Grey Forest swayed back and forth, the branches creaking and heralding the approaching storm. The hay field rocked back and forth in the breeze, a sea of golden color rippling like a tide cresting.

Under the canvas roof of the command tent, the two men hunched over a table of parchments and maps in the middle of a farmer's field.

The farmer had objected to the army marching through his land, but they removed the man's concerns. They tied him to an 'X' shaped cross in the center of his land, and conscripted his children to serve the army in any manner needed. As for the man's wife, she'd fill a different need for the army than her offspring.

The legion was a hodgepodge of mercenaries, thugs, and conscripts. Old men and teens barely old enough to shave were the mass of the force, and that was good enough for Manalo. Fodder was fodder.

The elite troops were a collection of other warlords and their personal guards and retinue. They were the horsemen, used for fast attacks, flanking, or causing chaos. And they did cause chaos, on and off the field.

Tymere didn't understand the need for them, thinking that one could just conjure up a force of loyal, fighting men. He didn't understand the need for camp followers, booze, and other distractions. The man barely understood that an army traveled on its stomach.

He was too used to his old life in Seawall City, under his old master. He forgot the city ran with many cogs in the wheel of bureaucracy, and that in the real world the minutia had to be handled personally.

There was also their shadow ally, who'd provided so much information. That one would have to be watched, if not for anything else, then because they were cunning. Manalo was excited and scared by the promise of another army, one who could wield magic.

The wind shifted, and the first light taps of rain tippled on the canvas roof above the joint commanders of the largest force seen in these lands for nearly a century.

The pavilion was small, only ten paces across, but they could keep the sides up and not get the papers wet in a storm if they kept the table in the center. Manalo eyed the horizon, and the darkening, roiling clouds over the wood, and wondered if they'd need to roll down a few panels of the canvas walls this time.

"That damned witch and her magics," the warlord muttered.

Tymere looked at him, then snorted.

"This isn't her work; she rarely plays with the weather. And she's never left carved symbols behind as a source of her magics. The sigils we've found are like nothing I've seen. Haven't you read any of the reports I've given you? She likes grander gestures. She's flashy and egotistical and doesn't think we're worth an effort unless it spreads the rumor of her power. This is the forest…"

"What does that even mean?" It was Manalo's turn to snort.

"It means the wood is an ancient place, full of old dangers, ancient magics, and things that make legends become whispered fears over evening fires. The Grey Forest was once home to the aeifain and the dasism, and those two abominations of races could teach the trees to stir the wind and sing down the thunder and lightning."

"Very poetic, but I think you're exaggerating for effect," the warlord dismissed Tymere's words, drawing him away from the topic.

Manalo moved to the side table, which was an acting larder loaded with wines, cheeses, smoked meats, dried fruits, and other easy-to-eat nibbles.

Picking up a pewter plate, he slapped a meat flap of ham on it, followed by wrinkled and shrunken plum-sized tomatoes. Sprinkling a handful of dark burgundy olives over it, he added a wedge of dense yellow cheese and a hunk of coarse bread.

"Listen, Tymere," the warlord caught the alchemist's eye and held his attention, "I appreciate your skills, intention, and drive. But, let's face it, your skills are minor, and your drive falters as often as it catches. As for your intentions, they waver. I don't think you actually know what you want."

Tymere opened his mouth to say something, but the younger man held a hand up to stop him.

"What I'm trying to get across to you is that, as long as you're useful to me, I'll keep you around. I like the fun little things you know, and that you're trying to get better at magic. Remember those little flaming balls you made a few weeks ago? They were kinda useful until they spread across the dry grass and made it impassable for my troops. But you're trying. And as long as you have some use, I'll keep you around. But the moment you don't, or if you try to overreach your authority…"

Manalo's eyes drew into a tight squint, and his mouth formed a straight line cutting across his unshaven face.

"I'll remove you from my list of problems with no effort or second thought. Do we understand each other?"

The older man's expression flashed from surprised to offended to dawning understanding. Fear crept in, and his face changed to an open expression of bewilderment.

Manalo could see the conflict of fight or flight behind the expressions, and wondered if he should be proud or worried his pet magician didn't cower.

"I see we understand each other," Manalo smiled a tight-lipped grin, and holding his plate in one hand, reached up and patted the alchemist's cheek, smearing grease and juices across Tymere's face. He wiped his hand down the man's neck and tunic, turning it over to get the last of the juices from the back of his fingers.

"Did you get your little scrying device working?" the warlord changed the subject.

"Yes," the alchemist sneered. "I got it working. But it won't do any good if we can't get it into their possession somehow. Why do you ask?"

"Because my hairy contact with the hooves has told me that the wizardess has left the burned village where she'd been hunting someone."

Manalo tossed a slice of ham into his mouth and chewed, watching his lackey.

"And?" Tymere pressed. "How does that help us?"

"I know the guy they're hunting. It's Kazzek Tel Virian." The warlord grinned.

"Wow! Isn't that the guy who took out the Witch of Winter a few years back?"

"Yup," Manalo nodded, "and the guy who took out the Bounty Hunters of Kresk."

"And our little aeifain friend is going to him for help?" Tymere asked. "That's going to make this much harder."

Still smiling, Manalo held up a finger to forestall any further interruptions.

"And I know someone who was betrayed by him during a heist job."

"Who is it?" Tymere was interested now.

"Kionna the assassin." Manalo's smile grew wider.

"Hasn't he been raising a small army of his own?" Tymere asked.

"Yeah, he's been growing it slowly, but doesn't have very many men," Manalo said, "and I think he'd be willing to throw in with us. We just offer him a place in what we're doing and set him on the trail. Give him your device, and he gets it into the pockets of one of the people we're hunting. As a bonus, we hand him the guy he's been hunting. He'll get things done."

"How will he find this Kazzek?" Tymere asked.

"With our benefactor's help, we can get him and his men in place in time," Manalo said confidently, "and we send a contingent of men to help him out. They can also deliver a trinket or two from your toy box, like that ring that does the battering ram trick, and some potions that make them run without tiring. It gives him authority over our men, a few cool magic tricks, and does our dirty work for us."

"And once Aiyana is being tracked," Tymere said thoughtfully, "we'll know exactly where she is."

"And our friend is going to nudge them when they need it," Manalo smirked, "and in the meantime, we can turn our force towards her eventual goal, Icon Hall."

"I'll go gather the things and then get back to my research!" Tymere turned to go.

"Of course," Manalo sneered, "maybe you'll get good at it one day. Why don't you do something useful and go outside and take a walk instead? The men hate you because you're weird, and it wouldn't hurt for you to make a couple of friends in the camp. It might come in handy in the future."

Tymere stalked off and Manalo laughed.

Chapter 7

The ruins crawled with thieving raiders, and by their livery—if you could call it that—Reggie guessed they were from Runsk. Twenty men shouted back and forth as they came and went from the structure, which once was some sort of fortification spanning the road. Carved runes decorated each wall and arch, faintly glowing sigils glinting in the afternoon sun.

Thick thorn bushes grew straight up to the double buildings, which were mostly human in design, but foreign elements blended into the stonework. A graceful line of vines, made of marble, had patches of green moss decorating it on the leaves.

Reginald crouched in the underbrush a dozen paces away. He recognized some men from the life his body had before he came into it. He couldn't quite figure out where he knew them from, but three stood out to him.

A tall, lanky man with an oiled goatee, greasy hair, and a feral look pushed at broken boards with his foot. He shouted orders at the men entering the structure and gestured upward to show they should check the top floors.

He stood with two others who could've been twins, if the first hadn't been a head and a half taller than the second. They both wore leather studded with metal disks, carried hand axes, and had bushy beards that were only rivaled by their eyebrows. Both looked like overgrown rokairn, right down to the swagger of the rock people.

"Daizjah and Danayia," Reggie muttered, "and that would make the other guy Kionna."

Pulling from his decades of archaeology knowledge, he focused on the building, drawing out details. The barbican resembled western European designs; twin towers on each side of the broken and weed-strewn road, and an arching span connecting them. A wall extended outward from each tower, crumbling, and disappearing into thick underbrush.

The embellishments—even dilapidated as they were—were starkly out of place on the bland and blocky building. They had a natural flow, and though etched from stone, looked more lifelike than some of the surrounding foliage. Besides the vines running up the walls and columns, the crenellations looked like foam-capped waves, swept by high winds. But it was the markings along the archway that held Reggie's attention.

They were a script of some sort. It was like hieroglyphics and cuneiform had a baby. Not grouped together to form words, they stood alone as graceful figures, elegant and artistic, and formidable though delicate. The way they glinted almost pulsed, making them lifelike. It could be a trick of the light, but the movement along them—inside them—couldn't be attributed to the sun, even with the wispy clouds trailing in front of it.

"Aeifain designs," he whispered, excited by the idea of the find.

The wind whipped across the clearing in front of the structure, tossing dust and dried leaves into the air. The bushes in front of Reginald bent low to the ground, and he dropped to his belly to avoid being seen.

Kionna squinted towards the movement.

"Daizjah, Danayia," the wind carried his voice as he gestured toward the hidden archaeologist, "over there, in those bushes. Go see what's hiding there. We may have rabbit for dinner, or something a bit more…sturdy."

The two stocky men lumbered towards Reggie, tilting from one foot to the other with each step. They fingered their axes but didn't pull them from the loops on their belts. They didn't even appear wary or curious; they were just doing what they were told.

They headed right for Reggie's hiding spot, and options flashed through his mind. He tossed the idea of staying still and hoping not to be seen aside immediately. It wouldn't do him any good. They'd spot him without difficulty. That left running as a viable option. But darting pell-mell into the thick forest at a dead run, his back to men with things easily thrown between his shoulder blades held little appeal either.

That left one option, which could lead down a few roads depending how the men reacted.

Reginald leapt to his feet, throwing his arms wide—both in a friendly gesture, and to show that he wasn't going for his weapons—and smiled his most charming grin.

"Danayia! Daizjah!" Reggie sounded like he was greeting an old friend whom he hadn't seen in years. "How are you two? It's been too long, and boy, am I relieved to see you out here!"

"He's Daizjah," the shorter one jerked a thumb towards the taller one, "and I'm Danayia."

"Yeah, I know that. I was looking back and forth between both of you. Must have just called it out wrong." Reggie shrugged.

"And we just saw you two weeks ago," grumbled the taller one, "or don't you remembers?"

"Of course, I remember. How could I forget?"

"Maybes the same ways you forgot to split the haul with us?" Daizjah asked, his hand idly twirling the hand axe in its loop.

"Or how you forgots to hear us when we was calling your name? Maybe like that?" Danayia grunted.

"Or maybes like how you forgots to not call the watch on us, so half of Dioneze City was chasing us, and we had to run for our lives to get aways from a right good hanging? Maybes like that?" Daizjah was a few steps away from Reggie now and had a short-hafted axe in each hand, twirling them in slow circles at his side.

Reginald's mind swam, trying to find purchase. He had vague impressions of the events, but only after the men mentioned each one. It was like remembering the plot of a play that you saw forty years ago, when in college and overwhelmed by classes, and trying to woo Annabelle Mcgurski to be your belle, and let you be her beau. It was muddled and confusing.

He was a good talker and had talked his way out of many problems, and into a few, as well. But these guys threw a pretty convincing argument out and had definitive grievances with him—or the previous him— and weren't likely to back down no matter what he said.

He could draw his rapier and main gauche and fight the two men. That would lead to the others coming at him, though, and those odds were not ones he cared to play.

Then there was Kionna. Something tickled at Reggie's brain about that man. There was something more to him than met the eye, but the archaeologist couldn't put his finger on it. He'd run cons with the man not too long ago. He remembered something about the dark, and the man having a way of knowing more about people than he should.

Danayia and Daizjah slowed when they reached the other side of the bushes, both holding twin axes. They looked Reginald up and down, their eyes drawn to slits, and their mouths matching.

Kionna drew up behind them.

"Kazzek," Kionna nodded, as if he'd been expecting Reggie the whole time.

Kazzek, the name imploded in the archaeologist's head. That was the name this body went by before Reggie showed up. But that man had died, the body abandoned of any spirit or soul. Kazzek Tel Virian was his full name, though further memories seemed distant. It was as if something had completely evicted the mind of the previous inhabitant, including past experiences. But the skills remained, the things ingrained into muscle memory, and hints of things beyond.

"I think you have some explaining to do." Kionna smiled, and it darkened his face rather than brightening it.

The men searching the ruins had stopped, watching the newcomer at the edge of the clearing as their boss and his lieutenants approached him.

"Ah," Reggie hesitated, "y-yes, I guess I do. And right now, I am debating…do I tell the truth, or create a story that you're more likely to allow me to live if you hear it?"

"You were always a horrible liar, Kaz. Since we were children, you had an annoying habit of telling the truth." Kionna's smile turned grim.

"I brought you into the gang," Kionna sighed and looked upward, "even though I hadn't seen you for years, trusting you because you were good at your job. The best second-story man I ever knew, and not bad with a blade. Even if you'd a problem with killing people. I've never seen more hands with holes in them than when I ran with you. That was even more cruel than killing a man, and I tried to show you that. Death is a blessing, Kazzek, and an end to suffering and struggle, but you never understood that. So, do I bless you now, or do you have some truth that will let you live another day?"

"Boss," the taller twin-ish man interrupted, "you gonna let this guys join the crew again?"

Kionna held up a hand, stopping any further questions, and stared at Reginald.

"Well, I can give you all the money I have," Reggie started, but the shorter thug interrupted.

"We kills yous, we gets it anyway, so come up with something better," Danayia muttered, fingering the leather wrapped haft of an axe.

"Fair point, ol' chap!" Reggie reached out to slap the man on the shoulder and stopped as Danayia's face fell, and the axe rose.

"Right, then." Reggie cleared his throat, took a deep breath, and continued. "Some magical thing happened to me, and I've lost most of my memory. But I'm on the trail of something big. I think there's a lost civilization out here, and this building is nothing more than the entryway into it."

"What sort of lost civilization?" Kionna asked, his voice low and husky.

"Aeifain," Reggie faltered, surprised at his own answer. "They went missing…"

"I know all that," Kionna's voice was a dusky, impatient growl, "and I suppose you did something with most of our last score? Returned it to the people who needed it?"

Reggie hesitated, the tendrils of memory threading its way through his brain.

"Yeah…" he said slowly, "I think so. It wasn't ours, and people needed it. It was gypsy's, right? The colorful folk. That's who we stole it from, right?"

Kionna nodded, curiosity creasing his face and muting the annoyance.

"Why?" Kionna asked. "I never understood why you cared."

"They have…something. Experience in life. A delight at the small things. Family, friends. Making the world a better place for whoever comes next. Something more than most people ever even have a chance to see…"

"You'se so stupid." Daizjah barked a laugh. "Why care for the weak? They don't even know about how much money they could have. I want the good life, where women and men live to serve me. Not some stupid help others things."

"That's just it, isn't it?" Reggie thrust his hands forward, like he was begging for something to help him survive one more day. "They want something that most others can't even see, can't even realize exists. And that's why I took the…"

Reggie's words, so full of passion and wonder, cut off.

"Oh, just kill him. We'll get any remaining money from him once he's dead." Kionna said.

The death sentence was like a bucket of cold water on Reginald. He stood stock straight, his spine ramrod stiff.

Without a thought, the rapier and main gauche were in his hands. The tip of the long blade, piercing the shoulder of Daizjah, but only because the short man had turned at the last moment.

The parrying weapon in Reggie's hand batted one of Danayia's axes to one side.

Kionna's long sword was a flurry of steel and skill in front of Reginald's body, knocked to one side then the other by the rapier, followed by the main gauche.

The leader came on, not relenting, a whirlwind of danger and death.

Kionna was a master of the sword, though where he'd learned it was a mystery to Reggie. The man, as a boy, had used sticks and stones. Later in life, it was all daggers and knives. The sword had come from somewhere else, maybe intuitive, maybe learned in back alleys, maybe from some drunk he'd found in a bar and spent dark, moonlit nights sparring with. But the skill and training were unmistakable.

The leader of the ruffians stepped over the bent bushes, his blade a blur, and moved to close in with Reginald.

The others who'd been clearing the tower were running towards the fray. They nocked arrows, drew blades, and screamed like banshees.

Reggie backed away, dodging, each step a way to stay alive another moment. He watched the thick forms of Danayia and Daizjah move to flanking positions, and the flood of bodies from the ruins create a circle around him he couldn't escape.

He'd just got this life. Before this, in the other world, he was so old. His children, those that still lived, and his grandchildren had gathered at their ancestral home to comfort and encourage him towards death.

He couldn't even count how many had told him it was okay to let go and move on. The kindness barely hid the greed and certainty that they had something to gain by his passing.

Distributed throughout his manor house—almost a castle—were the priceless treasures he'd collected while living. But he'd done it to preserve what had come before him and been lost. But his descendants—encouraging him to go to the next...whatever—didn't want to remember the past. They wanted the things to secure their futures. Futures that didn't include working hard for everything they gained.

Reggie's weapons were in his hands, flashing parrying moves, blocking Kionna's blades from ending this new and cherished life. He was off balance and outnumbered, with a ring of men around him. He knew he couldn't last long against these odds.

The ground rumbled, then exploded upwards, rocks and dirt raining down, throwing him and his attackers back.

Chapter 8

From where she stood on the crest of a hill, Aiyana watched the man jump up from his hiding place through the eyes of her feathered friend. Captain Farrell circled high above, sending images of the scene back to her. The raven was a second pair of eyes, and the information from her familiar was invaluable to planning her next move.

She couldn't hear the conversation, but the body language of the men told the story clearly enough. The man they'd been pursuing was trying to talk his way out of something, and the others weren't buying it, plain and simple.

Sweat dripped down her temple, a rare occurrence for an aeifain, but the summer heat was blistering on the crown of the knoll. A cloud of biting gnats closed in, the high pitch trill-buzz chiseling at the woman's attention and patience. With a wave of her hand, the wind swept around her, shuffling the minute pests away.

The voice in her head was new. She didn't know if it was her super-conscious talking to her, or something outside of her mind communicating with her. It had warned her this place would be a turning point.

She watched Nathan move around the back of the hill, winding through the dry rain gully between the hillocks, working his way towards the ruins. He was a good friend, but he was too soft. He served a rock-hard god, but still didn't understand things had to be made to conform. Not everything ended well because you had good intentions.

The arguing drew her attention back to the men. Squinting through her own eyes, they were small forms easily covered with the tip of her thumb when held at arm's length, and hard to discern any details. Switching back to Captain Farrell's eyes, everything jumped back into crisp focus.

The greasy man's two brute bodyguards drew dual axes, and the men scrambling across the top of the barbican slowed and crept forward, drawing their weapons. One man drew his bow back, nocking an arrow, and lifting it skyward, towards the raven. A gust of wind guided the bird higher and out of range. The man's shoulders slumped, and he lowered his bow.

The approaching thugs saw there would be a fight, and began moving quicker, shouting. Aiyana could hear the shrill, piercing undulations of the men, and from as far away as she was it sounded like the banshee cry of a fox, mixed with the gurgle laugh of a hyena. She shuddered at the thought, having had more than her share of gnohls in her life.

The soldiers formed a ring around the lone man, and the wizardess considered the situation. She debated saving him, but it felt like a puppet master pulling her strings. From what Nathan had said, it always led to serving the greater good, but it also served someone's agenda.

Jack Tucker always seemed to be the one directly responsible for pulling people from her world to this one. So, she'd done some research on him, and turned up very little. She found interesting ties to The Walking God, as well as the mad mage, Transvartius of the

Third Age. Funny thing was, both men seemed directly tied to the events that led up to the Talisman before it ravaged the land. But there hadn't been much to find on any of it, just rumors and conjecture, but enough in enough different places for her to feel some truth must lie behind it.

A flurry of blades erupted, and the crisp, tinny ting of metal on metal bounced off the hilltops. Through Captain Farrell, Aiyana checked on her rokairn companion's progress. He'd taken a knee behind some scrub bushes, in the shade of the last hill before the flat land around the fortification.

The woman raised her arms, and the earth erupted around the surrounded, protesting man they'd hunted. She didn't trust him. In fact, she suspected he was the worst kind of person who collected things with no thought of the people whom he took it from.

Nathan charged from his hiding place—Marcid held high—though his usual battle cry didn't come forth because he was being as stealthy as he could be. The stomp of his thick boots tearing through the underbrush and his heavy panting should have been enough to alert any enemy, but they were dealing with humans who were traditionally stupid and near-sighted beasts that never realized what was happening around them.

Close your eyes, Nathan, Aiyana whispered into the priest's head, *but keep true on your path. Protect the lout, and I will destroy the interlopers.*

Through Captain Farrell's vision, she saw the rokairn's head jerk up to look up at the raven. He shook his head, slashing through the air with a hand, his lips moving in unheard words. He disagreed about something. But that was the beauty of her plan. She didn't have to listen to him complain. She was in charge; she held the power.

The wizardess raised her staff to focus the energy and pulled on a thread from the earthen ley line. Tying in a thin sheet of the fiery ley line deep in the earth's crust, she created an upsurge of flaming earth that rose like an ocean wave and churned towards the enemy.

The ruins sang to her, a faint harmony that pulsed to the beat of the sigils magically embedded in the walls of the fortifications. It spoke to her on a blood level, the rhythm of its magic syncing with her heartbeat, the heartbeat of her missing people, the Aeifain.

She'd always fought for groups, not for the individual. In her home world, the country of the United States of America, she'd stood up for the rights of others. The Coloreds, the Asians, the women who were still second-class citizens in their own country that touted to be the land of the free. But they weren't. So many people were still oppressed and brushed away or beaten down in the most literal sense.

In front of her was an artifact of an entire race who'd disappeared, persecuted for their affinity for magic, by every human who knew of that power, and wished to have it for themselves. This small bastion of a border represented a greater atrocity of betrayal. The people who'd once joined with humankind had been shoved to one side, so mankind could benefit.

Even if it meant the obliteration of an entire species.

Her anger swelled, and she screamed to the elements, calling upon them to destroy the invaders of this outpost.

How dare they so casually enter a place that should be almost holy for its meaning, just to loot it for trinkets and baubles that might bring a few coins from the curious, she shouted in her thoughts. *The whole human race is broken and needs to be brought to its knees so it can finally recognize it isn't the only species trying to survive.*

Spears of rock solidified from the molten wave, bursting through the chests of the men who made the ring around the four men in the center. Flesh melted away and bone curled, crystalized, and crumbed from the intense heat.

The staff shuddered in Aiyana's hand. The magic from the woman, focused through the magical artifact she'd created, was drawn into the ruins, the sigils acting as a whirlpool for the power. It gathered it in, behaving like a centrifuge, collecting the energies, and spinning them, separating them to make something purer…and more powerful.

It made the woman think of power grids back home. They took in the power of rivers, wind, or coal and oil, and created an energy that could be focused and sent back out into the world in small or great amounts.

She did just that, pulling out specific threads of magic to reach out and do specific tasks. It sputtered, like an engine given too much gas. It was flooded. She reached out with her consciousness to find something to control that.

It was elusive, dodging her questing mind and power. But no, it wasn't elusive. She was just being held back. She looked for what siwas restraining her and found her connection to Captain Farrell. He was anchoring her so she couldn't reach her full potential.

She cut him loose.

Her mind exploded as it expanded, her awareness and consciousness settling over the area, sinking into the land and the settling like a net over a school of fish. Tight, silvery fish-like impulses tried to escape her net, but she pulled it tight. Everything clicked into place, like oars falling into an oarlock on the gunwale, allowing her to propel herself with the power. It also snapped and filled, like a sail under a headwind, allowing her to push to greater things. Then the tiller of the magic jerked under the hands of her mind, and she turned back to the situation.

She'd lost the vision of the countryside and battle from the raven, but now her awareness was the entire land. The building was like a radar dish that allowed her to see everything for dozens of kilometers. Ley lines were bright torrents of energy in her mind. The minds of the men were golden blips in her circle of radar…but there was something else. A jade haze of reality overlapping and flowing like tides across the area.

The land, the entire area, was breathing. It pulsed and ebbed and flowed like tides and a heartbeat if the forests and clouds could have such a thing.

Aiyana blacked out, overwhelmed.

Nathan was worried about the girl, but now was not the time to be thinking of her.

It was hard though, he thought as Marcid shattered the shoddy craftmanship of a hand axe. *I've been hanging around with this girl for over three years now, and I care for her. She has a good heart, but her head keeps telling her that a cause is greater than a person. And yes, it is, but…*

The priest pulled on the power of his god—Jonath, God of Earth and Protection, praised be his hallowed earthen name—and Nathan felt his skin pebble into the toughness of stone as three other axes bit into what had once been flesh. The edges of the weapons chipped, stone calling to metal, and drawing the shards in.

Almost four years of that sort of thing had given the priest a battle skin that was akin to chain mail, almost plate armor, even though he wore his usual jerkin and breeches. It didn't alter his clothes—and he sighed as he about having to replace them, again—but made him a part of the earth that represented the power of his god.

One step closer to divinity, or just to becoming the clay of the gods? He thought.

Marcid was a beautiful gift in his hands. It was like holding a rose bush, thorns and all, if it was made of steel. It bit into his enemies but was beautiful to behold.

The magics of Jonath flowed through him, his skin taking on the qualities of the surrounding earth. His flesh shifted from stone to steel, so raw and untamed that weapons shattered against him. Or slid to a slick and dark configuration of mud, and weapons passed through him, slowing the attackers. He flowed, bending like wheat in the wind, or standing as solid as an oak, whichever suited the situation better.

Nathan watched the faces of the men turn to surprise, and he felt no pride in their inevitable defeat and likely death.

The two lackeys—because that's all they were, secondary players in the play and dance that was this battle—stumbled back under his attack. Their defenses were nothing. He broke their fighting stances, tore through their armor, shattered their weapons as his god claimed the very materials that were *his* domain.

The man that fate—and, indirectly, Jack Tucker—sent them to protect, moved away, his eyes wide and his stance turning defensive.

But am I protecting him, or is Aiyana bent on taking him down too? Nathan wondered.

The leader, the greasy man, faded behind a line of his subordinates, letting them take the brunt of the battle. Thick spears of stone broke through their chests, burning their flesh and melting their rib cages.

The two men—who looked like rokairn fanboys—backed away as their hand axes crumbled in their hands. They followed their leader, letting the other men die in their stead.

The battlefield slowed, dying men falling to their knees in steaming mud and lava.

Nathan wiped at his sweating forehead, his eyebrows curling in the heat.

"We should go," the priest said, turning to the remaining human he'd come to save. "We're here to rescue you, I think."

"Who are you?" The tall stranger asked.

"Nathan, but I'll explain more later. I think it's time to go."

He turned to leave, gesturing for the man to run into the hills.

The man sized him up, then looked in the direction he indicated.

"I'm Reginald," the man said, "but we'll talk more if we survive this. Shame about those axes. They were good steel."

"You want them?" Nathan asked and touched the symbol hanging on his chest.

The steel dust bubbled and melted, rolling together like quicksilver. More raw elements gathered from the lava and joined the puddle of metal. Two solid hand axes formed, but without the wooden handles. In their place were steel handles, curved and notched for grip.

"Impressive." Reginald tucked his blades into their sheaths, stopping to pick up the axes. Wrapping his hands around them, he winced. "Still a bit warm."

"Yeah," Nathan smiled, "and they're likely to stay that way. Call it a gift from Jonath."

The two turned and ran, the ground around them rumbling and erupting in geysers of dirt and lava. The ruins of the barbican melted, the walls flowing into the land.

Nathan glanced up and saw Captain Farrell fighting the wind currents, struggling to stay aloft.

The elements had turned against them. The air buffeted the raven, and the ground tore—in a very literal sense. Nathan froze, amazed. The very element that his god presided over, and who the priest had direct control of, now struggled to support his weight as it obeyed the commands of an elementalist more than a league away.

Running, the two stumbled, trying to keep their footing. They darted around the ground geysers and lava flows now creeping along their path. Leaping across rivulets of molten dirt, they moved away from the trees and sought higher ground, and hopefully safety from nature's fury.

"Did…you…do this?" the stranger asked.

"No," Nathan's voice was a panting shout, "it's my friend."

"Your friend? They don't seem to be…" Reggie stopped talking to scramble to the top of a rise, using his blades to dig into the ground to help his climb, "too worried about your safety."

Nathan nodded, reaching the crest of the hill.

The priest stopped, shouldering Marcid, and closed his eyes. He focused on the power of his god and called upon his blessing to calm the surrounding earth.

The rumbling slowed, then stopped.

"Yeah," Nathan panted, "I'm going to have a conversation with her about this."

Captain Farrell wheeled overhead, cawing a triple cry of complaint, and spiraled downward to land on Nathan's shoulder, claws digging in sharply.

The bird turned a beady eye to the rokairn, tilting his head in a question.

"Yeah, Cap, I know. I'm curious, too. She's never done anything like this. I'll talk to her." Nathan said, trying to catch his breath.

The scene below was utter destruction. The last of the ruins were disappearing into the ground, melting away, only green sparks of the sigils remaining.

The priest turned to the new man.

"I'm Nathan," he said, thrusting his hand towards the taller man.

"Reginald Betancourt," the blonde man said, and took the offered hand, gripping it firmly.

The two shook hands halfheartedly, both staring at the destruction below.

"It's a shame to see those ruins destroyed." Reginald sighed. "There was so much to learn there."

"Oh?" Nathan cocked his head at the man.

"Yeah," Reginald nodded, "I got some of it, a direction towards the Aeifain lands, but wasn't close enough to get much more than that.

"Interesting," Nathan grunted, "that might be enough to be helpful."

Chapter 9

"What the hell was that all about?" Nathan whispered harshly, crouching beside Aiyana, the newcomer standing awkwardly a little way behind him.

Aiyana pulled the cold cloth away from her brow and shook her head delicately.

"I don't know, but I touched something I've never experienced before." Aiyana mumbled.

"You almost killed us, and that means me also. What happened?" Nathan had Marcid strapped to his back again, and both hands balled into fists and planted on his knees.

"There was a connection…" Aiyana hesitated, "and it opened itself to me because I'm aeifain. It was the power of my people."

Nathan growled, "It was terrifying, and I don't know if that much power is worth it if you can't control it, and it takes over. It's like you were someone else."

"Hey," Reggie said, "give her a few moments to recover."

Both Nathan and Aiyana turned to look at him, glaring. Captain Farrell croaked from a branch in a scraggly tree that was offering the barest of shade.

Reggie held up his hands defensively and took a step back.

"My people, the aeifain," Aiyana gulped, "something happened, and they put a contingency plan into place in case someone returned or survived."

"You can tell all that from what happened today?" Nathan stood, raised an eyebrow, tilted his head, and planted his fists on his hips.

Aiyana looked past him, leaning to one side as she pressed the frosted cloth—made so from her growing elemental powers—to her forehead. She pondered the finesse and raw powers in the arcane arts she'd increasingly enjoyed over the past three years.

Turning, the rokairn saw the human had come closer.

"An intense experience," Reginald licked his lips, and continued in a calm, even voice, "even something traumatic—though you might not even realize it as such when it happens—can create a drive to move forward and change things. Often, these things can be the impetus we need to push us further, and…"

The man trailed off, reading the faces of the two in front of him. Neither wanted him to interrupt, but both were listening, though their faces were now twisted with annoyance.

"He's Reginald Betancourt," Nathan said.

"I know, you told me already," Aiyana replied.

"Wasn't sure if you were in any shape to remember." Nathan sighed.

"I was, and I am." Aiyana sized up the man, her gaze traveling from his boots to his hair and back down again. "You trust him?"

"Well," the word was a drawn-out sigh, "you said he's one of us, from our world. And he…"

"Do you trust him?" Aiyana asked again, her voice insistent.

"My gut says yes, and I think we need to figure out what the trigger is here and move forward. Okay? Can we try to do that? When I showed up, it was to stop a demon army. When you arrived, it was to stop a power mad wizard…"

"Alchemist," Aiyana interjected.

"Alchemist," Nathan corrected, "and when he shows up, you suddenly do something you've never done before. I think it may relate to and fit the pattern. I think we should trust him."

Captain Farrell cawed and fluttered in the tree, then flapped across the open space to land on Reginald's shoulder. The young man stood straighter, tilting his head to one side to make room for the bird.

Laughing, Reggie reached into a pouch and retrieved a wedge of cheese wrapped in cheesecloth. Unwrapping it, he broke off a bit, and held it to the raven.

The bird tilted his head, eyeing the man with an oil drop eye, then pecked at the cheese, taking it into his beak.

"Does he know Jack Tucker?" Aiyana asked.

"Did you say Jack Tucker?" Reggie interjected.

Both others turned to look at the new man.

Aiyana nodded.

"I knew a man by that name once, but it was decades ago, when I was a young man." Reggie looked himself up and down and laughed in a harsh burst. "A different young man. He helped me find some ruins in Central America, a lost Mayan city."

The rokairn and aeifain traded looks.

Aiyana opened her mouth, but Nathan spoke first.

"What are you doing here?" He turned his head upward to look into the man's eyes. "I mean, we followed you from that small town that had been set to the torch, Wiley's Station…"

"Wiley's Station was burned?" Reggie's voice cracked and his face paled.

Captain Farrell leaned over and inspected the man.

"Yes," Aiyana said slowly, lowering the cloth from her forehead and pushing to her feet.

Nathan offered a hand to assist her, and she accepted it, using it and her staff to gain her feet.

"Do you know what happened?" the wizardess asked.

"When I left, the place was still standing. There were good people there, they treated me well. Just regular folk, making their way in the world. It pains me to hear they were…"

His words slowed to a stop, and he swallowed hard, his face contorting.

"Point is, I'm searching for something. You've already mentioned you think I'm from the world you came from…Earth, am I right?"

He watched their reactions and nodded.

"In that case, yes, I'm from your planet, though your diction is strange, and perhaps we're from different places, or if I dare suggest it, from different times."

Reginald gauged their reactions from his words, drawing out any information he could. He knew what he wanted—to learn more about what was lost, and how it related to the current affairs of the world—but he needed to know what they wanted, and if it coincided with his interests.

His world…the thought jarred him. He hadn't denied it existing, but decades of training allowed him to immerse himself into the world he was currently exploring. Sometimes it was ancient Egypt,

Mesopotamia, Maya, Aztec, or any other lost civilization, but this time it was a living, breathing world. He never forgot the world he lived in, but this time was different.

His world had forgotten him as his day-to-day life existed in a world of deterioration and degeneration. He was a husk there, failing in a bed of starched sheets, and pillows too new to be comfortable. And the nurses, they were cautious automatons, more worried about upsetting his children and adult grandchildren, then tending to him.

Dying wouldn't be so bad…and that triggered a thought. It was a wisp of a memory, of an idea that delirium and pain had blown away. One more adventure. One more time into the breach, into the dark, into the unknown. One more grand adventure.

He remembered calling out for that, and the cool cloth on his head, shushing noises in his ears. Then the bitter, acrid taste of something that made his head swim, and his equilibrium to float on storm-tossed seas of dreams.

He popped back to the moment; the question coming around a second time—whether in his head, or they repeated it didn't matter.

"Yes," Reggie nodded, "I do have an agenda, but probably not like you think. I'm here for a reason that is selfish, but not hurtful to anyone else."

Nathan looked up at him, waiting patiently for the man to go on. Aiyana crossed her arms with a huffed breath and glared.

"Youth has no tolerance." Reginald gave a sad smile. "They want all the answers in plain speak, laid out for them. But the problem with that is that they won't accept someone else's answers, not when they already know so much more about their own self-proclaimed wisdom and experience."

Reginald sighed, Nathan nodded, Captain Farrell ruffled his feathers, and Aiyana rolled her eyes.

"I'm here for one last adventure, then I'm ready to move on to whatever comes next. But before I do that, I want to help discover the locations of this lost race and restore them to their place in history. The aeifain, I think that's what they're called. This body, who was named Kazzek, seems to know myths and legends about it, but they are a haze, little more than a feeling. But those ruins below, now melted into slag…" Reginald's words trailed off as he sized up the others.

"What are your intentions?" he asked, his hand casually falling onto the hilt of his rapier.

Nathan held his hands up, scoffing in disbelief.

"Now, wait a minute here," he said, "we're here to—"

"It's none of his business," Aiyana interrupted. "We don't need to prove ourselves to him or anyone else. He's the intruder, the interloper, not us. How dare he question me!"

Her voice rose in pitch and intensity as she went on.

"Come on, Aiyana," Nathan laid a hand on her forearm, "fair's fair, and he has a right to hear what we're doing here, too."

She jerked her arm back.

"No, he doesn't." Each word was short, bitten back.

"What's wrong with you, Aiyana?" Nathan stepped in front of her, holding his hands out to either side to draw her attention.

"You're behaving like a spoiled brat. Did the magic do something to you? This is not you. You're more understanding than this, smarter than this, more open-minded than this. What's made you condemn this man?" Nathan asked.

"Jack Tucker, if I had to guess," Reginald stroked Captain Farrell, "and it's understandable. She doesn't enjoy being manipulated. But I assure you, young lady, I'm not the one holding the strings, I'm just one more dancing puppet. What I'm saying is that I understand your distrust. I'm a product of what chafes you."

They met eyes, and Aiyana dropped her gaze, nodding.

"If it helps," Reginald reached up and fed Captain Farrell another piece of cheese, then stroked the raven's head with one finger, "your friend here likes me, and perhaps that can count for something?"

Aiyana forced a smile, but it showed an effort to break out of the mood upon her.

"Okay," Aiyana huffed, shaking herself, "let's say we're working together. Where are we going?"

"Into the woods, I would say," the lilt in Reginald's voice sounded musical, "and let's go find more of your people. I saw signs in the ruins that pointed west, and that's where the Aeifain center of power should be. Let's make it our goal to find what happened to them and restore them to modern memory in whatever way we can."

"By bringing magic back into the hands of people," Aiyana said.

"By protecting their legacy from bandits," Nathan said at the same time.

The three exchanged looks.

"It sounds like all of our ideas can work well together," Reggie smiled, "and not all the men below were killed. They may regroup and come after us. Shall we make our getaway while the getting is still good?"

The other two nodded.

The trio moved through the forest, the sky fading under the canopy of ancient trees. The sweltering summer heat was muted, but the humidity climbed in the enclosing foliage, making breathing feel thick and wet. It was a trade of nature, less heat, but more moisture.

Squirrels chittered in the branches above, and birds trilled and chirped. Chipmunks scampered across pools of dried leaves, and insects whirred through the air, seeking flowers, or rotting vegetation.

They traveled along a deer track winding between thicket and trunk, leading them deeper into the woods.

There wasn't much conversation, though Reginald (who told them they could call him Reggie) tried to strike up an exchange more than once.

He knew it was difficult to create an atmosphere of camaraderie and trust without conversation. The exchange of quips, ideals, stories, and experiences was important to bonding. He knew it from countless excavations and excursions into the darkest parts of six out of seven continents.

He guessed both of his traveling companions were not from his era. Probably from later, from key bits of information they dropped. Neither was in his professional field, and the archaeologist had to wonder why Jack Tucker chose them for this specific task.

Jack Tucker.

He turned the memories of the man over in his mind. He remembered someone who was passionate but not self-serving. The man had been driven, it seemed, to find the temples and city streets the jungle had reclaimed.

Reggie tried to picture him as a puppet master, pulling the strings of others and calling the shots for his own purposes, but just couldn't imagine it.

Aiyana seemed convinced that Jack was a monster bent on making others do his will. She was a driven woman, though, but he'd seen it happen to others before. They found a cause and lost themselves in it.

Nathan was different though, and Reggie couldn't quite put his finger on what drove the man. He seemed to come along for the wizardess. The rokairn was tired, tough, and never appeared to be proactive, but reactive and trying to put out fires as they cropped up.

They were sitting around the campfire on the third night of their trek through the forest, when a rustling in the surrounding underbrush drew their attention. Moments later, dozens of rats—each the size of an emaciated terrier—with bumpy, graveled flesh burst into the clearing.

The three leapt to their feet, reaching for weapons and their magic, when the night sky erupted with drawn-out, high-pitched screeches. The noises were barely audible over the noise of the rat stampede, mixing with the terrified squeaks. The second sound resembled the noise of a dozen people running their nails down a chalkboard.

Bat-like beasts, with a wingspan the size of a grown man's spread arms, and six tentacles writhing below their thin, rubbery bodies, descended from the night sky.

The things swooped at the rats, lifting them with their half dozen tentacles to jaws that split on the bottom, to a half dozen fangs—two on the top jaw, and four on the bottom, two on each half—biting into the prey. Flapping heavily, the creatures lifted their burdens back into the night sky.

Two of the creatures landed on Nathan, wings enveloping him, and rubbery appendages entangling his arms and fouling his axe before he could bring it to bear.

Reggie launched himself forward, rapier flashing. The blade slipped off the monster's wings.

"Step away, I've got this," Aiyana commanded.

Aiyana chanted, and an icy wind swept through the clearing.

Reggie glanced behind him to see the wizardess moving her hands like she was playing a game of cats-cradle with a piece of string he couldn't see.

Turning back, he watched the motions of the beasts slow, and the rokairn shrug them off.

Nathan raised his axe to kill the things, but Aiyana stepped forward and stopped him with a hand on his shoulder.

"No need for that, my friend." She slid her hand down his bicep to his forearm and guided his axe down. "They'll crawl off until they thaw, then head back to their lair. They're part of the ecosystem here, and there's no reason to take from the woods what it needs to survive. No harm was done."

"No harm was done?" Nathan groused, watching the things flap-crawl for the tree line, rubbing the circular marks on his arms and neck. "They left two dozen hickeys on me. I look like fifteen horny teenage boys attacked me while on ecstasy!"

Reggie snorted, his hand covering his mouth as he turned away.

"They were fezels, also known as soul eaters. Relatively harmless to something our size, unless you're traveling alone and unprotected," Aiyana said, watching the creature's drag themselves into the tree line. "They didn't even exist until after the Talisman, and in the past few decades, they evolved into a fully developed species. As have many others."

"The Talisman," Reggie said slowly, "is the comet that brought the Downfall, right?"

"Yeah, that's right." Nathan rubbed at the red circles on his arms and neck. "Will they be back? Do we need to set a watch? Or build the fire higher?"

Aiyana surveyed their campsite with her hands on her hips, then sighed.

"No," she said, "but I guess it's time to pull out the Citadel."

"Really?" Nathan scoffed, amused. "In front of Mister Betancourt and everything?"

Aiyana rolled her eyes and turned away from the rokairn, untying the roll of canvas from the bottom of her pack. She shook out the material, and it spread to cover most of the clearing beside the fire.

Twenty minutes later, they were inside of the Citadel, clearing a sleeping spot for the newest member of the group.

"This is impressive." Reggie turned in a circle, trying to see everything within the tent. "Did you do this?"

"Yes," Aiyana mumbled, like she was being forced to share a secret.

"She's pretty good at making things that are cool and useful," Nathan said, his tone amused.

"Oh, shut it, fuzzy face," Aiyana groused, moving to her cot.

She glared at Reggie as he moved around the room, gazing at odd trinkets and inspecting corners.

"She didn't want you to know how much of a badass she is," Nathan whispered conspiratorially to Reggie, but loud enough that Aiyana was sure to hear. "In case you tried something shifty, she wanted to have the jump on you."

"She's a smart woman," was all Reggie said, thinking that less was more, and caution was the wiser side of prudence.

Besides that night, there were no other encounters of significance. They spent the days weaving through trees and around underbrush, heading in a generally southwest direction.

After traveling deeper into the Grey Forest for ten days, the forest broke, and a roiling river lay in front of them. The journey had been an easy one, though they'd seen local wildlife, nothing worse than a small black bear who avoided them as much as they avoided her and her two cubs.

They stood on a broken ridge overlooking the river, a ten-meter drop to the white water below them. It would've been a beautiful vista to pause and take in, if it hadn't been for the score of bare-chested men and women who stepped from hiding, bows drawn and arrows nocked, all aimed at the three of them.

Chapter 10

"What the hell is this all about?" Nathan growled, his hand twitching towards Marcid's handle.

Aiyana sent Captain Farrell skyward and rolled her head across her shoulders, feeling her neck pop a few times.

Reggie slowly raised his hands, a friendly smile plastered on his face.

"Aww," Nathan moaned, "it's like Indiana Jones all over again, ain't it?"

"What's Indiana Jones?" Aiyana and Reginald asked together.

A man stepped forward, lowering his bow, and shouted words in an inhuman language. It was guttural yet flowed with an elegance of a whisper during a storm.

At least, that's what came to Aiyana. A flood of memory broken into images tore through her conscious mind. Strict schooling, the idea pushed into her as her instructors reminded her she was an animal, and pain taught her what was a negative action, and a treat showed her what was a positive action.

The image of decades of training that her body underwent, learning the language of the primitive cousins of the aeifain, the dasism. Connected to the elements in a way no other race was, they steeped their existence in following messages given by Senaria, the goddess of the wood and nature, an embodiment of how the natural world viewed honor.

It was followed by a second torrent of memories, decades spent with these people, learning their ways.

When she was a mere eleven decades old, she'd defied the council and left her people to find the dasism and learn the ways of the ley lines. Her people believed in study, methodology, and ritual. They favored mind magics and alchemy, shunning summoning and elemental magics. As for ritual magics, they played it safe and followed gods when they felt they could take advantage of what that sort of magic offered, though many became devout priests, even fanatical by aeifain standards.

Aiyana understood the price one paid for power.

The dasism were primal and primitive, the same way the Native Americans (that was the proper term, according to Nathan in his time), were compared to the citizens of the United States military that constantly worked to overpower them. But that didn't mean they didn't have knowledge the other race couldn't, or wouldn't, ever know.

Reginald stepped forward and cupped his hands around his mouth to answer the man. The name—Reginald—stuck in her mental throat, like that snobbish character in the Archie comics, so full of himself.

"Hello!" Reginald shouted in the stranger's language. "We mean no harm!"

"Who are you, and why do you come to our lands? You are not welcome here," the Speaker of the Dasism, as Aiyana knew the title to be, called to them.

"We are seekers," Reginald called back, "not of your resources, not of the land, though we use what it offers, but of knowledge. We look for the lost peoples of the Aeifain, or their dead homes."

The human's words were clumsy, but elegant in his tone and demeanor. The phrases may have been simple, but the way he carried himself spoke of experience with the dasism people.

Aiyana looked at Reginald, surprised.

Nathan had turned to look at Reggie, as well.

"What did he say?" the rokairn asked.

Reginald held up a finger, glancing at the priest with a look that told him to be patient.

Nathan nodded.

The Speaker paused, shooting a look over his shoulder where his people stood at the ready to pincushion the strangers and let their dying bodies plummet to the river.

The dasism leader raised his hands, a sign of parley. The men and women behind him relaxed the pull on their bowstrings and lowered them enough so they weren't an immediate threat.

The dasism were darker of skin than Aiyana's people. Her race was pale and fair skinned and almost glowed in the sunlight. These people were ruddy, their flesh almost the same color as clay from the hills to the north. They spent almost all their time in the sun, working with the land, and their coloring was similar to the soil they valued so dearly. She also knew they disdained by her people, as the aeifain looked down upon them. In turn, the sway Aiyana's race didn't embrace the magic of the land saddened them.

"I am Shyam," the man stepped forward, "the Speaker of the Dasism, and will allow you a moment of peace with me to speak. If you will also give peace to myself and all dasism, then perhaps we will all learn this day."

"Shyam," Reginald said the name clumsily, "I am grateful for this moment, and hope our speak can be words that make peace for the time it can last."

Aiyana shuddered at the human's poor grasp of the language but said nothing. Reaching out with the mind magics so common to her people, she linked with Captain Farrell to see if any other dasism were hiding.

"He says we can talk, and they won't kill us if what we say works out." Reginald mumbled an explanation.

Nathan nodded, lowering his hands from his shoulder where his axe rested. But he didn't totally relax, still ready to call upon the power of his god, Jonath, or pull his weapon from his back if needed.

Aiyana nodded also, keeping her understanding of the language a secret, and letting the human speak for them so she could gather her power to her.

Captain Farrell showed her the lay of the land, circling higher and higher to catch the wind currents to glide. She could see the river and their encounter, and not too far upriver, a settlement of dasism.

Their small group walked right into the dasism's territory.

"We…" Reginald hesitated, formulating what to say, "are running from many humans. These other men seek to get good things and destroy anything they don't want. We want to know what happened to the aeifain."

"You say words that sound like you want something and want us to fight your enemy." Shyam said, still moving closer to the trio.

The dasism was without fear of the strangers. He walked with a calm confidence towards them. As he came closer, out of the shadow of the trees, Aiyana could see his dark hair, almost indigo, in the sunlight. He wore deerskin breeches, and a wide belt of hide with a buckle of silver-flecked quartz. His obsidian blade shimmered in the sun, and the wood of his bow was as red as his skin.

"Yes," Reginald nodded, "but no. To speak clearly, I do not ask you to fight a battle that is mine and not yours. I tell you this so you know an enemy may be within your land. I am not that enemy, though, and hope you can see that."

Aiyana caught herself nodding, then sneered. She didn't want to agree with the human, but he'd said it well, considering his poor grasp of the language.

Shyam considered this information, tilting his head and taking in Reginald, the de facto speaker for the group.

He nodded.

"Yes," he said, "I will take this and speak to my group."

The Speaker turned his back to the three, a sign of confidence, but more importantly, a sign of respect and trust of a potential enemy or ally.

He walked a steady pace towards his fellow dasism. A stout woman with a thick braid, darker of skin than the Speaker, lowered her bow and returned her arrow to the quiver at her hip, another sign of trust, and moved forward. A shorter, tattooed dasism—thin to the point of either being a runner or constantly hungry—broke away from the other side of the group and approached the Speaker.

Threes, Aiyana thought, *the dasism love threes. The number of balance and of firm support. It held much importance in their culture, but not in the magic of elements.*

Another flash strobed across Aiyana's perception. The fifth element. Most people thought that fire, earth, water, and air were the only elements. But there was a fifth element, the one that bound the other four together to create a cohesive effect: spirit. Nature provided the first four, but the consciousness of sentience provided the fifth, allowing the previous four to be guided for definitive effect.

Aiyana broke from the flash of bodily insight and saw the three dasism in conference. A thin mist—not physical, but something more ethereal—coalesced around the trio, and their words became distant and muffled.

The wizardess pulled awareness in tight, gathering her mind magics, and then released it slowly. It spread outward. She could feel the thick summer air and the spray of water particles from below. The roaring of the rapids blended with birds' calls, insect trills, and the crackle of leaves and the roll of gravel underfoot. The smell of dried grass, the sweat of the people, and the briny urine smell of an animal who had marked its territory rose to her nose.

Her sight from Captain Farrell clarified and focused, and she turned her full attention to the dasism in conference. She smelled the oils on their skin and in their hair, their features sharpening in her sight, and the gentle rhythm of the dasism language flowed through the air to her ears.

"…we knew people were coming, we've seen the signs from the winds and the animals," the woman was saying.

"That means nothing. It could still be them," the tattooed man countered.

"The spirits spoke of this to the elders in their vision tent, telling of invaders in our land who come to take the spoils of another land, all driven by the hand from another place. I do not think three people of three races would be that invading force," the woman sneered.

"Takia," the tattooed man sighed, "you are young and gullible. Do not think that seventy years makes you knowledgeable, not compared to my thirteen decades, or Shyam's seventeen."

"Chirai," Shyam looked at the man with a reprimand in his voice and eyes, "we do not do that. We respect the other's view, without prejudice. Argue against the argument, not the person."

Chirai looked chagrined, then smiled, bowing slightly to Takia.

"I am sorry. Shyam is right. I just like to see you get angry, as young people do." Chirai smirked, watching to see if it got a reaction from her. "But they could be the enemy the elders saw in their vision."

"Weak," Takia waved a hand dismissively, "you repeat your words with no stone or fire behind them, just wind and water, hoping to erode mine with no force. These people come here. They look lost, bewildered, and honest. I say we trust them, bring them to the village, and hear their tale."

Aiyana recognized what the three were doing. One was the good cop, the other was the bad cop. But this was also a dasism method sof judgement, where the third—Shyam, in this case—played the judge.

Shyam, Aiyana mused, *means Forest Song, though more literally translated is Dirge of the Broken Wood. Takia means Fire Spirit or Wind. And Chirai means the Child of the Chameleon. And this ritual they're performing is a traditional way for two to argue a different side, while the third decides based on all the information.*

The three continued their council as the wizardess withdrew her attention, and magic, pulling back into herself. She saw Shyam watching her and wondered if he'd noticed her intrusion. His smile could mean anything.

Reginald watched the line of warriors—who'd broken into smaller clumps, chattering and laughing, but still watching them—shifting from one foot to the other, trying not to rest a hand on the pommels of his weapons.

Nathan dropped to the grass and was running his hands across the top of the green blades, his eyes far away.

She'd traveled with the rokairn for over three years now, and he seemed so…plain. He didn't have any real motivation, but he was a good man, always wanting to help folks, but never wanting more than a meal or friendship in return. He brushed off praise or gratitude. She could understand resisting her praise, but his gentle refusal from a family he saved from their burning farmhouse was another matter.

As if he was missing something, he was sad and distant. She never could figure out what, even when she'd asked him directly. He'd brush that off also, never giving a solid answer. She doubted he even knew what he wanted.

Aiyana's reverie was broken by the three approaching. Reginald stiffened and stepped forward, stumbling on a loose stone.

Shyam smiled, and opened his hands, palms up, and spread them away from his body at waist level. It was a dasism sign of peace, and to be at peace.

"We invite you," Shyam said solemnly, "to join us as cautious guests, but not welcome ones, at our village."

Reggie smiled, delighted as they entered the grouping of structures that the Dasism called home. His head turned constantly, trying to take in everything at once.

The village was a collection of yurts, each decorated with bright swirls and symbols of reds, blues, greens, and oranges. He watched children run between the hide domiciles, shouting, and chasing one another. The older kids, ones who'd reached a decade or more, worked with the adults, though Reggie guessed they'd join the other kids in play after the sun rose to its zenith. At fifteen, the children were in training for adulthood. At two decades, they'd join the grown-ups and begin learning the skills to support the tribe.

Reggie noted that women and men shared tasks, depending on their skills and abilities. The elderly, those past three-hundred years old—though the oldest known dasism was nearly seven hundred—generally tended children, weaved baskets, shared skills, or taught the tribe's history through stories.

In this village, everything moved like a well-oiled machine. Reggie smiled at a group chatting around baskets of beans, cotton, and berries, a trio of each plucking, peeling, or beating their specific plant to make food, fibers for clothes, or dyes. A dozen dasism were at the riverside, waist-deep in the slow current, tossing nets. And a score were upriver fishing with poles.

In the distance he saw a group stringing up hides on steepled frames, tanning them well away from the village so the smell didn't taint everything.

He noted the dozen cook fires that held iron pots or spits, making a meal, or turning meat to be striped and dried for the winter.

People turned to look at the procession of three strangers, flanked by Takia and Chirai, with Shyam leading them. The warriors, who once aimed arrows at them, trotted along in a loose circle around them, bantering with one another or the odd passerby who asked what was going on with the new people.

Looking at Aiyana, Reggie noted she was stiff and withdrawn, lost in her thoughts. He wondered if she'd had experiences with these incredible people or was always like this in new places.

Reggie, as Kazzek, had studied the Dasism from afar. He'd heard tales of these folk in battle and celebration and asked any merchant or traveler who'd met them for more information. He knew they were distrustful of strangers and harsh in their dealings with outsiders. But once you gained their trust, they would accept you as one of their own.

He focused on the present. There was a trial going on, and he wasn't sure what he'd gotten them into.

Nathan, though, acted as if he'd come home. He crouched and waved at children, grinning like an uncle with a hidden present, and a secret waiting to be told. The rokairn pointed at warriors and their weapons, giving a fist pump in the air, smiling, and waving after.

The dasism recognized the symbol of Jonath swaying from a chain around the warrior-priest's neck, bowing slightly, until Nathan grinned, fingered the talisman, and winked or waved. Then the man or woman would grin, nod, and hold up three fingers on an extended arm.

The trident, Reggie realized, was the symbol of Jonath, and represented the pitchfork that worked the harvest, and used to till the soil that provided it. The people of the land and the elements were giving recognition to the priest of a god that the human's thought of as a god of protectors, guards, and battle.

Lessons trickled into his mind. The gods all represented many things. With Jonath, some things represented were flashy, like battle. Other things were mundane, like tilling soil and gathering the crops.

The layered aspects of the pantheons in this world fascinated Reggie. Every god had this type of layering. Promethene, goddess of sound and light, represented the sun—which did many things—and song, which was used in many ways. Latress, goddess of wisdom and weather, covered much more than those two things. Every god spanned the spectrum from good to greed, in one form or another. Gods were what you made of them, and you were what they made of you.

The procession slowed in front of a great yurt, at least compared to the others. Reggie inspected the thick walls, cracked with age and countless times being packed into carts to be moved to follow herds or the seasons. Ornate and simple paintings decorated the outer walls, depicting stories, histories, and tales in addition to children's hand paintings, showing they were learning the old ways and traditions.

A thin stream of smoke rose from the center peak. The Elder's Pavilion, Reggie realized.

"Speaker of the Three, Reginald," Shyam intoned, his voice solid and heavy with ceremony, "are you prepared to face the wisdom of ages, given by the elements and the gods which represent them?"

Reggie pulled his shoulders back and stood straighter, then nodded, and bowed at the waist.

Shyam raised a hand to his mouth, hiding a smile, but turning it into a gesture of respect as he pulled his flattened palm away like he was blowing a kiss.

Reggie wondered what that gesture meant.

"Son of rock and Jonath, Nathan," the Speaker said in the same voice as before, but this time in broken rokairn, "are you ready to face judgement of our people, and offer wisdom or consent to our needs of decision?"

"Yeah," Nathan sighed, jerking his head to one side, then rolling it around his shoulders to crack the tenseness from it, "I am. Let's do what needs to be done."

This time, Shyam grinned openly in reaction to the man's bluntness.

"Daughter of the aeifain, and elemental student of the Dasism Elementalists, are you prepared to face our judgement at your broken covenant?" Shyam asked, his face dropping to a serious look.

Aiyana stumbled, her knees buckling. She nodded, mutely.

"Then, I am to give the invitation to accept the command of the Elders," Shyam said, drawing back the flap of the entryway to the grand tent, "enter and face what is to come, with or without your consent and invitation."

Chapter 11

"What the hell is this all about?" Nathan mumbled, walking under Shyam's uplifted arm, and entering the tent.

Aiyana stood stock still, growing paler than the time she passed out from blood loss after being gored by a three horned bull.

Reggie moved past her into the tent. The human—Nathan realized he was thinking in terms of race and wondered when that shift had happened—gazed around the tent, his mouth quirking, shifting between childlike wonder and adult awe.

After traveling together, Nathan knew enough about Reggie's archaeology background to see why the man would be amazed. He was seeing a culture that had never been witnessed by humans, firsthand. The rokairn had been around long enough that it didn't faze him in the same way. Or perhaps, he was just less tuned into the same things.

The interior of the tent was a haze of scented smoke—reminding Nathan of hippies and sandalwood incense—coming from spagmoss in the central brazier, attended by a teenage girl.

He blushed and looked at the floor when he realized she was topless, as were most dasism he'd seen. While it was easy to avoid looking at girls' chests outside, in the intimate confines of the yurt his eyes turned to the ground with sudden bashfulness.

Most of the adults and children in the village were shirtless, though a few of the more endowed women had their breasts bound. The elderly usually had tops on, though Nathan thought it might be more for protection from the sun than vanity.

These people weren't primitive, but their bodies seemed as natural as the soil and weather, and they dressed as fit their mood.

Like the outside, they decorated the tent on the inside with painted runes or scenes. Panels displayed swirls of elements, an elegant design flowing from one to the next. At points, the representations of fire, earth, air, and water clashed and collided.

Bouquets and wreaths of dried herbs hung from many of the support poles, and the rokairn debated if it was for function or decoration.

Probably both.

Dozens of floor coverings layered the hard packed dirt, overlapping woven rugs blended with hides of herd animals. Displayed antlers and horns hung from support beams, including several blowing horns and musical pipes. Drums adorned the walls, some with stretched hide with horn and bone beaters, others were hollow percussion tubes.

Fifteen elders—men and women—stood in a circle formation, three close to the center brazier, and twelve along the walls, indicating their rank in the council. Six empty cushions were in the center circle. Shyam, Takia, Chirai, and the remaining elders lowered themselves to hassocks along the outer ring.

"Sit, join our circle," an older dasism said in the common tongue, his inflection accented but clear, and gestured at the remaining cushions. "I am Mekiya, the chief elder. To my left is Neyla, the second leader representing the middle generation, and to my right is Gokia, representing the youngest generation."

Nathan sat on the center pillow, Reggie settling to his left, and Aiyana stumbling to his right to plop down.

"Aiyana of the Aeifain," Mekiya looked at the woman, "thirty years ago you went to the Rain Dancer Tribe begging for knowledge. They sent you to us, the Wind Song Tribe. You asked to know of the ley lines and the elemental magics, promising loyalty in your quest for wisdom of the travelling ways, the portals. Then, you left in the night, taken by winds to the gods know where. Now, you have returned to us. Tell us your tale and let us understand why you broke your promises."

The room fell silent. Muffled sounds of children playing and people working and calling to one another came from outside the walls.

The sounds faded, and Aiyana drew a breath.

Nathan turned to look at Aiyana. She'd composed herself, her staff across her lap, and Captain Farrell on her shoulder, though he couldn't remember when the raven had joined them.

"My memory is not whole," the aeifain began, "but I have pieces. I came to you, as you said, a humble petitioner, wanting nothing but to know more of the secrets of magic. I was young, eager, and willing to pay any price to gain as much knowledge in a short amount of time as possible. I tried to cheat wisdom with shortcuts."

She paused, and Mekiya nodded and gestured for her to continue.

"I took your knowledge of portals, how to harness them from any point along the ley lines to bring me to a junction and sought more power and learning. It brought me to Seawall City, where I…died."

Aiyana coughed, choking back an emotion that bubbled to the surface.

Nathan watched his friend, understanding her sense of duty and commitment. She always wanted to do what was right, even at great cost to herself or those around her, driven to shake things up.

"I was reborn," she continued, "a new soul taking this body, a spirit, from another place. This man…"

She gestured at Nathan, who raised his eyebrows in surprise.

"…and a human warrior named Torrents rescued me and took me in as one of their own. In the time that came, we rescued the portals from someone who would use them for his own means…"

Aiyana continued, telling a story Nathan had only known parts of. She spoke of the battles, of Jack Tucker and his inn, how they'd traveled the land for years to find more knowledge, and the day faded into twilight.

At the end, she slumped on her cushion, exhausted, and waiting for judgement to be passed.

"She has learned much, and faced many trials," Neyla, the second in the trio of elders, said, "and she broke the word of the covenant, but not the spirit of it."

"Yes!" Gokia interrupted. "She protected the ways, and from what she told us, created a great artifact that is a key to opening the lost paths throughout the land. And she knows Jack."

"I agree with you both," Mekiya nodded, "and if she is to be believed, her mind was as new as this soul she claims to have taken her form. But how are we to trust her again?"

"I have an idea…" Reggie raised his hand, his voice quiet, but drawing all eyes to him.

"Then, though you are a human, and a traitor to the land," Mekiya's voice held a hint of annoyance, but an overtone of amusement, "I invite you to speak."

"Okay," Reggie drew in a deep breath, letting it out slowly, "she protected me and our friend Nathan in her story. We are both from that other world from which she came, both of us inhabiting a body when it died, and the…something, healing it as we did so. We are like her."

Gokia straightened and opened his mouth to speak.

"But…" Reggie held up a finger to stall the man and pressed forward, "I know of one of your people, a dasism, held prisoner by an ogre, in a tower that once housed great magical power. If we were to rescue them, would that restore your trust in her, and us, at the same time?"

"Why not?" Nathan shrugged, gripped Marcid's haft in both hands, and considered the glowing blue circle.

Hidden in the forest not too far from the village, the dasism had a wood tower, just barely more than the height of two men, with the lower ring made of waist high stones. Inside was a wavering glimmer of a wall, like a reflection of the stars on a pond, but vertical instead of horizontal.

The three entered, promising to rescue someone named Arkeshia, which translated in dasism to the Treasure of the Sun.

That damned human, Reggie, and his loose lips. Nathan's internal thoughts came out as mutterings and grumbles. *Because of how free he was with his words and promises, the three of us are being sent to fight an ogre in its own territory. And all with just a small meal before going. We didn't even get to the drinks, and I really wanted to know what dasism aperitifs were like. They sent us to bed early and woke us before the sun came up.*

The makeshift portal thrilled Aiyana, who almost danced with excitement. She looked everywhere at once, her hands raising to point at various details. Apparently, this was one thing she'd always wanted to see, but forbidden during her decades of living with the people of the wood.

Captain Farrell croaked and hopped on her shoulder to keep his balance as the woman inspected the interior.

But it was her staff that caught Nathan's attention. It hummed—a deep thrum, barely audible—and when he looked around to see what the noise was, he saw Aiyana's hand shaking. But it hadn't been. It was the Key of Aiyana vibrating, apparently attuning itself to the magical doorway. It was what would allow them to come back to this place when they completed their mission.

Reginald looked excited, also, but not in the same way as the wizardess. He had a gleam in his eye, and a smile quirking his lips. He looked like a child who'd been told he was going to Disney World.

Reggie strode forward into the circle and disappeared in a dazzling burst of blue sparks.

Nathan stepped through.

The feeling of being ripped apart at the core enveloped him as it flung him across the world in magical transport.

The rokairn stumbled out of the light and into a clearing, of sorts. He felt the ground crunch under his feet and the smell of soot around him. Hints of sunlight tickled at the surrounding trees.

He blinked the afterimages from his eyes and saw Reginald bent over, losing his meager breakfast into a burnt spray of weeds.

Nathan recalled the first few times he'd travelled like this, and the stomach lurching effect it had. It still had that, and he didn't know if he'd gotten used to it, but he didn't get sick very often anymore.

Another flash of light from behind him announced Aiyana's arrival.

The surrounding land was a charnel house. Swaths of blackened grass created a partial arc leading away from a stout tower, and the trees over the area had shriveled and dried leaves on the branches closest to the structure.

Desiccated bodies hung by rough ropes, hunks of meat cut from ribs and thighs, each belly emptied—no doubt by the ogre for the delicacies within. Punctures in the withered flesh of each corpse showed where the sturine had fed…and fed well.

A swarm of fat, black insects erupted from the chest cavity of a hung man, and the aroma of fetid rot drifted across the area.

"The precision is amazing," Aiyana said from behind him.

Nathan turned to look at her, his face contorting in a blend of disgust and confusion.

"Look how close their portal brought us, and it isn't even a prepared and linked place. You can't say that's not amazing, can you?" she asked.

Reginald lurched and bent over again, having realized the surrounding scene.

"Do you see what has happened here?" Nathan waved his hand around the area, indicating the atrocities.

"Of course, Nathan, I'm sorry," Aiyana said, but her voice wasn't apologetic. "But they're just humans and intruding on the land, to boot. They got what they deserved. They should've never come here."

"What?" Reginald's voice was a harsh whisper. "These are my men. We came here to find traces of the dasism, or your own people. We came to open trade, create a negotiation, or at least find out what happened to the people who once lived here, protecting the land."

"Unneeded." Aiyana waved a hand dismissively.

"We should make a plan to get into the tower," Nathan said, trying to avert the confrontation that was brewing. "We can discuss this another time, or not at all."

The last four words came out in a grumbled whisper.

"Yes," Aiyana and Reginald said together, her looking around and surveying the area, him glaring at her.

Aiyana thrust her wrist under Captain Farrell's belly. He'd been crouched on her shoulder, fluffed up in obvious distress. He stepped onto her forearm, and she launched him into the sky.

"Captain Farrell will scout the tower and check the windows," she explained.

"Is he a storm crow?" Reginald asked.

Aiyana turned to regard the man, looking down her nose at him even though he was taller than her.

"Why does it matter?" she asked sharply.

Reginald shrugged and pointed at the tower.

"Three stories, a partial basement, and parts of the interior floors are crumbled, allowing the monster to move from one floor to another without using the stairs." Reginald held Aiyana's gaze, still pointing. "The bottom level is mostly refuse, which means bidj, bones, and other things along those lines. The second level is his cooking and resting area, and I don't know what's on the top floor, but do know it has access to the roof, which he's built a lean-to over, so the rain or snow doesn't come in. The beast has covered most of the windows to stop sunlight and weather, but has traps set to stop people from getting in when he's sleeping."

Reginald dropped his arm.

"How would you like to go about this, your highness?" he asked, his voice a glare.

Nathan heaved an obvious sigh of frustration.

"Okay, kids," the rokairn muttered, "I'm in charge, since you both are being brats."

Each turned to look at him, their mouths opening to say something.

"No, dammit!" Nathan made a chopping motion with his hand. "This is how it'll be until both of you learn to get along, or at least behave and tolerate one another. No arguments, so shut it unless you have something constructive to add."

"My breakdown of the tower was constructive," Reginald muttered.

"Actually, it was," Nathan agreed.

"The beast's asleep according to the captain," Aiyana's voice was subdued, "and he tells me that the roof is dangerous but can't tell me how. That's constructive."

Nathan pressed his lips together and looked back and forth between the two.

"Really? You're competing to see who'll be in less trouble by offering help?" Nathan's face broke, and he laughed, a short, sharp bark. "Okay, you're both starting to make up for your mutual attitudes. Looks like, under the circumstances, it's a frontal assault. Reginald, if he has a prisoner, where would they be kept?"

"Third floor," Reggie said without hesitation. "They can't just run out and must go past him to get to the ground level. They're shackled, but I don't know why the ogre would keep them alive when he did…this…"

Reginald flapped a hand over his shoulder, gesturing at the gutted and flayed men in the trees.

"…to everyone else," he finished.

"Because of magic, or someone else who has their hooks in him wants them," Aiyana said, her eyes distant, and her voice barely a whisper.

"Damned mind magics," Nathan growled. "Lass, you grow new powers quicker than a lizard grows a new tail. It's like you've found the fast track to power."

"So, how're we going to do this?" Reginald asked.

"The same way we do everything…" Aiyana grinned.

"With a little style, and a lot of kick ass." Nathan finished.

Chapter 12

"Watch this," Nathan nudged Reginald, and pointed at Aiyana.

She raised her staff in the air, perpendicular to the ground, and began weaving an intricate pattern in the air with her other hand.

The air chilled, and the humidity spiked, becoming thick. Tendrils of fog writhed lazily upward from the soil, like the ghosts of plants on fast forward in some otherworldly nature documentary.

Reginald fidgeted, shifting from one foot to the other, unsure of what to expect or what he should do

Nathan stood with his arms crossed, a tight, proud smile on his face as he watched his traveling companion.

Reginald followed the rokairn's lead, dropping his hands to the pommel of his weapons and leaning his weight onto his rear foot. He took a deep breath—like he would before entering the tomb of a five-thousand-year-old dead emperor—closed his eyes, exhaled slowly, then opened his eyes like he was gazing at a piece of art in a quiet museum, instead of a field of carnage.

The fog covered the ground to waist height. It grew higher, and Reginald stared in fascination. Within minutes, it reached the top of the tower.

"We have cover, boss," Aiyana said, barely visible, though she was only an arm's length away.

"My turn." Nathan swaggered forward like he was on the deck of a rolling ship, his thumbs tucked into his belt.

Reginald and Aiyana followed, the woman raising her arm to receive Captain Farrell.

"How'd he find you in this fog?" Reginald asked.

"Magical tele-location," Aiyana answered in a hushed voice, "like radar or sonar, but we can find each other wherever we are."

They came to a wall halfway between the front door and the back of the tower.

Nathan grunted, amused. He raised his hands, pressed them together, and began moving them, his thumbs in constant contact with one another.

The movements the priest of Jonath made reminded Reginald of those puzzles of sliding tiles, trying to form a pattern or picture.

The side of the tower opened, stones sliding and pivoting from the wall to form an entryway of fitted stone, others shifting to make a step-formation from the top of the opening to the ground two paces from the opening, meeting the newly created floor.

"If you guys can do all this..." Reginald swallowed, "how am I supposed to help?"

"Relax," Nathan chuffed, "and try to look cool. Other than that, keep your sword arm loose and jump in when you can."

Reginald took another deep breath, nodded a quick jerk, and walked forward and into the structure, ducking under the newly made entry.

"What the hell is this?" Nathan mumbled, looking around the foyer of the lower level.

Wispy humanoid shapes swayed, a few gathered around ornate sculptures of bones decorating the walls, strewn in patterns of complex geometric shapes. Antlered skulls hung on the walls, the height of two men, and shapes scurried in the shadows.

"Rats," Reginald mumbled from behind the priest.

"Um, no…" Nathan growled, "those aren't rats. That's the dead without bodies."

Reggie moved up the last step and into the room, looking over Nathan's head. Seeing the incorporeal figures, he shivered and tried to pull himself together.

"This beast is a necromancer?" Aiyana's voice was a mix of disgust and wonder.

"Maybe?" Nathan shrugged.

"Or someone else is lending help in the form of…these things." Reginald's voice was matter of fact, and the others looked at him curiously.

"Our new friend may know some things," Nathan laughed.

Aiyana grunted noncommittally.

The shadows lunged forward.

Reginald's rapier flashed, his main-gauche held across his midsection in readiness. His blade cut through nothing, as a misty, black humanoid form reached for his throat with ghostly tendrils of fingers.

He stumbled backwards with a squeal.

"Jonath, protect us from unnatural specters!" Nathan roared, lifting his holy symbol in front of the beings of darkness.

Dozens of figures surged past the priest, avoiding him as they slid towards the other two.

Aiyana spoke an arcane word, or perhaps it was a phrase, Reginald couldn't tell, the sounds twisting in his head.

The enemy didn't slow, but the one reaching for the swordsman hissed—the agonizing sound like a teakettle winding down when you turned off the heat—and disappeared from existence.

"I can only disconnect one at a time," Aiyana's voice was strained, and a harsh whisper, "they'll overpower us."

"Then we better find a better way." Nathan's booming voice was a counterpoint to the woman's soft words.

Reginald's mind whirred, his real-world experience having nothing of value to help. But the vague recollections of his body—the impulse to run, and thoughts of magic and how it works—overlapped, and a thought occurred to him.

"The connection," he gasped, catching his footing, and balancing to dodge instead of attack, "a priest can shatter those, right? And a mind mage can feel them, right? Can you two work together? Aiyana, find the connection, show it to Nathan, and then he clouds them, breaks them, and sends these men to their rest?"

"Men?" Aiyana asked.

"These…beings, and don't ask me how I know, are my men. The ones I brought here. I'd guess the ogre, or those that empower the monster, can't keep the spirits around for long," Reginald's voice was tinted with sadness and a dash of revulsion.

Aiyana and Nathan traded looks, and the woman shrugged.

The wizardess drew on the intuitive powers of her people, the power of a mind mage, and her brow furrowed.

Reggie saw Nathan stagger, as if a great weight had hit him. The rokairn pushed to an upright position, squared his shoulders, and set his feet. He wrinkled his brow, his lips flattened, and his teeth showed as he ground them together.

"Got it," the rokairn growled, "I think…"

The priest of Jonath sucked in air. Drawing in the atmosphere, the essence of what made up the surroundings, he pulled it into himself.

Reginald sidestepped a form of darkness, slashing out with his weapon. His hand went cold, as if he pressed his open palm to a piece of metal in the middle of winter. He moved back, then zig zagged forward, to avoid two others, trying to stay in between the two magic wielders.

Aiyana broke the connection of another and drew the attention of three more. She shrouded herself with energy matching theirs, and they passed to each side of her, seeking living flesh.

Reaching over his shoulder with one hand, Nathan tore Marcid free of her restraints and swung the axe. His other hand clutched the medallion of the trident balancing a scale with mountains behind—the holy symbol of Jonath.

Watching the priest, Reggie zagged when he should've zigged, and a hand gripped him. Half his body went numb, and his breath faltered, coming in short, harsh gasps. His main gauche clattered to the floor, and he fell to one knee.

This was Thomas. The man he'd trained since the soldier had been a boy was now feeding off his very essence, his soul. Reggie couldn't define it any other way, and though he'd been raised a good Protestant, he'd never put much thought into the soul.

When you explore ancient cultures with other gods and beliefs, he thought, *you became more open to concepts outside of the Holy Bible.*

Images of Thomas's life rolled across Reggie's mind. It was more like the fog outside, present, but not something he could grasp and inspect. The man, though barely so, always wanted to journey to the Great Desert and find the Prison of Verl'zen-luk, a lich who later became a god. The stories and research of the tomb buried under the sand came into Reginald's thoughts, like a tide, his dual lives rolling into the shadow being feeding off his identity.

Falling to the broken stones of the floor, Reginald clutched at his chest, the rapier still in his hand. He knew the feeling of a heart attack—having suffered more than one in his time, in another life, in another world—and briefly wondered if he'd ever breathe again.

The world twisted, and his vision narrowed, like a picture with a vignette creeping inward from the edges.

Then everything released, and Reggie sucked in deep breaths. His vision filled with Thomas's face, waning from the shadowy form to a more human one before fading like a dream.

Hands gripped Reginald, pulling him to a sitting position. He heard voices from a distance, and tried to focus on them, but his hearing and other senses were swimming as much as his sight.

The thick miasma of offal cut through his awareness, other sensations returning with the smell. Nathan and Aiyana were kneeling beside him, asking him questions.

He shook his head, and everything spun.

"How could you know to do that?" Aiyana's question came to him sharply. "Have you studied the arts? Why would you know something like that?"

"Prisoners only fight…" Reginald gasped, "when they're forced to do so. Why would magic be different? It just felt like common sense."

Aiyana let him go and stood up, the side of him supported by her falling towards the ground. Nathan's firm grip took up the slack.

"Just breath, buddy," the rokairn said, "catch your breath, then we'll see about standing."

"He's mocking me, calling me stupid." The wizardess's tone was sharp, her fingertips rubbing her temples.

"No," Nathan shook his head, "he's answering your question. Not everything is a personal attack on you. Most people, when they say things, are only talking about themselves, and not too worried about other people."

"My apologies," Reginald coughed, and pulled his legs under himself, pushing to his feet with Nathan's help. "I meant no offense. It was just the logic of the elderly."

The three fell silent and went in three different directions. Aiyana called upon her abilities to find other life within the building. Nathan explored the room, finding the stairs up and down, and investigated the support columns. Reginald steadied himself and worked on regulating his breathing.

"We go up. I can feel three beings up there." Aiyana pointed at three points in the ceiling.

"How do we want to do this?" Nathan asked.

"I'm tired of pussy-footing around," she answered. "I will lead and take out the beast."

Before either of the men could reply, Aiyana stomped up the stairs, the thump of her staff sounding like a third footfall, Captain Farrell flapping after her.

The rokairn and human followed, Reginald taking up rear guard.

Reaching the next floor, they saw the potbelly stove and broken furniture scattered about. There was a large lump of furs and bedding on one side, a massive form atop it, snoring in a gentle buzz saw of breathing.

Her hands twisting, Aiyana drew on the power of the elements. The pile burst into flame.

The gigantic form sat up, roaring a scream and lurching from the furs.

Shards of ice shot from the wizardess. They were the length of swords by the time they pierced the ogre.

Gripping her staff, she threw her arms wide, and the stone floor beneath the behemoth melted into mud, and the monster fell downward.

The building shuddered when he hit the lower level, and Aiyana firmed the mud back to stone and let the bricks rain down on the enemy.

"Okay, then," Nathan said, looking through the hole that remained at the wreckage of the ogre below.

With a prayer to Jonath, the priest softened the stones once again, then solidified them into a mounded tomb for the monster.

"Now, let's go rescue the dasism, and whoever is with them." Aiyana said, her tone sharp.

The three ascended to the third level of the tower, and as predicted, two forms were crouched together on the floor.

The people peered from between arms crossed over their knees, dressed in less than rags, more of tatters of cloth. They were elongated bags of bones covered with taunt pale reddish skin, and dark hair.

When the three crested the last step, the two people looked up. They struggled to stand, helping one another.

They were neither male nor female. Gender was a thing that could be determined in most people's minds by genitalia, but the two figures in front of them defied that simple, physical determination.

"They are sun-moon folk," Aiyana's voice was full of wonder, "they are Yulima-Milwen, and carry the balance of masculine and feminine in one body."

"Dual spirit, twin spirit, or two spirit in Native American lore," Reginald added, "respected because they have the balance of both sides of nature within their body."

"You know," one of the tattered people croaked, in broken human language, "we're right here, and we can hear you."

"And we can speak for ourselves," the other said.

"I am Arkeshia, and this is Chevae," the first one said, "my soulmate, partner, and bonded."

Something heavy hit the wall, and it cracked, the building wobbling on its foundation. Dust trickled from overhead, and the stones of the wall dented inward.

"Surrender," a human voice boomed, "and turn over the treasures of the tower, or face your annihilation."

"Is that...?" Nathan started.

"Tymere?" Aiyana asked. "The lackey of the damned dead alchemist of Seawall City?"

"Khizhane? He had someone take his place?" Nathan looked worried.

The structure shook again as something battered it.

"Oh, no they didn't…" Aiyana muttered, spinning towards a window on the wall where the building blocks had buckled inward. "I'm in no mood for this crap."

"Uh oh," Nathan muttered, "she's in one of her moods. Lad, get those two ready to run, or at least ready to get out of this place."

"Gotcha," Reginald nodded.

He moved towards the prisoners, tucking his main gauche into its sheath, and drawing a knife.

Slicing through the ropes that bound the two, Reggie smiled at them.

"Don't worry," he said, "we're here to rescue you and bring you home. My companions will take care of this new threat. Oh, and the ogre is dead, so don't worry about him. I'm Reginald Betancourt. That's Nathan, he's a priest of Jonath, so all about being fair though judging others."

The human gestured towards the rokairn with the small blade, and then the aeifain.

"And the woman is Aiyana. She's a wizardess, taught by your people, and temperamental. But she's good, deep, deep, down inside. But, like us all, she has her issues."

The side of the tower erupted, but outward rather than inward, and Aiyana glided out into the open air of a fine summer morning.

Nathan sighed and his shoulders slumped.

"Here we go again," Nathan muttered, and a cloud of dust coalesced into a semi-solid stair leading downward in front of him. "Shall we go meet the people who knocked?"

Reggie drew his weapons and moved forward. Arkeshia and Chevae moved to follow, exchanging concerned glances.

Chapter 13

Aiyana descended like an avenging angel, her robe whipping around her, staff held in front of her, and Captain Farrell circling her like a dark messenger of doom.

The voice whispered retribution in her head, encouraging her to take out those who would stop her from opening and controlling the portal network.

She raised her staff, and lightning crackled from clouds forming overhead. A flock of hundreds of storm swallows launched into the sky. The cumulus mists became a thick grey mass, roiling and swirling with sudden intensity.

Blue-white lines, tinted with lavender, jerked towards the ground, jagged spikes of power hitting the soil, glass divots larger than a wagon appearing where they touched down. A shower of dirt and limbs rained down on the assembled army.

"You…have…no…power…here." The wind carried the wizardess's voice like the shrill scream of a harpy.

Men at arms scattered under the onslaught. It was that or face death, head on, without prejudice.

Nathan bounced down the steps he'd made with the blessing of Jonath; Reginald, Arkeshia, and Chevae followed.

The priest looked worried when he should've looked triumphant, his eyes locked on his friend wreaking havoc on the assembled army.

Wind and rain answered the cold call of the elementalist, and the ground rumbled and cracked under her power.

The Key of Aiyana was made to open portals across the continent—even the world—but was now being used to channel the forces of fire, air, earth, and water to decimate a gathered force who only wanted trinkets that would bring them gold.

Men screamed in their death throes, lightning breaking the earth and their bodies.

Nathan reached the ground and turned to check on Reginald and his charges.

A thunderous explosion from behind him, followed by a pelting rain of stone shards, threw the rokairn forward. He tumbled from the steps of debris he'd been descending. He flashed a look behind him, only to the see a cloud of dust from the collapsing tower rolling across the three and towards him.

He fell to his knees, pulling a cloth from a pocket to cover his mouth, nose, and eyes.

When the dust settled, Aiyana was a glorious and horrifying specter hovering above the cracked and broken earth. Dozens of men lay at her feet, as shattered as the tower behind the priest.

Turning back to the building, he saw Reginald supporting the two dasism, one shoulder under the arms of each, and stumbling towards him.

"How dare you!" The wizardess's shriek tore through the trembling air. "I will tear you apart for this cowardly attack!"

Nathan hesitated, wanting to assist Reginald and the prisoners but needing to go to Aiyana. She'd been under a lot of pressure, and he knew it was good to release it, but killing a small army might not be the healthiest way to do it.

Bolts crackled from the heavens above, slashing through the small army. Men shrieked as it threw them a dozen paces back or were silenced as it fried them on the spot.

Nathan moved towards the wizardess.

Reginald stumbled under the weight of the two dasism, their legs weak from being restrained for however long they'd been here. The two had a distinct, sour smell. It was more than just sweat. It was poor diet, urine, and other things that came with treating prisoners poorly.

How long have they been here? Reggie wondered. *And where did the designs for how the ogre embellished the hall come from? Were those specific designs and styles to their race? Or was it just a hodgepodge of what the beast had seen?*

Chevae let out a brief scream and tore away from Reginald, diving for the ground.

Reggie turned to see what had caused them to react and barely lifted his rapier in time to block an axe thrown at his head.

Spinning the rest of the way around, the swashbuckler directed Arkeshia towards their friend, hoping the two would be safe enough with him between them and the three simen coming towards the trio.

Kionna, flanked by Daizjah and Danayia, swaggered from around the front of the tower.

"So," Kionna shouted over the explosions behind Reginald, "this is what you've been up to, Kazzek.

Going for the big loot, rather than some long-abandoned ruin, eh? Smart, and an ogre, too? That must've added some extra loot to the pile. Ogres spend little but collect all kinds of things."

The bandit paused, looking at the dasism laying in the dirt.

"Trafficking now?" Kionna raised an eyebrow. "Kidnapping and ransom? Looks like you're branching out. Smart."

Reginald watched the mismatched bodyguards move away from their boss, looking to flank him. The swordsman shot back an insulting and witty retort, but wasn't even listening to himself. He was gauging the lay of the battlefield.

Kionna was adept at his long sword, and the other two were bulls in a China shop. They'd come at him, throwing axes, or chopping at him. They'd be wild, but dangerous. Kionna would be like a swaying snake, though, waiting to strike when he was distracted by the attacks of the others.

Waiting would not make things better.

Reggie knelt, set his rapier down, drew a stiletto from each boot, and threw one at a time in a sidearm toss. The first flew towards Danayia, and Reggie turned to throw the other at Daizjah without waiting to see if he'd hit his first target.

The second blade sunk into the taller bearded man's, Daizjah's, chest, sliding between his ribs. He kept coming.

Picking up his rapier and gripping it in a trigger hold, Reggie drew his main gauche, and did a shoulder roll towards the wounded man, coming up in a crouch.

Daizjah tripped over him, and Reginald stood, throwing the attacker higher. Putting his weight on his back foot, he thrust his rapier out towards the sound of Danayia, locking his arm.

The shorter man impaled himself on the blade, and Reginald parried the axe with his blocking blade, knocking the man's arm to the side.

The swashbuckler shoved his main gauche into Danayia's belly, pushing upward to slide between the layers of studded leather armor, and felt it hit bone.

Danayia barreled into him, knocking him back and under him.

Shoving his attacker off, Reginald heard the soft steps of Kionna moving towards him fast, and rolled in the opposite direction of the wounded man, jerking both of his weapons free.

A blade slithered across the dirt next to his face, and Reggie looked up to see Kionna standing over him, smirking.

Flat on your back is not the place to be when someone is trying to kill you, Reggie thought.

Reggie kicked upward, aiming for Kionna's belly, but the bandit easily sidestepped.

It gave Reginald the time he needed to get to his feet, but barely.

Kionna's sword came down in an overhead swing, and Reginald batted it aside. The strike aimed for his head bit into his shoulder, and Reggie grunted.

Stumbling backwards, Reginald tried to take stock of the situation. Daizjah was on the ground, rolled onto his back, and clutching the stiletto that had been pushed to the hilt in his chest. He was gasping, his breath coming in gurgles. Danayia was curled into a ball, his fingers spasmodically gripping at his bloody armor.

That slight distraction was enough. Kionna lunged forward, his weapon centered and steady for a killing blow. Reggie knew he'd never get his blade up in time and wondered what exactly Nathan and Aiyana were doing.

Kionna's head jerked to one side, a bright splash of blood appearing on his temple as a rock bounced off it.

Reginald moved his main gauche sideways across his body, swept the imminent blade tip to one side, pulled his right shoulder back, and thrust his rapier into the throat of his old partner-in-crime.

Looking over Kionna's shoulder as the outlaw crumpled to the ground, Reginald saw Chevae and Arkeshia leaning against one another with a stack of fist-sized rocks in front of them.

He nodded thanks at the two, and they smiled back, each giving a little, tired wave of friendly dismissal.

Stepping forward, Reggie pushed his blade forward, the tip bursting from the back of Kionna's neck. Twisting the weapon, cartilage and bone popping around the blade, the swashbuckler shook his hand left and right, tearing the hole in the man's throat wider.

Pulling the blade free, Reginald moved to dispose of the other two.

A fitted stone beside Nathan wobbled, and rose into the air, another rolling under it, as a third fell on top. A similar pile was being constructed a meter away, and they took the shape of thick, rock legs. A waist and torso formed, Aiyana's magic continuing to construct a rock golem.

"This is getting out of hand," Nathan grumbled.

He lurched to his feet, set them at a shoulder's width, squared his shoulders, and walked toward his friend. The construct behind him grew with each step the rokairn took and was twice his height before he stood below the wizardess.

"Gotta do this the hard way…" he sighed.

Calling upon the power of his god, the priest rose on a column of dirt until he was eye level with the woman.

"Aiyana, you need to stop now. They're running, you've stopped them. You're getting carried away, and you could end up hurting someone you don't mean to." Nathan tried to speak calmly, reasonably, but his voice had a granite edge to it.

The huge block fist of the rock golem came out of nowhere, moving right at Nathan's face.

Nathan caught it in one hand and crushed it.

Aiyana turned to look at him, her face a mask of twisted anger.

"No, Aiyana." His voice was quiet now, just below conversation volume, but with a rock-solid quality to it. "Do you think even an elementalist as skilled as yourself could best me in my own element? The element of Jonath? Spoiler alert, the answer is no."

Nathan lifted his hand, the one not holding his double-bladed axe, and slammed it downward. An unseen force crushed the rock monster.

With another gesture, a hollow column of soil and rocks erupted upward, encasing the wizardess, and cutting off the flow of air that kept her aloft.

A soft thump came from within the makeshift well, followed by a frustrated screech. The black earthen walls melted away, flowing into the surrounding area, revealing Aiyana with her wrists and ankles pinned to the ground by stone fists.

"You…" Nathan stabbed a finger at the helpless woman, "have crossed a line, and I bet you don't even know it. I've supported you as you learned the '*great mysteries*', and let you have your way in so many things. But when it comes to dealing death with a nonchalance and high-handedness, I will not allow it. I will shut you down. Do you understand?"

Reginald and the two dasism came up behind Nathan, looking down at the powerful elementalist. The surrounding area was filled with the remaining humans fleeing the scene.

Aiyana tightened her jaw, and the restraints cracked. Then she nodded.

The five moved away from the crumbled tower, scattered corpses, and the tattered remnants of the bandit's little band of ruffians who moved in the opposite direction.

Glass divots, the size of wagons, dotted the burnt landscape, and fissures in the ground steamed with sulfurous tendrils of smoke. The heat radiating from the cracks caused dried grasses near them to burst randomly into flames.

Aiyana walked in front of everyone, her posture stiff, as Captain Farrell scouted ahead.

Nathan helped support Arkeshia, who looked at the surrounding desolation, their face pale from more than the rigors of their captivity.

Reginald lent a shoulder to Chevae, and looked at them, his mouth forming to ask a question.

"Ask, human," Chevae sighed.

"Okay, I didn't want to seem forward, but since you're open to conversation, I will ask…" Reggie drew in a deep breath, as if pushing past some inner wall of caution or reluctance, "your name means Desert Moon, right?"

Chevae glanced over at the man, a small smile quirking the edge of their dry and cracked lips.

"Yes, it does. You know the Dasism language?" they asked.

"A little, but I wouldn't say I'm as fluent in your language as you are in mine," the man shrugged, a bit chagrined.

"Why are you asking what my name means?" Chevae asked.

"I know of your people's connection to nature, and I was curious if you have any connection to the Great Desert to the west of this forest," he said it as a statement, but the question was implied.

"What does your name mean, Reeg-an-ald?" Chevae countered.

"My name?" Reginald laughed. "It means 'counselor', but some would say it means 'ruler or King'. And you can call me Reggie if it's easier, all my friends do."

"So, we are friends, then?" Chevae grinned, then grunted as their ankle twisted on a root.

Reggie took their extra weight and helped them steady themselves.

"Sure, at least in my mind. You can decide on your own what you think of me as, though." Reggie smiled and shrugged.

"I was born on the edge of that desert you asked about," Chevae said, "on a clear night. I have long studied the shifting sands and know quite a bit about it. Why? What is your interest in the Great Desert?"

"The dead men in the tower—the ghosts, or wraiths, or whatever they were—were men I once worked with. When one touched me, Thomas, I saw a great tomb in that desert, and I knew it was *that* desert, but I don't know how. I've always been curious about lost places and have spent decades searching for lost civilizations."

"Decades?" Chevae looked the human up and down. "If that is true, then you are older than your body looks."

"Yeah, that's an interesting story I'll share with you sometime in the future…" Reggie trailed off, scoffed, then shook his head at his thoughts.

Chevae nodded and began speaking of the Great Desert. They told about the man entombed there, Verl'zen-luk, who later became a god. The details of the people who'd built the ancient prison were lost in time, but some things were not forgotten.

The conversation was interrupted as the group slowed to a stop. Reginald craned his head to see what caused the delay.

A looming, horned form rose from the bushes in the tree line.

Nathan released Arkeshia, stepping away and loosening his axe. Reginald did the same with Chevae, drawing his rapier and main gauche, and Aiyana took a wide stance, her staff held in front of her.

Chapter 14

The creature stepped from the dappled shadows where it had been well camouflaged in the speckled sunlight. It moved with an odd gait, slightly hunched forward, rolling its shoulders with each step.

At first, Aiyana thought it was a man in baggy trousers, a leather cuirass, and a decorative helm, with a wide blade hanging across his back. But then she saw the stranger was a woman, and the pants were really fur on *her* legs, and the wide helmet was horns scrolling outward from her head. The leather breastplate was real, but the woman's skin was a similar light reddish-brown that almost matched her armor.

Her head was larger than a human's, to accommodate the mass of the winding horns that balanced on her head. The furry legs ended in cloven hooves, and her hands were covered with fingerless gloves.

Nathan set his feet a shoulder width apart, squared his chest, and dropped the haft of Marcid into his open palm. Reginald moved up beside the rokairn, each of them flanking Aiyana. The wizardess wobbled, exhausted from her earlier exertion, but steadied herself and began gathering elemental forces.

The stranger held up her hands in a sign of peace, splaying her fingers and showing they were empty.

"Kajuun," Arkeshia limped forward, putting herself between the group and the newcomer, "she's a friend. She's the one that told us about the ogre tower and what was going on there."

Aiyana turned to the dasism and raised an eyebrow.

"She's the one who sent you to a tower of a monster who had just killed a couple dozen men to turn them into shadow beings that kill with a touch…and you call her a friend?" The wizardess's voice dripped with sarcasm.

"They were violating nature," Chevae moved up to stand beside Arkeshia, "warping it, and needed to be stopped. We had to find out who was giving the beast this kind of power and follow the trail back to whoever it was."

"And did you find out who it was?" Nathan asked, not taking his eyes off the strange woman.

"No, but…" Chevae began, only to be interrupted by Reggie.

"Is she a satyr?" the swordsman asked, his voice almost a whisper. "Like straight from Greek and Roman mythology? A faun? A child of Bacchus or Dionysus? Do all those pantheons live here too?"

"What?" Nathan asked, shooting the man a glance.

"No," Aiyana answered, "those are not of this world, those are of the other world. And let's not speak of them here and now. We have other things that are more pressing."

The dasism and the satyr looked at the human, each of them curious, but cautious.

"Please," Kajuun said, her accent heavy and ponderous, "be letting me to explain. My people once were new to this forest, but the Dasism come and say to be the welcome. They give gift of winds and water with magic, letting us know them. The Aeifain also come, and they share the secrets of the mind, to speak and make things of who we are. We learn to write the symbols of language, and the magics, and make our own. We take all the gifts, and we thrive with them."

The satyr stopped speaking, her brow furrowing. She looked back and forth between the group, then her face opened with a distressed, 'oh', of worry.

"This, I am doing the wrong!" She held up her hands like she was trying to stop traffic.

Kajuun stood up straight, pressed her palms together in front of her, and bowed to a thirty-degree angle.

"I am Kajuun, of the Torck, who your people call the Rammen. I welcome you to Grey Wood, and invite you to our humble city, Rauhen, to take our hospitality."

The satyr bowed again.

Cocking her head to one side, she struck a pose, one fist on her hip, and the other—with open palm facing upward—gesturing across the gathering.

"There," she grinned, "I do-ed it right that time. So, now I wait to see if you will be friend to the Rammen and to Kajuun, which is me."

"Your people made the sigils we saw?" Aiyana squinted at the woman. "The ones on the bastille? The ones inside of the ogre tower?"

"Yes, we people do those. That is our language, and it is the language of the trees, the wind, and the land." Kajuun nodded.

"What about the one in Wiley's Station? Were those yours also?" the wizardess asked, her voice taking on a dangerous edge.

"Oh…yes," Kajuun looked down at her hooves, "I put those myself, when I found the human place burned. I do that to stop the thing that destroy it, so it do not find it again."

"Who?" Reginald took a step forward without realizing it, his hand dropping to the hilt of his rapier.

Nathan put his hand on the man's forearm.

Kajuun looked at the human, her eyebrows rising.

Chevae put a hand on the swashbuckler's other arm.

"She sent us to find the ogre," Chevae said softly, "she'd set the sigils in the tower to contain the magic."

"Yes," Kajuun nodded, "and it draw away magics, so it is not as hard to beat for my friends. And I see it is to be helping you when there."

A scatter of small, black birds passed overhead. The flock became thicker, until it was a blue sky full of black, tittering specks far above them.

"A storm is coming," Arkeshia said, "we should get moving."

"I can't portal us without a stationary hub," Aiyana watched the birds, noting the blue-white sparks moving between them, "but maybe the dasism will teach me how to make a temporary point I can use one day."

"Ahem," Nathan stepped forward, "we need to move, no matter what. Do we take the long way back to the dasism village, or do we go with Kajuun to the city of the Rammen?"

Standing on a grassy knoll, Reggie stared at the home of the Torck. The city rose from the Grey Wood like an island. Gleaming white marble towers with bulbous tops thrust above the trees. They came to a point at the top and grew thicker and rounder at the bottom. These were mixed with other structures that were more familiar, square, and crenelated.

"Look at that," Reggie sighed, "the architecture is completely unique, but has elements similar to the Ottoman Empire or the Byzantine style that influenced Russia in the early part of the century."

"Those things?" Nathan pointed at the structures atop the towers. "They look like upside-down onions, or maybe beets, to me."

Reggie laughed.

"That's funny," he said, "because in Russia they're called onion domes. But look at the blended styles. Oh! I know! It reminds me of Islamic architecture, with their domes and square towers, delicate arches and scrollwork, but solid buildings.

"And look!" Reggie pointed at the rounded roofs, sighting down the length of his arm.

Nathan leaned forward and squinted, looking at the people moving across the rounded roofs, walking on them as if they were hills, or stairs wrapped around a hill.

"They're not just walking on them," Reggie went on, the words coming out in a rush, "they're high stepping and hopping. Some are using them like a rooftop street, bounding and bouncing towards their destination. Those there are probably youths. Look, they're making a game of leaping from one platform to the other to a path, and so on. This is incredible! It's like mountain goats on the heights of a craggy cliff."

"That goat thing might be an offensive comparison, don't you think?" Aiyana said.

Reggie looked at his companions.

Kajuun was grinning at his delight, her hands on her hips. She nodded at him, showing her pride in the city, and Reggie blushed and looked away.

Nathan stood to one side, and Reggie wasn't sure if the man was more comfortable that way, or if he was keeping his distance from Aiyana for her comfort. Reggie felt a kinship to the man, and he liked him for no solid reason. Well, besides, the man was kind, caring, and driven to help others.

Arkeshia's and Chevae's strength grew stronger with each passing day, and Reggie couldn't tell if it was good nutrition and exercise, or being connected to the elements again, that helped them more.

Aiyana shifted her footing, drawing the man's attention. Captain Farrell perched atop the fist holding the crystal at the top of her magical artifact and looked at Nathan with a tilted head and a knowing eye.

Reggie bowed his head slightly at the raven, and Captain Farrell bobbed his twice. It was like the bird understood more than he should ever be able to. But this was a world of magic, and that was an easy possibility compared to the incredible things Reggie had seen in his short time in this reality.

The woman shifted again, and he thought she seemed impatient. Her face changed from wonder at the sight in front of them to a hardened expression meant to mask her true feelings.

She wants to be grown up so badly, Reggie thought, *but still wants to believe in the world and people. Those two things often aren't the same thing, though. Experience breeds bitterness.*

Reggie wondered if he was bitter about life, people, and the world. Or worlds. He was—at least potentially—dead in his world because of disease, age, and the 'kindness' of his family.

He'd always wanted an exciting life. He never needed to be the center of attention. He enjoyed helping people find their happiness. Give others a boost in what they wanted. After all, a rising tide raises all ships, or something like that.

He refocused on Aiyana. He was worried about her. He knew she needed to find her own way in life, and offering advice only made her bristle. It saddened him when he tried to help and she took it as a personal affront, like he was trying to belittle her or tell her she didn't know anything.

He'd learned to keep silent and offer help from the background when she looked like she needed it.

Maybe after she found out what had happened to the Aeifain people and culture, he'd be able to help her enjoy what this world offered.

Shaking his head, he coughed a laugh. This world wasn't like Middle Earth; this was a broken and fragmented place.

Actually, he grinned as the thought rebounded, *in that way, this world is like those other worlds. But in this world, instead of having the usual fantasy creatures, it had birds that bring the weather, demonic and undead herds roaming the land, and blood-sucking octopus-bats. It's like a wasteland of magical, mutant monsters.*

Looking at Kajuun again, Reggie realized she was one of the most normal things he'd encountered in this world, as far as a mythology-type creature. Sure, aeifain and dasism were like elves, and rokairn were similar to dwarves of classic literature, and humans were humans…but anything else had been a warped version of a mythical beast, at best, and completely foreign most of the time.

Reggie thought back to the trip here, which had taken a few days. He and Kajuun had talked often, and at length. He asked questions about the land, the Torck, and her.

She'd explained that thirty years ago her people lived on the southern spur of the Wandering Hills, a few weeks' travel to the north. They were little more than a primitive tribe traversing the highlands, gathering various wild berries and vegetation. Then a voice whispered to a member of the tribe, giving them advice and knowledge. Shortly after, they planted their first crops in the cracks and crevasses of the mountainside.

Encouraged by the tribe's unseen advisor, her people befriended the minotaurs who roamed the hilly lowlands surrounding the mountain range, and the fauns of the forest to the south. The three peoples merged, united, and migrated slowly south under the advisement of their mysterious councilor. Within five years, they'd reached the northern edge of the Grey Forest and met the dasism.

Reggie considered the city as the group approached as they continued on their way. It was less than two decades since the Torck had laid the first stone. They'd built it in a handful of years. As an archaeologist, he knew that was an incredibly fast rate of change for anyone.

Emerging from the forest, a couple kilometers of cleared land lay between them and the city wall. Where the trees ended, a pure white cobblestone road started. Marble columns and arches flanked the alabaster path, wide enough for two wagons to pass over the thoroughfare. Farmland, with crops in neat rows, replaced the grass nearest the city wall. Distant figures moved between the greenery, weeding, pruning, and caring for the plants.

Kajuun whispered something, and a breeze swept across her.

Reggie thought of something she said earlier: that she spoke the language of the trees and wind. He wondered if she'd just spoken that language and sent a message to someone.

This morning, she'd changed from her armor into something more official. The outfit had the look of a ceremonial outfit. It was a single, long, red tunic sort of thing. It reminded Reggie of an Indian kurta, which many of the men wore when at official functions. Her broad-bladed sword still sheathed across her back, she added bronze bracers and a shoulder piece to the outfit. All in all, it was very striking.

The group started towards the city, but before they were halfway to the crops, a military contingent emerged from the open gates. A dozen minotaurs trotted towards them, pikes on one shoulder, their armor glinting.

They came alongside the travelers, flanking them, and moved as an escort and an honor guard.

"It's okay," Kajuun reassured. "This is being customary. We like to be greeting emissaries from four different peoples with a little bit of the pomp and circumstances and be letting our people know that everything is good and in the hand."

Five minutes later, they passed through the gates, towering three stories overhead in a grand arch.

"This city is a work of art," Reggie breathed, his voice full of delight, "look at all white graced with greenery. I love how the ivy vines climb the buildings, giving it contrast and bringing a natural feel to something so stark. And look, fauns and minotaurs are tending the small islands of grass and fruit trees with buckets and pump sprayers. Ingenious!"

"Let's keep moving," Aiyana said, and moved forward, the group keeping up.

Smaller fauns and satyrs ran alongside of the newcomers, shouting cheers and questions, most of them to Kajuun, who appeared to be a bit of a local hero and legend.

They passed through the marketplace, and the differences between here and other places crept into Reggie's awareness.

People, though of a different species, still crowded stalls and shops, buying food, supplies, jewelry, and tools. The storefronts were open affairs, wide and welcoming, and the wares offered were like any other place, but with variations specific to the people of the culture.

Green grocers were everywhere, offering fresh fruits and vegetables. Flower shops had plants instead of cut stems. The clothing offerings were bright colors, and almost exclusively saris or toga-like wraps, with leggings and pants being scarce.

There were no butchers or shoe shops. In fact, there were no leather workers of any kind, and Reggie noted the lack of the acrid smell. It made the city feel cleaner than other cities he remembered from the experiences of Kazzek. Hawkers still called out their wares, though, and metalsmiths still clanged.

They left the marketplace, and the gentle upward slope of the road wore on the dasism, who were still recovering from their ordeal. The two leaned in close to one another, talking in whispers and attempting to be subtle as they pointed out people and places.

The Torck had laid out the city in tiers, reminding Reggie of the rooftops he'd seen from outside the city. Circular streets wound upward to the top of the hill.

Reginald looked everywhere at once, gawking, though his background allowed him to do it with style. His eyes darted between the living culture of a whole other race, and the dazzling architecture that was built for a whole unique body type. The fauns, satyrs, and minotaurs were built to climb, and it showed in the architecture. The Torck had bracketed the low road they traveled with thin, high steps that led to narrow ledges of second or third story store fronts or living quarters.

Aiyana was the picture of collected calm, her staff tucked into the crook of her elbow, and her hands tucked into her wide sleeves. She kept her eyes forward, but Reggie saw her studying the honor guard beside them.

The minotaurs' armor was a thick, woven hemp. The glint and glimmer they'd seen earlier was from metal studs atop circular plates layered at points to protect vital organs, but still allow for flexibility of movement.

Captain Farrell flew from rooftop to rooftop, keeping pace with the procession. Reggie wondered if Aiyana was watching for tricks or traps through the bird's eyes.

Nathan probed at his connection to Jonath, searching for the element of earth. It was all around him, and it sang of unity and completion. That was odd in his head. He was used to human cities, where the stone was dead, as was the wood used to build the structures. Clay tiles were common, but here…they still had veins of connection to the ground, allowing the energy to flow upward in the same way it does in rokairn underground fortresses.

These people had created a civilization that allowed the land to remain within their buildings, rather than being separate.

The priest wondered at that, spinning in a circle while he walked, his mouth hanging open.

Kajuun laughed and dropped a hand to his shoulder.

"Jonath is being here, always, my friend," she said, as if she'd heard his thoughts. "We welcome the wind and the rain also, building so the elements can flow as they would anywhere they are being."

Nathan could only nod and smile.

The palace, the only word Nathan could give the structure on top of the hill they entered, was a work of simple art. The columns of the gates and the city continued here. The outer rooms were open to the sky, with the upper floors only providing partial cover from the elements.

There were no guards posted, either, the ones attending them being the only ones in sight.

Moving deeper into the building, the ceiling closed over them, and Nathan missed the open sky.

Entering what he thought should be the center of the building, the roof opened again. A shaft of light poured from above, making the white stone gleam and glitter with the tiny crystalline shards imbedded in the marble.

Tiers of balconies were above, filled with rows of the populace, and covering the areas closest to the walls. Their honor guard led the group to the center of the open area and then moved to the shaded parts past the albino columns.

A huge satyr stood in front of a stark stone throne. He was larger than most of the minotaurs and dressed in a thick coat and a wide belt, a barbed whip on his side.

To Nathan, the ruler's face seemed cruel, twisted in an expression between a grimace and disgust at the visitors.

"Show respect," Kajuun muttered, patting the rokairn's shoulder.

Nathan stepped forward, in front of Aiyana, and bowed.

It was something they'd agreed upon. Nathan would do the talking when meeting new people. He was better at it than her, and it allowed her to observe and take in everything.

Reginald followed his example, and Aiyana gave a stiff incline of her head, Captain Farrell standing tall and slim on her shoulder, bobbed his head in imitation.

"I am Rauhen, leader of the Torck. Welcome honored guests and visitors," the huge being said, nodding in return, "and speak freely and plainly to your purpose and intentions."

The man's voice clashed with his demeanor, and felt false to the priest, but sounded sincere. The being wasn't a satyr, or a minotaur, or a faun, but something different altogether.

His horns were large and spiraled upward and out, ending in sharp points. He had a long tail, which ended in a tuft, like a lion. His deep-set eyes, and nose, were almost human, with a series of ridges that rose between his eyes and his thick, pointed eyebrows. He stood, his dark brown fur, almost black, and muscles rippling with the grace of a predator.

"I am Nathan, rokairn priest of Jonath, and we come seeking nothing more than knowledge of what happened to the Aeifain to the west."

The chamber fell quiet. The only noise was the shuffling of the people of the Torck on the balconies above.

"Simple, and to the point," Rauhen said after a long pause, "and it is good to hear, but I have to wonder if there is more. A human is among you, and not known for their...good behavior. Then there is an aeifain, which is not surprising considering your goal, but it is surprising considering their fate. And two dasism, who are always welcome as friends, mentors, and allies to our people."

"Oh," Nathan said, stepping forward as he saw both Aiyana and Reginald open their mouths to say something, "yes, that makes sense. That you would be cautious about them. But Reggie—Reginald, the human that is—is different from other humans, and desires to discover things that have been lost, as it relates to...um, peoples of cultures that are lost."

Nathan had to wonder why Aiyana thought he was better at this as he stumbled over his words.

"Aiyana, the aeifain," he continued, and thought his hesitation wouldn't help put this ruler at ease, "she's an elementalist, unlike most of her people. And she seeks lost knowledge—did I say that already?—and doesn't want to disrupt anyone, individual or society, that is."

Aiyana moved forward on one side, making it apparent she was ready to speak. Reggie moved up on Nathan's other side, ready to take over the conversation.

"Ugh," the priest heaved, putting his arms out wide to stop his companions without touching them. "Yeah, this isn't coming out so well. But I hope that shows my sincerity, and that I don't have some speech prepared to make you relax and believe me…"

Nathan trailed off with a sigh and a shrug, still wondering why they had assigned him the job of speaking for the group with new people.

Overhead, the shuffling stopped as the silence stretched out in awkwardness.

Nathan dropped his eyes, noticing the sigils on the throne, silver runes sparking with an inner light.

The leader of the Torck stared at him. The man's nostrils flared, as if he were testing the air for truth, then he shook his head, the short strip of a mane on his neck and head waving.

"Har," Rauhen guffawed, "I think we can help one another, but there will be conditions and consequences."

Chapter 15

They moved through the forest, eyeing the sky overhead. Storm swallows scattered in thick swaths of black spots across the dark clouds. Thunder boomed, promising a challenge for anyone left outdoors when the storm struck.

"No, really," Reginald was saying to Nathan, a few paces in front of the wizardess, "I thought you did fine, and the verbal stumbling came across as authentic."

"Do you really think so?" Nathan glanced at the human, trying to gauge the words. "I mean, it turned out okay, but I don't think that was because of me."

The two men continued talking, and the aeifain lost track of their conversation, her thoughts coming to the forefront.

Aiyana smiled, pleased with how the meeting with Rauhen went, even though it wasn't quite what she'd hoped for. The leader had promised to give them assistance and directions to help them reach the aeifain land, and that he'd deliver the dasism back to their people.

Arkeshia, Treasure of the Sun, and Chevae, Desert Moon, had given each of them an affectionate hug, and a promise of friendship when they met again. Aiyana hadn't even seen the two swept away by a courier and escorted south to their people. She was more focused on what she wanted.

The wizardess was seeking an island enclosed by a looping tributary of what they commonly knew as the

Cracks. The Cracks were a series of wide, but shallow, waterways in the hills between the Grey Wood and the Lower Swamp. Icon Hall—the mythical ruling structure of the Aeifain—was reputed to be in the center of the island. It was not just a single structure, but a building complex.

The Grand Libraries, (she'd seen five of the twelve, the others reserved for those of higher circles within the studies than herself), called to her, offering the histories of magics, and the Arcane Codexis of her ancestors. That was where she'd first discovered the theory for her staff, that night when she'd snuck into the Tomb of the Tome, the Fifth Library.

That series of buildings also housed the College of Studies, which taught everything from a child's first letters to the basics of the society's structure and housed the laboratories of the highest wizards and mages among her people.

"I believe in structure and law," Reginald was saying, "I even embrace it. But I see the need to work outside of such constraints, as well. I guess that's why I follow Parsay Gevies, both of his aspects, luck and dreams, as well as the Walking God."

"Jonath isn't about rigid law…" Nathan held up a hand to tell his chatting buddy he had more to add, "well, actually, he's often seen that way. Senaria is much more about the laws of nature than the laws of man, and much more fluid than Jonath. But even order needs to be changed and rearranged occasionally, and any set of rules that doesn't allow for that are doomed to failure."

Aiyana's mind wandered to the Gallery of Law, the long, thin building that housed the histories of the government, all the books of current law, and the tiered rows of chairs for the ruling council of Icon Hall and surrounding territories. She remembered sitting there, as a girl who'd barely entered her teen years, watching the gathered law makers argue, shouting and banging the hollowed, wooden columns next to each chair.

She reminisced about the seating. The lowest sat in the highest seats, which were nothing more than a railing to rest their rumps on, and a railing in front to hold on to. The aisle was barely enough to squeeze through sideways. Their columns were hardly more than a spindle.

The bottom row of seats on each side of the hall was separated by a carpeted walkway wide enough for two to walk, and the chairs—almost thrones—were up one step. This seating had tables beside each chair for wine and finger foods, and their columns were as wide as the barrel chest of a barbarian (she smiled, thinking of Torrents), and when a lawmaker pounded one, they issued deep booming noises.

All those things—the laws, the histories, the knowledge—should be accessible through a single place, the tower in the center of the city that was the heart of information and ran the entire city.

"You have to let things happen sometimes," Reginald was saying, his hand on Nathan's shoulder, "and other times you take charge and move forward with purpose. The secret is to accept the times you can't do anything and recognize the times you can. And look graceful as you do, like you know what you're doing to those around you, no matter which situation you find yourself in."

"Yeah," Nathan grumbled, drawing the word out, "it all sounds easy, but it isn't. You almost feel like you're lying. You know?"

Aiyana thought about looking like she knew what she was doing. She did that a lot, but she always had an idea of what she was doing. She never floundered.

She knew if she could only reach those hills, cross those rapids, find Icon Hall, get into the structure—that was little more than a smear of a blur in her memory—and find what happened to her people, and recover the bulk of their magical knowledge…then, she'd be prepared to move forward.

"I just want to bring people together," Nathan said, "show them they can work together to make incredible things."

"Yes, and that's admirable," Reginald laughed, causing the rokairn to look up at him suspiciously. "Seriously, I love the idea. But people push to be different while yelling that they want everyone to be equal. They want to stand out, while claiming everyone can do it, but secretly not wanting others to ever be their equal. It's a bidj habit."

The wizardess thought that sort of behavior was something the humans did. Back in her world, humans were the only race, thus the only species who could cause harm and misery for others of their own kind. But they found ways to segregate their own people every chance they got, and then torment anyone different from themselves.

Aiyana didn't see why humans should be any different in this world. If anything, they'd be more like that, because they had other races to cast aspersions on (at best), or annihilate, enslave, and decimate (at worst). She'd already seen it hundreds of times in thousands of ways, small and large, and most of them done to her personally.

She couldn't go on letting mankind treat her like they had. Instead, she'd find what they desired the most, and use it against them. If she had to bring the whole human race to its knees to get them to understand that they were not superior—usually not even equal, and often inferior—to the aeifain, and the other races, then that's what she'd do.

The sky let loose above her, and with a flick of her hand, she redirected the air and water away from herself. It was as if an invisible umbrella had opened over her. The downpour still misted her. Captain Farrell hunched on her shoulder, but the rain didn't drench the aeifain nor the raven like it did their companions.

Aiyana pet the bird absently, thinking about how much she enjoyed having him around. He'd chosen her, not the other way around. It was nice to have someone to talk to, work with, who didn't second guess everything she did. Being questioned or doubted annoyed her. Her actions always showed results, and people should respect that.

She looked at Reginald Betancourt and studied the human, hunching his shoulders in the torrential rains, and pulling his oiled cloak tighter around himself. He was young, mid—or maybe late—twenties, but he walked with a grace of an older man.

Nathan had once explained that older people didn't move with that grace for the reasons most people thought. It wasn't from years of style and practice. It was because moving too fast led to hurting themselves. So instead, those that grew older and wiser would move with deliberate pacing, making each gesture or step a thing of beauty to those of younger years.

That's how Reginald moved, but he wasn't older, at least not in body. He had said something about having been older, or lived a long life, or something like that…hadn't he? Well, he moved like it.

She also watched how he walked, how he placed his feet, and how he reached out for support when younger men would've jumped over whatever was in his path. Reginald had been old once, but he was definitely feeling much better now.

Nathan had been middle-aged and looking at him as he marched stoically forward, she thought this body may be older than his body back home. The rokairn was solid, in body and personality, and never complained. In fact, it seemed like he was talking much less than he'd been before. But that was probably just her imagination, she thought. The man knew how to speak up and speak out if he had something to say. It's not like she'd shut him up. He could stand up for himself and didn't need anyone else's help to do it, not even hers.

Over the last three or so years, he'd grown on her. He wasn't a father figure so much as a…maybe an uncle? An older cousin? A college professor? Yes, that was it. If you could have a college professor of life, but who didn't know they were a professor, and hadn't ever gone to school to learn to teach, that was Nathan.

A guru? Could that be the right term to use? With his calm confidence in Jonath, Nathan was a stable point in the chaos of constant change. His humdrum stories about his grandmother, or ordering coffee at a diner, or making change for money-strapped newlyweds, or any number of mundane exchanges, were all quaint and charming.

The man had no agenda of his own, and Aiyana felt she would know if he did, she'd looked for one. He was simply there, solid and as unchanging as a rock.

The elementalist laughed to herself, thinking how rain would wear down a rock, air could carve it, and lightning would shatter it, and she was all those things.

She stumbled with that thought. Was she wearing him down? Gently pushing him to a point where he wouldn't be what he once was, and instead be something much smaller?

No, she scoffed internally, *I'm not that. And Nathan is…Nathan. He'll be around longer than any human*, she thought.

Her eye fell on Reginald Betancourt, a fop in a graceful body. The old-young man would show his true colors soon enough, and she'd be waiting for him to do so, and would be there to respond in kind.

A deep rumble growled from the north.

Were those the rapids? Aiyana wondered. *They sounded wrong for rapids. Rapids should be, well, rapid, slappy, and chuckling over rocks and sandbars.*

The new sound was much deeper, slower, and louder. She knew that sound, but it had been some time since she'd last heard it. She couldn't remember if it was from her human past or her aeifain one, but she knew it.

The rumble became a distant roar, a misty but solid sound at the same time. She was still debating where she knew the sound from when the memory of what it was bubbled to the surface of her thoughts.

Flash flood.

The trickle of water in the valleys between the hills at the edge of the aeifain lands was swelling, a small wave running along the rivulet. Soon, those low areas would fill enough to create an archipelago with a torrent of muddy waters separating each hilltop.

The two men had stopped talking and walking and were looking in the direction of the sound.

The wizardess closed her eyes, searching for the ley lines with her mind. Air and water were thick here, intertwining above her. She wound her consciousness into the threads of energy, tapping into their power.

Her eyes went wide with the realization of what was coming.

"Move," Aiyana shouted, "we have to get to the lake before we're cut off from Icon Hall!"

The wizardess pushed between the two—the rain letting up on them as she passed—and took the lead.

Nathan squared his shoulders and barreled after the aeifain. Captain Farrell fluttered from her shoulder and lighted on Nathan's head, digging into his thick mane of hair with his claws.

Reggie's hand dropped to his blade as he followed the other two, his long strides allowing him to catch up. He slowed, so he didn't pass them.

Aiyana sprinted down the hill, leaping the widening rivulet, and running up the next slope. Nathan followed, and the two synced in their movements, showing years of working together. The rokairn's hand reached out to steady his lithe friend, and then dropped once she recovered her footing.

Not that she needed assistance often. She was sure in her steps and fleet footed, leaping from hummock to flat parts, turning with gusts of wind. She dropped a hand, her palm out flat, and the sharp current of air ripping between hills softened for Nathan, but buffeted Reginald and knocked him three stumbling steps to one side.

The human's cloak whipped around him. He grabbed it in the center, knotted it, and dropped it behind him to give the wind less leverage and material to grab.

By the time the trio had moved across a half dozen hills, the trickles had become rapidly burbling streams. By a dozen hills, the rivulets were white water streams too wide to leap across.

Raising her staff, Aiyana waved it to her right as she approached a stream that was becoming frothing rapids in the low area they needed to cross. The water slammed into an invisible barrier, rising against it to form a waist-high wall.

"Cross, quickly," Aiyana shouted against the winds.

Nathan did as she said, and Reginald followed, his boots sinking into the wet ground of the small valley. Aiyana moved across, keeping her body facing the blockade that held the water back.

Stepping upon the rising slope, she dropped her arm and the barricade of rain sloshed to the ground and rushed forward past their backs.

They repeated this a half dozen more times, each time the wall of water held back becoming higher, before they reached the edge of a larger waterway.

In the grey mists of the rain, they could see a mass of land across a massive river. The Mighty Mississippi might give this waterway a run for its money, but add in rain and gales of wind that bordered on the intensity of a tropical storm, and even The Big Muddy might have to bow out.

"How the hell will we cross this?" Reginald asked.

"You'll see," Nathan smirked through his drenched whiskers, looking like a beaver surfacing from its pond. "She's in her element, literally."

"That's it, old man," Aiyana said through gritted teeth, "*shower* me with praise, and *rain* down the compliments."

They lost any other words as the wizardess extended her arms above her and reached out her hands. Aiyana grappled with the energy lines above the river, calling upon the forces of nature to obey her.

The temperature dropped and their breath fogged in front of them. Reginald unknotted his cloak and pulled the wet cloth around him, the material stiffening as the moisture turned to ice.

"What's going on?" the swashbuckler asked, his voice quavering with shivers.

"Just watch and be ready to move. Keep an eye on the water in front of us." Nathan pointed at the roiling surface of the river.

Waves lapped against the shore, and Reggie saw them slow. The surface of the floodwaters crusted with slush and solidified into ice. A muddy white disk formed in front of them.

Aiyana stepped onto the slippery surface and waved the men forward with the hand that wasn't holding the staff.

"Come on, and I suggest you crouch once you're on, so you don't slip off. I'm going to give us a push towards the island." Nathan stepped onto the newly created ice floe.

Reginald scrambled onto the rough surface of the ice plate and squatted in the center.

Aiyana stood at the leading edge. Nathan planted his feet on the opposite side, squaring his shoulders and taking a deep, calming breath.

The rokairn reached towards the muddy shore, closed his fist in front of him, then pulled his arm in like he was drawing something towards himself.

A thick shaft of rich, black loam burst from the shoreline, a vaguely human shaped hand at the end, and connected with the back edge of the ice plate, shoving it away from land and into the rapidly flowing river.

"We're free," Nathan yelled.

"I see that," Aiyana shouted back, the ice floe slowly spinning in the current.

She turned around to face the place they'd just left, and threw her arms wide, her staff extending to the east. Slowly drawing her arms closer together, she caused a swell to rise underneath them, propelling them further into the river.

The ice tilted, the leading edge higher than the trailing side, and the three slid on the slick surface.

"Now what?" Reggie asked, crouched, and holding on as best he could.

"Now," Nathan said, "we pray."

Chapter 16

The ice floe cracked when it struck the shore, catching between a few trees. The water level had risen to the tree line, well above the usual watermark. There was no sandy beach, any coastline lost to the torrent of water flashing past the group.

Jumping from the disintegrating sheet of ice, the trio stumbled into the copse of junipers, which provided some small protection from the storm.

Captain Farrell fluttered from Nathan's head to the top of Aiyana's staff. Eyeing the woman, he tilted his head and shook the rain from his black feathers.

Aiyana pulled the hood of her cloak up and looked at the raven. Muttering, she reached up and stroked the bird.

Captain Farrell cawed and leapt to the branches of the closest tree, half flying and half jumping up the limbs to a better vantage point.

Nathan stomped his feet and shook his cloak off. Turning in a circle, the rokairn got his bearings and smiled.

"Good to have my feet back on Terra firma," he said.

Reggie looked between the two, slicking moisture from his short cloak.

"I feel I must ask, and please, forgive me if this is a less than appropriate question..." the swashbuckler paused as the two turned to regard him, "but, Aiyana, if you're an elementalist, why not just dispel the storm?

Why not part the waters and let us cross on dry land, rather than changing the whole environment to create ice that was unstable and foreign to this climate at this time of year?"

"Heh, that's a lot of words for one simple question." Nathan said.

"It might be a simple question, but not a simple answer," Aiyana said, "but I will explain this time. First, I sensed that someone or something had already tampered with the weather, tapping into the ley lines to create that obstruction. I didn't want to fight the power that changed it for control, or alert someone of our presence. It may be a defense of Icon Hall, or someone else who doesn't want us to reach our goal."

"Yes, that makes sense—" Reggie began.

"Also," Aiyana interrupted, irritated at being interrupted, "altering a local ecosystem can create backlash. Either directly as the ley lines fight to maintain what they were already doing, or worse."

She held up a finger to stop Reginald's next question.

"It's like rerouting a river or creating a dam." She continued, "it suits your purpose for the moment, but it can change the whole ecology of an area."

"I've heard about that," Nathan grunted. "I heard there was a river rerouted in…Yosemite or Yellowstone Park, and it made the wolf population drop. That, in turn, made the deer and other herbivore populations explode."

"How could one river do all that?" Reginald asked, his tone genuinely curious.

"Because when the river was rerouted, it went through plains, and the prey species could see the predators coming, so they weren't taken down as much. They, in turn, ate more plant life, which made certain flora die out from consumption, and new trees never grew because they were chewed to nothing before becoming trees, and so on." Nathan explained.

"Wow, old man," Aiyana smiled, "you sounded very educated there."

"Well, I didn't get out much back home, and watched a lot of documentaries." Nathan blushed and shuffled his feet.

A low roll of thunder echoed across the island. All three looked inland, the shush of rain surrounding them.

The island itself was about seventy kilometers long, from southwest to northeast, and twenty kilometers wide, wider at the south end than the north end. The city was on top of the central rise, a hint of a dark smear in the weather, details hidden by the grey sheets of the downpour.

"It'll all be uphill," Aiyana pointed towards the dark blur far away, "my people had terraformed this island. It used to have terraced plateaus every so often, each circling the entire island. It was a work of art, made from the living, breathing network of plants and animals…"

The aeifain trailed off, eyes distant and her mind somewhere else. She shook herself so subtly, Reggie wasn't even sure if he'd seen it.

"It's been a long time," she continued as if she hadn't stopped speaking, "decades at minimum, since anyone maintained it, some erosion and change are bound to have taken place. I don't expect anything more dangerous than a mudslide or a lightning strike until we reach the city. But once there, well, we may face things beyond the word dangerous."

"More dangerous than a mudslide or a lightning strike?" Nathan choked.

"You, of all people, could redirect a mudslide with minimal effort," Aiyana sighed, "and I'm configuring my staff to absorb any lightning into the ground like a lightning rod. Nathan, you and I are essentially like superheroes in this world with our levels of power. We have little to fear. Besides, there hasn't been any ground lightning in this storm yet. Let's get moving."

The wizardess gave action to her words. She stepped out of the shelter of the trees and into the open of the upward sloping plain of grass.

"Yeah," the priest muttered, following the aeifain, "right up until someone finds our kryptonite."

"I have faith, don't you, favored of Jonath?" Aiyana teased.

"Arrogance can be a weakness," Reggie mumbled, then quickly went on, speaking louder. "Where are the gods, anyway? I mean, since they're real here…are they on their own version of Mount Olympus, hanging out on the moon, or in some celestial plane of paradise? And have you noticed that the constellations are almost the same as they were back home, and the moon is pretty similar too?"

"What?" Nathan stopped in his tracks. "Really? What would that mean?"

"It means we should keep moving," Aiyana shouted over her shoulder from in front of the two.

Nathan started trudging forward again, Reggie taking up the rear.

"It would mean that we're still on Earth, our home world, but the differences in the heavens and the craters of the moon indicate that we're in a different time." Reggie explained.

"In the past?" Nathan asked.

"I thought of that, but I don't think so." Reggie said. "I think we're in the future, but my mathematics and astrophysics aren't what they should be to do the calculations to figure out exactly *when* we are."

The two fell silent as they turned into the wind, and uphill, following Aiyana, who was getting much further ahead.

She's in a rush, Reggie thought, *and excited. She knows what we're going to find, at least partially. But I wonder if she knows everything.*

Reggie observed his surroundings with his archaeologist brain. He'd been out in much worse than this. This storm wasn't as bad as most monsoon downpours, and this land was cultivated and tamed, though it had gone wild since anyone had been here last.

Each step sunk into the rich, wet, soil on the soft ground. The lowest plateau had once been a beach. At least that was what Reggie guessed from the traces of sand, and the half-submerged little houses—possibly changing houses, possibly small shelters for weather—that sat in waist-deep flood waters.

The next level up consisted of pines, cedars, and junipers. Three types of trees planted in a very specific order, the pines being the furthest out and acting as a windbreak. The junipers and cedars grew in alternating groupings. All the older trees were in orderly rows, with newer growth at the edges and randomly among the elder trees.

Reginald guessed the aeifain used the pines and cedar for wood for furniture, and the junipers for their berries. Each plateau was a kilometer across or more, and each level up was about a meter higher than the last.

The next level appeared to once have been farming land; wild onions, tubers, and carrots still grew on the flat area. Broken-down houses dotted the distance in the gray rain, showing where the people who'd farmed the land had most likely lived. Open air stables were also in evidence.

The houses were simple, but elegant. The eaves sported curling latticework and carved spirals of wood on every column. Each building had a porch on the east and the west, allowing for seating that was always in the sun or shade, depending on the time of day.

This was a well-thought-out community, planned down to the smallest detail. It had a rural feel, but with the attention to detail of the great cities of Persia and Egypt. It was an odd dichotomy, and something tickled at the archaeologist's thoughts.

"Where did everyone go?" Reggie asked, directing his question to no one in particular.

"That's what we're going to find out." Nathan pointed at Aiyana. "She doesn't remember much from her host body's past, but she thinks she left before they disappeared. She's spent the past three years preparing for this, that, and opening the portal network."

"Portal network?" Reggie looked at the shorter man, rain running down his face.

"Yeah," Nathan nodded, "we opened up a few nexus points. They're essentially underground safe points that lead to a handful of places. But she thinks that the greater mages and elementalists could teleport to anywhere they wanted. She's even suggested that the conjurors had designed a kind of reverse conjuring so they could go places, and that the holy practitioners of specific gods could do it, too. She's not sure if alchemists ever figured out a way, but they're a crafty sort and may have, as well."

"There's five magics then?" Reggie asked.

"As far as we know," Nathan sighed, "but in her research, Aiyana discovered hints of other types. She's not sure if they're lost disciplines, or hybrids of the five we already know."

Reginald wanted to know more, but thought he'd have to ask the wizardess for any true insight. She didn't trust him, though. He'd have to find a way into her good graces, but that would be difficult. That woman carried a chip on her shoulder the size of a sphinx, and he wasn't sure if she'd let anyone close enough to earn her trust.

Maybe the way was through Nathan. He was a good, solid chap, but he was tired. Reginald had seen this before, after the Great War, when he was campaigning with the Legion on the Dark Continent. Men who'd seen too much but went on because they couldn't sit idle. Their thoughts would eat away at them, and they'd...well, give up.

But it seemed Nathan wasn't ready to give up, any more than those other men with their bushy moustaches were back home. They'd found their crusade, and Nathan's was this girl and her mission. It was admirable, and if he could help her, she'd change this world.

The three found a wide stone path that led from the water towards the city. Reggie looked back over his shoulder and could see dilapidated docks jutting into the floodwaters far below.

The plateaus here weren't like the ones in the Torck city. The Rammen had built ridges into everything, and their steps were often knee height, and they'd jump from one to the other. They even designed their rooftops that way, people using them to travel as much as they used their roads.

On the Aeifain island, they'd dedicated the earthen layers to different uses. They passed through flat areas crowded with berry bushes, grapes, and other fruit and vegetable crops, or at least what had once been crops. They also moved through spaces that had probably been grazing land, as well as recreation areas.

Closer to the city, they passed by small, abandoned hamlets. A cluster of a dozen buildings with weathered picket fences, behind which were flowering plants that had gone wild. Ivy covered most of the buildings now, but Reggie thought someone had once tastefully pruned it for shade, comfort, and beauty. Lattice archways buckled under the weight of decades of disregard.

Nathan drew upon the powers of Jonath a few times to calm the natural issues that happen in a torrential downpour—things like the ground turning to slush underfoot—calling upon the gifts from his god to firm up an area or reinforce a dirt wall.

One such area showed exposed baked clay pipes, suggesting that the aeifain had plumbing and sewers that may have matched the era Reginald had come from.

The archaeologist pointed out each of these features as they passed them. Using his experience and knowledge to extrapolate the uses and function of the designs of each place to Aiyana. He hoped to create a bond between the two of them, or a conversation at least.

The woman paid little mind to him, her attention on her goal.

"If she doesn't learn to stop and smell the flowers once in a while, she's going to die young from a heart attack," Reggie muttered.

"You're telling me," Nathan said, "I've been telling her that for years. She's very focused."

"That's an understatement," Reggie sighed.

It took them two hours to cross the terraced plateaus to the city. When they reached the wall of Icon Hall, they stood, staring for more than a few minutes.

It was a massive wall, towering four stories above them, which was quite an engineering feat for any civilization, let alone a world where most things were up to a medieval level of technology at best.

"Magic?" Reginald asked, pointing at the smooth surface.

"What?" Aiyana shook her head to clear her thoughts.

"Did they make this wall by hand, with laborers, or with magic?" Reggie expanded.

"Both." the aeifain looked down the length of the wall, an air of pride in her posture.

"Where's the entrance?" Nathan leaned back, looking down the length of the massive structure.

Reggie looked around, turning in a circle.

"Follow me," he said, walking back the way they'd come.

He led the others back to the closest crossroad and knelt on the overgrown street.

"They had roads," Reggie said, pulling up a handful of grass and exposing cobblestones underneath, "but they're covered. We follow this to the wall, keeping the drainage trenches on each side of us, and we should find the entrance."

They trailed behind Reggie, heading back to the wall, but ending up in a different spot.

"It's here," Reggie said confidently, "but well hidden. We just need to find the keyhole to open it."

He ran his hands across the weather-pocked stone of the wall, stopping at a particular point. With his free hand, he drew out a horsehair brush and some picks.

The others watched as Reggie scrubbed at the rock-face, then picked away dirt and debris from a square stone with a handprint-shaped depression set into it.

"Maybe it got sealed up?" Nathan shrugged. "Maybe I can create an opening large enough for us to get through?"

The priest lifted his amulet and began to pray, but stopped when Aiyana laid a hand on his shoulder.

"No need for that," she said.

Pressing the open palm of her other hand to the depression in the stone wall, she closed her eyes. Her lips moved in silent words.

Nathan felt his connection to the earth intensify, and the power of the element course through his feet, up through his body, and into the wizardess.

The rain stopped like someone had turned off a spigot, a final gray line landing on the surrounding ground. As the sun set, the clouds parted and drifted away.

The stone of the wall softened and peeled away like the curtain of an enormous stage being drawn back for the opening act of a grand production. It made the sound of sand falling in an hourglass, if that hourglass was the height of seven men standing on each other's shoulders.

The gap widened, showing a city within, and a wide street with tall buildings on either side.

Captain Farrell launched into the air, screaming a croak, and flew through the dim opening.

The human and rokairn leaned in for a better look, their eyes drawn to the huge guardians on either side of the passage through the thick stone wall.

Tree-men, the height of four full-grown adults, and about as thick as a man, leaned forward, gnarled hands outstretched towards the trio.

Chapter 17

"Are you sure they've entered the city?" Manalo stopped pacing, his hands clasped behind his back, and looked at Tymere.

"Yes, absolutely." Tymere leaned against a table, idly taking bites from a flap of ham. "I've sent in a bug. You may recall the small insect constructs I made? I have them watching everything they do, and I monitor it on the silver plate I attuned to them, so I see what they see."

Rain pattered on the top of the canvas tent, soldiers rolling up the sides since the storm had subsided. The camp outside had grown, men joining as they picked up stragglers from the small force that the hunted had torn up. More had come from the contingent they'd sent to deal with the dasism, and the small army was becoming a sizable force.

The alchemist had changed—transformed, if Manalo wanted to use Tymere's word—his confidence becoming innate instead of forced; calm instead of insistent. His magical abilities had improved and expanded, blending some of the other schools of magic's tricks into his repertoire.

Tymere stood straighter. His clothes were pressed, instead of being constantly wrinkled. He didn't sweat as much and spoke with confidence. The men were responding better to him, and he almost never raised his voice.

It made the warlord wonder if the man had been playing at being bumbling, nervous, and incompetent, or had finally hit a plateau.

It made the warrior nervous.

"At least the rain has stopped," Tymere smiled, his eyes on the sky, "though I'm unsure if it was the elf's doing, or some other power that had been employed."

The alchemist looked meaningfully at the warlord.

Does he know about my deal? Manalo thought, shifting where he stood. *What am I doing? Jumping at shadows. Nothing has changed. This is all in my head. I'm just worried because we're almost at the end.*

"We're on the brink of winning this, conquering the Grey Wood and ridding it of the vermin hiding under its branches." Manalo moved to the sideboard, covered with food and drinks. "With your sudden epiphanies and new toys, it'll be that much quicker."

The warlord reached for the ham, but then stopped, not wanting to look like he was following the other man's lead. Instead, he reached for a hunk of bread and a wedge of cheese.

Tymere smiled again, watching Manalo choose his fare.

"The men are building the rafts for the ferries," the alchemist said, waving a hand towards the tree line and the river beyond it, "and once they've completed them, I'll strengthen them with my magic, and set the pull ropes on both sides of the river."

Tymere reached across Manalo to pick up the decanter of wine and pour a cup for himself.

The warlord glared at the man, having been reaching for the same decanter.

"Are you sure you can handle the witch?" Manalo asked, his voice unintentionally harsh.

Tymere laughed.

"Oh, yes. Very sure." The alchemist pulled a bunch of grapes from a bowl and sucked one into his mouth.

Chewing, he added, "I know exactly where she'll be, and with the priest blocked from his god by the elven magic of the city, and her being distracted by her search, she'll be easily handled. All we'll have to deal with are the two men with metal weapons and no magic. No warrior will be a match for my power, and the army at our beck and call. Oh, and your sword."

Sucking in a breath between clenched teeth, Manalo held it for a moment, then let it out slowly, forcing his muscles and mind to relax.

"I'm going out to check on the men," he turned and walked out, calling over his shoulder, "you should start getting your toys ready, just in case we actually need any of them. No reason to get cocky, Tymere, that only leads to problems."

The alchemist watched his partner go, a small smile quirking his lips.

Manalo walked away from the command tent, the smell of fresh rain and trampled grass all around. He could hear the shouted orders of his lieutenants and the sharp retort of axes on trees.

He didn't miss how Tymere put him last and dismissed him as one sword.

He wanted to backhand the jackass, who looked so smug and superior. A few weeks ago, the man couldn't make a fireball go where he wanted, but now he thought he held all the cards in this game?

The warlord held one card that the alchemist didn't know about, and that would keep him on a leash.

Never go into battle tense, he told himself. *It only blocks you up, makes you unable to be flexible and roll with the punches.*

Rolling his head, then his shoulders, Manalo heard his joints pop.

He moved towards the sounds of the axes until the clearing where the tent sat disappeared behind trunks and leaves, then he changed direction.

The few soldiers he passed stiffened and gave hasty salutes, watching him.

They still respect me, he thought. *Or at least, fear me. One is as good as the other and will get the job done.*

These men never feared Tymere, and they never would. Sure, they laughed with him, and were happy— even eager—to do whatever crazy thing the alchemist asked. Fetch herbs, chip crystalline deposits from rocks, or even collect a bit of sweat or a drop of blood from each man in their unit.

As if his magic could actually improve their fighting. Alchemy doesn't have that kind of stuff in it.

He kicked at a stone and wound his way between the trees, deeper into the gloom of the forest.

Why am I so bothered by that? The men will listen to me, Manalo Maqsher. I am the Warlord, the commander, and the first and last word that this army obeys.

"You seem troubled, human," a rumbling tenor said from behind him. "Is there something to be concerned about?"

Manalo turned to see an immense man step out of deep shadows of low-hanging branches. Huge, twisted horns on his forehead made him look impressive and fierce, but not dangerous. It was the squint of his eyes, and the tilt of his smile that looked dangerous.

"Rauhen," Manalo bowed his head slightly, "it's good to see you."

"Is it?" the leader of the Torck asked. "What has you concerned, my friend?"

The last two words sounded like an afterthought to Manalo, and even mocking.

"Tymere, the alchemist," the title was added in a rush, creating almost a verbal stumble, "is getting big for his breeches."

"Will that be a problem?" Rauhen asked, leaning forward.

Manalo took a step backwards, feeling like the taller man was looming over him.

"No," he said, a bit too quickly, "no, I have everything under control."

The torck studied the man for a long moment, then nodded.

"Of course you do," Rauhen smiled. "I have every confidence in you."

The smile felt predatory.

Pull yourself together, the man hissed in his mind. *You let that weasel get in your head, and now you're jumping at shadows.*

Or maybe I'm finally seeing what I was blind to before, he thought.

"My scouts report that the three have crossed the river and are completely unaware of our presence." Rauhen put his wide hands on his hips and turned to face the west, his eyes going out of focus as if he could see the enemy in the distance.

"Where are the rammen you promised to help in this battle?" Manalo asked.

"I sent my people away," Rauhen looked at Manalo. "You won't need any extra help, or anyone else to claim the spoils of a war that will take nothing to win."

The leader of the rammen turned to the west again.

Manalo watched him, wondering if that was the only reason the torck sent his people away.

"They are disarming the city's defenses as we speak," Rauhen continued, "and all we need to do is give them time. Four or five days should be enough. We will strike after they shut down all the guardians, opening the streets to our troops. Let the little aeifain get to her tower, discover what we need, and open the floodgates of power. Before she can open access to her rokairn lackey, we will strike. She will be most powerless right before she becomes the most powerful she's ever been. More powerful than she ever imagined possible."

The torck's voice was full of excitement and expectation.

"And once we help you get the city, we get access to their magical knowledge and trinkets, and then we leave," Manalo added.

"What?" Rauhen turned to the human, his reverie interrupted. "Oh, yes. Of course, then you leave with the protection of all my forces. And we will have the forest as our domain, and you will have the plains to the south and all points east. Free to go and conquer your own kind, building an empire that your people haven't seen in generations. If left to grow, it could cover half the continent, and be greater than anything seen in a thousand years."

"I'll always hold you as a friend," the warlord said, placing his fists on his hips.

"I am sure you shall," Rauhen laughed, and clapped the man on the shoulder, nearly toppling him, "right up until your dying day. I shall be the lynchpin of your destiny."

A shadow slipped backwards, away from the clandestine meeting. Kajuun melted into the forest using decades of skill earned the hard way, without magic, and at the loss of many lives on both sides of many battles.

Tymere watched the small raft with six men move into the rapidly churning river. They had six ropes, tied end to end, uncoiling on the deck as they paddled furiously to get to the other side. They were good men, but he couldn't recall any of their names.

The alchemist usually sat with those men, or others just like them. One thing he'd learned in Seawall City was the importance of loyalty.

You didn't get the men to trust you and love you by offering wealth or power. That only made them join you. But no one was loyal to promises or coin. It was the person who made them decide to stick around when times were lean, or the battle hard. It was the leader they loved who made them throw themselves into battle, and even die if that's what it took.

A different campfire every night, and a different group of men each time. Sometimes he asked questions, other times he told stories. It was as simple as knowing his audience.

Tymere's father had been a bit of a rogue and a wanderer. He'd been raised by his mother and apprenticed to a bleeder barber by age nine. He'd picked up a knack for chemistry and had been traded to the local herb and hedge witch by twelve. He was fifteen when he met his father for the third time. His old man was a troubadour, and traveled from place to place, earning coin with tales and songs.

That was when he'd learned how to make people love you with words. It was also how he'd landed a job in Seawall City when his father abandoned him there. It was just a few years before he was assistant to the man who wanted to rule the city, and much more.

All those trials and tribulations, he thought, *taught me when to look the fool, so some other man who needed his ego stroked could feel confident. That's how I came here, with Manalo. He's a coward, and rules by fear. But he lives in that same state, terrified of his own weakness. But my time with him is almost at an end.*

The army crossed the river on ferries before dinner and settled into an abandoned farmstead an hour before dark.

Rauhen had come across on the second to last ferry, but Tymere had crossed on the second.

The alchemist had led the men on the hard march through the pines and junipers, and across the thickets of berries with their thorns. At every leg of the journey, he'd encouraged the men to pick up anything they could eat. After all, an army traveled on their stomach, and they thought of it as a kindness when he provided fresh food, even though it was there for the taking to anyone passing.

After they had set his tent up, something the men insisted on doing for him—though a few weeks ago they'd laughed at him as he did it on his own—he'd insisted they take the house.

A good roof over their head would do them well, he'd told them, and had even used his magics to clear it of vermin.

A simple concoction of herbs, and a high-pitched emitter whistle made every rat and roach abandon the place, and the men lived like warlords themselves. Full bellies and a building to call their headquarters.

At least, that was the idea he'd put into their heads when he offered the ramshackle quarters to them. He brushed off offers of joining them, saying they deserved it for all their hard work.

He wouldn't step into the place. It was old and rotted, and it smelled of droppings and mold. But the soldiers didn't know better.

Yes, he thought, *when it comes down to the deciding moment, these men would follow my commands, not those of the pretender, Manalo Maqsher, Warlord.*

Shortly after the sun had set, a shadow moved hand over hand across the ropes spanning the river. When Kajuun reached the island, the army's trail was a wide swath of destruction. The beauty of the unspoiled land shattered.

She passed within a stone's throw of the encampment, making for the city. She knew she had to get to it first if she wanted her people to survive what was coming. She'd have to bid her time. Revealing her presence too early would cause Rauhen to act before the woman had completed her tasks. Acting too late, and things would be much worse.

Chapter 18

Nathan and Reggie jerked back, looking at their companion to check her reaction, unsure if the giants were a threat or not.

The tree-men lurched forward to duck through the aperture, their leafy tops brushing the underside of the passage. They didn't have legs in the way bipeds did. Instead, one had an extended roots system, and moved as hundreds of dark tendrils propelled it forward. The second guardian had more than a half dozen thick leg-like appendages and lurched in a rolling gait.

They also didn't have two arms, rather, they had a dozen arms. Each ended in twisted fingers that looked like thin branches braided together.

Knotholes along the bark bodies blinked, turning and shifting to look at the intruders of their long, undisturbed home. A vertical crack, about head height to Reginald, split both trunks, widening with a creaking noise. Ropey threads of sap stretched from one side of the jagged maws to the other.

Aiyana had her eyes closed, her hand still on the wall, her lips moving, a melodic and soothing sound coming from the wizardess. The woman didn't react; her face enraptured as she connected to the magics of her people after so long.

"What do we do, Aiyana?" Nathan gripped Marcid in his thick fingers, staring up at the walking trees.

"I don't know how much good my sword and dagger will do against these things," Reggie said, patting the pommels of his blades with a shrug.

One abomination let out a deep groan, sounding like a tree bending in a heavy wind, reaching for the wizardess.

"Okay, then," Nathan huffed, "I'm making an executive decision."

Nathan squared his shoulders, set his feet, stomped forward, dropped his axe low, and swung upward.

The magical vines wrapped around Marcid's haft writhed as the rokairn cut into the guardian. The creature's misshapen wooden hand flew upward in a spiral shower of splinters.

Reggie appeared at his side; the two steel hand axes that Nathan had created from lava in his hands. He chopped at smaller branches reaching towards them, slicing through them with ease. The limbs smoked where the magical blades cut them.

"Hey," Nathan grunted, swinging at the guardian's seeking limbs again, "I know those weapons!"

"Yes sir," Reggie chortled, "not my forte weapons, but I think they're better in this instance. But if you could ever make a rapier and main gauche like these, I'd be eternally grateful!"

"We'll see…" the rokairn's words fell away as clouds of termites flew from the severed branches, and right into his face.

The priest stumbled backwards, sputtering and waving a hand. He swatted at the swarm, trying to clear his vision and mouth of the insects.

"What the hell?" Nathan shouted, clamping his mouth shut as he breathed in the bugs.

"They're infested," Reggie said, pulling up a bandana around his neck to cover his mouth and nose. "You go for their…feet, and I'll get their arms. I think our weapons are better suited for those tasks."

The second guardian reached them, and a dozen limbs stretched out from the two monstrosities to grab the men.

Reggie surged forward, stepping in front of the rokairn to hack through the thin branches reaching for the duo. The limbs cracked and broke, fragile and thin.

"Dry rot?" Reginald asked as Nathan ducked past the man.

"Tell you when they're not trying to kill us," the rokairn shouted, raising Marcid above his head and hewing at one giant.

His blade cut into the trunk, just below the gaping mouth of the guardian, and wet chunks tore away from the core of the monster. Gooey sap dribbled from the wound, and the head of the axe sizzled where it was coated with the viscous liquid.

The two men wove in and out of each other's path, switching places to attack or defend, as agreed.

Nathan glanced at Reggie, noting how the man fought with reserve, pacing himself and looking for the best opening, rather than throwing himself into the fray.

Jack chose well, the priest thought. *He knew this guy would be useful. But I have to agree with Aiyana. Why does Jack do this? Unlike her, though, I don't think there's a malicious motivation behind it.*

The rokairn spun towards the second foe, the one with thick stumps for legs, and his axe passed completely through the limb. The thick supporting leg erupted in a spray of splinters, as well as dark, glistening, wriggling things.

Centipedes and beetles scattered across the ground, and the tree-man reared back like a massive, leafy elephant who'd just stepped on something sharp.

The insects poured from the hole that had once had a leg, landing with pops and clicks on the stone path. They moved away in a wave, reminding Nathan of dripping a drop of soap into a bowl of water with pepper scattered across the surface.

Reggie danced out of the rokairn's view, the magical hand axes flashing in the sunlight.

Reggie screamed, and Nathan turned to look.

The man was hanging upside down by one foot, a tree-man having grabbed him by his ankle and lifted him high above the ground. The behemoth was lowering the helpless man towards its maw, which was bent into a sideways oval, much wider than should be possible.

Insects scurried about inside the hole, some running along the cavernous walls of the mouth, and others moving along the stringy filaments of sap.

Reggie couldn't curl upward far enough to get a clear shot at the entrapping branches, not without risking his ankle.

Nathan charged forward, looking up, knowing he couldn't reach the branch holding his companion. So, he went with option two.

He brought his axe down on the mouth of the guardian, and the scene from moments ago repeated itself, the shattering of the bark and the scatter of insects.

The things didn't react to pain, not in the way other creatures did. They drew back in silence except for the creaks and groans of their branches and trunks. To Nathan's mind it was a scream, but muted and atmospheric.

Reggie slammed into the trunk, right beside the mouth, sliding along the bark towards the opening.

The rokairn looked around for some way to stop the man from being devoured.

The small warrior ducked and ran beneath the monstrosity with the dozens of root legs. Crouching, he swung Marcid and spun in a half circle.

Hundreds of the thin tendrils supporting the guardian were severed, and the thing tilted. Nathan threw himself into a roll in the direction opposite of the guardian's fall.

Coming back out into the open and regaining his feet, he leapt into a thick patch of roots, bounded off it, turned in the air, and brought his axe down on the branch holding his friend.

The limb shattered, and Reggie hit the ground, insects scattering across the road, landing on and around him.

"Thank you, I think?" Reggie gasped, rolling to all fours, and flicking bugs away.

"Let's take them one at a time. Stop splitting our forces." Nathan's voice was a tone of authority.

Regrouping and refocusing their efforts, the two men moved to the other side of the guardian they'd been fighting, putting the tree-man between themselves and the second attacker.

The first guardian spun to face them, but it was a slow process, with a large part of its mobile root system missing.

The two men took advantage of the time, hacking at the trunk, lopping off limbs, and, in general, chopping down a walking tree.

Nathan watched the vines on his weapon twitch and spasm each time he hit the enemy, and he had to wonder if the druidic magic endowed upon Marcid was reacting to attacking something of similar magic.

The knotholes still blinked at the two, shifting and pivoting to focus on them like wooden eyes. It was eerie, and the whole situation didn't seem right to Nathan.

The massive trunk cracked and splintered, and the first foe fell, the rokairn having chopped a large wedge into one side of the trunk, and the human having made a smaller one on the other side with his two weapons.

Reggie vaulted across the trunk while Nathan ducked under it, meeting on the other side to begin the same attack pattern on the remaining tree-man.

Less than a minute later, the two stood among scattered bark, rotted tree chunks, and wilted branches with pale, sickly green leaves.

Aiyana stood in the opening, on the outside part, staring at the scene, her face a mix of horror and wonder.

"What happened here?" she asked. "I only took a few seconds to open the gate…didn't I?"

"No, Aiyana, you didn't." Nathan shook his head and brushed insects and mulch from his beard. "We tried to talk to you, but you were mesmerized, caught up in whatever you were doing. You didn't respond at all. You were…occupied…for about five minutes."

"And these things," Reggie gestured at the fallen tree-men, "were waiting for us, or maybe for you. Because they didn't look like they were coming for us, but for you. We stepped in between you and them and did what we had to do."

"You had to kill them?" The aeifain's voice was sharp and angry. "Is that what you *had* to do? Destroy the guardians of my people's magical sanctuary? Do you think because we shared a few words on the trip here, you're allowed to attack the land of my people?"

The wizardess took a threatening step forward, her staff clacking loudly on the stones.

Captain Farrell descended from the sky with loud caws and flutter of wings, landing on Aiyana's arm holding the staff, and blocking her view with his wings.

"Yes," Nathan stepped between the woman and the target of her ire, "we did. He followed my lead, not the other way around."

Aiyana glared between the raven and the rokairn, her eyes narrow slits. Then she let out and breath and her shoulders slumped.

"Yes," she said, her voice quiet, "you're right. I'm sorry. I'm just tired. Actually exhausted, I've used a lot of power today, with little food or rest, so am a little short-tempered."

The rokairn nodded, the lines around his eyes and mouth creased with worry.

"Shall we close the way in?" Aiyana asked. "The city spoke to me because I'm an aeifain. No one could gain access without being one of my people."

"I think it would be wise to shut it." Reggie nodded. "As a backup, it would keep us safe."

"Why would we?" Nathan asked. "No one knows we're here, and we're powerful enough to ruin the day of anyone who does find us."

Aiyana considered.

"I agree. I think we're strong enough to turn anyone who arrives away," she said, "and as Nathan said, no one is looking for us. There's no reason for anyone to come here. Besides, the city has built in defenses. It created that storm, right? It has guardians, right?"

"Didn't you just shut all those down when you opened the gate?" Reggie asked.

"Icon Hall has stood for a long time without anyone breaching its walls," Aiyana said dismissively. "We'll be fine."

"We should find a place to rest, now that we're in the city." Nathan said. "Now that's settled, can you recommend a pleasant inn?"

They stopped at the first place they found, a quaint but broken-down inn named 'The Willow Way', which was two blocks past the wall. The door was open, creaking on its hinges, and the place was devoid of inhabitants of any kind except a few bugs.

They'd passed other homes and businesses but didn't want to explore and try to find somewhere more suitable. Aiyana didn't want to spend hours looking through places that may not have what they needed.

Nathan inspected the rooms, looking for danger or anything worth using, like beds. The mattresses housed more vermin, and even the blankets were moth eaten. He found plenty of furniture they could use for firewood, and a few oil lamps that still had fuel.

Reginald went into the kitchen to see if he could start a cooking fire, but not expecting anything to be edible that remained in the larder. Any foodstuffs left behind were bad or infested with small black insects. They could eat it, but it would be best to avoid it. Dishes, utensils, and other kitchenware were still in reasonably good shape, and he claimed a skillet and a small iron pot, along with a wooden spoon for his pack. The gem of his search was a working well pump right inside the room. Fresh water for cooking and cleaning would be nice.

Aiyana prepared the common room, moving tables from the center, but leaving one near the fireplace. She gathered glasses and a variety of wine and spirits for them to choose from. Beetles and other insects had bored into the casks holding ale and beer, so she avoided them.

The three bunked down in the common room, wedging the door shut, and shuttering the windows. It was summer, making the room stifling, but the small sense of security in a deserted city was worth it.

"It's eerie," Nathan said after they'd cleaned up their meal of dry biscuits, jerky, and cheese, "the quiet in a city of this size, but the random noises. It's like a giant house, creaking and settling around us."

The three sat around the sturdiest side table remaining in the room, glasses of spirits in front of each of them. The aeifain of Icon Hall were known for their gin, made from the junipers ringing the island, and Aiyana had been pleased to find a few nice, sealed bottles.

"I don't find it that bad," Reggie smiled. "It reminds me of exploring long forgotten ruins when I was young. And there's still birds and bugs, but even the rats have moved on for the most part. I saw a couple, but without a constant renewing food source, most of them are gone too."

"Squirrels," Aiyana said, and the men looked at her. "Tree rats, my father used to call them. But they're still here. Saw some in the trees, they can live off the acorns, and make nests in the attics and such."

"So, what's our plan for tomorrow?" Nathan asked.

"Well, I really want to get to the city center, which is a tower between the libraries and the Hall of Law." Aiyana looked at the two men, and they nodded. "Once I get in there, I can get to work. You two can explore, or whatever, but I really want to get there as quickly as possible."

"Will there be any more of those tree guardian things?" Reggie asked.

"There are more out there," Aiyana sighed, "but we'll take the main routes, avoiding the outer wall and the parks where they usually go to rest and feed on the soil. But considering the shape those two were in, I think that there's a good chance that most of them have…become a *deadfall*."

"Ugh," Nathan moaned, "I knew you *wood* go there!"

"I didn't want to *birch* the subject, but the topic *willow* go where it goes." Aiyana giggled, sipping at her Aeifain gin.

"Puns?" Reggie slammed his whiskey glass on the table, his tone indignant, and the other two looked at him. "Is this some sort of *oak* to you two? I think we should *leaf* the jokes alone and focus on *branching* out our plans."

"Oh, ho!" Nathan guffawed, raising his glass of brandy to the man. "Are you trying to *stick* it to us now? Do you think I'm some sort of *sap*?"

The pun war went on for a while before they settled down to sleep.

Chapter 19

They left shortly after dawn the next morning, before the sun got too high and the heat became draining. Gathering what supplies they could scavenge, each claimed a bottle of their preferred drink to add to their packs.

Aiyana led the way through the streets, stopping frequently to get her bearings. She'd returned to the city where she'd been raised—or at least the body she inhabited had been raised—and tried using the memories that weren't normally available.

"It's like trying to recall a dream from ten years ago," she explained. "It's fuzzy and muddled and comes in bits and pieces."

"Well, I don't mind the breaks," Reggie gestured at the canyon of buildings rising around them, "it lets me study the architecture. It's amazing, because I keep trying to compare it to something from our world, and there are similarities, but it doesn't fit any one specific culture or society at all. It's mind bending to me in many ways."

Most of the businesses were three stories tall, with living quarters above, but the residential areas were two stories at most, and all had yards and fences. The once manicured lawns and pruned bushes had all returned to a wild state, but still held a shadow of the care given to them.

The street was designed with foot traffic in mind, but wide enough for a wagon to move down the center while leaving room for pedestrians. There were no sidewalks, just a wide boulevard. Broken down carts and other transports all faced the same direction, indicating that the entire city layout was meant to be one-way streets when it came to wheeled vehicles.

"With the city's high walls," Reggie explained as the aeifain studied the crossroads, "and all entrances being closed, there hasn't been much cross-pollination of flora or fauna. Winds and birds have carried some things in, but for the most part, it was probably pretty close to what it is now, except much better kept. The ivy climbing the buildings has toppled some of the stonework, but the way your people incorporated the trees into their houses is amazing. It's like full-sized bonsai trees, carefully cultured to a specific purpose."

Aiyana grunted an agreement, not really listening.

The trip from the river to the city had been filled with the new man's knowledge and insight, and Nathan had been fascinated with the comparisons to their world, and how the archaeologist related it to the structures they'd seen.

"Yeah, amazing," Nathan said, so the man didn't feel like he was talking to himself. "The plants grew, and the animal populations dropped."

A small metal object shot across the road, glinting silver in the midmorning light. It was ankle height and round.

It's about the same width across as a white five-gallon bucket that normally holds paint or drywall compound, thought Nathan.

"What was that?" Reggie asked, pointing.

"Hm?" Aiyana grunted again, glancing in the direction the man had pointed. "Scatter can. They're small magical devices used to clean the streets of litter.

Either dirt and leaves, or things dropped by people. When they're full, they drop it off at designated places to be used as mulch or recycled if it's something reusable."

Her voice was distant, like the words were falling out of her mouth and her mind was somewhere else.

"As a kid," she continued, "we used to follow the scatters to the depots, hoping to find any coins they had picked up. I once found a very nice pen knife. Another time, my friend found a beautiful sapphire ring. She kept it since it was of a common design and not marked in any way to indicate an owner."

"She's recalling the memories of her body, isn't she?" Reggie whispered, leaning toward Nathan.

"Yeah," the rokairn nodded, "it looks like not trying to do it makes it easier than trying."

"Like riding a bicycle…" Reggie stopped talking, his head snapping to the right. "What was that?"

Another device zipped from under a broken-down wagon, dragging a metal wheel spoke behind it. Three others buzzed around the corner and stopped, whirring back and forth in a small circle.

"Are they watching us?" Reggie asked.

"Yep," Nathan nodded, and reached for his connection to Jonath so he could mold the metal and components of the machines.

He felt the power of his god rain down towards him, then it stopped, like that rain had hit a window.

"I-I can't reach Jonath," the priest muttered.

"Hm?" Aiyana turned to look at him, returning to the present. "Oh, no, you can't. Not until you're cleared by the priests. They set up a shield of sorts, so magic is muted, unless they clear you for those connections. It messes with everyone. Well, except the alchemists."

"You think you might have mentioned this earlier? We're going to talk about this, but right now, what're we going to do about those?" Nathan pointed at the humming disks.

"Oh, them?" Aiyana laughed, "they wouldn't hurt anyone, their harm—"

The three devices spun and shot towards the trio, whirring in tight circles. Wire brushes descended to scrub the stone street, and small blades slid out of the sides to cut overgrowth that crept into the road.

Nathan leapt on the base of a streetlight, gripping the metal pole that held the reservoir of oil to stop himself from dropping back to the street.

Reggie jumped onto a wagon, and the back tilted towards the street as the rear wheel collapsed from the missing spokes the scatter cans had taken.

Aiyana floated upwards, her feet rising to knee height and well out of reach of the machines.

"That's new." The rokairn pointed at the aeifain with his chin, indicating her levitation trick.

"Yeah," she nodded, "I got access to a few basic things when I connected to the magical network around the city. I'll study what I can and hope to retain it when we leave."

"Now what?" Nathan asked, looking up and down the street.

A dozen more of the machines were moving in from the four streets that converged here.

"Aw," Aiyana smiled, "I think they missed cleaning up. They're just eager to do what we made them to do."

"I think," Reggie's voice was annoyed, "they're a bit too eager."

He pointed at the one closing in on the back of the flat buckboard he perched on. The device spun up to it and started cutting into the wood with the spinning blades extended from its sides.

Aiyana was in the middle of the intersection. Nathan had moved to one street corner, and the wagon that held Reggie was on the opposite side of the road.

The wizardess looked around, stepping forward in the air. She looked up at the tower in the center of the city, which was still quite a way away.

"Can you float us all, like you're doing?" Nathan asked.

"No," she shook her head, "nor could I carry you if you both held on to me. Even if the magic would support the weight, I could not."

"I could run off," Reggie suggested, "and maybe they'd all follow me?"

"I don't think so," Aiyana shook her head again, "they'd probably divide their numbers. And even if they didn't, there's more of them waiting to come out."

"Okay, then," Nathan said, "what do we do? Can you blow them up? Destroy them?"

"No," the aeifain drew out the word, "I don't want to damage my city, and it would only bring more out to clean up the ones we blew up."

"How about a distraction?" Reggie asked. "If these things only want to do their job, let's find a way to give them that. We make some sort of mess, and while they're cleaning it up, we run the other way."

"Hm." Aiyana's mouth curled downward in thought. "What do we use to do that?"

"Blow up a tree? Or a few wagons?" Reggie suggested.

She nodded slowly. "Yeah, sure. That might work."

Aiyana looked around, searching for things she could use for the plan.

"Can you get off that wagon and get somewhere else?" Nathan asked Reggie. "Then she could blow that up."

The human sighed and looked around for how to get that to work.

"Okay," he said, "I think I got it."

He moved to the front of the wagon, and his weight made the vehicle shift, the back end lifting off the road.

The scatter can that was cutting into the aged wood rose in the air, continuing to take apart the back end. Small doors opened on the top of the machine, and metal arms came out, clamping onto the wood.

Reggie perched precariously on the seat of the wagon, the vehicle see-sawing up and down. Leaping into the air, he reached for the metal poles of an awning, the canvas hanging in shredded tatters.

His hands wrapped around the framework, and the wagon detonated behind him. Splinters of wood and metal exploded around him, and he turned his head, tucking it into his shoulder to protect his face.

The machines whirred towards the detritus, blades and metal claws greedily snatching at the chunks of wood and metal.

"No fire? Nice." Nathan said.

Reggie hung above the wreckage, looking down at the half dozen scatters going to town on the pile of scrap. The railing he held groaned, and with a loud pop, pulled from its mooring in the wall.

Reggie dropped an arms-length lower, still holding the awning frame. His feet dangled a hand-span above the hungry little machines, and one oriented on the motion above it.

The device's pinchers came up, seeking the booted feet, and Reggie pulled his legs up.

"Now what?" the man asked.

"Drop and run?" Nathan suggested, laughing.

"What direction are we going?" Reggie asked. "Aiyana, start moving in that direction so I know which way to run."

"This way," the wizardess walked on air, moving away.

Nathan dropped to the ground and trotted after the woman.

The metal Reggie was holding creaked and groaned again, grinding as the next bracket on the wall came loose.

With a shrug, the swashbuckler swung his legs to get some distance and launch himself over the gathered machines.

The awning gave way. He dropped, his legs swinging forward, and landed on his butt on top of one of the scatters.

The machine turned in a tight circle, and the swashbuckler tumbled off into the street.

Three machines spun towards him.

Pushing to his feet, Reggie jumped on top of the closest scatter, leapt to the next one, and then to the street. The force of him pushing off the machine shoved it back into the wreckage of the wagon.

He ran towards the others, whooping loudly, lifting his knees high and leaning backwards, moving away in a comical motion.

"He's like a cartoon character running from something trying to grab his bum!" Nathan laughed again, picking up his pace and passing Aiyana.

She laughed as well.

"Glad you find this amusing," Reggie said, drawing up next to the rokairn, "but remember, I don't have to run faster than them. Just faster than you."

The human picked up his speed and shot ahead of the other two, laughing.

"Damn it," Nathan dropped his head, and pumped his legs and arms to run faster.

Aiyana laughed harder and threw an arm toward another cart. The conveyance shattered with a loud boom, pieces of it shooting across the street behind them.

The tower loomed above them, scatters whirring at the base of the stone steps behind them. The machines soon lost interest and moved on in search of easier cleaning duties.

"Are those mechanical devices?" Nathan asked, watching the scatter cans scatter.

"In a way," Aiyana answered absently, intently studying the path in front of them, "they're one of the alchemical creations. Using the magic of chemical reactions to power and repair themselves. They actually keep part of the trash they pick up, breaking it down and using it to repair themselves on a molecular level."

"Wow," Reggie chimed in, "that's pretty high tech for this sort of world, isn't it?"

"It is, and it isn't," Aiyana said vaguely, "and some of it may be me mixing knowledge from both worlds."

"Alchemy is often underrated and overlooked from what I've seen," Nathan said, "but a few years ago, we ran afoul of one guy who could do all kinds of interesting things with alchemy. I'm just worried about one day someone inventing a gun or something with it. But fireworks, explosives, and so on are all alchemical."

"Is it just chemistry, then?" Reggie asked,

"Not really," Nathan shook his head, "but I suspect that some of the laws of physics are different here, or they've just gone about it in a different way than anyone in our world thought to do. But I also think that the brain developed differently here, and it allows us to tap into forces with our minds that we couldn't in the other world."

Reggie nodded and looked.

The architecture had changed, moving from the blended style of trees, stone, and wood to almost exclusively stone. The buildings were predominantly reddish, but not quite clay or brick. It was still solid blocks of stone, but seamless like the outer wall.

They'd passed the libraries, massive four storied structures that took up a few city blocks each. Set into the walls were glass windows with wooden shutters bracketing them. Arched bridges flowed from one building to another, giving access without having to descend to street level.

Fountains replaced the wells that were common in the center of the streets they had passed through to get here. Statuary was everywhere, in the fountains, in plazas, and along the middle and top of the government compounds.

Shaped to look like aeifain, the middle row of statues on the ledge circling each held a sword, a shield, and a short spear: literal stone guardians. The row that circled the ledge at the top of the buildings held gryphons, monstrous gargoyles, and a few that looked like bulky, squared off suits of armor with weapons built into their arms.

The air was dryer here, hints of lavender wafting from the trees further out, but there remained an underlying taint of dust. Birds weren't as prevalent either, staying mostly in the places where there were trees, like the parks and residential areas.

A massive rose-colored tower dominated the center of the plaza at the top of the stairs. Balconies buttressed by scrolling stonework jutted out from dozens of places. Dried and dead foliage hung limply from the railings surrounding the stone plateaus.

The tower was almost twice as tall as any other building, surrounded by dead gardens, showing where people had once lounged and relaxed. Massive double doors stood at its base, huge carved wooden barriers interlaced with brass and copper that hadn't tarnished, even without maintenance for decades.

Movement caught Reginald's eye, and he turned to squint up the wide, white marble stairs they stood on.

"Did that statue just move?" the archaeologist asked, pointing.

"It's possible," Aiyana said, looking where he'd pointed. "We set up non-living guardians here to help support the militia if needed. You know, in case something happened, like the entire city population disappeared. We should be fine, though; my presence should be enough to keep them in place."

"Wait," Nathan said, pointing at the two rows of statues lining the buildings, "are all of those able to animate?"

Aiyana shrugged and began walking up the steps.

"So, what's the plan?" Reginald asked, following the wizardess. "Do we just walk up and knock? Will a cranky guy with a huge, bushy moustache pop open a little window in the door and tell us we can't get in without a horse of a different color or something?"

"Wizard of Oz?" Nathan asked, the edges of lips quirking upward.

"Felt appropriate considering the company we're keeping," Reggie smiled. "I remember when that came out in theaters. It was only a couple of years ago, and my grandkids loved it. But those flying monkeys scared the hell out of them."

A dozen statues turned towards them, stepped off their short pedestals, and moved to block the way up.

Their smiles faded.

Chapter 20

Statues clumped forward, holding weapons aloft and at the ready, forming a staggered double line across the landing, one flight up. They were statues of heroes, some carved in full armor, others in robes and armed with staves, and still others in flowing garments of politicians bearing daggers.

Aiyana stepped forward, raised her staff, and threw her arms wide. Shouting a word in aeifain, she slammed the butt of her staff on the step in front of her.

A dull boom echoed off the stone of the surrounding buildings—louder than it should have been—rattling windows in their frames and causing birds to take wing.

Captain Farrell crawked and ruffled his feathers, hunkering down on Aiyana's shoulder.

The animated stone figures stopped and lowered their weapons.

Aiyana placed her foot on the next step, speaking in the tongue of her people. The words were flowing and melodious, but she spoke with force and power that made the song of the language sound more like a march. She bit each word off, barking the next syllable, and taking a step higher each time she paused.

"Is that magic, or just the aeifain language?" Reggie whispered to Nathan.

"It's aeifain," Nathan said slowly, "but I think the intention behind it holds more than just commands.

Could be something to do with this place, the same way she opened the wall for us to get in."

The wizardess continued her methodical advance, thumping the stones with the Key of Aiyana every few sentences, as if she were adding auditory exclamation points to her message.

Halfway to the landing where the statues waited, she looked back over her shoulder.

"Keep up," she hissed at the two men, "and stay close."

Reggie and Nathan exchanged glances, both shrugged and bounded up the stairs to catch up.

Reaching the step below the stonework guardians, Aiyana gave another command, and they turned sideways—each facing the center—and took three steps backwards, creating a pathway between them.

The trio walked past the honor guard towards the enormous double doors. The massive entry was deep, polished reds of ancient cedar, offset by traced gilt and gold. Inset panels of the darker wood showed that the softer cedar was a veneer, and the solid walnut underneath had inlays of ivory and silver creating flowing patterns of vines and berries.

The wizardess raised her arms. Creaking and cracking, the two-story portal opened. The metal inlays shifted and slid into new positions, creating new trees of gold and silver.

The line of stone guardians behind the three stamped twice, acknowledging their entrance, spun on their rock heels, and returned to the pedestals and alcoves to await the next threat.

Stepping forward, the trio crossed the threshold. The temperature dropped, shedding the oppressive heat and humidity that comes with summer and the closeness of trees to a subtropical region.

"It's cavernous," Nathan whispered. "This hall would challenge even the grand halls of Tariluine of the Rolling Mountains."

His opinion carried weight as a rokairn, one of the mountain folk, who knew impressive stonework.

They'd seen the depth and breadth of the structure but didn't truly realize the immensity until they'd stepped inside. The ceiling was over two stories above them, and showed a series of etched frescos, each image separated by a short wall jutting from the high dome.

The walls were long alcoves, extending from floor to ceiling, with three individual platforms spaced at regular intervals in each. A statue of a bird of prey occupied the topmost level of each. A dozen hawks, eagles, and other raptors looked down at the circular floor. A shimmer of color and form moved across the alabaster forms in the uppermost alcoves.

"Illusions," it was Aiyana's turn to whisper in wonder, "they've covered the constructs in illusions!"

The floor was a checkerboard of rose and aquamarine, but giant game pieces sat in place on the appropriate squares. Knights, rooks, bishops, pawns, kings, and queens hovered a hand span above the tiles, each with a very real and dangerous looking weapon in their hands.

A passage was open across the gameboard, showing a hallway out of the round tower, and stairs led up in two passages, one to the right and one to the left.

"Looks like the engineers of this tower had a bit of humor," Reggie said, a bit too loudly, and the sound of his voice echoed. He continued, quieter, "Sorry, is this a challenge we have to beat, or what?"

"No," Aiyana chuckled, "but that would be funny."

"It's like in that brand new book that just came out," Nathan said. "What's it called? Oh, yeah! Harry Potter and the...something. But people are going crazy about that book, and some kids at a magic school have to play chess to get past a thing. Or something like that."

The other two looked at him, and the rokairn shrugged.

"I heard the author is writing more in the series, in case you're interested," he mumbled.

"Great, I'll look it up in thirty years...if I ever go back," Aiyana's tone was sarcastic, but then grew serious. "Heck, if I get back, I'll look you up and try to stop that guy with the shotgun."

"What guy with a shotgun?" Reggie asked, looking back and forth between the aeifain and the rokairn.

"It's how I died, back home," Nathan shrugged, "or at least, I guess I died."

"Ah..." Reggie drew the word out slowly, then turned to Aiyana. "And you?"

"Race riot in Chicago in sixty-six," she said nonchalantly.

Reggie stopped in his tracks.

"1966?" the archaeologist asked.

"Yup," Nathan laughed, "and I took buckshot to the gut in 1997. So, if she ever went back and lived, then she could come find me and warn me. Weird, right?"

"And if I went back, wait...can we go back?" Reginald asked.

"Jack Tucker," Aiyana spat, "is toying with us. He apparently offers for each of us to go back at some point. I can't wait to see him again, and…"

She trailed off and lifted a hand to point at the level between the ground and the shifting raptor statues.

"Mirrors," she pointed, her eyes staring upward, "but they aren't showing this floor. They're showing…somewhere else."

"Security cameras? But two ways?" Nathan suggested, and both glanced at him.

"In my day," he started, then hesitated. "How do I put this, so you'll understand? Okay, it's like a television—"

Reginald shook his head, showing that it didn't exist in his era, and he didn't know what it was.

"Lemme try again," Nathan said. "Movies, moving pictures, came into homes in the 1950s, like radio, and everyone had more than one in my day. Most had nineteen-inch screens, though some had larger, and others had projection televisions which were…"

The rokairn held his arms out as wide as they'd go.

"This big, or larger, my arms aren't really long enough," he continued. "It was like a personal movie theater in your house. Anyhow, they had live camera feeds of places for security. They'd watch for problems."

"That's huge!" Aiyana said. "My parents had money, but we still only had one, but it was in color!"

The three stared up at the mirrors, which were each a meter in height, and about half that in width. Each one showed a high-back wooden chair that sat empty.

"Let's go," Aiyana said, breaking their individual memories, "we have things to do. Once I'm in the top chamber, you two can explore anything you want, and bond over…whatever."

She walked forward, and Captain Farrell launched off her shoulder. Neither of the men knew if the raven had done it on her command, or of his own volition.

The raven flapped upward, circling the room, then dove through the exit to the stairs. The bird landed on the floor between the stairways and looked down the hall that led into darkness.

Moving further into the room, globes of light flickered into brilliant white bursts in the alcoves as they passed, tearing away the shadows to reveal the hidden corners. Peeling painted scenes were in each nook, showing heroes, battles, and other significant events.

The woman stopped at the base of the steps, each winding in opposite directions, leading up.

"We go our separate ways here," she said, "and if you have some patience, you should know when it's safe. In the meantime, you can roam the city without threat or danger from the defenses."

"We should go with you—" Nathan began.

"No," Aiyana cut him off, "this is my home, and you coming with me will just divide my attention. I don't have the time or energy to protect you or stop you from stepping in the wrong place. Please, listen to me. Trust me. I need to do this next part alone. I'll come to you when I'm done."

Nathan sighed and shifted from one foot to the other, lowering Marcid from his shoulder and settling the haft of the weapon on the stone floor.

The rokairn nodded, and Reginald looked at him, then nodded as well.

"But don't forget to unlock whatever is blocking my ability to call upon Jonath, okay?" Nathan said.

"I promise," Aiyana nodded, waving absently, "I won't forget."

Aiyana reached the uppermost floor, having ignored the two other landings she'd passed.

The floors were shorter than the ground floor, barely three meters tall. Compared to the ten-meter-tall bottom level, these levels felt cramped in comparison.

She knew where she was going, but wasn't sure if it was her body's memories, or because of her mental journey into the magical latticework of the city she'd taken when she'd opened the outer wall.

The men didn't know, and couldn't understand, what she'd done while they were fighting the tree guardians at that entrance into the city known as Icon Hall.

The name of the city was much more than a name. It was a title. This was where the Aeifain had come after leaving the west a couple thousand years ago. Sure, they'd had the peninsula with the hourglass mountains—a waypoint of the portals that had been discovered by a group of adventurers some hundred years ago—but that was more of an outpost.

Was it a hundred years? Or more? Less?

She shook her head.

It didn't matter. She wasn't there, but she felt the destruction of it in the aftershocks of the Talisman.

Most of the aeifain had fled across the oceans to their homeland. But some had stayed here, a contested decision by her race.

A few strongholds of her people remained, repositories of knowledge and power, and Icon Hall was one of the handful that hadn't been overwhelmed, destroyed, or abandoned.

Aiyana could feel the emptiness of her missing people, and her gut ached with the void. It was odd though, because her conscious brain didn't know these people, but her vague impression of the past held the aeifain in high importance and regard.

Her human memories battled with the aeifain brain she currently inhabited.

Move forward, child, that unseen presence whispered in her head. *You must hurry before the others come and take the power.*

She pulled herself together, discarding the pressing emotions, shifting to the thoughts that weren't in the forefront of her mind.

The room at the top of the stairs was circular in more ways than one. She'd passed through the observation room—a dozen small palm-sized mirrors showing the lower level where Nathan and Reginald moved through the statues that were game pieces, observing the art and architecture—arriving at the place where the…archmagius?

Was that the right word? She wondered.

Yes, it is, she thought. *The archmagius would sit in this room, that now stands dusty and empty in front of me, and manipulate the magics of the city.*

The room was a blend of a government dark site and a magical laboratory. It felt like there should be G-men standing on each side of the door, and a black limousine waiting downstairs. But only if the square-jawed muscle had a wand in a holster under one armpit, a gun in the other, and a bracelet of charms on one wrist, to balance the gleaming silver watch on the other.

Built into the walls on three of the four sides of the room were long, wide tables. Crystal orbs flashed winking lights throughout the city, and polished panes of silver displayed vistas of plazas and open spaces.

Aiyana settled into a tall back chair with a padded seat and back. The magic drifted over her, enveloping her consciousness, and she pulled it around her like a warm blanket. It spoke to her aeifain side, responding to her thoughts and feelings.

Her mind connected with the city again, as it had at the gates. But this time it wasn't just the city defenses she could feel. It was the whole of the aeifain knowledge.

She gripped her staff, opening channels of power within the magical artifact to store that knowledge, and began searching through the magical chronicles for arcane knowledge and the histories surrounding them.

It would take days, but soon the Key of Aiyana would hold the ability to open portals anywhere, as well as the ability to access all the magical paths.

The promise she made to Nathan slipped from her, and she dove into learning about her people.

Nathan and Reggie were like kids at recess. Though Nathan was well past forty in the 'real world' and Reggie over seventy, they ran through the streets, laughing and doing what only could be called frolicking. They explored hidden recesses and open spaces alike.

Reggie insisted on looking for libraries and exploring the abandoned structures, explaining that this had been his life's work. To learn about extinct cultures was paramount to his nature. He scribbled notes into a small notebook he'd found, adding questions to ask Aiyana later.

After a day of this, Nathan insisted they should check the 'common folks' dwellings to learn more about the people who once lived here.

Moving through people's homes, they held up tattered clothing, cookware, and portraits to one another, making inane comments. They swung from light posts and ran across rooftops, avoiding the scatters on the street below. They mocked the gargoyles and heroic statues, drawing eyebrows, moustaches, and goatees in dark indigo inks they'd found in dyers' shops.

It was days of freestyle bliss like they'd hadn't experienced since their early teens, and they bonded in that time, doing things together that 'real adults' would have never done.

The two men stopped in the tower occasionally to check on Aiyana, offering food and drink. Engrossed in her task, she sometimes grunted and waved them away, but rarely responded.

On the fourth day, they sat under a tree in a raised mulch bed filled with wildflowers, sharing a lunch.

Reggie made a horrible pan bread—that he claimed everyone loved—over an open grate fire on a cleared area, and Nathan compared to it eating Plaster of Paris with a hangover, which both men had more than once in the past few days.

They were nibbling on pickled fish, pickled eggs, green-veined cheese, and pickled sausages they'd found in a noble-esque home they'd explored. Perhaps it was good canning skills that kept the rations edible, as Reggie argued, but Nathan thought it was a magical enhancement.

Five scatters bumped against the squared-off wooden barrier around the tree, and a family of something akin to flying squirrels had arranged themselves on the branches above, competing with a particularly buff and angry group of pigeons.

The two men leaned against the trunk of the tree covered with greenery, vines, and the scent of jasmine mixed with something that smelled very citrusy. Small, reddish fruits hung above, thick skins protecting them. Reggie said it was like a cousin of the mango had had a threesome with an apple and an orange, but neither had worked up the drunken courage to sample one.

The birds and 'winged tree-rats' above weren't eating them, and the two men took that as a warning.

They were bickering, sort of, comparing Marxism to creating things with magic, the heated exchange intermingled with sloshing more drink into their respective drinking vessels. Nathan settled on a steel brandy snifter, and Reggie took to carrying a metal flagon with a thumb-operated flip top.

The gentle rumble and the echo of noise bouncing off the buildings went unnoticed…at first. Dozens of armed men interrupted their debate, coming into sight with shouts of battle cries echoing off the buildings. The two friends stared bleary-eyed down the street at charging men with raised swords rushing towards them.

Surrounded and bound before they even thought to reach for their weapons, they dropped face down in the wildflowers beside them.

Led away from their place of comfort, and to the enemy camp just inside the walls of the city, they could only guess what was in store for them.

Chapter 21

Nathan stared at his hands strapped to the chopping block. His head spun in a fog of alcohol, trying to sort out his thoughts. His face and head felt cool, and the rokairn remembered someone roughly cutting his beard and hair with a dagger. Scattered clumps of hair jutted from his scalp, cheeks, and neck.

Reggie hung by his hands—his toes barely scraping the wooden planks of the porch—from the overhead beam of the inn the army had taken as its makeshift headquarters. They'd stripped the human down to his breeches, beaten him with axe handles and scourges until blood and bruises showed along his ribs, back, and legs.

A vaguely familiar bearded man stood over Nathan, Marcid balanced on one shoulder.

"Tell us," the man said, "or we'll take your hands and melt them down, like we did with your holy symbol. Your god can't help you within the shielded confines of this city."

"Manalo?" Nathan croaked, his voice hoarse. "Tell you what? I haven't seen you in years."

"I won't repeat myself!" The warlord shouted and kicked the rokairn in the face with a muddy boot.

The priest's head jerked back, but the bonds holding him to the chopping block moved to the middle of the street stopped him from falling.

A ragged cheer mixed with rough laughter rose from the men surrounding them.

"Stop it! You haven't asked him anything!" Reggie screamed from where he hung. "You're going to kill him!"

A huge bald man stepped behind the swashbuckler and swung a weapon with a half dozen knotted leather straps at Reggie's back.

Arching his back, he screamed, the device tearing his skin and reopening wounds.

"Just tell us what you want, and we'll talk!" Nathan shouted, trying to interrupt his friend's punishment.

"Don't play stupid with me, dwarf! Tell me what I want to know!" Manalo shouted back.

The man laughed, a short, harsh bark. He walked in a circle around the chopping block and the rokairn.

"I'm tiring of this," he said, raising his head to the men gathered around the gruesome scene. "Who else is getting bored with this?"

He brought his free hand to his ear, cocking his head to listen to the shouts of agreement from his audience.

"Who wants to see some blood?" Manalo stopped in the same place he'd been before, raising and twirling Marcid in a slow circle at his side.

The men shouted, stomped, and banged weapons on shields.

"Who wants this priest to give them a hand for all the hard work of taking this city?"

The crowd roared again.

No one noticed the solitary figure on the rooftop a block down the street, lying flat to remain unobserved.

Kajuun moved to the back of the building and dropped into the alley, making her way towards the tavern.

The warlord raised the magical, double-headed battle-axe above his head, gripped it in both hands, and held it there.

"Get the branding iron ready so he doesn't bleed out," Manalo shouted, "and let's hear some noise for this gift which the priest is about to bestow upon us!"

His men started chanting his name.

"Man-a-lo! Man-a-lo! Man-a-lo!"

Manalo Maqsher brought the axe down in an arc towards the chopping block, the vines on the shaft quivering.

Tymere smiled. He stood at the base of the tower, looking up at its pristine surface.

Arrayed behind him were three dozen soldiers, glancing nervously at the statues around them. The guardians shifted but didn't advance.

"Do not worry," Tymere said in a raised voice, "the witch has subdued them, made the city safe for her little friends. I have her scent, and we will control all the magic of the city soon enough. You will all be heroes in this battle and won't even need to raise a weapon."

A murmur went through his men, some of them agreeing, others nervous.

Tymere adjusted his device, a brass and wood box with switches and dials, and it crackled.

The alchemist checked his vest and bandolier. A hand crossbow hung from each hip, and a dozen quarrels lined each strap of the leather belts crisscrossing his chest. At the bottom of those were bottles of the mind-numbing chemical that would cloud the wizardess's mind.

A wide leather girdle held small metal canisters that would create a fog that made people choke, and a breathing mask—which had the appearance of a crow's head—hung from his front like a macabre codpiece.

Strapped to his thighs were thick metal wands, and a coil of conduit wound to a chemical battery attached to his back. This could shock someone and render them senseless.

The largest advantage of the magic of alchemy in this city was that the shield restricting magic did not block it. All the arcane energies were already instilled in the devices and components, so his powers weren't blocked because he wasn't drawing on any outside source.

All the gear was overkill if things went right, but he'd rather be loaded for bear, then unprepared.

Manalo had mocked him, saying he looked ridiculous, but Tymere didn't care. One way or the other, the warlord would be at his mercy soon enough.

The one ace in the hole the man thought he had was up the alchemist's sleeve. Rauhen had come to Tymere and told him he'd rather the humans be led by someone who understood and wielded magic. The leader of the torck people claimed the idea of a simple man of violence leading the way into the new era was short-sighted.

Not that Tymere trusted the horned ally, and neither did Manalo—one of the few things the two humans agreed on—but he was a means to an end and would be a problem to deal with later.

The alchemist smiled and stepped into the building, following the crackling of his machine, following the energy of magic, following the path taken by Aiyana and her magical staff that would change the world.

Aiyana felt the world open to her mind. Locations of static portals popped into existence across the city, and the Grey Wood. The continent followed, and in turn, the other six continents and the ocean archipelago.

A weary smile crossed her face, and she sighed, slumping in her chair.

She'd spent three days scouring the archives for the knowledge she'd needed to do this, a day opening the portals, and had another couple of days of work to find the remaining information about her people to locate them.

She took breaks to eat, drink, and move her bowels, but hadn't slept. When she was inside the network of information, it was like sleeping anyway. Her body was well rested, but her mind was exhausted. This was still much easier, and quicker, than going through thousands of books in the libraries.

Aiyana sat up and wondered what to do next. A mischievous grin spreading across her face, she decided to spy on her friends. She'd have plenty of time to do the other stuff now that she'd done the hard work. Oh, and take down the shield blocking Nathan's magics; she hadn't done that yet.

Captain Farrell was her first thought because he was the way she usually spied on people. She felt him, in the west, sunning on a branch. Then she remembered she'd already linked to the quickest way to find anything in the city.

Opening the conduits of energy to eyes of the statues and reflective plates throughout the city, she searched for Nathan and Reginald.

She knew she could do it with her staff after she removed the shield and toyed with the idea. Reggie had suggested the magical network would be like the sewers—disgusting comparison, but aptly put—and would interlace throughout Icon Hall. Her mind wandered with that thought, filtering through the magical files and waypoints that acted almost like aqueducts for the flow of arcane within the city walls.

"Oh," she muttered, "this is easier than I thought!"

She'd already attuned her staff to the information, and to give it remote access wasn't anything more than changing this one gateway, so it went both ways.

Smiling at her cleverness, she shifted her attention to finding her friends. She sought movement, leaning back, her eyes closed and her awareness within the system of magical surveillance.

"Hm, that's a lot of movement. What're they up to?" she giggled.

Focusing on the activity, pictures formed on the various receiving mirrors in the room. She opened her eyes and gazed amusedly at them.

Three mirrors showed dozens of soldiers moving around the base of the tower. A single mirror revealed a satyr slipping into the back of an inn and disappearing inside. A half dozen others displayed a group of men around a short wooden chopping block, chanting and thrusting weapons above their heads. A bearded human with rippling muscles was raising a double-bladed battle-axe over his head. Nathan was below the blade, bound to the wooden block.

"Holy bidj!" She sat bolt upright. "We've been invaded."

Her hand gripped her staff, and her mind whirled.

"I need to activate the defenses!" She shouted to the empty room.

Her hands shot out, looking for something to do. Forcing herself to stop, she calmed her mind and stilled her body.

Slipping back into the network, she sought the nodes that controlled the guardians. Dim pulses of light showed they'd been deactivated, and she pushed magical energy into them.

She felt the statues animate, but they were slow, sluggish, as if something limited their abilities.

"The shield!" she mumbled fiercely.

Shifting her attention, she sought the anchor points at the gates at the cardinal points of the outer wall. That was where the shield generated from, drawing on the ley lines under and around the city to fuel it.

She flicked ethereal switches, halting energies from passing the city walls, but those within could access their magics. It had already been set so energies could pass out of the shield, but nothing could be used within the limits, so it hadn't mattered.

She felt the staff, and her awareness, blossom with the connection of the arcane. A trickle of energy poured into the location where she'd seen Nathan strapped to the chopping block, the axe descending towards him.

A torrent of magical energy pulled her attention to the north. Someone…or something…there was drawing in a lot of power. Focusing on that direction, she sought to pinpoint this new threat.

She felt a biting pain in her arm, then another in her neck, bringing her back to the present.

Her hand, that wasn't gripping her staff, shot to the place where it hurt, and she fingered the small shaft with feathers embedded in her neck.

Wrapping her fingers around it, she tried to pull it out, but her hand had gone numb and gripping anything was difficult.

Spinning in her chair, she saw a man covered in leather belts and bottles. She knew him, and that thought triggered the memory of the man standing over Nathan.

Bottles shattered at her feet, acrid fumes rising to invade her nose and mouth.

Who were these men? She thought, consciousness slipping from her, and she collapsed in the seat.

Tymere smiled and stepped forward to retrieve the staff that had clattered to the floor when the woman slumped over the arm of her chair.

He bent and picked up the magical artifact. Sparks flew as he wrapped his fingers around the shaft. Images and knowledge flooded through him. He gasped with the intensity of the mental barrage.

"Sir? Sir?" someone said, shaking him. "Are you okay?"

"Yeah, fine, soldier. Unhand me and secure the prisoner and the perimeter."

"But sir, you were just standing there for almost ten minutes. We were worried. The prisoner is unconscious, but we've bound her hands and feet and gagged her," the soldier said, stepping back.

"Good work," Tymere nodded, his vision returning, "and the perimeter of the tower?"

"Secured, doors shut and barricaded. Men on the walkway around the entrance, armed with bows. No one will get in," the soldier reported.

"Well done," the alchemist nodded again, "now remove her and give me some privacy. I need a few more minutes before I am ready to leave."

Settling into the chair, Tymere watched the soldiers drag the unconscious wizardess from the room. Holding the staff, the Key of Aiyana, the alchemist opened his mind to the power and potential it held.

Tymere grinned.

Manalo held the axe high above his head, his eyes wild and angry. The circle of men chanted his name, and he knew that everything he'd worked for, struggled to achieve, would soon be his.

No one would stand in his way. He'd already destroyed the dasism in the south. The most powerful force in the area—Rauhen—backed him. And his lackey, Tymere, was about to claim the power of the magic in the area.

The three people who'd stood in his way had become his pawns. They did all the heavy lifting for him when they tramped through the forest, fought the defenses of the storm that protected the city, and then opened it for him. It was just waiting here like a fruit waiting to be plucked. He only had to come in and do a little cleanup, and the city of the lost elves and all their magic would be at his beck and call. He wouldn't rule a lone city or even just a region. With this much power, he could conquer the eastern seaboard—including Rauhen and his people—from the northern barbarians, the magical wastelands, Seawall City, and Land's End now that they'd cleared the demons out.

Which meant destroying his enemies.

Marcid came down, cutting into the flesh and bone where the rokairn's hands met his forearm, severing both of Nathan's wrists.

In response to the blow, the vines on the weapon shuddered. The axe rang as Manalo pulled it free, and a dissonant tone rung with uneven vibrations.

The dwarf fell backwards onto his ass, and four men rushed forward. Lifting the priest to his feet, the guards forced his arms out in front of him.

Blood shot across the chopping block in short, rapid spurts in rhythm to the small man's panicked heartbeat. The rokairn's hands scratched lightly at the wooden surface as nerves reacted.

The big, bald man who'd been whipping Reggie on the porch just a minute ago rushed forward, a branding iron in his grip, and pressed it to one of the priest's stumps.

The flesh hissed, a cloud of steam puffing out as the red, glowing metal seared and cauterized the rokairn's injury.

Nathan's knees went out from under him, his head falling back, and he screamed. The men on each side of him held him up as the man pressed the red-hot poker to the other wrist.

The ground rumbled, and men looked around nervously.

Manalo gritted his teeth in a smile, and turned in a circle, the magical axe held above him. A drop of blood fell from the blade and stung his eye. The warlord blinked it away as movement on the porch of the inn where the second prisoner hung caught his attention.

A figure slid across the shadowed decking, cutting down his men. A half dozen soldiers fell in quick succession, blood filling the air.

Manalo wiped at his face, trying to clear his vision. One rammen whirled in place, a broad sword slicing through the soldier. A blurred form of steel, fur, and plates of leather armor cut through the guards surrounding the prisoner.

The strung-up enemy dropped to the ground as this new threat cut his bonds. A belt with weapons and two packs hit the wooden slats in front of Reginald, and he reached for them with a determined grimace.

Kneeling on the wood porch, Reginald looked up to see Kajuun smiling down at him. The newly released prisoner picked up the belt and wrapped it around his waist as the rammen defended him from the onslaught of soldiers rushing the porch.

"Kill them!" Manalo screamed, pointing at the two in front of the inn with the magical axe.

Men surged at Reginald and Kajuun. The four men holding the rokairn dropped him to his knees and joined the rush.

"You're insane," Reggie wobbled to his feet, "and you're probably going to die."

"I am not thinking the same as you," Kajuun said, "because if you do not be protecting me, then you and Nathan will both be dying."

Their conversation ended and Reggie slid his rapier and main gauche from their scabbards with shaking hands.

The swashbuckler blocked a short sword with his parrying weapon and fell to one knee. The attacker looked down at the slim blade Reggie thrust through his abdomen.

Manalo clenched his teeth and hissed, echoing the same sound that had come from the wrists of the priest at his feet moments ago.

The air shimmered, and the sky shifted, becoming sharper and bluer. The rokairn surged upward under Manalo's gaze, his chest puffing out and his arms flying wide.

Nathan sighed.

"Jonath," the priest muttered, "bring me the weapon you granted me with the blessing of Senaria. I call Marcid to defend me in this time of need."

"You're a pemtie," Manalo said, turning to the priest.

The warlord raised the axe to strike and swung the blade down at Nathan.

Vines writhed down the haft of the weapon, wrapping around Manalo's limb, and burrowing into the man. His arm bent, and the blade turned in his grip, falling towards him.

Manalo screamed and threw the weapon to the side. Tendrils clung to him, and the axe fell straight down, cutting deep into his calf.

"Jonath," Nathan continued, "I beg of you, with the power of the earth and the power of growth of crops and plants, return my hands to me."

Marcid dropped from the warlord's calf, falling at the priest's feet. Nathan reached forward with his stumps and gathered the weapon to him, cradling it in the crook of his elbows.

The vines tore from the human standing over him and wrapped themselves around the priest's forearms.

On the porch, Reggie stood and thrust his rapier into the eye of another man. He pulled his blade free and took a step forward. Stopping, he reached down and pushed each blade through the straps of the duffel and backpack at his feet, pulling them to his elbow and shrugging them onto his shoulders. He winced as they hit his bruised and torn ribs and back.

Kajuun whirled in front of him, blocking a blow from a spear, and slashing a second man across the throat.

The shirai leapt from the porch into the mass of a dozen soldiers rushing towards the swashbuckler. Hooves met one man's face, and another's chest. Bone crunched and the two men went down, rolling away with shouts of surprise and pain.

The satyr tucked one sword under an arm and pulled two daggers from her waist, throwing them into the oncoming attackers. Two more foes fell to the cobbles of the road.

"You could have carried these better than I could," Reggie complained, pulling each strap over his head with the hand holding his parrying dagger.

"Yes, that is being a truth," Kajuun said, slashing a double stroke across the abdomen of an attacker, "but you are being broken and hurt, and I am not so. It is better that you be slow than me."

Nathan took a deep breath and rose to his feet, Marcid attached to his arm by vines that grew and dug into his flesh. Each step steadied, and where mud had coated the stumps, crusts of rock grew on the torn skin at the end of his wrists.

"Reggie!" the rokairn shouted. "Quit your whining and come to me!"

"Roger that, boss," the human shouted, stumbling down the two steps to the road and falling to his knees with a grunt.

Three men closed on the swashbuckler and the priest, each swinging long swords.

Kajuun covered the human's retreat, blocking and striking at the men pouring from the inn.

"Hands of stone!" Nathan shouted, his voice cracking.

Columns of stone burst from the street, connecting with each of his attackers, meeting flesh, and shattering ribs and groins.

"You're all—" Reginald's words cut off as he thrust with his rapier into the eye of one man, parried another blade with his main gauche, and twisted past the third blade.

Reggie grimaced when the second man punched him in the face, and he responded by shoving his main gauche into the man's chin and into his brain.

Pushing the surprised soldier into the third man, Reggie slashed across the remaining man's face, slicing through both of the soldier's cheeks.

Nathan squared his shoulders, set his feet at shoulder width, and spoke.

"We're not gonna win if we stay here," he said through gritted teeth. "We need to get away."

The ground shook again, and something huge and leafy blocked the sun. A massive form of a tree-man lumbered forward, the ground vibrating with each step.

It swung a dozen massive arms down, and Nathan sighed in resignation, falling to his knees.

The branches passed over him and slammed into the next wave of attackers.

Marble forms darted in, heroes of old carved from stone cut into the army of invaders, forming a circle around the three.

Satyr, rokairn, and human all looked up in surprise. But who the guardians of Iron Hall aimed blows at surprised none of them as much as their enemies.

Soldiers fell, knocked down in swaths.

"Retreat!" Manalo and Nathan shouted at the same time.

The warlord limped into the inn, now cleared of combat.

Nathan looked at him but had no way of attacking from afar.

"We go west, towards the setting sun," the rokairn grunted, and lumbered that way, swinging Marcid across the calves of a soldier in his way.

The other two followed; Reggie panting, barely able to keep his sword up, and Kajuun walking backwards, defending them from anyone coming up from behind.

After limping a city block, the battle fell behind; the army occupied by fighting for their lives against the statues and the rotting tree-men.

The three cut southwest, keeping to back alleys, avoiding the main roads. Peeking into the street, they saw an opening in the outer wall.

"What about Aiyana?" Reggie asked, his back against a building and his breath coming in short, sharp gasps.

Kajuun stood at the mouth of the alley, watching in both directions as Nathan leaned on his axe to catch his breath.

The rokairn was pale from shock and loss of blood, and it didn't look like he or the human would make it much further.

"I know, I know," Nathan muttered. "We're going to have to hope she is safe up in her tower. Pray that her magic is enough to fight off anyone trying to get to her. After all, she was the one who set the guardians onto the army, right?"

Reggie nodded.

"So, do we leave the city? Or do we risk it being safe enough to hole up here somewhere?"

"Um, friends?" Kajuun whispered, pointing up the street in the direction they'd come from.

Nathan and Reginald leaned over to look around the corner.

A dozen soldiers, weapons drawn, were moving across the road. Four statues and a tree-man trailed behind them. They moved as one unit, not as two groups of enemies.

"I think," Kajuun said once they were out of sight, "that Aiyana is not being in control of the guardians any longer. These magical constructs may be able to track us if we hide in the city."

"Yeah," Nathan nodded, "that makes the choice easier. We leave and hope she can get away and come find us."

The three checked the street again, turned towards the city gate in the outer wall, and disappeared into the twilight outside of Icon Hall.

Chapter 22

Aiyana jerked awake, her breath quick and panicked, a keening sound escaping from her throat. In her dream, she'd been at the drive-in theater. The noise had been the distant squeal of tires on asphalt as a 57 Chevy took a corner too fast in the movie. It took her a moment to realize the sound was coming from her, and she was trying to scream.

Cold stone was under her cheek, her face moist. She was confused, unsure why it was wet, and wondered if she'd been crying.

She raised a hand, trying to wipe at her face. Her forearm and wrist dragged across the floor in front of her blurred vision. The limb felt disconnected, like a bloated water balloon. It was cold, and she only felt anything when she put pressure on it. She stared at it and wondered if she could open and close her fingers.

Mildly fascinated, she watched the hand do what she wanted. But she couldn't feel the fingers curl, or scrape against the skin, or flex open again.

She opened her mouth to speak, and the sound that came out was a formless group of wet vowels. Testing a few words, the most recognizable thing was the heavy sigh.

Pushing herself to a sitting position, she looked around. Seeing that she'd raised herself on one hand, with palm flat on the ground, she noticed she'd folded the other hand over the opposite way and pushed up using the wrist and back of the hand.

She flopped it back and forth in a mild panic, hoping she hadn't hurt it when she'd done that. She shuffled her feet to push herself upright, and had to look down to see them moving, unable to feel them either.

Her muddled thoughts were as rubbery and disconnected as her limbs. She wondered what had done this to her, though her mental equivalent of the question in her head was closer to, *What do this?* Except her thoughts had less finesse and style than that sentence.

She fell over again, slapping against the damp stones of the floor. It didn't hurt, but she saw a trickle of blood winding away from her face in the trench between the large, flat-fitted stone of the dim room.

Need new brain, Aiyana thoughts drifted, *need new body. Can't work these.*

She must've fallen asleep because she thought she'd been flying. Everything had been clear above the treetops, watching the clouds scutter across the crescent moon. She could see, and she could think.

Aiyana understood she'd been taken. Someone had come into the room, and she'd known the man. He had devices and shot her with a miniature crossbow.

Her mind shifted, rising away from her situation, unconsciousness sending her into another place.

She saw a house, well, a broken-down structure that had once been a house, a familiar form in the doorway. It was the man who'd given her cheese! Circling, she watched the figure turn away and go back inside.

Checking her wings and the air currents, she aimed for the open window. She had to tell her friends what had happened.

Reginald shuffled back inside the ramshackle house. He looked around at the others and moved across the room to settle in.

The three holed up in a broken-down homestead not far outside of the city. It hadn't been the first place they'd passed. They'd rejected those, not wanting to be too close to the walls that now protected the invading army, the magical guardians, and imprisoned their missing friend.

The shack—which had been much more than that at one time—had a floor of wooden planks, but half of them were missing, showing hard-packed earth underneath.

Nathan sat in that bare spot, his naked feet digging into the dirt with his toes. The ends of his arms, where his hands had once been, were now capped with stone. He trailed them along the small trenches he'd dug beside him, mumbling to himself or in prayer. Marcid leaned against the broken boards, its vines sunk into the ground around the massive axe head.

Kajuun sat on an overturned crate in the doorway, watching the crescent moon and the landscape for movement. The satyr ran a whetstone along the edge of a sword, the gentle scraping singing counterpoint to the loud buzz of insects, and a gurgled, basso echo of frogs providing rhythm to the night.

Reginald sat leaning against a wall, his duffel wedged into the small of his back, and flicked cockroaches that scuttered across the floor with faint clicking noises. They wrapped his ribs in torn strips from bed sheets found in a small chest with preservation magics on it. Vermin didn't infest any of the cloth within.

That same chest had yielded a shirt and tunic for him, and they recovered his boots from his belongings. Kajuun had applied some salve to the wounds, and now the cuts from the lash, and the bruises from the beatings, were a dull, constant throb, rather than sharp, burning pain.

The three had scoured a few other places before choosing one, looking for anything of use; weapons, food, tools, or something they hadn't thought of. They replaced some things they'd lost, but they couldn't replace Nathan's hands.

Reggie looked at the priest, the corners of his mouth drooping, and his brows coming together.

"You think he'll be okay?" Reggie asked no one in particular.

Kajuun looked back over her shoulder, glancing at the rokairn, then the human. She shrugged and turned back to watch the night.

"I cannot be knowing," she breathed, "everyone is different. Even the strongest have their breaking point, and only he will be knowing if this is his."

Reggie nodded.

The silence drew out.

"I'll be fine," Nathan said. "I still have something to do, so I have no choice but to be fine."

The other two looked at the priest, who pushed to his feet with a groan. He used his legs, unable to use his hands to help.

"We have to find Aiyana," Nathan continued, "and get these people out of Icon Hall. We can't leave that kind of power to this sort of people."

Reggie snorted, and Nathan looked at the man.

"What?" Nathan grunted, his tone challenging. "Say it. What's on your mind?"

"We should've shut the gate." Reggie said shortly. "If we'd done that, none of this would've happened. And if we'd used Captain Farrell more effectively, we'd seen this coming. But because of sheer arrogance at you two being 'superheroes', we didn't bother covering the basics with the tools we had on hand."

"Is that helpful?" Kajuun asked, her accent thickening with her anger. "I followed you in the city, saw the men to be coming in. I went to the tower, but Aiyana was in a trance, plugged into the magics of the city and wouldn't respond. You two were off being drunk, and I couldn't find you. So many things were to be could've done, but it wasn't to being done. What is being done is done. We should focus on what can be done."

The two men exchanged glances, Nathan looking chagrinned.

"We're beat to hell," Reggie shrugged, "and that's only the beginning. I can't take a breath without feeling that sharp pain in my ribs, meaning one or more is probably broken. You're…well, hurt. We do have Kajuun, but she's only one person. The enemy is entrenched in a magical city, and they have control of a second army of magical things made of stone and living trees. Our most powerful person is missing in action, and…"

The swashbuckler trailed off with a sigh.

"So," Nathan squared his shoulders, and set his feet, "if we can find Aiyana, this would be much easier, right?"

"Well, it would be a start." Reggie snorted. "We're going into a high-stakes poker game, and the deck is stacked against us. We're low on chips, and luck and the odds haven't been going our way."

"Yes," Kajuun said, "but there is one more thing, but I am not knowing if you are knowing this."

The human and rokairn looked at the satyr.

"Rauhen is with these enemies." Kajuun shrugged.

The other two stared at her, waiting for her to go on.

"Rauhen, the leader of my people? You met him at my city?" Kajuun said. Her statements were half questions.

The other two waited for her to go on.

Kajuun sighed, then continued.

"He came from the mountains and united the tribes. He brought magic with him, then traded for more. Once he thought we'd learned enough, he began playing the different races against one another. Trying to get them to kill each other, or at least weaken one another so he could move in and take over.

"He was the one who destroyed Wiley's Station, the reason I was marking it with the sigils you saw," the shirai continued, "he was the one who sent the dasism to the ogre tower, trying to get the secrets within. He is wanting to know how to travel through the portals. And he was the one that left a trail of information for your aeifain to follow. He couldn't get into Icon Hall. The only one who could unlock the city was a powerful aeifain arcanist."

The two stared at her.

Reginald rose gingerly to his feet, wincing.

"What are you saying?" he asked. "Why are you telling us this? Do you mean to betray us?"

His voice was level, but his fingers twitched, and he glanced at his weapons leaning against the wall three strides away.

"Calm down, Reggie," Nathan said, cocking his head and watching the satyr. "She wouldn't have rescued us if she meant us harm. There's no reason to keep us alive, and she could've killed us anytime. Just let her explain."

"No," Kajuun set her sword down and held her empty hands in a gesture of peace, "no, I am not meaning any harm. Nathan is being right. I am telling these things to you because I am not agreeing with Rauhen. I think he makes much danger for our people. I do not want to conquer anyone; I just want my people to be safe. This is the things that I work for, for many years. I think he makes that harder. Maybe even to be impossible."

A flutter of noise came from outside, and the three turned towards the door. Kajuun knelt and picked up her discarded sword. Nathan stepped to Marcid, vines twining around his wrists and forearm, so he held the weapon steady. Reginald moved across the room, pulling his blades from their sheaths, and dropped back on his left foot into a guarded stance.

A black form flew in through the window, and Captain Farrell lighted on the rafters overhead. The raven tilted his head, one beady eye taking in the three beings below him.

Cawing, the bird leapt down and landed in the upper curve of Nathan's double-bladed battle-axe.

"Yana," the raven croaked.

"Did the Captain just speak?" Reggie asked. "Or did I imagine it? He reminded me of a man they commissioned me under, back in Africa, in my twenties. We had a troop of us, and we were heading down the Congo in a tiny steamer boat…"

He trailed off as his thoughts wandered, and he realized the other two were staring at him. And so was the raven.

"Nathan," Captain Farrell said, clear as if anyone else had spoken, "help."

"No," Kajuun said, holding up her hands, "we cannot be of helping to anyone."

"Are you talking to the bird, yourself, or someone else?" Reggie turned to look at her.

"He said 'Yana'," Nathan said, "he said it. Aiyana needs help. We have to go back for her."

"You are wanting us to go into a heavily guarded and fortified city—" Kajuun began but was cut off.

"Yes," Reginald said sharply, then sighed. "Yes. We have to do this, but we don't expect you to go with us. We'll face the army, a magic guy, and your boss, Rauhen. It's our mission."

"Nope," Nathan shook his head, "neither of you needs to go."

The rokairn held up his stone stumps, looking back and forth from one to the other.

"I can't promise to protect anyone else," the priest muttered. "Hell, I can't even protect myself. I can barely use my axe, and my connection to Jonath and the magics he gives me is…well, I don't know how well it will work. If it will even work at all. Reggie, you're beat to hell. Kajuun, if you help it would be treason to your people, if it isn't already. I will go alone and tear that cursed city down stone by stone if I have to. But that woman, Aiyana, wizardess, mind mage, and so much more, must be saved at any cost."

"Why, my friend?" Kajuun almost pleaded. "Why is she so important?"

"If she was able to open the portal passages at all," Nathan said, "even in a small area, then these armies will be unstoppable. They'll be able to cross great distances and attack with surprise, killing countless folk who are just trying to survive, to rebuild what once was."

Nathan stared at Captain Farrell for a moment before continuing.

"The Dasism, the Rokairn, the Rammen—excuse me, the Torck—and even the humans don't deserve to die or be enslaved because one woman had a dream of restoring the knowledge of the Aeifain. This one, small, simple choice, can influence the entire world. And I, for one, won't back down because I'm missing a couple of hands and there's no hope against the odds we face."

"The thing about betting the pot on long-shot odds is," Reggie drew in a breath through his teeth, "the risk is high, but the payoff is incredible. And think of the stories to go with it."

The man stepped between the satyr and rokairn, looking decades older than his years. He shuffled forward, shoulders bent from time, and the shadows showed crags on his face that hadn't been there before.

"I've been in places like this," Reginald continued, "situations like this. They're hopeless. But I can't walk away from them. Because I'd rather die doing something worthwhile than live with the idea that I couldn't do what was right."

He stood up straight, and was the young man again.

"You do what's best for you," he said, looking at Kajuun, "but I think you didn't follow us across the Grey Wood, helping from the shadows and defying your master, so you could back out now. But if you did, then I respect folding when you know you can't possibly win the hand."

"Ugh," Nathan groaned, "you just had to upstage me? Had to do a better speech than mine?"

"Whatever," Reggie laughed, "you inspired me, if that helps?"

"A little," Nathan nodded, "but you really don't have to—"

"Great," Reggie interrupted, "then we agree. Let's get ready, as much as our broken bodies and minds will allow, and go in there like gangbusters, relying on our spirits to carry the day."

"That's stupid," Kajuun stomped a hoof, "we can't just go running in!"

"What else can we do?" Nathan shrugged.

"We call on whatever dasism still live. They have portals." The satyr looked back and forth between the two men and the raven. "We call my people. They are crossing the river to the east as we speak. We use your god's magic, and we make tunnels into the city. And we go in with a plan of attack and use that talking bird to find the wizardess."

"That *is* a better plan," Nathan said, looking up at Reggie.

"It is," the human agreed, "maybe we should do that. But instead of digging tunnels, I have a better idea. Sewers."

Chapter 23

Fifteen dasism answered the call, bright blue flashes of portals bursting in the night, washing over the overgrown fields of long-dead farms. Nathan thought it looked like alien fireflies invading, remembering the glow from so many movies that showed strange life forms emerging.

Each dasism was heavily tattooed, and armed with a spear, bow, knife, and shield. They'd come from across the continent, or that's what Arkeshia and Chevae had said at least. They were all warriors, but these were also the elementalists of the tribes they represented. Shyam the speaker, Takia, and Chirai had come along, and Nathan was glad to see them. Gokia had showed up also, his hot temper displayed the way the others showed their tattoos.

The other nine were strangers, though, and Nathan couldn't remember their names. He'd been sleeping when the first of them arrived, a couple hours before the sun rose.

More than a hundred torck stood in the chilly morning rain, milling about in a dozen different groups. Some had a talisman or some small ability of magic and would act as forward stealth scouts. The mass of the torck people would be shock troops.

Each of these groups had more invested in the outcome of this battle than either the human or the rokairn that had called to them through Kajuun. Both would face the army if it wasn't stopped here. The dasism was the target of genocide, and the torck would face death for treason against Rauhen. Nathan and Reggie wanted to free their friend; the Dasism and Torck wanted to free their people from an oppressive regime. Together, they wanted to stop the advancement of an evil empire.

The priest moved through the crowd, surprised by the warm greetings. Many of these people had heard of him and his sacrifice. Some hesitated but asked for the blessing of Jonath. As a god of protection, guards, honor, and earth, many people looked to Jonath before battle even though war wasn't his domain.

Nathan was humbled—and happy—to offer something to the upcoming battle, knowing he wouldn't be much help in any other way.

The two healers among the group looked at the rokairn's stone capped wrists, but just shook their heads when asked if they could restore his missing hands. They did what they could, magically and mundanely, to restore Reggie's torn body, and Nathan's broken spirit, but there were limits.

"Reggie!" a gruff voice called out, causing heads to turn.

Nathan wasn't sure if that voice was excited or angry and turned to see who was calling for his friend. It was people from Wiley's Station, brought by the dasism.

An older, rounded man with steel in his hair and beard who strode towards the swashbuckler, a sword slapping his thigh. A younger man walked fast behind him, trying to keep up. They were both followed at a distance by a half dozen other humans, who looked lost in the crowd and bewildered.

"Teorge! Collin!" Reggie shouted back, and hastened to the two men, then slowed and stopped, a worried crease in his forehead.

The men stopped in front of him, the older one crossing his arms across his chest.

"Teorge? Elda?" Reggie spoke slowly and quietly.

Teorge's face tightened, and the older man shook his head.

Reggie bowed his head for a long moment, then looked back up.

"You brought this ragtag bunch together?" Teorge asked.

Reggie shrugged and gave a small nod, and Captain Farrell bobbed up and down on his shoulder.

"And you intend to take on the ones who burned Wiley's Station, show them what's what?" Teorge asked.

"Yes sir," Reggie sighed, "I guess I am."

"Good," the older man's lips quirked up through his pain, "then me and the boys will follow you into battle, and we'll get our pound of flesh for what they did to our town, and to our…"

Teorge lowered his eyes, and his shoulders shook a little.

Reginald stepped forward and grabbed the big man by his arms. Teorge looked up.

"Yes, sir," Reggie nodded. "We'll do that. Damn right, we will."

Teorge reached out and pulled the younger man into a tight hug.

When they pulled apart, Collin stepped up, grabbed Reggie's hand, and pumped it up and down.

"Time for some of that adventure you told us about," Collin said, then stepped back.

The other men came forward, greeting Reginald, shaking his hand, or thumping him on the shoulder, making Captain Farrell squawk under the jostling.

When the group moved away, Nathan sidled up to the swashbuckler, who looked emotional.

"Friends of yours?" Nathan asked.

"I guess so," Reggie said. "They were the ones who…they didn't deserve what they got. They're good people."

Nathan nodded and bumped the taller man's arm with his shoulder.

"So are you, Reggie," Nathan said without looking at him. "We should get this show on the road."

"We'll enter the city through the sewers. Are you going to be able to widen them so we all fit?" Reggie asked, wiping at his eyes.

"It was a good idea you had, but I don't know if I can," the priest shrugged. "I don't have hands."

"You don't have to dig them out personally," the swashbuckler teased, nudging the man back, "and I think maybe your god will lend you a *hand* in this task."

"Puns?" the rokairn asked, smiling. "Why not? Well then, let's go get our *hands* dirty."

"You're not very good at this, are you?" Reggie scoffed. "Can't use the same pun more than once. Just thought I'd *point* that out."

"Aiyana is the one who loves puns. I just play along to help lift her spirits. I imagine I see more of the real her when she does, instead of what she's become in this world." Nathan sighed.

"I can *dig* it," Reggie said.

Nathan sighed again, but smiled.

On the plateau closest to the city was a sewer pipe that sloped downward and widened to become a passage. As the sun broke the horizon, the last of the makeshift army disappeared down it. The ridge of the land hid the entrance from anyone in the city.

Reggie was right, Jonath had answered Nathan's call. The earth surrounding the sewer parted at the priest's command, rocks in the loose soil knitting together to create supports and arches along the tunnel. The one hundred and fifty invaders disappeared under the soil more than an hour before a single guard of the newly dug in army thought to look out across the farms outside of the walls of Icon Hall.

Within the old marketplace, the cobblestones cracked and spilled aside as the invading force erupted from the ground like an angry nest of ants.

At Nathan's suggestion, and backed by Kajuun and Reginald, they broke into fifteen squads of eight, each with a spellslinger and an armed contingent. The plan was to split up, covering three blocks wide and five deep, staying a block apart from other groups, but close enough to see others at all times. Everyone would follow the raven as it tracked where Aiyana was being held.

The plan was that every ten blocks on the main road, a group would stop to help cover the retreat and prevent attackers from approaching the lead group from the rear. Those groups took to the rooftops and balconies, hoping to use the heights as lookouts and high ground to attack with bows.

The plan went flawlessly for about two blocks, then marbled statues dropped from the eaves and nooks of buildings, falling into the gathering of people, laying about them with swords.

Metal clanged on stone, and green sparks danced from the city's guardians, their magical protection blocking damage from the intruders' weapons.

"Nathan," Reggie shouted, "can you take them out?"

"I dunno!" the rokairn shouted back, "But I'll try!"

The priest lowered his missing hands to the ground and called upon the power of Jonath.

"Jonath," his voice was excited, almost in song, "if you want to see this city in the hands of those that will help the world find balance and justice, grant me the boon of melting these bastards to slag!"

Three of the marble monstrosities lurched towards the priest, their ankles twisting, melting under their weight as they turned to mud.

A rough cheer went up from the attackers, and the ragtag group of humans fell onto the guardians, pummeling them with clubs. Chips of stones burst upward as arms cracked on the weakened forms of the magical constructs.

A two-story tall man of oak lumbered around a corner, and leafy limbs swept the street. The advancing monster threw dasism, humans, and torcks against storefronts.

"Chevae," Reggie shouted, "turn up the heat, and let's get this party blazing!"

The dasism, Chevae, stopped in their tracks, turning to face the new foe, the group led by Arkeshia following suit. Flame arced forward, shifting from a stream to small, fist-sized balls exploding on the tree-man.

Blue flame raced along the limbs of the natural guardian. The attack reached its leaves, and the dried and withered behemoth burst into flames. The creature jerked upright, stumbling backwards, its flailing arms—all seven of them—slid along the wood and stone buildings, catching the wood alight.

Magical flame raced along anything in its path, igniting it and turning the golden dawn with dispersing rain clouds into a glowing red light.

The carefully constructed groups of units shattered into a chaotic onslaught as everyone raced to join the fight.

"Keep in your group!" Reggie shouted; his voice lost in the tumult.

"Tighten up, you pemties, pull back and attack as a unit. We won't win if we don't stay with our groups!" Nathan's voice was preternaturally loud, like he had a megaphone, and men and women fell back into their assigned units.

Kajuun leapt atop a broken wagon and raised her sword.

"It is being the first time we met the enemy, and we will be beating them with our minds and skill, not our numbers," the satyr yelled, "remember your training, and stay with the people you know, and we shall win the day. Torck, we are the ones showing the example. Do not fail now by being the blind!"

The groups reformed, some pressing forward to attack the crippled enemy, and others falling back to wait to see if they were needed to support the units in the lead.

A dozen people limped, but within a minute they won the first battle, and the mass of the invading force moved forward.

Five blocks later, their force was cut in half as two lines of human warriors streamed in from side streets. The city defenders were quiet until their commander shouted the attack command, and dozens of soldiers boiled onto the street.

Arrows streaked from higher vantage points, piercing the dasism, the enemy aiming for the casters wielding elemental forces.

"Jonath!" Nathan screamed the name of his god, not wanting a repeat of the previous encounter. "Give your protection to these people!"

A shimmer of gold scattered through the advancing force, and arrows and swords alike slid sideways, deflected off many of the surprised force led by the rokairn.

A dozen screams rose as others were injured. Two dasism crumpled to the paving stones, and more than a dozen torck fell in the first push of the ambush.

Reginald leapt over a fallen faun, his rapier flashing across the throat of an attacker. His main gauche slapped away the broadsword of an overconfident bearded man who towered over him.

"Are you a giant?" Reggie breathed, his eyes going up the enormous man's body.

The larger man smiled down at the archaeologist, and Reggie's knees buckled.

A huge two-handed sword came down towards him, but he hit the ground and rolled, his parrying weapon slicing across the giant's calves, cutting muscles and tendons.

The massive warrior collapsed, and Reggie bounced to his feet and stabbed the enemy in the base of his skull, just about even with the swashbuckler's shoulder.

The opposing fighter fell, gurgling blood.

"The bigger they are, the harder they…" Reggie's words died off, and he pulled his weapon loose to block another incoming attack from two wiry men.

"Wizards," Nathan shouted, his voice heard above the fight, "hit the archers!"

The dasism followed the command, and calling on the power of wind and water, lightning arched from the tattered remnants of the clouds and exploded on the balconies holding archers.

"I am being to think," Kajuun said, pressing her back to Reginald's, "that your friend Nathan should not fight, but lead. He has a knack for this thing we need!"

The shirai was a whirlwind, spinning away from Reggie, her wide blade making quick work of three men.

The melee died out, and the groans of injured men crawling or limping away in retreat filled the street.

"We move, now!" Nathan commanded.

"There!" Reggie pointed towards the sky.

Captain Farrell wheeled above the group and soared towards the tower.

Aiyana breathed slowly.

Deep breaths, she told herself, *don't try to figure it out. Let your body react and trust your instincts.*

She wasn't bound, and she'd crawled to the door. Leaning against it, her head swam.

It's like the worst fever brain I've ever had, she thought, *but I'm able to move, so I can do this.*

Her mind connected with Captain Farrell again, feeling the bird's thoughts.

Help comes, the raven thought, or something close to it.

The wizardess saw through his eyes that the skirmish in the streets was ending. Nathan was facing forward, and Reginald was pointing straight at her in the sky.

"That man," she breathed, her awareness back in her body, "may actually be okay."

Then she felt the arrow cut through her wing.

No, not hers, but Captain Farrell's. She screamed from the pain and fainted.

Chapter 24

Reggie saw the raven gliding on an air current, and the black streak of an arrow rising into the sky.

It's a wasted shot, foolhardy, a one in a million play, he thought, *but it could…*

He winced as the shaft hit the bird, and a burst of black feathers scattered across the sky.

"No, Captain Farrell!" he shouted, and took off at a run towards the falling avian.

The group of people assigned to him followed, Teorge and Collin flanking him, and Chevae close behind. There were no longer eight in their group. The other humans injured, or worse, were left behind.

Reginald could hear Nathan shouting to stay with the group but ignored him. He knew the man was right, but this was Captain Farrell. That raven was one of the team, and he wouldn't leave him to this fall any more than he'd leave Nathan.

A contingent of men broke away from the enemy army, moving to intercept them. Fifteen battle-hardened and tested soldiers flowed towards them, their footfalls nearly in unison. The group cut them off, coming between Reggie and the bird struggling to slow his plummeting descent.

Teorge overtook Reginald, shoving him to one side as the enemy engaged. The older barkeep's skill showed, the weapon that once hung over kegs of beer flashing and striking. He gutted a warrior that came screaming at the break-away group, his wide broadsword dragging across the man's belly and spilling his guts.

Collin darted around Teorge, his long sword biting into the shoulder of another soldier. The opponent fell to the ground, and two others moved to replace him.

Reggie saw a spray of red erupt from Collin's back, followed by the bloodied tip of a blade. A second hole, then a third, appeared. He doubled over; the soldiers stabbing him over and over again.

Without breaking stride, Reginald flicked his rapier towards the two men, striking one in the eye socket and pushing the blade in until it scraped along the inside of the man's skull.

Twisting his wrist, he made the now shrieking soldier's head turn, and his body followed. He stumbled backwards and to the side, his arms and weapon flailing as he clawed at his face with his free hand.

The soldier's sword, now over his shoulder and pointed behind him, bit into the shoulder of the second soldier who'd stabbed Collin.

Pulling his weapon free and glancing at the sky, Reggie poured on the speed. There were more men between him and Captain Farrell, and he didn't have the time to fight them all.

He juked to his left, his foot falling on the tongue of a small, single-axle wagon. Running up the support, he launched himself onto the driver's bench. Reggie hit the center of gravity of the cart, and the t-shaped crossbar he'd just traversed lifted into the air. He twisted his body and swung at a soldier rushing towards him. His momentum, with the added impetus of his strike, made the cart spin in a circle, the tongue of the transport slamming into the gut of three of the soldiers still standing.

He'd almost made it to the area where the bird was coming down, just a half block more. He launched himself off the back of the small wagon and heard Chevae's voice rise. A wind whipped around him, matching the intensity of the elementalist's voice.

The buffeting gale had three effects; it knocked the remaining soldiers backwards; it slowed Captain Farrell's fall; and it lifted Reginald up and towards the bird.

The sky roiled above the raven, grey clouds falling over one another, with fist-sized blue circles erupting randomly.

Reginald twisted in the air, jamming his main gauche under his belt, and reached up to scoop the raven into the crook of his arm. Looking down from the apex of the arc, two-stories up, he wondered how he'd get down without breaking a leg.

Eyeing an awning, he turned his back to the gusts, making them push him towards it. Flipping the grip on his rapier so the weapon pointed down, it caught the canvas, and Reggie locked his wrist. The wind pulled him to the awning as he fell downward, his blade cutting the canvas and slowing him.

His wrist hit the metal pole at the bottom of the sidewalk cover, and he flipped down towards the ground. Twisting in the air, he landed in a crouch, Captain Farrell nestled against his ribs, his rapier pointing directly at the solider charging him. The man impaled himself on the fencing blade and fell to one side with a shrill scream.

Chevae and Teorge caught up, along with others, forming a ring around Reginald as he inspected the bird's wing.

"It's okay, buddy," Reggie said, setting his rapier down on the cobblestones, and running a hand along the torn wing.

Captain Farrell's head whipped towards the man's hand, biting at the fingers, but there wasn't any malice in it, just an instinctual reaction.

"Sh, sh, sh," Reggie murmured. "I don't know if you can understand me, but I need you to try to be calm. I'm going to break the shaft off so I can pull the arrow out. This'll be over soon, and I'll get you somewhere safe."

Actions followed the words, and Captain Farrell screamed a caw when Reginald snapped the arrow, and another as he removed it.

The bird lay limp, his breathing shallow, one beady black eye watching the human smoothing his feathers and wrapping a cloth around the wing. Captain Farrell didn't look at the wing and the hands touching him, like most animals would have. Instead, he watched Reginald's face.

"We have to go," Teorge panted. "The others are making sure we can get back to them, but it won't last long."

Soaked with sweat from exertions his body was no longer used to, the barkeep had a half dozen cuts along his hands, arms, and chest.

"Teorge," Reggie said, "I need you to do something for me..."

"Yeah, anything," Teorge said without hesitation, then looked down at the bird, "oh, you want me to..."

"Yeah, take Captain Farrell," Reggie explained, "he's important to me. Bring him to Collin, check on the boy. But the three of you stay at the choke point we're creating at this intersection until I come back. Will you do that for me?"

"You sure you're not just trying to get rid of an old man who'd slow you down?" Teorge gave a small smile.

"Nope," Reggie handed the bundled bird to Teorge, "I just want you to take care of my friend for me, so I have him when I get back. I think you can understand that."

Teorge looked up, surprised, and tears filled his eyes, just above the puffy blue-grey bags. He nodded and smiled again.

Reggie jogged up to Nathan, who was standing at the bottom of the steps leading to the tower. A ragtag group of mismatched warriors waited on the high ground, one man in the center standing out.

"That the guy you mentioned when we were drunk on that rooftop a couple of days ago?" Reggie asked, pointing, as he leaned over to his friend.

The rain changed to a drizzle, and almost four score of torck stood arrayed below the two in the wet streets surrounding the tower.

"Yep," Nathan nodded, "that's Manalo, Warlord of Dioneze."

"He doesn't look so tough," Reggie said with a shrug.

"What about the guys around him, and all those flapping guardians and shifting statues around him? Do they look tough?" Nathan asked.

"Well," the human drew the word out, "tougher than their boss."

"I don't think that's their boss," Nathan sighed. "I think he's hooked up with someone who has magic, and that's who's holding Aiyana."

"Hooked up?" Reggie asked, and Nathan looked at him with a frustrated look. "Never mind, I think I get it. How about this, I take out the mean guy with the sword, and you handle all the stone bastards with the help of the dasism?"

"Sure, why not?" Nathan shrugged. Raising his voice, the rokairn addressed his troops behind him. "Wizards! Target the statues. Let the ground troops handle the humans!"

Reggie started running forward before the priest finished shouting commands.

Nathan watched the man slash his way into the broken line in front of them, the satyrs and fauns pouring around him like a wave of swords, flesh, and fur. Battle cries from both sides rent the air, and the clash of steel on steel punctuated their shouts.

The handful of remaining dasism gathered around Nathan, raising wands and staves—their magical focuses—towards the animated constructs swarming down from above and down the sides.

The warlord shouted commands of his own, directing the warriors and statues around him.

Lightning strobed down from the remnants of storm clouds, which thickened with the magics agitating them, and the rock bodies of aeifain gargoyles erupted into sprays of pebbles and detritus.

Nathan stood alone at the back of the group, feeling useless, but still shouting commands and warnings to his troops.

He thought of Aiyana, alone and surrounded inside the tower. Either she was still alive and out of commission or she was dead.

The last thought made him shudder. He'd spent years protecting her, to lose her when everything hinged on her would be more than disastrous. It would be a personal failure on his part.

He'd spent his life taking weeks to design and chisel gems until they were unique works of art, only to sell them to someone who'd never truly appreciated the work that had gone into creating it. They'd put on the bracelet or ring, and never give it another thought, other than to impress someone else.

But Nathan didn't create to impress people, he did it to make something lasting, that would change a single person's world with a thing of beauty.

He thought of his time with Aiyana in the same way. He hadn't created her, no more than he created a gemstone, but he had chipped away at the excess to make something greater than what he'd first beheld.

So many things had slipped from his grasp, lost to the world beyond his reach. Priceless gems and works snatched up by the greedy and arrogant.

He didn't want his friend to end up the same way.

Nathan squared his shoulders, set his feet, put his head down, and charged forward.

Marcid bounced on his forearm, her vines wrapped around his stunted limb, and he slashed at the warrior in front of him.

The man fell with a shrill scream.

Kajuun fought a dozen men to one side. The cluster of spellslingers chanted and called out arcane words to bring down flashes of lightning from overhead, or to unbind the enchantments that held the living statues, so they crumbled.

Nathan kept moving, weaving through the broken line of soldiers, and heading for the huge double doors of the tower.

The coppery smell of blood mixed with the scent of ozone, the second from the rain on the cobblestones and the electrical charges tearing through the magical forms of the ancient guardians. Rain fell in fat drops, breaking on the priest's face and clothes, and the sounds of warriors from both sides dying flooded his ears.

He focused on the door and ran for it, nothing else mattering in that moment except helping Aiyana.

Reginald pulled his shoulders back and rolled them, his rapier spinning in a circle at his side. Three men ran at him, and he turned the movement into a figure eight in front of him, his main gauche in the center.

The leading blade batted away the attacker's weapons and sunk into stomachs and throats without Reggie having to think about it.

"Hey," he laughed at the next man to step in front of him, "I'm pretty good at this. You might want to reconsider playing the cards you were dealt. It looks like a bunch of the other guys have already folded."

The swashbuckler rose on his toes, pushing his posterior to one side as a sword passed his midsection. He lashed out, stabbing the man through his ribs and into the center of his chest.

"Gotcha!" he sang, laughing.

A man with a beard stepped in front of him, a clean long sword held between the two.

"Manalo, right?" Reggie pointed with his parrying dagger. "Heard so much about you. None of it good, I assure you."

"You speak as if I care," Manolo said. "You'll die as easily as your friends."

Reggie leaned back as the warlord slashed carelessly. The blade slid past him.

The swashbuckler's laugh was cut short as the warrior reversed his swing, bringing it in low at Reggie's knees.

Jumping up and over the blade, Reggie's blade thrusting up, the swashbuckler felt the boot to his knees as he came down.

The warlord kicked the legs out from under the laughing fighter, and Reggie's knee popped audibly. The nimble swashbuckler came down on the cobblestones, face first.

His head cracked on the cobblestones, and the surrounding sounds washed away in a wave of pain, his brain rattling in his skull.

Reggie's vision swam, and everyone around him blurred. He rolled to one side, tucking his blades close to his body, and felt his enemy's sword cut in his sleeve, pinning him in place.

The larger man stomped down, his hobnailed boots filling the younger man's vision as it cleared.

Jerking his head to one side, the boot landed beside Reggie's head.

The warlord's calf was bound in bloody bandages, but he fought like he didn't feel pain. A blurred recollection of the man holding the axe over Nathan's head—moments before the bastard removed the priest's hands—crossed his mind. He saw the stolen axe coming down again, a magical artifact made for the rokairn being used against him.

The swashbuckler thrust upward with his main gauche, jamming it into the man's inner thigh of his wounded leg. It slid under the rectangle of armor and bit deep into the flesh.

Manalo stumbled backwards, the weapon tearing from his body, and Reggie kicked the man's groin. Boot met tender bits, and the warlord let out a grunt that became a quiet squeal. Blood trickled down the man's leg, the rivulet becoming a stream in gushing bursts, and Reggie knew he'd hit the artery in the thigh.

It was only a matter of time now. Even if the warlord didn't realize what had happened, it would be a slow but assured victory.

Pushing to his feet, favoring his good leg, Reggie fell into a defensive stance. It would be a battle of attrition now, and he only had to stop the warlord from hitting him, while chipping away at the man until he lost enough blood to collapse.

"Kill him," Manalo's raised voice and pointing finger drew the attention of the surrounding forces, "everyone kill this man. A thousand gold kords to the one who deals the killing stroke!"

Dozens of eyes and blades turned towards Reginald.

Chapter 25

Kajuun looked across the skirmish outside of the tower. The winds picked up, throwing dust and debris into the air, buffeting the incoming stone guardians. The beings reminded her of the torck horses, the constructs of her people, created by Rauhen, and she didn't trust those either.

She held her broad blade across her body, ready to block or strike, her hand held to one side to knock away any incoming blade.

Nathan dodged between groups of fighters, working his way towards the double doors with a single-minded ferocity. She admired the priest. Few she knew could bounce back so quickly from having their hands amputated in a show of dominance. She didn't know if she could.

Her mind shifted to his tactic. If he was heading inside, instead of waiting in the back, he must have an objective in mind, probably to save the aeifain he'd been body-guarding this whole while. Kajuun didn't think Aiyana realized the fierce protectiveness Nathan felt towards her.

She called out commands to the torck, shouting for them to protect his path and make sure he got to his goal. Her people reacted without question, making her proud.

The sound of exploding stone made her duck her head, and a low-flying guardian rained down around her, in pieces. Lightning blinded her for a few seconds, the elementalists calling upon the winds, rain, and electricity to do their bidding.

Seeing Reginald fall to the master of the enemy army, Kajuun waded into combat, calling for her group to surround and follow her. They responded like an extension of her, flowing to make a circle around her.

The handpicked elite group worked together flawlessly, each guarding the one beside them, blocking or attacking any threat.

This was grunt work, clearing the mass of the army, but it meant something. If she could fight next to the humans, rokairn, and dasism to save the aeifain city, then there was hope. Her master had turned traitor to his people, long before she'd turned traitor on him, though the council may see it differently.

Kajuun swung her sword, shrugging in answer to her thoughts. If doing the right thing was wrong, she would die for it, whether that was on a battlefield or in the halls of the ruling council of her people. It was because of Rauhen that she'd stayed in the field, rather than settling down at home for old age. Well, that and the fact that she could still do this; fight the fight and help others. She wasn't ready to train others, and not be in the thick of it.

It was an odd thought, but it felt right. She'd rather stay here until she was a detriment to her people, instead of living a soft life in the protected walls of a city. She'd give it all up when she was more of a hindrance than a help.

With a shout to her group, her friends and fellows, she raised her sword and barreled into an enemy group. They were winning, but she knew this minor battle wasn't what would win the war. That was up to one rokairn with no hands, and a young girl of a magical people. And if she could do one thing, it was to give them the chance.

Two more waves of stone guardians swooped down, falling on the dasism, and the screams told Kajuun this battle wouldn't be won easily, if at all.

Nathan stopped in front of the closed double doors, raised a stone capped wrist, and punched forward with all the power he could muster. The magic of his god backed him up, and the obstruction shattered inward.

Barreling through the doors of the tower, Nathan saw objects barricading the opening, scattered across the chessboard floor, and the statues moving to block his progress. He called upon the power of Jonath through clenched teeth and hissing breaths.

The axe weighed heavily on his arm, the stone caps where his hands had once been, throbbed in a rhythm to match his pounding head. He was exhausted and knew this would be his last battle, one way or the other.

He'd spent his life hiding behind his mother's wishes, then books, and, finally, a counter and his work. He avoided confrontation as a rule, but now had to charge headlong into it just to survive.

How'd he come to this? He'd only wanted to make the world a better place, help others, or at least make their day a little bit better.

Nathan's entire existence had been a series of efforts similar to his jewelry making. He'd tried to create small pieces of beauty, something that someone could long cherish after he was gone.

That wasn't so much to ask, was it?

The power of his god trickled into him, guided by the druidic energies that flowed through his enchanted axe. But instead of shattering his foes, he felt his body grow heavier, but not in weight. His muscles thickened and strengthened, growing firm and solid. His breath came easier, and he knew what he had to do. The same thing he'd always done. Take one step at a time.

Nathan squared his shoulders, set his feet, and took one step forward. Marcid's vines tightened around his forearm and he swung his axe, colliding with the first guardian.

The blade connected and green tendrils shot out to wrap around the stone construct, entangling it. He felt the magic of the thing surge up the weapon and into him, strengthening him further. He stepped forward again, his free hand—which is how he still thought of it—connecting with another foe, and it burst into pieces and rained down on the floor.

Three of the things piled on him, punching with their stone fists, and slashing with their stone blades. They hit with so much force that the rokairn slid backwards, but their hands shattered against his strengthened body. The blades slid along him with a grinding noise of rock on rock and fell away harmlessly.

He pushed forward, meeting each enemy with renewed and reinforced power. They fell around him, Marcid wrapping some, and him shattering others. He reached the stairs that led to where he last saw Aiyana and turned to look at the room behind him.

It felt like it had been only moments, but the wreckage of the room argued that. A dozen shattered forms or more littered the area, and Nathan nodded emphatically.

"That'll show them," he laughed. "I'm a force of nature, and they're just stone. One will overcome the other every time."

He moved up the circular stairs, passing the openings on each floor until he reached the top level, hearing a strained voice swearing in frustration. Moving through the first antechamber, he peeked into the gloom of the next room.

The chair he'd last seen occupied by his friend now showed a thin man hunched over what Nathan thought of as the control panel for the security for the city. The chair swiveled to face him, and the person in it glared at him through sunken eyes, a familiar staff across his lap.

"You can't stop me," Tymere said, his voice angry but tired, "I've already started the process, and others will be here soon."

Nathan looked around, wary.

"Who do you think is coming?" Nathan asked, his breathing relaxed and even. "The army is being torn to shreds. Your friend Manalo is losing."

"He's a pemtie, nothing more than a tool, a means to an end," Tymere spat, "just a steppingstone so I could control the portals and bring back true power again."

"You want to finish what your boss started?" Nathan's brow creased in confusion.

"Khizhane was a short-sighted fool," venom laced Tymere's voice, "he only wanted to increase the magic. I'll bring back legions to fight for me, cut a contract with lords of other planes so they will fight for me!"

"Demons…" Nathan breathed, "you want to bring back demons? Didn't you see what they did to this world? How could you even…"

Nathan trailed off, shaking his head. He wanted to talk to this man, reason with him, convince him of what was right or wrong. But he knew the type of person Tymere was, and it was the mentality of a madman. So convinced that he was right in what he was doing, there was no other way.

"I shall have you," Tymere muttered, almost to himself, "and use you as I'm using the witch Aiyana. I'll pull your magic, use it to power the portals…"

The man's voice dropped to a mumble, and he pulled the Key of Aiyana from his lap.

Nathan knew the staff and knew it connected different magics, like a tributary of rivers of arcane energies. If brought to bear, the priest wouldn't stand a chance.

The rokairn charged, swinging Marcid. At the same moment the alchemist stood and raised the artifact.

It was only a handful of strides to get to the man, but Nathan felt the magic swell in the room. He'd waited too long, talked too much, trying to ward off what was coming with words instead of violence. He should've known better, acted sooner.

Tymere raised the staff and objects rose into the air. A hand crossbow launched darts at the priest, the clip dropping in the weapon's shaft and loading the next quarrel, firing repeatedly.

The projectiles reflected off the priest's stone hardened skin, the blessing of Jonath still protecting him. Three daggers followed, to the same effect.

Nathan was upon him then, the axe coming down in an arc.

The alchemist slammed the butt of the staff against the floor and a hollow crack echoed throughout the chamber. A blue spark exploded at the point of impact and the battle-axe bounced off an invisible barrier.

The rokairn stumbled backwards, shaking his arms, his weapon bobbing and its vines quivering.

Tymere tittered, a high-pitched, unhinged noise, his eyes slitted in merriment.

"You thought you could actually hurt me!" The alchemist giggled again. "I have all the power now; it flows through me. I've connected with the raw arcane energies of all the magics, and I cannot be stopped. Your wizardess couldn't do it. How do you—a lowly leech of a priest, suckling from a forgotten god's power—expect to stand up to me?"

"You're crazy," Nathan muttered. "You can't think that you can handle all this. The energies will burn you up. It's already doing it."

"Energies?" The alchemist sounded thoughtful. "Yes, that's a good idea. Let's see what that sort of power does to you."

Raising the staff, Tymere wobbled and turned his head upward. A guttural squeak came from his throat, like he was choking, and then transformed into a scream.

The tower rumbled, and stone exploded above the two. Chunks of rock rained down, bouncing off the spellslinger's shield and battering Nathan.

A hole in the ceiling opened, showing the darkening sky outside. The grey clouds roiled, thickening into a deep green. Lightning arced across the sky in purple-white streaks.

A drizzle fell into the room, spattering everything with fat drops of rain. The drizzle grew into a downpour, which became a deluge within moments. Jagged branches of raw energy multiplied overhead, reaching out like skeletal hands, then shot downwards.

Lightning blasted buildings, and booming echoes reverberated through the streets below. A single arc came through the overhead opening, crashing into the floor in front of Nathan.

Electricity ran along the wet floor and found the rokairn's booted feet, throwing the priest backwards into the wall. He slammed against the stone, and his vision swam.

Shaking his head to clear it, a sharp pang accompanied a dull thumping. Nathan blinked the tears of pain from his eyes, trying to focus on the shadow moving towards him.

Tymere's voice was high and strained and broke with intermittent giggles as it grew closer.

"Now, it's time for you to die and give your magic to me, dwarf!"

Aiyana woke to the building shaking, threads of sand filtering onto her from above. She sat up, holding her arm. It throbbed where the arrow had hit her. No, not her, Captain Farrell.

"I know where you're from," a thick voice cut through the darkness, "I've been to your world and know why you're here."

"You've been to Earth?" Aiyana's words sounded rushed and confused in her ears.

"Yes, though it was a long time before you were born," the shadowy figure coalesced in front of the wizardess, "and I was looking for something very specific. Something which you have."

Aiyana's head spun, and she stumbled over words.

"Um, what, I don't understand," she said.

"Of course, you don't," the strong masculine voice answered.

Her vision cleared, and the hulking form of a being appeared with dark fur covering his body, large twisting horns rising from his head, and a tufted tail swishing around his goat legs. A pair of knee-length breeches and an open leather jerkin tucked into a wide leather belt were all he wore. A spiked flogger hung from the belt.

"I've sought something for a long time, and you shall give it to me," he said.

Aiyana closed her eyes, trying to clear her head, but snapped them open just as quick. This thing was coming closer, the clomp of his cloven hooves a dull sound with each step.

The building shook again, more dirt falling from the ceiling.

"You're Rauhen," she said, "the leader of the torck people. It was you at court when we visited."

"Yes, simple one, very good," the creature sneered, "and you have played pawn long enough. Now, I give you the choice to join me, or become nothing more than a disposable tool to help me achieve my goal."

"What goal?" was all Aiyana could think to ask.

"To move back and forth between the worlds, open the portals so I may begin my campaign to conquer all the people, realms, and worlds I've been working for, for centuries."

"No," Aiyana mumbled, "you can't."

"Can't what?" He glared at the helpless woman. "You have one choice, and mere moments to decide. Remember, a choice not made is a choice in and of itself. I shall accept any answer, or none, and still get my way. It's as simple as you choosing if you're willing or not. I'd rather you come along willingly, but I'm fine with burning you out and destroying your mind."

A huge hand reached down, pulling Aiyana upright. She stumbled to her feet, her hands going to her forearms, and pushing up the sleeves of her robe.

She felt the raised flesh of her tattoos.

The wizardess, in all her research, had become adept at finding, activating, and using portals. But on the journey of knowledge, she'd learned and excelled at accessing interdimensional space. This is how she'd made the Citadel, her tent, with its extra spaces and abilities. This is how'd she created her robe, which held many mundane items, such as ropes, ladders, oil lamps, shovels, and other items. She'd also learned how to imprint that dimensional anchor to her flesh through tattoos.

Pulling at the puckered scarring of ink and magic she felt her hand wrap around the daggers burned into the skin of her flesh, one on each arm. They shifted from the space beyond, entering the world she existed in, and with a blue spark appeared in her grip.

She pulled them from her sleeves and slashed at the torck godling gripping her shoulder. Bright ribbons of scarlet appeared across the beast's biceps, coloring his dark fur.

In her past—in what she considered the real world, as opposed to this world that was so real, but she thought of as a fantasy world, a dream world—men had often pushed her around and manhandled her. Men always thought women were a weaker and inferior version of themselves. Just because the female form didn't have the upper body strength, the musculature of the male form, they thought they could dominate them. They even referred to them as the weaker sex.

They were wrong.

Being strong wasn't just in the body. No. It was so much more than that. It was in the mind, knowledge, experience—and dammit—just in the raw force of willpower and determination.

She cut Rauhen a half dozen times, causing him to step backward with a sharp gasp of surprise and pain.

Rising to her full height, she pushed her power into her aura.

That was another thing she'd learned here, in her special fantasy world. Spirit and soul meant more than anyone back home in the real world ever knew. Her aura was something to be contended with, and so many—in both worlds—never realized that simple fact.

She'd practiced expanding her unseen influence, pushing her confidence around her, causing a physical reaction in those around her.

She did that now.

Rauhen laughed.

"Oh, child," he sighed between chuckles, "I feel you, and though it may be impressive or imposing to others…I am not them."

His fist shot out, connecting with her nose, and a popping crack sounded in her head. A bright, white flash of sensation that translated to pain blinded her, and she fell back.

When her sight cleared, Rauhen leaned over her, grinning through his cleft palate.

"Stupid girl," he chuckled again, "you cannot win this. You are inferior in every way. All I need you for is to open the passages between places. First this world, then your world, and then all the worlds."

Aiyana's head spun. The chemicals and magical assault Tymere attacked her with still clouded everything. She was acting on instinct and gut reaction, unable to do more than trigger a response on an animalistic level. Her higher brain was blocked.

Though realizing this was a victory in itself, it was too little, too late.

Rauhen's large hand slid around her upper body, his long fingers meeting under the opposite arm. She only now realized how large he was, or maybe it was how small she was. Without effort, he lifted her. She saw the wounds she'd inflicted moments before had sealed, leaving thin lines of blood on his intact flesh.

"I will tell you this," Rauhen's tongue, elongated and black, slithered from his mouth and swirled towards her, "you are my savior. It is because of you that I am out of this prison. This very cell once held me, my mind in a cloud and lost. Put here by your people, so long ago, I mouldered here long after they left this land."

He shook his head, and his black, spiral horns moved back and forth. The hand holding her was almost gentle, one finger sliding up and down her neck in something that almost seemed like affection.

"Then, after being in the dark for a long time, I saw the light." A braying laugh tore from him and broke all around her into a coughing cackle. "Literally, the light. The light caused by you when you reopened the portal network, a portal that you'd opened without even knowing it. Three years ago, I escaped because of you."

He pulled her closer, his tongue trailing under her hair and around her neck to flick at her opposite cheek.

"Do you understand me, little one?" His breath, moist on her parted lips, smelled of cinnamon and brandy. "You freed me. The last thing your people did was to make sure I never got away, since I couldn't be killed. And you, the only one left on this continent that could do it, set me free. You have set a series of events into play that will destroy the last of what your people held dear."

Rauhen snapped a sack open with his free hand and shoved her inside. Her body folded, her knees bouncing off her lips and teeth. She felt his hand and thick nails—almost claws—intertwine in her hair and heard him mutter arcane words.

She knew the words; they were the phrases she'd created to open portals.

Then she felt that cold, enveloping energy of shifting from one place to another.

They were traveling through a portal, and Rauhen was using her as the compass to guide him.

Chapter 26

Reggie dove to the side to avoid the weapons of the men attacking him at the command of a megalomaniac.

His knee screamed with a sharp, shooting pain under the kneecap, his attempt to dodge failing, and a sword bit into his shoulder.

This is a great body, he thought, *so much younger than my old one. But a torn ligament in a knee will slow me down, no matter my age. Now, how do I take on a dozen bloodthirsty pemties with a dozen more waiting in the wings, without getting killed?*

He brought his rapier up, knocking away a blade, and stabbed into the abdomen of another soldier with his main gauche. He pulled the weapon to the one side, and the man's entrails splashed on the cobblestones. The warrior fell, and another soldier stepped into his place.

Reginald had been in lots of tough spots, though usually it was a territorial hippo, and on one occasion, the locals along the Congo defending their homeland. He'd always had moral issues killing natives. After all, they were just protecting their homes. But these guys were here to support a usurper. A man who'd built himself up as a hero, when in truth he only wanted power.

Worse than that, Manalo wasn't trying to help others. What he did was out of selfishness and greed.

Reggie was back on his feet with a flourish of his rapier, a twist, and a lurch. But he stumbled on his wounded leg, his knee barely supporting his weight.

His skill was instinctive, the previous inhabitant of his body well practiced with the weapons the swashbuckler now wielded. Amazed by the ingrained ability, Reggie let his body take over the combat and he considered his options.

Swords turned aside with a gesture of his blade, and delicate thrusts deterred attackers, making them step back. But another over-confident warrior immediately filled any hole in the wall of aggression.

I need to get to Manalo, he thought. *Cutting off the head of the snake makes him harmless.*

His rapier and main gauche danced with a practiced skill that dazzled him, blocking and cutting through opponents, and it had a similar effect on those rushing him.

Soon, the wall of combatants thinned, and he focused on the leader, Manalo.

Killing was not in Reginald's nature. He didn't enjoy ending the life of anyone, but words wouldn't stop this man, or even besting him in single combat.

Manalo, the warlord, must be slain. Reggie realized. *He would fall soon enough with the wound, but if he got away, he'd be able to recover.*

The others, the fodder of men rushing at him, weren't of the same mind.

Seeing Manalo, his hand pressed to the wound in his thigh, creep backwards out of the circle of attackers, Reggie knew he had to take him down.

Around him, the few dasism left and the rammen barely held their own against the stone guardians of

Icon Hall. They were no help, only he could face and defeat the leader of the invading army.

Melodramatic, aren't you? He thought, a small laugh coming out.

Remembering a time he'd faced overwhelming odds—well, two different times, once in the jungles of Borneo, and another time at a poker table—he considered his tactics.

Nodding, he hoped the same bluff would do here.

"I'm holding all the cards," he shouted, "and it's inevitable that Parsay is with me! I shall call down the might and wrath of the gods; The Walking God, Torgoth, and others, to end this farce!"

"Kazzek Tel Virian?" a soldier asked, his voice filled with wonder. "Is that you?"

Reggie hesitated, then nodded, a sly smile crossing his face as he remembered the name of his body.

"You're a legend," the man muttered, then raised his voice to the others around him and backed away. "He took down the behemoth of Milestone. Killed the ogre of the south. He fricken slew the Witch of Winter when he was more boy than man! They say that he can't be killed!"

"Don't forget the Battle of Wine in Runsk," Reginald added, rising to his full height, and batting away a hesitant attack with his parrying dagger and stabbing a soldier in the thigh, "and the bounty hunters of Kresk. They all fell to my blade, even when they had the upper hand. I am death to those who attack me!"

The last word ended in a shout, and the men around him took a step back.

Without hesitation, he limped forward, favoring his uninjured leg, and closed the distance between himself and Manalo.

"Kill him!" The warlord's voice was shrill and panicked. "Defend me! He isn't immortal, he's just a…"

Reggie's rapier slid into the man's throat, cutting off his words.

Manalo gurgled, his sentence cut off as Reginald slid his main gauche into the man's ribs, angled upward towards his heart.

The circle of soldiers broke and scattered.

"What do you know?" Reginald asked the backs of the fleeing men. "Looks like the gods *do* favor me! Well, in battle, moreso than at the card table."

Kajuun ducked under the clack of stone wings. Her fellow torck screamed in the onslaught of magical constructs.

Looking around, she gauged the battle. Reginald stood over the warlord, and the enemy army were falling back, but the creatures created to defend the city still swarmed them.

"Chevae! Arkeshia!" she shouted, seeing them remaining out of the all the magic-wielding dasism still standing. "Can you be unbinding these things from their earthen bonds?"

The two-spirit spellslingers, bewildered and bedraggled, drew close to the woman and looked at her.

"I know the wind and water," Kajuun went on, "but not the element of rock and stone! Can you be tearing the magics that keeps them to this world?"

The elementalists looked tired and at the edge of breaking. The two dasism exchanged an exhausted look and shrugged.

"Do it," Kajuun encouraged. "What you be doing right now can save your people. Stop this army from destroying everything that you be holding dear."

Kajuun saw a beautiful gargoyle falling towards the duo, and leapt forward, knocking the magical being away with the flat of her massive blade.

"Do it," she shouted, "doing it now, or be dying here, and condemning your peoples to the same fate!"

The torck were separatists, excluding others from their society. That was something Kajuun never thought was a good idea. She'd always believed including others was the best way to help her people to flourish and thrive. She stood in front of the two dasism, putting her thought into action.

Slamming her sword into the sheath on her back, Kajuun stooped down to pick up a stone bench on the edge of the plaza, and came up from her crouch, swinging it.

She knocked the first statue back, and it spiraled into the flagstones of the courtyard with an explosive result. Shards of stone from the bench and an animated statue flew outward, causing the torck to throw an arm across her eyes to protect herself from tiny bits of marble.

That opened her to the attack of the next guardian. It bowled her over, and she hit the ground on her back. The creature thrust a spear at her head, but she pivoted her body to one side.

The magically hardened and sharpened marble weapon missed the woman's head by a finger's width, and instead slid deep into Kajuun's shoulder, just under the collarbone, jarring her as she heard the spear scrape the flagstones underneath her.

From her prone position, Kajuun saw the clouds churn, turning over and around themselves. It reminded her of her babushka and how she'd mix potatoes when Kajuun was just a girl, sitting on the counter next to her grandmother, giggling and trying to taste everything.

But the sky wasn't the creamy white of that long past recipe. It was deepening to a bright verdant color, and instead of being puffy, the stratus bubbled and boiled in the sky overhead. It was like the folktales of Baba Yaga coming to life and made her think of a dense witch's brew from childhood tales.

The searing pain in her shoulder brought Kajuun back to the present. She wrapped her hands around the shaft of the spear. Her grip was weak from the pain, but she pressed her feet against the midsection of her attacker and pushed the statue away.

It stumbled backwards, and a bolt of lightning shattered it just a few steps from the warrioress, leaving a crater in the plaza.

Kajuun skidded away on her back from the force of the blast, her vision a white sheet from the pain and the lightning. Blinking, a double image of a photo negative of the statue being struck lay across everything she saw.

Looking around, she saw buildings bursting as bolts of lightning struck all around. Then the tower exploded outward.

Chevae and Arkeshia raised their arms, their fingers grasping at the air like they were reaching for something. They thrust their limbs towards the guardians, and the energies of sky and nature bent in their trajectories to strike the statues. The dasism did this again and again, redirecting the lightning towards targets of their choosing.

Within moments, they decimated the guardian gargoyles. Broken and shattered, parts of stone bodies littered the ground around them.

An open hand came into Kajuun's line of sight. She followed the length of the arm upward to see Reginald smiling down at her.

"Come on," he said, "I'll help you up, then we can get inside and help our friends."

She let him pull her to her feet, almost pulling him down instead.

"You are being hurt?" she asked.

"Yeah," he nodded, "my knee got bent the wrong way. Maybe we can lean on each other so neither of us falls?"

"Dah," she nodded back, "this is sounding like a good thing."

Together, they and the rest of their forces headed towards the huge double doors of the tower. Chevae and Arkeshia had their arms around the waist of the other, helping one another walk.

Those who weren't injured, or not hurt as badly, helped the wounded torck, and the group limped towards shelter, and the final battle.

Nathan sighed. He felt a warm trickle down the back of his neck. Probably a concussion, or worse. He wouldn't be getting to his feet, not easily at least, and the madman was coming towards him.

Jagged arms of lightning burst forth from the alchemist, and with an exhausted wave of his hand, Nathan called up short walls of stone to catch the magics.

The alchemist's confidence was bordering on insanity; Nathan had never seen anyone like this before.

No, that's not true, he thought. *There was that one time when a guy was high on something. Meth, or maybe PCP. He thought he was immortal, invulnerable, and couldn't fail.*

Reasoning with the man is out of the question. The only way to beat someone who can't feel fear is to overpower them quickly.

Nathan felt a peaceful calm fall over him.

If this is it, he thought, *then I'll go down doing what I can to protect my friends.*

He drew in a breath, and with it the power of Jonath. He felt his connection to the earth, far below him, and the runnels of power threaded into the structure of rock all around him.

Drawing in that energy, the priest slapped his stumps on the floor, sending it outward and away from him.

The ground rippled like an ocean wave, rising higher as it flowed away from him. Stones tore free, holes appearing in the floor, and Tymere was thrown backwards.

Nathan pushed his forearms into the stone and felt it soften to mud under his wrists. He pushed again, and a second wave followed the first, rolling away from him towards the stumbling alchemist.

The bubble of arcane protection balanced over a large hole underneath the man, but it had pushed him more than halfway across the room.

"You cannot break my shield," Tymere screeched. "I am impervious!"

"I thought you might say something like that," Nathan breathed, "but let's see if your shield can break you."

The priest called upon his will, gripping at it with the invisible fingers of his spirit. If he failed, everyone in this world he cared about would die. He knew he wouldn't remain conscious much longer, and this would be his last chance.

Raising his stone-capped wrists, he slammed them on the floor, and a third wave rose and rippled outward. It caught the sphere of magic and tossed it up and back. When it came down, it landed in the tossed, muddy surf of the remaining floor, and slid out of the crumbling hole in the wall behind the alchemist.

Nathan heard the man's scream, becoming distant as the alchemist fell. It stopped and a sudden silence filled the rokairn's ears.

Unsure if the quiet was because the madman was dead, or if he was losing consciousness, Nathan pushed to his feet. Stumbling forward, the ground solidifying with each step, Nathan moved towards the hole in the wall. He had to know if he'd stopped the man, or if he'd just doomed the people fighting in the courtyard below.

Reaching the breach, Marcid dragging at his side, Nathan put one stump on the wall and leaned over the edge to look down at the plaza.

Tymere was still in his bubble of safety, the Key of Aiyana clutched in one hand. But the man was twisted, his bottom half facing down, and his upper body facing up. The man's empty eyes stared at Nathan, a look of surprise etched on his face.

The rokairn's knees buckled, and he fell forward, towards the opening and the ground below.

Hands gripped his shoulders, and others grabbed his belt, wrapping around his waist, pulling him backwards.

They were gentle, even caring.

As blackness washed over awareness, Nathan heard voices.

"We've got you, my friend," Reggie said.

"You're being safe now," Kajuun said. "You can being resting."

Everything faded.

The wash of travelling caressed Aiyana, clearing her mind. It was like stepping out of a smokey room into fresh air. She knew this area in between wasn't a place. This was her space, and it refreshed her in ways that even a good night's rest could never do.

Others often felt dizziness or nausea when travelling, but not her. This was what she loved doing more than anything else.

The bag made the air close and thick. She panted to get her breath, but with her head clearing it was easier to feel the flow of energy of the portals. Her captor's hand still gripped her hair, using her to help guide him.

She felt something else. A thin tendril of mind magic, drilling into her, pulling her innate knowledge of the ways to be used by her kidnapper.

Aiyana had training. First from her childhood with the aeifain in the ways of mind magic. Later from the dasism in the elemental magic. Back in her own world, she'd been studying in college, learning how to hone her mind to do many things at once. It was an era of struggle for many people, the 1960s, but also a time of opportunity to bring about change. She'd been on the edge of those events, riding it like a surfer in an Annette Funicello beach blanket party movie.

The thought of this young girl who'd been a Mouseketeer flooded her mind, and it made her think of Sally Field in Gidget, a situation comedy that was popular. And she'd heard about Sally Field doing another show called The Flying Nun.

These women were entertainers, but they showed the power of women growing, allowing the chance for change. The opportunity for women to lead and influence the next generation.

Aiyana Riandell—once known as Donna Russo in a different time, place, and world—thought of those who inspired her and gave her strength. Others, more important in what she believed in, came to mind: Betty Friedan, journalist and co-founder of the National Organization for Women; Gloria Steinem, journalist, and activist; Angela Davis, African American political activist, and author; and others flooded Donna's memory.

Aiyana would be damned if she'd fail at the last moment when anything she'd do would make a lasting difference.

She drew upon the strength of memories, hope, struggle, and her will. She remembered how she'd slapped away Nathan's helpful hand in the first moments she'd met him. She was more than this. She could stop this monster who'd grabbed her to be used. She would overcome.

Chapter 27

The power of the portals' 'between places' flooded through Aiyana, snapping back to the present. No time to linger on what had been. She had to deal with what was happening now.

Reaching up, the wizardess gripped the wrist of the beast using her and unleashed her power up his arm.

Flames erupted, and the smell of singed hair and flesh flooded the sack that imprisoned her, the fire burning away the fibers of Rauhen and the bag.

She fell.

Tumbling through the cosmos that was the space between places and worlds. Reveling in the sensation, her mind reaching out to find familiar anchor points. She saw where Rauhen wanted to go, the Nine Towers of Magic. She saw all the places she'd been: Red City, Durgan's Keep, Land's End, Seawall City, Runsk, Wiley's Station, and more.

Aiyana also saw Icon Hall and turned her focus there. But she'd have to bring Rauhen with her. Reaching up through the aether, she found her captor's wrist.

No, he is no longer my captor, she thought. *He's my passenger, and at my mercy now.*

Gripping the man's arm, she flashed to Seawall City. The tatters of the bag fell away and bright sunlight flooded her sight.

Rauhen stumbled.

A crowd in the courtyard where she'd once been hung gaped at the duo, and she opened her mind to travelling again.

She tore open another passage through time and space, and they shot across the space to Durgan's Keep. Sewers opened around them, and surprised rats squeaked and scurried in all directions. The stone guardians of the chamber lurched to life, lifting weapons, and she shifted again.

The air of the recently renamed Crescent Plains filled their lungs, full of moisture and fresh growth. Aiyana saw the tower where she'd defeated Khizane and his armies. Grass covered what had been a desert three years before, and birds flitted through the sky.

Rauhen bent and vomited, trying to pull free of her grip, and she shifted again.

This was her game now, and the man who'd tried to use her like a pawn—no, a tool—had no choice but to but come along with her.

The short, gray walls of Runsk appeared around them, then the brown wood buildings of Dioneze City, then the white marble and stone of Icon Hall.

Rauhen tore free, stumbling backwards, still retching.

Aiyana pulled at the daggers tattooed on her calf, and two metal weapons shimmered back to reality from the plane where she'd stored them.

With a feral scream, she launched herself at the torck, stabbing him in the neck sand chest. Pulling the blades free, she plunged them into the man again and again.

He stumbled backwards, throwing his hands up to protect himself. She slashed his forearms and shoulders, shredding his burnt flesh.

"You won't," she panted, "you can't…control me! You will not take what I made and use it!"

Rauhen fell under the onslaught. She dropped on top of him, plunging the daggers into him over and over again.

"This world is mine," she screeched, "not yours! I will protect it! I will…"

Her words trailed off, and the world around her came into focus.

A crowd of torck stood in a wide circle in a plaza littered with broken white stone statues and buildings. Dark clouds rolled overhead, parting and scattering, allowing the sun to creep tentatively across the city.

A gentle, but husky, voice was speaking to her.

"Aiyana," Nathan croaked, "I think you got him. You can stop now."

The rokairn reached out a severed limb towards her, the stone cap at the end covered with mud and blood.

"Dah," Kajuun leaned against Reginald, both injured, "I am thinking that you have made him regret what he did."

The swashbuckler nodded, his leg buckling under him.

The shirai took up his weight, wincing as her hand went to the scarlet bandages across her chest, and helped him stand.

Reggie grinned sheepishly at Kajuun.

Chevae and Arkeshia looked down at her, their smiles turning to frowns of concern at her gore splattered form.

A dozen paces away lay Tymere in a shallow crater, his broken body still clutching the magical artifact that Aiyana had created to connect the different arcane arts.

"Oh," Aiyana looked back down at the mutilated form under her, "yeah, I guess so."

She dropped the daggers, pushing up with her knees to stand.

Rauhen's bloody hand shot up and gripped her throat, and she gasped in surprise, but it turned into a choking sound.

A blue oval shimmered around the torck leader as Aiyana turned her eyes back to him, her mouth shaped into a grimace of pain and hate. She slammed both of her hands into the man's chest, and his hand tore away from her neck.

Rauhen fell backwards into the portal open beneath him, his eyes wide and his hands flailing for purchase.

He found the edge of the flagstones and pulled himself up and back into the time, place, and world where Aiyana stood over him.

The aeifain stomped on his face, kicking at him, and reached into her robe, pulling the first thing off it she touched. A cloth patch of two lines, intersected by a dozen other lines, ripped free. A wooden ladder solidified into reality, and Aiyana jammed it downward into Rauhen's chest. Wood met ribs with a crack and the torck's hands lost their grip.

The master of a race, the puppet master of this world, and invader of her home realm, fell backwards into the portal she'd called into being, and it cut his stifled scream off right as it started.

"I guess you *rung* his bell," Nathan mumbled, which turned into a coarse laugh, which became a cough.

"I can say," Aiyana said with a small smile, "he won't be *climbing* any social *ladders* anymore."

"He won't be *stepping up* anytime soon," Reggie chimed in.

"Maybe he needs a *step-by-step* guide to know how to get back?" Aiyana chuckled.

Nathan burst into a guffaw, and it turned into a hacking cough.

"Stop," the rokairn gasped, holding up his two stone-capped wrists, "I gotta pee, but don't know how I'm gonna do that, I'm *stumped*! I think I'm going to need a *hand* with that!"

That caused others to join in the laughter, but only for a moment. The merriment died into an awkward silence.

"*Urine* trouble then," Aiyana muttered.

The following days weren't easy. Most people were seriously injured, and food and medical supplies were difficult to find. The clear, blue sky silhouetted the broken towers. Charred holes across rooftops and walls, some with smoke still trailing upward, the smell of smoldering cloth and furniture wafted through the streets.

Roadways littered with stone, brick, wood, and glass dominated the city. Remnants of lightning strikes showed black scoring marks along the thoroughfares and avenues. The once beautiful city was a ghost town, with scattered survivors wandering the streets in twos and threes.

Most of the people remaining were injured, but spirits were high. Scouting groups found what food they could, scavenged from the shops and homes, or harvested from the wild growth in the surrounding countryside.

A group of the torck returned to their city, promising to bring back help for the injured. Kajuun accompanied them to make sure the council understood what happened, and the part Rauhen played in the events.

The other torck regarded Kajuun as a hero of their people, though they'd always held her in high regard. Now they bowed or saluted, depending on the person, and deferred to her suggestions or opinions.

It drove the shirai crazy.

She tried ignoring the people, giving them a buffeting reproach, insisting she wasn't anyone special. This just made them love her more. They spoke of her humility, and how she never thought she was better than anyone else.

The dasism twin-spirits sat with Kajuun one evening, as the setting sun cast scarlets, burnt umber, and indigo across the celestial expanse. Chevae and Arkeshia laughed at Kajuun good-naturedly, but also offered advice.

"They've just experienced a betrayal at the hands of the one they thought of as a leader," Arkeshia explained, one hand on the shirai's arm, "and you are very much his opposite. They gravitate to you. It is the nature of people."

"If it helps," Chevae waved around a skin of wine, "give them a month and they'll start talking bidj about you. It's only a matter of time. They'll find something you did, and disagree, then tell others how horrible you are. Others will still think you walk on water and are more intoxicating than this wine—and it is quite strong, wouldn't you agree?—and they'll defend you against the others."

"It's true," Arkeshia agreed, putting a hand on Chevae's wrist to stop them from waving around the goatskin flask, "it is the nature of people."

Kajuun looked like someone had struck her, her eyes wide and a bit panicked.

"But..." she gulped, then took in three short, sharp breaths.

Chevae laughed.

"She takes on an army of magical constructs," the tipsy dasism said, still chuckling, "faces hundreds of warriors, and barely breaks a sweat. You tell her people are people, and she looks like she wants to vomit!"

"Kajuun," Arkeshia said with a gentle smile, "you're going to be fine. Soon, you will just be one in the crowd again."

Kajuun breathed out, nodded, and gave a weak smile.

"Unless you decide you want to lead them, then it's another story," Arkeshia finished.

Kajuun looked pained again, and Chevae burst into laughter. When Arkeshia shot them a look, they raised the skin to their lips.

The next morning, Chevae and Arkeshia gathered the other dasism and set out to reunite with their tribe, promising to tell them what happened. They also offered to come back and help with the rebuilding of Icon Hall and finding the lost people of the aeifain.

Aiyana reassured them she knew what happened, and where they'd gone, and that they wouldn't be returning anytime soon.

"A thousand years isn't soon," she'd told them. "I'll lock down the city and leave it in a condition, so when they do return, it'll be waiting for them."

"Did you find what you were looking for?" Arkeshia asked.

"Yes," Aiyana smiled wistfully, "and no."

Aiyana returned to the tower between the times she spent with Nathan. She'd insisted on taking care of him personally, brushing away other offers of help beyond tending to his wounds.

The rokairn wasn't his old self. He'd never been outspoken or exuberant, but now he was often in a funk. The pleasant word was melancholy, and people could see he wasn't the same man he'd been before.

When in the tower, she activated the latent magics of the city. First the guardians slowly reformed, pebbles and shards of stones creeping towards one another to bond together until the beautiful gargoyles became whole. The constructs returned to their posts and perches, taking dutiful watch over Icon Hall once again.

Aiyana assigned the scatters to clean up the streets and asked the remaining torck to go into the mountains to a quarry to get new stone to fix the buildings. She used the gargoyles to lift the blocks, and the torck did the masonry to repair buildings. The work went on through the summer into the autumn.

The tree-men were another story, though. Aiyana had the dasism—those that were left—plant the magical seeds of those guardians in the enchanted soil of the parks throughout the city. The cousins of the aeifain were born for the work, their magics helping to accelerate the process. It would take years, or even decades, before the tree-men would freely roam again, but to Aiyana it was just a blink of an eye compared to her lifetime.

The leaves were hues of gold, orange, and red before she locked down the city, and everyone gathered outside the gates.

She stood, head bowed, and her hand on the outer wall. The gateway into the city closed, reversing what they had witnessed months before.

The torck stood far back, bags and satchels over their shoulders, ready to return to their home before the winter snows came.

The handful of dasism stood near her, lending their magical strength to hers as she closed a city that had once been a jewel of knowledge…and arrogance.

Teorge and Collin, and the dozen remaining humans—some taken in from the broken army of the warlord—waited as an honor guard.

"Where to now?" Reginald asked.

"Back to the beginning." Nathan's voice was quiet.

"What's that mean?" Reginald looked at the rokairn, concerned.

"He means we go back to where our paths first crossed," Aiyana said, "before we met. We go to Wiley's Station. Teorge needs to go home. Maybe we can help them rebuild and start again."

"Wiley's Station?" Reginald asked. "Perhaps it's time for a new name? Would it be forward of me to suggest Elda's Rest as a new name for the village?"

Epilogue

Nathan stood at the bar of the Traveller's Inn. Cogsley, the odd bartender, prepared a tray of drinks, and the priest looked down at his stone-capped wrists and sighed.

A grizzled old man, Croaker Norge, hunched on a bar stool next to the rokairn, and raised a crystal glass of whiskey to him in a toast with a nod. It held respect and sympathy.

Nathan hated that last part. He'd never wanted pity, but appreciated the gesture, so he nodded back and gave a grim smile.

Something as simple as carrying a round of drinks to his friends was impossible for him now. He couldn't even raise a glass for a toast. Sure, he'd found a workaround, but it wasn't the same as holding the handle of a mug and throwing his hand high into the air, clinking flagons, and downing a pint.

A large golem shuffled up. Nathan thought their name was BroomSweeper, or something like that. They were huge, double the rokairn's height, which meant that most men would only come up to their armpit. They were made of molded clay and looked…almost human.

The construct lifted the tray, their shoulders slumped, and moved towards the table that Nathan indicated with one of his stumps.

Aiyana, Kajuun, and Reggie sat together near the hearth, at a table in the center of the room. Aiyana's staff leaned against the chair where Captain Farrell perched. Nathan thought about how others he'd traveled with would've never sat anywhere except with their backs against a wall.

The inn—which had magically appeared a couple of weeks ago in the ruins of Wiley's Station, now Elda's Rest,—was filled with a scattering of people. Townsfolk mingled with 'regulars' and employees.

A shirtless, muscled man—Nomed—sat with the halfling Wanderly, the smaller man leaning in and whispering to his companion. Everyone could hear every word since he did it in a stage whisper meant to carry.

Nathan knew the pair too well to think it was done by mistake.

A crowd of dasism were at a corner booth, Shyam the Speaker leading them in some song from their tribe. Takia, the braided woman, was standing and swaying, her mug held high. Chirai, the tattooed warrior, was laughing too hard to join in, and Mekiya, the tribe's leader, was slapping the man on the back. Neyla, the tribe's second leader, rocked back and forth, eyes closed while Gokia belted out the song, more than a little off-key. Arkeshia and Chevae saw Nathan looking at them and raised a hand to wave at him.

The proprietor of the inn, Jack, was around somewhere. He came and went, often appearing in clothes drastically different from what he'd been wearing just moments before. It was part of the man's charm.

Aiyana glared at Jack every time he made an appearance. She'd made her distrust of him apparent to Nathan for years now and had become more vocal around others as well. Especially to Kajuun, who'd been travelling with them since they'd passed through the Torck capital on their way back to Elda's Rest.

The two had become good friends, and Nathan thought Aiyana had wanted another woman to talk to. Whenever the aeifain complained about Jack, the torck just laughed and asked how Aiyana could know such things to be true.

Jack always brushed it off with a smile and a wave. Nathan felt the man was genuine. He never made excuses, or tried to deny anything, nor did he change the subject.

Teorge, Collin, and others sat at a long table in the center of the room, laughing and drinking. Dirt and soot, after a long day of hard work, marked every person at the table.

The rokairn knew the place would fill more as the evening wore on, as people of the village came wandering in. It was usually someone who'd been working on the rebuilding. But occasionally someone who'd been lost, and thought dead, would come in.

That always caused a reaction.

The crowd would hush as they realized one of their own had come home. Then they'd creep forward, an indistinct murmur blanketing them. Someone would shout the person's name, there'd be a sudden flurry of hugs and movement as loved ones made their way to the person, then the crowd would cheer. It guaranteed that the next few hours would be full of song, drink, food, and stories.

It always made Nathan choke up a little to witness. After so many years of dealing with callous, uncaring people who laughed about bombings on the news…it was refreshing to see human beings displaying signs of humanity.

Nathan had been here for most of the day and had seen the flash of windows and doors along the outer wall more than once. He wasn't sure what that meant but knew some magic or another was part of it.

He approached his friends, following behind the golem. The construct lifted the drinks from the tray using two massive fingers, and set them on the table, and even the largest mug looked like a child's tea cup in the golem's grip.

Kajuun, Reginald, and Aiyana were leaning in close, their whispered words slurred in the buzz of sound around them. Nathan pulled out his chair and picked up the thread of the conversation.

"Where did you send Rauhen?" Reginald leaned towards Aiyana on his elbows.

She pulled a fork from her mouth and stabbed at the plate of greens in front of her.

"Where he hopefully can't cause any more trouble," she sighed, "the sixteenth century, I think."

"Our world?" the swashbuckler asked, astounded.

The boy had healed up well.

Nathan chuckled to himself. This young man was probably thirty years older than Nathan on Earth, and though Nathan's body was older in this world, he didn't think it was older than Reggie was back home.

Kajuun nodded to something Aiyana had said, her face sympathetic.

"Yes," Aiyana nodded, and took a bite of her food thoughtfully. "No magic, no technology, and, well…"

She hesitated.

Nathan settled into his chair as the golem shuffled off. Captain Farrell sat on the top of one of the six ladder-backed chairs, nibbling at a strip of meat at his feet.

"I couldn't just kill him," she sighed again, "it's just not in me. Can you understand that?"

"I think so," Reginald nodded. "I never like killing when it can be avoided."

Nathan nodded, agreeing.

"He also claimed that he couldn't be killed," Aiyana sighed, "and he healed fast enough that I think he may have been telling the truth."

The table fell silent, the wash of sound from voices around the room breaking across them like they were walking in the surf on the shoreline of conversation.

Aiyana forked a piece of meat and held it towards Nathan, who shook his head.

The priest had lost weight, partially because he was embarrassed by accepting help for his most basic needs. He'd worked out a way to do a few things, using the blessings of his god. A shallow bowl of clay sat in front of him at the table, and he could manipulate it to make a hand that he could use to feed himself or get a drink. But it always drew attention, which wasn't something he wanted.

"So, what do we do now?" Reginald asked.

"Well, I'm kinda glad you asked." Aiyana said.

She took another bite, and they waited for her to continue.

"Rauhen wanted to use me to open a portal to the Nine Towers of Magic," she continued. "Something about using it to find a way to destroy my people, and invade other worlds. He said I was the cause of it, and because of that, I want to look into it. Perhaps find more lost magic and bring it back to the people."

A flash of bluish light from the side door caught Nathan's attention. He tried to remember if he'd seen that side door before this moment, but couldn't quite put his finger on if it had existed before.

The door opened, distracting him from the thought, and two figures entered. A tall, lean warrior dressed in furs with a long blade on his back, and a short young man with delicate features, and daggers decorating his belt and thighs. The former had the ruddy skin of a northern barbarian, and the sleek, black hair to match. The latter was slight and wiry, his own dark hair pulled back into a short ponytail that didn't even reach his collar.

Nathan immediately recognized the duo and darted a look at Aiyana. The woman hadn't noticed and appeared to be lost in thought.

Nathan watched the newcomers scan the room for a table and choose one that had chairs with their backs to the wall. It was a few tables away, but close enough to observe, and probably overhear if the new arrivals weren't trying to be surreptitious.

"It's Torrents and the Kid," Nathan whispered harshly, jerking his head towards the two that were settling onto a bench.

"What?" Reggie said, turning in his chair to look at the two settling into their seats and waving at the serving maid.

"Don't look," Nathan grunted. "They may not want to be recognized."

Aiyana craned her head to look.

"They're old friends," she said, waving at them.

"Look," she smiled, "they waved back."

"Well, I can't wave," Nathan muttered, thumping his stone caps on the table.

"Here," Aiyana lifted a glass of brandy, "have a drink, you need it."

She moved the glass to Nathan's lips and tilted it upward.

The rokairn made a nominal effort of turning his head to refuse, but opened his lips to drink rather than spilling the alcohol.

Aiyana lifted it more, forcing the man to drink it all, or risk wasting it.

Nathan gulped, sputtering, but getting it all in his surprise. The clay in the bowl formed hands and one attached to the one of the rokairn's stone stumps. His arm rose, and he took the glass from the aeifain, smudging her and the glassware with streaks of muddy fingerprints.

"Now," Aiyana said sweetly, discretely wiping the smears off, "stop being a dour dwarf, and welcome some old friends. Use your clay hand to wave if you feel the urge."

Nathan looked up to see the Kid standing between him and Aiyana, Torrents standing beside the rogue, and towering over him.

Nathan smiled weakly, raised his hand to greet them, then pulled it under the table and nodded instead.

The clay hand rising from the bowl in front of the rokairn waved frantically until the priest shot it a scathing look and it collapsed back into a lifeless lump.

"Thanks for the invite," the Kid said, sliding into a chair.

Torrents looked the group over, and Captain Farrell screeched, launching himself to land on the big man's shoulder. The raven nuzzled the barbarian, rubbing his head on the man's chin.

"I think he likes you," the Kid laughed.

Torrents laughed as well. He pulled out the chair the raven had occupied, picked up the dropped strip of meat from the seat, and sat down. He offered the rare-cooked treat to the bird, who pecked at it eagerly.

The Kid pulled out a skein of yarn and knitting needles from a satchel, and began counting rows of the strings. The clack of needles followed.

"The Traveller's Inn," Torrents muttered, looking around the room, "is this place like a chain restaurant or something?"

"It's called a franchise, sweetie," the Kid said. "Don't be simple."

"Well, I am simple, Kid," Torrents smiled innocently, "and if I ever forget that, you make sure and remind me fifty billion times a day."

"Don't exaggerate," the Kid said without looking up from counting the rows on his knitting, "I'd bet it's almost never more than fifteen or twenty times a day. But sometimes, someone as simple as you needs reminding, or you tend to forget."

The sixth chair slid back, and Arkeshia dropped into it with a smile.

The scraping sound of another chair being slid over cut through the murmur of noise in the inn, and Chevae—drink in hand—shoved it between Torrents and Aiyana.

"Looks like we're all here," Kajuun said, "and that must mean something."

"It must, indeed," came a voice from above their shoulders.

It was Jack Tucker, proprietor of The Traveller's Inn.

The man was nondescript to the nth degree. He had hair colored hair, eye-colored eyes, and was neither tall nor short, and looked to be of an age between thirty and fifty, depending on the light.

"Uh, oh," the Kid said, "we've hit this moment. I know what's coming!"

"How did we go from three of us," Aiyana said, glaring at Jack, "to nine of us in the space of a few moments?"

Captain Farrell croaked and gave Aiyana the side eye.

"Excuse me, so sorry, Captain. Ten. Better?" the aeifain asked.

The raven fluttered and settled down to attack Torrents's knuckles, trying to get to a crust of bread.

"Magic?" the Kid suggested with a smile.

"Manipulation is more likely," Aiyana grunted. "Isn't that right, Jack? You do like to create a situation, don't you?"

"Do you know about the Troll Lords?" Jack asked the table, ignoring the aeifain's question. "And the troll migration towards the Nine Towers of Magic?"

"PepperGarten knows about it!" A shrill voice crackled, and a deeper, scraping sound cut off all conversation in the inn.

A thin, old man dressed mostly in rags and sheets of moss—though the latter was worn like an expensive mink drape—dragged a full length, solid oak picnic table across the room towards the group. The man shoved another table, almost a twin to the one he was dragging, aside with his hip sand shuffle-clumped his table to one side to get around the one in the way.

"Here, old man," Kajuun stood and moved to the other side of the approaching barge of a table, "allow me to be helping you."

The torck grabbed the table and with a single movement, lifted it and moved it until the short, flat end butted up against the round table everyone else sat at.

Chairs were shuffled and redistributed, and food was passed down the table to give everyone room and access to fresh breads, roasted meats, fried potatoes, and other delights.

"Eleven!" PepperGarten cackled. "And that's a magical number!"

"I could call Edsumar in and make it twelve, nothing like a dragon to round out a party!" the Kid said.

"I think he might be a bit too big to get in the door," Torrents said.

"Jack could be fixing that," Kajuun suggested, "couldn't you, Jack?"

"I'm sure Jack is a master of fixing many things," Aiyana said, holding her staff upright beside her.

"Can we get on with this before PepperGarten has to go pee?" the wizened druid asked.

"Speaking of going pee," The Kid turned to Nathan, "how's that work for you now? Or going number two, for that matter? I mean, I guess you could bring your plate of clay hands with you, but that would leave muddy streaks on your…um, areas, and then you'd never know what to wipe, until the hands were totally gone."

"Oh ho!" PepperGarten exclaimed, standing up to look at Nathan's hands. "You could do like PepperGarten does. PepperGarten just drops trow in the woods and does like the bears do. But of course, PepperGarten's diet is mostly nuts and berries, so

PepperGarten just poops hard little nuggets, and not much sticks to PepperGarten's butt."

"Enough!" Aiyana said, half rising from her seat. "Nathan had help, and I think that's enough of this discussion. Am I understood?"

She said the last words individually, breaking them apart, glaring around the table.

Everyone fell silent, and a small squeak came from PepperGarten. Something like a sugar glider ran from his tattered waistcoat pocket, over his chest, and into the hood flopping on his back as he nodded.

"Thank you, Miss Riandell," Jack said, earning him a glare from the wizardess, "and I think we need to return to the subject of the troll migration to the Nine Towers of Magic. Are you all familiar with how the trolls, aeifain, and dasism were all once the same race?"

Torrents paused in the middle of stacking a plate with steaming meats, potatoes, and bread, snorting.

"Oh, don't tell them that," he laughed, "the idea might offend them!"

"You mean the trolls?" the Kid asked, snickering.

"What do you mean?" Chevae asked. "I am not familiar with this."

"PepperGarten knows!" PepperGarten half rose again.

"Perhaps I should tell this story, my old friend," Jack said, laying a gentle hand on the wiry man's shoulder, guiding him back into his seat.

"Jack was always being the bossy one," Kajuun nudged PepperGarten, "ever since the three of us were coming to this land."

"Yes, well…" Jack mumbled before he was cut off.

"Wait a cotton-picking minute," the Kid said, before being interrupted by Torrents.

"You can't say that anymore," the barbarian said, but with a smile.

"I'm an old woman, allow me my slips," the Kid said, then added teasingly, "you whippersnapper."

"Wait, how old are you?" Reginald asked. "Older than I was? I presume you're from Earth also, as are most of us here?"

"We're not," Arkeshia said, thumbing a gesture towards Chevae.

"Wait," the Kid huffed, "stop interrupting my interrupting!"

Everyone quieted and looked at the young street rogue.

"Jack," the Kid began again, "do I understand correctly that when PepperGarten came here, you and this horny lady came with him?"

"Well," Jack hemmed, drawing the word out, "it wasn't my first time here, but it was the first time I drew a trio into the world to help things out. But that's a story for another time…"

"I'll wait for the movie," Torrents muttered, and a chorus of laughs rose from the table.

The big man smiled sheepishly, and the others fell silent for a few moments.

The mood around the table calmed, feeling almost nostalgic as each person held their own thoughts triggered by the barbarian's words.

"The point is that it was on the site where the Nine Towers were later built that the ritual that caused the split in the races happened," Jack continued, "and I think it bears looking into."

"And Rauhen wanted to go there," Aiyana said, looking at Jack with suspicion, "and I'd already planned to go there. What a coincidence..."

She trailed off, and Jack smiled softly.

"Aiyana," their host started, "I did bring each of you here for a reason, and in that way, I do guide each of you. But that's about it. I don't manipulate you any more than bringing you in at the right time and place. Any of you can leave at any time, like Esperanza did. Or just go off and do your own thing, as the Kid and Torrents did."

"Speaking of which," Nathan spoke in a rush of words, "I'd like to go back home."

The table fell silent, and Aiyana stared at the rokairn with wide eyes and her mouth open before dropping her head, her hair falling around her face to cover her reaction.

"Look," the priest sighed before going on, "I can't do this anymore. I feel like I've done as much as I can to help people here, and all things considered..."

Nathan trailed off and held up a stone-capped wrist and a clay hand.

"I'm not that handy to have around anymore..." his words broke off with a choking sound.

Aiyana looked up at her friend, her eyes brimming, glistening trails moving down her cheeks.

"Nathan," the wizardess reached out and laid her small hand on his forearm, "you've done more than you can ever know. I understand why you want to leave, and don't think we need to point out the reasons."

"Yeah, buddy," Torrents dropped a huge mitt on the bearded man's shoulder, "I got nothing but respect and good wishes for you."

"Nathan," the Kid stood to put his hand against the rokairn's cheek, stroking his beard, "you've been a great friend, and a quiet inspiration to everyone that's had the honor and pleasure of meeting you. You never ask for anything, but always offer to give something. You never complain, but always listened to us when we did. You were our silent leader from behind, doing it by example, and not words. I think we all support you in whatever you do."

The Kid wiped at his eyes with the back of his free hand.

The rest stood and moved to gather around the priest. Kajuun was nodding as she put a hand on his other shoulder, and Chevae and Arkeshia leaned over to wrap their arms around him. Reggie stood just outside of the circle, looking in and meeting Nathan's eyes. The human nodded, a tight smile on his lips, and an understanding look in his eyes.

Captain Farrell flapped across the table and dropped a piece of cheese in front of the rokairn, then looked at the man with his head tilted and a beady black eye watching him.

"Ha!" PepperGarten screeched. "Even the raven knows how cheesy this is!"

The group chuckled—but it didn't have any genuine humor in it—and broke up, moving back to their individual seats.

"When do you want to go home?" Jack asked Nathan, leaning around the man to look at his face.

"Soon," Nathan breathed out, and it sounded like relief, "can we do that? But not right this second!"

He held up his hand and stone capped wrist in a gesture to slow down, then his eyes caught sight of them, and he pulled his arms back to his sides, hiding his missing hands under the table.

"Maybe later tonight?" he asked quietly. "Can we do it after…this?"

"Of course, Nathan," Jack laid a hand on the man's shoulder, "you can't travel on an empty stomach or a heavy heart. So, take this evening to fill your belly and lighten your soul, and we'll leave when you're ready."

Jack moved away, and the table broke into excited chatter. The clink of glasses, the clank of mugs, and a raised cheer indicated the group was toasting the man of the hour.

Jack smiled without looking back, his eyes rimmed with moisture.

"You deserve this, Nathan," he mumbled to no one in particular. "You've earned it."

"So," PepperGarten said with a grin showing missing teeth, "do you think you'll die when you get back home?"

"PepperGarten!" Kajuun admonished.

"No," Nathan interrupted, "it's okay. And no, I don't think I will. I don't think I went through all this, only to die. I don't know how I'll live, but I think I will. And even if I don't, that'll be okay, too. I've lived a good life…here and there. Here was more than good! The past few years here have been more exciting than all the rest of my life put together!"

"Nathan," Aiyana said, her voice forceful, "you won't die. I promise you that, with every fiber of my being, I promise you will live long beyond the day that brought you here."

"Chick is intense," Torrents said.

"You can't say that anymore," the Kid teased, punching the large man in the bicep.

The table roared with laughter, but it felt forced.

When it died down, Reginald leaned towards Nathan.

"What're you going to do with Marcid?" Reggie nodded towards the double-headed battle-axe.

"I'm glad you asked," Nathan grinned, "because I think I have one more prayer that might be answered. Grab her."

The priest jerked his head towards his back, where he'd strapped the weapon.

Reginald stood and moved behind the rokairn, lifting the weapon reverently, and returned to his seat.

Others cleared the space in front of Nathan, and Reggie laid the axe on the table.

"Aiyana," the priest smiled at the wizardess, then looked at the druid, "PepperGarten, would you both lend help to this?"

The two nodded, and the Kid perked up.

"Torrents and I were there when it was made," the Kid said. "Can we help also?"

"And us," Chevae smiled, "Arkeshia and I will lend our abilities to whatever it is you want to do."

"Good enough," Nathan nodded, his grin widening, "but be gentle, no huge pushes of energy. Just support what I'm doing."

The group fell silent, and the priest bent his head in prayer to Jonath. He stayed that way for many minutes before raising his missing hands. The clay hand collapsed into the bowl, and he touched the weapon with the stone caps at the end of his wrists.

Each person, no stranger to rituals, acted accordingly. Some closed their eyes, others raised their faces to the unseen sky outside of the inn, but they all focused on the weapon.

The flash of blue magics outside the windows caught Nathan's attention, and he felt the immense, but subtle, power of The Traveller's Inn join in the magics.

Looking around the room, he realized it had fallen silent. Nomed's and Wanderly's lips moved in soundless words. Croaker turned around on his barstool, leaning towards them. The dasism in the corner booth all held their hands palms up and whispered quietly with closed eyes. Cogsley, behind the bar, held the golem's hand, his other hand pressed flat to the bar, and his clear, glass dome shone with an inner light. Jack stood in the shadows of the corner and nodded at Nathan when he looked at the proprietor, a small smile on his lips.

Even the humans were silent, holding their breath as they watched something most people never dreamed of seeing.

Kajuun put a hand on Nathan's shoulder, and he felt a rush of sensation push out of him and fill Marcid, the magical weapon that had been at his side for almost every moment since he'd entered this world.

"Put the hand axes I made for you beside her, and then pick her up," Nathan said to Reggie.

Reginald pulled the two steel weapons from his satchel and set them so their blades were touching the larger blades of Marcid. He reached out slowly and laid his hand on the shaft of the weapon, then wrapped his fingers around the grip.

The battle-axe melted, her wide head pulling into itself, and the haft becoming flat and thin. The two smaller weapons became puddles and were drawn into the larger blade like mercury rolling to find the greater puddle of the same material.

Something long, thin, and delicate formed under the swashbuckler's hand, an intricate woven guard swirling into existence around his knuckles. When he lifted his hand, he held a perfect rapier with a scrollwork guard around his fist. He raised it, and vines swirled and grew from the pommel, leaves caressing his wrist.

Reginald stared at the blade, his mouth open, and his eyes misty twin circles of emotion. Whether from generosity of the gift, or the beauty of it, Nathan couldn't be sure.

"Marcid is yours now," Nathan said softly, "and she'll be what you need her to be. Treat her well, and she'll take care of you, and guard you like no other weapon could."

Reggie nodded, unable to speak.

The weapon shifted, shrinking, and folding into herself, becoming a main gauche. Then bent again and reshaped to a stout hand axe.

"I can…" Reggie hesitated, "feel her. Without looking, I know where she is. I know that sounds crazy…"

"Nope," the Kid said, and then laughed before continuing, "I threw some stuff I learned from Edsumar into her."

"And we added awareness of the elements," Arkeshia said, Chevae nodding beside her.

"And berries!" PepperGarten cackled. "I added berries, so you can eat!"

The rapier reformed, and Reggie looked at Nathan, who shook his head.

"No," the priest said, "don't thank me. Just keep her well and use her to help others. Jonath has blessed her, and she'll do things you never expect."

"Now," Aiyana said, and all eyes turned to her, "there's a lot of magic left floating around here. How about I give you a tattoo like mine?"

She pulled back a sleeve of her robe and showed a dagger imprinted on her forearm. Pressing her hand to it, she drew it free of her flesh and held a thin dirk. She pressed it back to her arm, and it became a tattoo again.

Reggie nodded slowly in wonder.

"Um," the Kid said, "can I get a couple of those?"

"Yeah," Torrents pushed forward, "me too? Maybe a short sword on each thigh?"

The night flowed on, and the inn slowly emptied. Groups of people filtered out or went upstairs to their rooms. It was well past midnight when Jack came to Nathan and laid a hand on his shoulder.

"Are you ready?" Jack asked.

Nathan looked up, bleary-eyed from drink, exhaustion, and good company. Emotions rode high that night, and it showed on the posture of the six remaining friends, plus Captain Farrell, who was nestled on an empty plate, head tucked under a wing.

Aiyana looked pained, and Reggie confused. The Kid smiled nonchalantly, while Torrents belched and scratched himself.

"Yeah," Nathan nodded slowly and stood up. "I think so."

"Would you like to say your goodbyes?" Jack waved a hand at the table.

Nathan nodded again and turned to the group.

The Kid stood up and moved to the rokairn, pulling the priest to his chest.

"You did good, big man," the Kid said, "now, go take care of yourself. You deserve it."

Torrents took the Kid's place when the younger man stepped back.

The barbarian knelt.

"Look," Torrents said, "I kneeled down, so you don't hug my crotch, because I'm cool that way. You do you, and you'll be okay, because you're awesome."

The barbarian hugged Nathan, who awkwardly thumped the big guy on the back.

Torrents pulled away and held the man at arm's length.

"Yeah," Torrents laughed, "I suck at words, but you know…"

Nathan nodded and the big man moved back.

Kajuun stepped forward and stared down at Nathan.

"Dah," she said, "you are being okay, once you know one thing. It is one thing you need to know, and I will tell you now what that thing is, Nathan. You are being the most important person in your life. You understand, dah?"

"I think so?" Nathan raised his eyebrows and shrugged.

The woman clapped him on the shoulder and stepped back so Reginald could move forward.

"My friend," Reggie held out an open hand, and Nathan put a stone capped wrist into it, and they shook, "tell me, any advice for my time here?"

Nathan considered, looking over the man's shoulder at the corner of the room.

"Things are more than they seem," the rokairn said, meeting the man's eyes, "but they still boil down to the basics. Take care of Aiyana, she needs looking after, no matter how much she thinks she doesn't need any help."

Reggie nodded and moved away.

Aiyana stared at Nathan, her face tumultuous. A mix of emotions contorted as she slowly moved to him and dropped to both knees.

"Come here," Nathan said, embracing her.

She clutched him, clinging to him, tears streaming down her face.

"I love you, Nathan," she choked out through her tears.

"I know," he said with a smile that was echoed in his voice, "and I love you. You're going to be okay. Just keep saving the world, this one or the one we came from."

She nodded violently against his shoulder and pulled away, turning from him.

Nathan watched her back, a confused look on his face.

"Ready?" Jack asked quietly.

The priest shrugged.

"You know," the rokairn said, "I've been so many things since I've been here. Hunted. Scared. A hero. A mentor. A friend. But I think that last thing was the only thing I really ever wanted. I've never had friends like I've had here. Thank you all, it's been a wild ride, but I'm ready to get off thing crazy thing…called life."

"Was that from 'So I Married an Axe Murderer' with Mike Myers?" the Kid asked.

Nathan smiled, shrugged, and turned to Jack.

Jack smiled down at him and put a hand on Nathan's shoulder.

"Let's get this show on the road, then," the proprietor said, and led the rokairn towards a door that hadn't been there earlier.

Aiyana tilted her head, as if listening to a voice no one else could hear.

It was dark, except for a simple blue light. It came from the blade laying on the dusty floor, the spiral horn that made the pommel jutting above the white metal casting a shadow on the rock.

Raven Stealer stirred, and the sentience in the weapon woke fully, and reached out to call to the one person who would find it, and free it.

End of Sigils & Satyrs, Portals, Book 4

Sneak Peek: Towers & Trolls, Portals Book 5

Chapter 1

The dense jungle foliage waved far above his head. A cool wind moving the leaves was little more than a sluggish humid caress on the jungle floor. Insects buzzed around him, and sharp, little pains made him aware of their feeding on him.

The fetid smell of the trees and rotting plants clung to his nostrils, and the coppery taste of blood in his mouth. Muscles rippled in his belly, threatening to cramp at any moment.

"I am Griffon, the monster masher," he shouted out his gamer title and laughed, staring up at the canopy. "And, OMFG, a bus just crushed my ass. TPK, total party kill, and here I am…wait, where the hell am I?"

Another thought, so different from what he'd just experienced on the busy street downtown, rose to the surface. A dark, magical ritual and the gore of a gladiator ring came to Griffon's mind, and something not that deep inside of him screamed of danger. Something had gone horribly wrong in more than one place.

He remembered dying. He remembered the goblins, kobolds, and green-skinned, pig-faced warriors he'd slain, one after another, just before he died.

A flock of colorful, long-tailed birds burst from the trees above, distracting him from his thoughts. He smiled, wondering if there was any danger of them dropping a dookie on him. A dark blur leapt across the space he was watching and snatched a bird mid-flight.

"Oh, yeah!" he muttered, his mind returning to what he'd been doing before he woke here. "I was playing that game…wait, no, I wasn't. I was out picking up Doritos and Mountain Dew. But if this was the game, wow! They really did a VR graphics upgrade on this week's patch!"

A different memory of a wavy kris knife gutting him—first across his rippled, muscular stomach, then up and down from solar plexus to his pelvis—flooded across him.

His hand shot to his belly.

It wasn't his usual flabby gut that bulged over his low hanging jeans. It was taut, and he thought it read like braille under his fingers. His sister was blind, and he'd messed with her books, trying to figure out how she read anything with those tiny bumps when he would barely figure out where the light switch was in the dark. He always thought it was funny that their parents had named her Melody. How did that make any sense when she was blind?

Sound clicked back into his awareness, like he'd unmuted his game. Chanting surrounded him, blending with the screams of the hunter and the hunted in the branches above the clearing where he lay.

He shot bolt upright and looked around.

Thirteen witches stood in a circular pattern around him, the thirteenth still stood above him. She gyrated like a pop diva on XTC at a rager rave, her arms thrust up. The women's chanting grew louder and more intense, a rippling blade in one hand, and the other hand covered in blood.

His blood.

She brought it down and smeared it across her face, from one earlobe, across her mouth and nose, to the other earlobe. She brought her fingers to her lips and thrust four of them into her mouth, licking and moaning loudly.

Griffon couldn't quite put together what was going on. This had to be the game, right? He was the hero of this game, and he'd just barely recovered from a killing blow. That was the only thing that made sense.

Everything felt so real that it was all surreal. He struggled to wrap his mind around the situation and scrambled to remember the events before and after he'd walked into the crosswalk.

A conflicting memory fought for attention. Him killing a dozen others in a fight in front of the hundred gathered creatures in the rough wooden stands around the arena, which stood in for a ritualistic summoning circle.

"Crowd?" he muttered, then turned his head to look around.

The valley surrounding him rose in all directions; the spectator stands ringing the natural depression. Bent trees jutted up in the middle of the partially scraped logs that made the rough bench seating. Hundreds of forms writhed and undulated, matching the woman standing over him. Most seemed to be caught up in the fervor, but a few spotted he wasn't dead, and were pointing and shouting.

The women surrounding him still hadn't noticed the fact that he was still alive, inspecting his healing abdomen with his fingers.

"They sacrificed me!" he mumbled under his breath. "They meant for me to be the last thing in their magical…"

Magical what? He thought. *What game is this? The graphics are great, it must be VR.*

I don't have a VR unit, was his next thought, *so I must be at Tony's house, using his box that he just got! Let's see if I can level this bitch up!*

Griffon reached out, snatched up his two-handed sword from the sand next to him, and jumped to his feet. He hunched his shoulder and slitted his eyes and glared straight ahead to lock his menacing gaze on the woman's…

"Belly button?" Griffon shouted, looking down to the ground, then up above him. "Where's the rest of me?"

The woman finally noticed the small man in front of her, the top of his head barely reaching her midsection.

"Are you feckin kidding me?" Griffon whined. "Hey lady, are you a giant? Please, please, please, tell me that you're some sort of huge amazon warrior! I'd never make a short toon! I hate dwarves, halflings, and especially gnomes."

Griffon held out his sword crossways to indicate he wanted the woman to pause, to give him a time-out, and he began feeling his features with his other hand.

"Hold on a second," he said.

He patted at his face, staring at the jaw, and moving up.

"Uh oh," he said, "a short beard, a long moustache, and huge sideburns, a big bulbous nose, bushy eyebrows, and anime hair…oh, no."

He looked into the polished surface at the base of his sword, where the blood hadn't covered the blade, and surveyed his features.

"Oh, no. Oh, no!" his voice rose to a shrill scream. "Imma fricken gnome, aren't I?"

The woman in front of him, who a moment ago was performing a sinuous dance, her ankle length loincloth swaying, now stared at him, her eyes commanding his death. She screeched and brought her wavy blade down at his shoulder.

Instinctively, his blade came up to block her blow, the tip of her dagger a fingers-width from his eye.

The witch pulled the blade back and slashed side to side, stepping forward with each stroke.

Griffon stumbled backwards, unable to get stable footing or predict the rhythm of her attack. He fell onto his butt, leather small-clothes pulled tight between his nether cheeks, and leather straps and metal buckles biting into his chest and arms.

"What the hell am I wearing?" Griffon glanced down at himself, taking in his outfit for the first time.

He had leather sandals with leather ties wrapping around his calf. Leather greaves covered his thighs, barely more than an oval to protect the front from attack. His wrist and forearms had bracers, one shoulder a pauldron, and his chest and back had a sort of half cuirass that met the leather girdle across his midsection.

She'd gutted him just below his wide belt and right above his…

"Leather underwear? And I'm a gnome? Really?" Griffon moaned. "And who designed this? I'm barely covered, and things are hanging out all over the place! Is this meant to protect me?"

The last words trailed off as he looked up to see the woman who'd been trying to kill him moments ago now leering at him. Her eyes tracked along up his shapely legs, across his muscular thighs, and paused at his leather pouch, which had nothing to do with holding coins, but did hold his family jewels.

"Hey, lady!" He shouted, waving his free hand back and forth across her line of sight. "My eyes are up here!"

"I've always liked the short ones," the woman's voice was a gruff hiss, and she wiped at the corner of her mouth with the back of her free hand, smearing blood across her lips, "they always make me feel powerful when I am smothering them with my— feminine wiles."

The other women in the outer magical circle noticed the kerfuffle in the middle of the arena and looked back and forth between each other. They continued their chant, never dropping a syllable from their incantation.

One woman pointed at their leader standing over the gnome, and flapped her hands at a second woman, indicating that she should go in and see what was going on.

The second woman shook her head vehemently, refusing to move from her assigned spot.

Slapping his thighs together, Griffon swung his sword at the woman's midsection.

She stepped back and the tiny gladiator missed. She laughed at him.

"Aw, does the poor little man feel uncomfortable?" Her voice was mocking as she drew the words out. "Who do you think dressed you in that?

Who do you think cast the spells so you couldn't take it off?"

"Um, you?" Griffon mumbled, looking around for something to distract her.

There wasn't much out here. His steel buckler lay to one side of a circle drawn into the sand with silver dust, runes marking points inside of the arcane ring. The magical markings glittered, the metallic symbols shining as the ritual pulled power into them.

"No!" the woman screeched. "I'm no servant! I had one of the novices do it. Touching something like you is below me!"

The gladiator's fingers dug into the sand under his hand, and his face lit up.

"Oh, you like the idea of the eunuchs undressing you, bathing you, putting on this adorable wittle outfit, and then an acolyte running her fingers across your taut and tight body to seal your armor to your flesh?" she asked.

Griffon threw the handful of sand at the woman's face and rolled to his shield. Acting on instinct that wasn't his own, he slid his left arm under it and into the waiting strap without thinking, and his hand gripped the second strap.

He lurched to his feet. The woman screamed and frantically wiped at her face with her hands, trying to dislodge the grit from her eyes.

Turning his shield parallel to the ground, he dropped the flat of his blade atop it, clanging the two and stepped forward. He pulled the weapon sideways, even with the ground, and pushed with his shield arm to give it more momentum.

The sword cut along the woman's midsection, and she screamed again, her hands dropping to clutch at her belly.

Stepping back with his right foot, Griffon bent his elbow back and lifted his weapon to eye level for a thrust. He angled it up and pushed forward. The tip of the blade caught the woman on the solar plexus, unbalancing her, making her tumble backwards, landing across the outer circle with the magical runes.

She screeched and writhed, one hand on her face, the other on her belly. Silver and sand scattered underneath her. The women at the outer circle began gesturing furiously at Griffon, crossing their waving arms above their heads.

Placing the tip of the blade at the throat of the witch on the ground, the gladiator looked to the crowd in the age-old expectation of the onlookers choosing the fate of the fallen.

Griffon shook the buckler to his forearm, freeing his hand. He lifted his arm, his hand clenched into a fist and the thumb jutting out parallel to the ground. He waved it, bobbing the thumb up then down, indicating that the crowd should choose the woman's destiny.

Spare her…or kill her.

The crowd went wild, leaping to their feet, screaming. The screams slowly morphed into one word: kill.

"Kill, kill, kill," the mob chanted.

The gladiator inside of him was coming out, and he smiled. He'd done this dozens of times. He was one of the best. His small size made everyone underestimate him. Though his reach was short, he was clever and quick.

He leaned sideways, the blade sliding easily into the bumpy length of the woman's neck, piercing her larynx, and sliding deeper. With a jerk of his wrist, the gladiator cut the woman's throat, tearing a wide hole across her neck.

The spectators went into an uproar, clapping and shouting and stomping. The women at the edge of the arena stopped chanting, watching their leader's lifeblood drain onto the sand inside the arcane circle of runes.

Griffon drew the sword out of the woman and held it aloft, spraying a line of blood across himself and the sands.

Then he danced.

"Oh yeah, oh yeah," he shouted in a singsong voice, wiggling his hips and dipping his knees, "I kicked your boss's ass, oh yeah, I'm the best!"

He laughed as the women at the rim of the arena pushed and shoved to get away. The crowd grew quiet and stared at him as he did his victory dance.

Griffon hammed it up, throwing in classic dance moves he'd learned from Fortnite and other bits from touchdown dances in football games. He closed his eyes, holding his sword above his head and spun in a circle, throwing his head back and howling.

The silence of the crowd grew eerie, the sound of shifting and sliding sand growing louder. Griffon slowed to a stop and opened his eyes.

A single shout from a man in the stands drew the gnome's attention. The man was pointing at something behind Griffon, who slowly turned to look.

Foul smelling, oily smoke, grey tinged with green, filled the circle in the center of the arena, seeping out from where the witch's body broke the magical ring.

The sand was pouring off something inside, a shadowy form rising to the height of two men. A long, scaly snout topped a massive set of shoulders that wound down to a tapered waist. Three tentacles writhed on each side of its torso where arms should have been. A guttural hiss came from the beast, sounding like a volcano in a teakettle, a rumble with an underlying angry whistle.

The creature took a step forward, showing thick legs with backwards bending knees. Two tentacles shot forward, extending well past where they should've been able to reach, and snatched up the still dying form of the witch.

The woman's head fell backwards, ripping her throat further. The beast lapped at it with dual forked tongues, tasting the blood offering. Its open mouth showed multiple rows of dozens of pointed teeth in a spiral pattern that led deep into its maw.

"Oh, bidj," Griffon used the native word for his swear word without realizing it and he stumbled backwards, "looks like it's time for a boss fight! But again, these graphics are insane!"

The summoned monster looked up over the body of the witch and eyed the tiny gnome far below it. It leaned its head down, pushing the woman's head into his mouth and bit down. It shook its head back and forth, bones crunching under the pressure of its jaws.

The body jerked and twitched, the arms severing and falling to the ground as the beast tore off half the torso.

The monster threw its head back, jerking it up and down, swallowing the portion it had bitten off, all the while staring at Griffon.

"Wow," he gasped, "that is intimidating!"

The abomination threw the corpse to one side and looked down at its clawed feet, which were halfway out of the magical circle.

"I-I am not," each guttural word came out separately, as if it had been a long time since the creature had used words, "restrained."

It did something with its face, which Griffon guessed was a grin. The sight made him shudder, and he suddenly felt the need to pee.

The beast stepped forward, out of the circle, and turned its head to inspect its surroundings.

"So, many, morsels," it growled, pausing after each word, watching the panicked crowd turn and run. "But a little snack first."

The creature looked at Griffon, and its face split again, the edges of its mouth twisting in unnatural ways.

Its body bent to leap, and shot forward, mouth wide, and tentacles flailing.

The world swooned for Griffon, the edges going blurry and the center misting. This didn't feel like any video game he'd ever played. Other video games didn't have that weird feeling of sweat trickling down your spine and into your butt crack. Other videos games didn't tell you, let alone let you feel, when your bladder released.

Something shifted and clicked in Griffon's head as he let go, perhaps even fainted. Something else took over, and he was merely a passenger in the body he inhabited.

Shoving the buckler into the beast's maw, Griffon swung his sword upward, cutting through two of the tentacles on one side of the monster.

The creature jerked back, but Griffon pushed forward, keeping the buckler in the thing's mouth, its two tongues dancing across his forearm and leaving red welts wherever they touched.

The gnome's feet came off the ground as the monster rose to its full height, and the gladiator pushed off the beast's torso, so he swung away. As he came back in, he pushed his sword in front of him, and the tip pushed into the beast's chest.

The thing roared and flicked its head, opening its mouth wider, and the miniature warrior flew across the sand, landing on his side, knocking the wind from him.

His exercises told him to breathe, and he'd exhaled as he hit, so his body was ready to inhale. Getting his feet under him, he rose right as the summoned monstrosity came at him. His sword severed two more tentacles, this time from the other side of the beast's body.

The monstrous maw of many miniature marrow mashers shot at him again, and he barely raised his bucker in time. The shield flicked flat, and dozens of fangs sunk into his arm.

Gritting his teeth, the gladiator glared into the cat-slit eyes of the attacker, reversed his grip on his weapon, and jabbed it sideways into the thing's eye socket. It burst out the other side with a splash of viscera and gore.

The thing screamed and pulled away, jerking the blade from the gnome's hand. The creature shuffled backwards, clutching at the weapon with its two remaining tentacles.

The gladiator pulled twin dirks from his wide leather girdle, and stepped forward, blades slashing and cutting the tender inner thighs of the beast. He ducked under its crotch, and came out by its tail, sliding each blade across the hamstring of a different thigh on the monster.

It collapsed backwards, and the gnome rolled to get out from under it before it came down on him. Rolling to his feet, one dagger fell from the numb fingers of the arm the beast had bitten, and the gladiator brandished the remaining blade.

The abomination thrashed around in the sand, legs useless, sightless, and a gushing wound in its chest.

This battle was over. The only thing that remained was showmanship for the crowd. It was time to grow his legend. Auric, the gnomish gladiator, was once again triumphant.

The crowd had stopped its panicked exodus, and he looked at them. He raised his one good arm, and a weak cry came from the spectators. He raised his weapon again, and the cheer was stronger. A third time brought a deafening thunder of clapping, whistles, stomping, and shouts.

He strutted around the flailing enemy, taking his time to stab his thin bladed dirk into sensitive areas, hitting arteries when he could.

He knew he'd won, but he'd have to make the closing quick. Whatever venom this beast had was getting into his bloodstream, and if he didn't tend to it soon, he'd be the final loser of the arena today.

Possibly ever.

He threw his blade into the back of the monster's neck, and then ran up the thing's back to grip his sword, still piercing the creature's head from one side to the other.

He pulled it free, wobbled on the back of the thing as it went into death throes, and thrust his blade down into the creature's skull. He hit the crease that he'd known would be there, and the well-cared-for weapon tore through the thing's head and the tip buried itself in the sand.

The crowd went wild, and the gladiator leapt from the back of the beast and held up his good arm in victory, the wounded one hidden behind the buckler.

Wiping his sword on the remains of the dead woman, he slid it into its sheath, then snatched up his dropped dirks and put them away.

Turning to the crowd, he made the universal sign of wanting a drink, spreading his pinky and thumb apart while leaving the rest of his hand in a fist, and tilted it at his mouth. He then pointed at the crowd.

Dozens of people jumped into the sands and rushed towards him and the creature. His adoring fans, coming to lift him up after his victory.

Then they rushed past him, a few tossing wineskins or flasks at his feet. The mass of people fell on the creature, slashing with daggers and tearing off hunks of scales and meat. They shoved gobs of bloody flesh into their mouths, devouring the monster.

Inside of the gladiator, a small urge to vomit fought against his sensible thought to grab the strongest liquor thrown to him and use it as anesthetic, orally and topically.

Snatching up a metal flask, he popped the corked and sniffed it. Powerful spirits tickled his nose, and he jerked back. Pouring the contents over his arm, he watched the mass of people turning on one another.

A few turned towards him, murder in their eyes. He stumbled backwards, then turned and ran as the mob set their sights on him.

Calendar

The basic calendar is a lunar calendar. There are thirteen months in each year. Each month there are twenty-eight days. There is a new moon on the first day of every month. The first day of spring is on the Equinox.

Seasons	**Months**	**Days**
Spring	Loen	1. Ginof
	Hapok	2. Bestuf
	Axara	3. Midā
		4. Therin
Summer	Surem	5. Uthr
	Santara	6. Dunwith
	Xaco	7. Lasin
Autumn	Harton	
	Thon	
	Ault	
Winter	Witen	
	Maleo	
	Frear	
Thaw	Milwen	

Glossary

Aborgas: Small hamlet near Red City.

Aeifain: Willowy race of beings with almond eyes, pale skin, and slightly pointed ears. Often more advanced in arts, culture, and magic than the lesser races.

Akar Lake: Body of water near Ruger Whitley Estates.

Ault: Ninth month of the year, and the third month of the autumn season.

Axara: Third month of the year, and the spring season.

Bestuf: Second day of the week.

Bidj: A swear word meaning waste or offal.

Binaple: a fruit that grows on binaple bushes used for make red, orange, and yellow dyes.

Changing Wheel, The: The god of cyclical change who all the other gods bow to.

Chuz: A harsh swear word.

Dangrazio: Subterranean metropolis and trading post.

Dasism: A race who follow the path of elements and nature. Physically, they are slighter than humans, with olive skin, pointed ears, and almond eyes.

Dioneze City: A broken city on the eastern part of the continent run by slavers. Known for its gladiatorial ring.

Dragon Estates: An ancient castle rumored to have a dragon residing in the caverns below it.

Dargaon's Hole: Ancestral home of dragons in the Wandering Hills.

Dunwith: Sixth day of the week.

Durgan's Keep: A city-state in the far east that was founded by a rokairn and his adventuring companions.

Edgewater: Medium port town on the coast of the Sea of Seron.

Everyway: Largest city on the continent of Teurone.

Ez'rainia-fromton: City of the dead located in the Great Desert. Was the city in which Verl'zen-luk had been imprisoned before his rise to godhood.

Fate's Run: Dockside gambling hall in Tarnish. Run by a woman named Fate.

Frear: Twelfth month of the year, and the third month of the winter season.

Ginof: First day of the week.

Glass Valley: A valley made of glass in the slim desert that was formed when a stone dragon fell from the heavens.

Gray Lands: Home of the Aeifain.

Great Desert: A large desert east of the southern Rolling Mountains, which is home to Rogen the Plague and the Great Desert Empire.

Great Desert Empire: A civilization built by Rogen the Plague and his nation slaves, located in the Great Desert.

Hapok: Second month of the year, and of the spring season.

Harton: Seventh month of the year, and the first month of the autumn season.

Highest Spire: A structure that is fifty kilometers at the base and spirals upward. Doors that lead to other places in time and space are spaced every six meters. The height of this tower in unmeasured.

Hope's Hollow: A small village on the on the borders of the Black Wood and the Wandering Hills.

Humbrey: A Kingdom of thirteen houses that embodies nobility and honor.

Icon Hall: Aeifain home on the eastern portion of Teurone.

Jonath: God of justice, protection, strength, and earth. His symbol is a trident and balanced scales.

Kez'et-dual: A demon enslaved by the Troöds.

Khelikian: God of Insects.

Kord: A twisted gold wire that is the standard currency.

Land's End: A demon-ridden peninsula on the south-eastern most portion of the continent.

Lasin: Seventh day of the week.

Ley lines: Elemental energy currents, invisible to the naked eye, from which wizards can draw energy.

Loen: First month of the year, and of the spring season. It begins on the spring equinox.

Mage, Mind: Practitioner of the art of psychic magics such as body alteration, telekinesis, telepathy, etc.

Maleo: Eleventh month of the year, and the second month of the winter season.

Malvor: Duchy in the Kingdom of Trysteria, south of the Kingdom of Humbrey. Run by Duke Malvornick.

Mida: Third day of the week.

Milwen: The thirteenth month of the year, and the transition month between winter and spring.

Nine Towers of Magic: Abandoned during the Wizard Wars, this secluded and elite university was dedicated to teaching magic. Located east of the Black Wood.

Nomed: A demon-human-aeifain hybrid.

Northwood Community: The largest city in Northwood, founded by humans, dasism, and other races.

Obsidian/Onyx: God of Magic who came to power when the Talisman appeared in the sky.

Obsidian/Onyx Towers: Black towers raised by the God of Magic to distribute magical tools, goods, and weapons.

Ocean Wood: Lands reclaimed by the Dasism from humans under Kala the Black.

Olde Kingdom: A fallen Kingdom in the southern portion of the Everyway Plains.

Oracle Plain: Grasslands north of the Common Wood, east of the Slim Desert, and west of the Rolling Mountains. Home of the mystical order of the Oracle.

Pantageas: City run by mages and wizards in the northern Everyway Plains, just south of the Kingdom of Humbrey.

Paradise Island: An island created by a dead volcano. Now a refuge for pirates and seagoing folk. Run by small governments and individuals, known for its waterfalls.

Parsay Gevies: God of Luck, Chance, and Dreams. Referred to as Parsay by adults, who pray to him for luck, and as Mister Gevies by children, who pray to him for dreams to come true.

Pek: A silver coin, worth one-tenth of a gold kord.

Pemtie: A moron, ignorant, or stupid person, idea, or event.

Phaz, Day of: A day that happens once every four years. Shrouded with myth and superstition.

Promethene: Goddess of Song and Light. Her clergy is almost always women. Wife of the Walking God, Mother of Chanian and Senaria.

Pyridom of Power: A landmark on the east coast of the continent that focuses magical energies.

Red City: Run down city once plagued by lycanthropes and undead. Located on the coast of the

Red Wind: Located in the Red Plains, this city is known for its crime lords and drug trade.

Rock Crag Wastes: a rocky area geographically located west of the Great Desert and east of the southern Rolling Mountains.

Rogen the Plague: Rokairn slave master and lord of The Great Desert Empire.

Rokairn: The Stone Folk. A short, stout race known for their attention to detail, organization, and dedication to fine craftsmanship. Both sexes are known to have beards.

Rolling Mountains: An immense mountain range east of the Oracle Plain, and west of the Northwood.

Rondarius the Foul: Insane Necromancer

Royale Bay: A bay north of the Sea of Seron and east of the Everyway Plains.

Rugber Whitley Estates: A small community known for the mind mages born there.

Rumay Bay: A shanty town on the shores of the Broken Sea that was once a hub of trade before The Downfall.

Runsk: A warlord-controlled city nestled between the Grey Forest and Diaz Wood.

Santara: Fifth month of the year, and the second month of the summer season.

Sea of the Great Plague: A body of water south of the Great Desert.

Sea of Seron: A body of water south of the Everyway Plains.

Seawall City: A fortified city run by spellslingers in a military fashion, located on the east coast of Teurone on the Eastern Ocean.

Senaria: Goddess of nature, innate honor, and woodlands. Daughter of The Walking God and Promethene.

Sharp: A brass coin, with one one-hundredth of a gold kord.

Shuglak (shug-lak): Horse-sized herd creature with large round ears, a single nose horn on a flat hog-like snout, and two tusks jutting from the bottom jaw of males.

Shulyar City: Dasism name for Silver City.

Silver Castle: One-time home of the god, Jonath, who built it.

Silver City: Also known as Shulyar City, a city built by the god Jonath.

Sinking Swamp: A swamp that hides the Library of time, west of Trysteria and north of the Everyway Plains.

Slim Desert: A thin desert between Everyway Plains and Oracle Plain.

Spellslinger: A generalized term for a wielder of one of the five types of magic; alchemy, mind magic, holy, conjuring, and elemental.

Stadia Isle: A pirate island in the Sea of Seron.

Surem: Fourth month of the year, and the first month of the summer season.

Talisman: A comet that returns on a regular basis, but now is in orbit around the planet.

Tarnish: Run-down desert city on the coast of the Sea of the Great Plague.

Tarra: Goddess of water and healing. Twin of Torr.

Teurone: Continent detailed in this book.

Therin: Fourth day of the week.

Thon: Eighth month of the year, and the second month of the autumn season.

Torgoth: God of Trade and Commerce.

Torr: God of fire and combat. Twin of Tarra.

Transvartius: A wise and benevolent man sometimes known as the Traveller, the Hidden Diplomat, and disciple of the Walking God.

Traveling God, The: God of innate magic, such as mind mages and wizards. Also known as the Walking God.

Troöd: A race from another dimension, that are reptilian in features. They have two distinct species, greys and greens. The former deal in summoning magics, and the latter are chameleon like soldiers.

Trysteria: Kingdom in the northern portion of the Everyway Plains.

Uthr: Fifth day of the week.

Vallenwood: a wood harvested from Vallenwood trees that is strong and beautiful.

Velentian Brandy: A strong alcoholic drink.

Verl'zen-luk: God of ritual Magic.

Witen: Tenth month of the year, and the first month of the winter season.

Wizard: Practitioner of elemental magics which tap into the energy of ley lines.

Xaco: Sixth month of the year, and the third month of the summer season.

Acknowledgements

This book took me a year to get out the door. That's significantly longer than a book usually takes me. The reasons for that are myriad, ranging from personal disasters to once-in-a-lifetime things. But there's a lot of people who helped make this happen, and I'd like to thank them here and now for all they did.

For the people who helped when my computer died, and went above and beyond to get the single tool I need to do this work, I thank you. This includes Ed Summers, John Millington, Kevin Crew, Maria, and Coldbrew Science.

To the people who stepped up and supported the Kickstarter, you are my personal heroes. Thank you Jamie Carrieri, Nia, Eleanor Terry-Walsh, Laura Parkinson, Crow NoYami, Emily, Eli Kwake, Zach Dunn, Rebecca Snow, Jenny, Roberta Guillory, Michael Brooker, Shane Heaton, Andrea Parkinson, Arthur Ni, Carolyn Rowland, Sara Ekstam, Joseph Kennedy, Tempie Wade, Debora Kerr, Marian Goldeen, Jeremiah Campbell, Rachel Morley, WirelessMous3, Adrienne Wood, Andrea D'Amico, and The Creative Fund by BackerKitt

Beyond that, there are countless folks who watch me write on my live stream on twitch.tv. People who write their own projects along side me. Those that just hang out and give company and encouragement. And everyone else pops in and out to say hello and check on me.

I especially want to thank those that support and help my subscribing on my live stream, Ko-fi, Patreon, PayPal, etc. Your tips, donations, and financial kindness have kept the lights on as I fight for my dreams. I love you folks and thank you for all you do.

Travis I. Sivart

About the Author

Travis I. Sivart writes Fantasy, Steampunk, Cyberpulp, Social DIY, and more. You can find him live streaming the writing and editing of his latest project from his home in Central Virginia, surrounded by too many cats.

You can find Travis on Amazon, Barnes and Noble, Books-A-Million, and other literary retailers.